PROVOKED

PROVOKED

PROVOKED

REBECCA ZANETTI

LYRICAL PRESS
Kensington Publishing Corp.
www.kensingtonbooks.com

This book is dedicated to all the loyal fans who sent me an email or Facebook question asking when Kane was going to get his happy ending. This is also dedicated to my amazing Facebook Street Team, who gives so much time, support, and encouragement. I really appreciate it.

ACKNOWLEDGMENTS

I have many people to thank for help in getting this book to readers, and I sincerely apologize for anyone I've forgotten.

Thank you to Tony, Gabe, and Karly Zanetti, my very patient family, for giving me time and space to write, as well as lots of love and excitement;

Thank you to my hard-working agent, Caitlin Blasdell, who is patient, logical, and a lot of fun when I get her talking about character arcs;

Thanks also to Liza Dawson and Havis Dawson for your encouragement, support, and hard work;

Thank you to my amazing editor, Megan Records, who I've missed while she's been on maternity leave—congratulations and I'm SO happy for you;

Thank you to all the folks at Kensington Publishing, especially Alicia Condon and Alexandra Nicolajsen because they're wonderful to work with;

Thank you to my critique partner Jennifer Dorough—you rock;

Thank you to Beckie Acree for sharing her wisdom regarding anatomy and decapitation;

Thank you to the crew at Hot Damn Designs—your covers are spectacular;

And thanks also to my constant support system: Gail and Jim English, Debbie and Travis Smith, Stephanie and Don West, Brandie and Mike Chapman, Jessica and Jonah Namson, and Kathy and Herb Zanetti.

CHAPTER 1

The demon destroyer was beautiful.

Kane Kayrs settled back in the worn booth of the bar and eyed the blonde solution to his devastating problem. Long strands of hair flowed down her trim back, a messy and free tumbling that whispered of cool nights rolling under the stars. An organized chaos that somehow worked. Sun had kissed her angled face, leaving her slightly freckled and rosy cheeked. The cowboy hat perched precariously on her head was all sass. She maneuvered around packed bodies, an island of calm and grace as she delivered beer, hard drinks, and an occasional bottle of water.

A slight sneer lifted her pink lips every time she plunked a water bottle on a table. Interesting.

She stood to about five foot eight—tall for a human female. Ripped jeans molded to full curves, and a low-cut peasant blouse guaranteed she'd receive excellent tips for the night. The woman moved like a dancer, easily dodging groping hands without losing a step. A good-natured laugh, low and sexy, rumbled from her several times.

Kane finished the local beer he'd ordered while waiting for her to show for her shift. Odd that she hadn't acknowledged him. They were the only two people in the bar with power.

The jukebox against the side wall had played a combination of hip-hop and country music all night, and his head was beginning to ache. Dollar bills hung stapled from the ceiling, and a television in the far corner highlighted local rodeo footage from last spring, regardless of the snow currently whipping around outside. The stale scent of old beer permeated the area. Several inebriated women rode saddles masquerading as bar stools, their excited yips a prelude to falling on the floor. The peanut-shell covered floor.

Kane shoved away impatience. Hanging with the locals had never interested him, and the pull of his laboratory called. He had work to do.

Finally, she approached his booth, her gaze going from the empty bottle to his face.

A punch of raw power slammed from her black eyes.

The woman smelled like wild heather just blooming. She smiled, a small dimple flashing in her left cheek. "Would you like another beer? Huckleberry Ale, right?"

He tilted his head to the side, allowing her vibrations of energy to run over him. They were almost as sexy as her smooth, slightly raspy voice. An unwilling smile played with his lips. "Are you serious?"

Curiosity widened her smile. "Yeah. Most people like another when theirs is empty. If you didn't like the Colorado Huckleberry, you should try the Cooper Ale. The brewery next door makes it for us. It's lighter and not quite as sweet."

Irritation and a hint of respect filled him at her calm look. She gave absolutely no indication she knew who, or rather what, he was. "I'm not here to play games, sweetheart."

She stilled all movement, wrinkling her brow. "Um, okay."

He leaned forward, clasping his tapered fingers on the

damaged table. "Are you really going to pretend you don't know why I'm here?"

Wariness filled her dark eyes, and she took a small step away. A quick glance over her shoulder toward the bulging bartender resulted in confidence tilting her lips. She focused back on Kane. "Listen, jackass. We're not selling the northern rocks. Do you want another drink or not?" The warmth in her smile had disappeared.

A chill swept along his skin. What the hell were the northern rocks? The animal within him, the one so rarely let loose, suddenly wanted to roar. He coughed. If she wanted to play games, he'd allow it until closing time. At that point, his patience ended. "I don't want rocks, northern or otherwise. Why don't you surprise me with the choice of beer?"

"Fine." She pivoted on beige cowboy boots.

Damn, he'd always had a thing for women in cowboy boots. Probably because opposites really did attract. Her ass was something in the tight jeans, too.

He shook his head and stretched his neck. Lust had no place in this mission. When was the last time he'd slept? Grabbing his phone, he speed-dialed his older brother.

"Did you find her?" the king growled across the line.

"Yes. She's broadcasting strong enough I'm shocked I'm the only one here." Kane eyed a couple of cowboys at the bar who'd zeroed in on the blonde. Human, drunk, and stupid . . . they might create a decent diversion so he could grab the woman and go.

"You won't be alone for long—I have no doubt the demons are heading your way." The sound of rustling papers came over the line. Dage must've been in his study. "Will she help us?"

"I don't know. So far she's acting like she has no clue I'm a vampire."

The woman sauntered toward him, a dark beer in hand.

Depositing the frothing glass on the table, she stared him in the eyes. "Robust Rude Dark Ale. Seemed to fit." Two seconds later and she was busing a table across the room.

Her husky voice had Kane thinking thoughts he really shouldn't. He cleared his throat. "I may have to just grab her." In fact, his hands all but itched with the need to get ahold of her. Damn enhanced human females. They instantly sent a vamp into overdrive. Even a logical one like him.

"I don't care what you do. Just get her to help us." Desperation and something darker lowered Dage's tone. "I haven't had a vision, but my gut is telling me we're running out of time. We need to find Jase and now."

Kane rubbed his chin, forcing back despair and a now familiar fear. "Don't worry, I'll do what I have to do."

"I know." Dage sighed. "Have you come up with a plan for when we get him back?"

Kane shoved emotion down, his eyes never leaving the woman. He leveled his voice into logical tones, because logic was what the king needed. "I have several plans, and we'll decide which one works best when we get him and assess the situation." The idea of assessing how damaged his younger brother had become after being tortured by demons had Kane's eyes morphing to his vampire mode and back—hopefully before anyone noticed. Yet he kept his voice calm. "Jase is strong, Dage. He'll survive."

But would he? The demons had taken him nearly four years ago. Demons tortured with obscene mind games, often rendering the victim stark crazy and suicidal. After years of such agony, could any man survive? Kane blinked twice. Wallowing in fear wouldn't help.

"We've been so close to finding him, so many damn times," Dage said. "New intel is that the demons have created a base somewhere in the southwest. I'm hoping they've moved Jase there."

"Maybe." Kane wouldn't have. He would've kept any prisoner at home base and away from the known vampire headquarters in the States. Of course, vampires didn't keep prisoners. But as strong as the king was, he was also an older brother who needed something to cling to. Some type of hope allowing him to function. "We'll find him."

"Yes, we will. So tell me about the woman."

Kane shrugged. "White blond hair like a demon. Black eyes. Tall, graceful . . . beautiful."

"Beautiful?" Dage breathed out. "Interesting. I always figured if we found a demon destroyer, she'd be a massive monster with warts. In my three hundred fifty years, I've never seen one. In fact, I'd thought they'd died out."

The woman certainly lacked warts or monstrosity. Kane took a drink of the dark ale, enjoying the rich hops. "Which begs the question . . . how has she hidden so well, and why stop now? Why is she broadcasting so damn strongly? I felt the vibrations the second I drove into this small Colorado town."

"Well, if there's a mystery to solve, you're the guy to solve it. Just get her to help us."

"I will." God help the woman if she refused.

One of the drunk women yipped loud, fell off her saddle, and crashed to the floor. A chorus of applause rippled throughout the bar.

Who the hell were these people?

Dage cleared his throat. "Ah, Kane, I know this isn't your kind of mission. But you were the only one I could send."

"Not a problem." Jesus. He knew how to deal with people—he merely preferred not to. "I have to go—see you soon." Clicking off, he took a deep breath, resisting the urge to cough from smoke and the scent of spilled tequila. Hunting werewolves was a hell of a lot easier than hunting one small woman.

He caught her eye and lifted his bottle in a silent toast. *Oh yeah, sweetheart. We're both about to leave our comfort zones.* Smiling as she flushed and broke eye contact, he swallowed a good drink of the brew. Let the real games begin.

Amber wove around another cowboy on his way to the restroom, her gaze on the full tray of tequila shooters, her mind on the guy by the door. Make that the *man* by the door. There was nothing guy-like about the smooth tourist. And if she didn't miss her guess, he was no tourist.

Wearing black silk trousers and shirt, he hinted at money. Dark hair that curled over his nape, deep eyes so blue as to be almost violet, and rugged features hinted at intelligence. Dig deeper, and the hints ended to a blatant display of . . . maleness. He had it.

Lounging in the booth, he apparently couldn't care less he didn't belong in the Western bar. And the rest of the patrons stayed clear of him. Quite unusual, considering most of the women had given him "come take me" eyes all night. But not one of them had the guts to approach the stranger. He might as well have had a "stay the hell away" sign on his chest. Or on his chiseled face.

She'd delivered no less than eight beers to him, and he appeared as alert after the last one as he had when she'd arrived for her shift. Thank God it was almost closing time and she could get away from his constant appraisal.

Those dark eyes never left her. They cataloged, watched, and kept track. But there was no leer, no creepy expression in them. He just . . . watched.

She'd had about enough of him. Her feet ached from being on them all night, and the muscles along her neck were killing her. But she needed the money, so she'd taken the waitressing job a week ago.

Too bad she wasn't trained in anything other than nurturing plants and trees. It was definitely time to sign up for some night classes at the college.

With a sigh, she headed his way, having to concentrate to keep from tripping over her boots. Something about the stranger reminded her of her femininity. The silly thought caught her up short. Man, she had to stop sneaking away from the group and reading goofy romance novels.

But she couldn't help herself. Sure, she'd been taught to rely on herself and that she had to create her own happy ending. But wasn't that what the heroines in those books did?

Finally she reached his table. "Last call, buddy."

A smile curved his full lips . . . one that had odd tingles wandering down her spine. The grin failed to soften the harsh angles of his face, making him seem even harder than before. Man, he was good-looking. Almost too much so. He slid the empty beer bottle across the table, his fingers long and tapered.

"Buddy? That's a new one on me. Thanks, but I'm finished." Reaching for a wallet in his back pocket, he slid a fifty toward her. "You haven't taken a break in five hours. Please sit down while you count my change."

Smooth, cultured, his deep tone zinged butterflies through her abdomen. She glanced around at the now nearly empty bar. She could spare a moment. Curiosity forced her to sit, even while warning whispered in the back of her head. She knew better. "Why have you been looking at me for five solid hours?" Not reaching for the fifty, and certainly not reaching for her change pouch, she stared him right in the eyes.

A flash of temper filtered across his face that he quickly banished. "I don't have time to dance with you. You know exactly why I'm here."

"I do?" She frowned. Her heart sped up. "You lied about the northern rocks?"

Danger lived in his frown. "Sweetheart, I don't know a thing about any rocks. I do, however, need your help."

Oh, for goodness' sake. Was this some sophisticated-guy *come-on?* "I'm really not interested." She softened her voice to appease him. While he appeared classy, there was no doubt the guy was dangerous. The way he filled out the expensive shirt showed toned muscle. But the danger lived in his eyes and on his skin. Instinct kept her alert.

Anger flattened his full lips. "You won't help?"

She inhaled deeply. The scent of cedar and musk—maleness—tickled her senses. Perhaps the guy was merely lost. "Maybe I've misunderstood. What kind of help do you need?"

He paused, taking her measure. "The demons have my brother."

Her mouth went dry. Alarm bells in her brain widened her eyes. "Ah . . . demons?"

"Yes." Calculation and an odd sorrow flashed across his face. "The demon nation captured him, and they've imprisoned him for almost four years. I need your help."

"Oh. Well now." Moving slowly, scooting from the booth, she sighed in relief when she reached her feet. "I'm so sorry to hear that. Those demons, well now." Subtly, she nodded to Butch, who had just finished wiping down the bar. "But, well, there's nothing I can do." Except send the wacko back to his spaceship.

Butch's cowboy boots clomped through peanut shells on the wood floor, all three hundred pounds of him showing grumpiness. "Problem?" His bald head glinted under the dim lights, and pure pissed-off male shone in his eyes as he glared at the crazy guy.

A nervous giggle escaped Amber. "Ah, no. It's just, this man should probably get going."

Butch nodded his massive head. "Pay and get out, fella."

"Kane." Most men immediately rushed to do Butch's bidding. Not this guy. With an appraising glance, he slid the fifty closer to Amber, his gaze on her. "Kane. Instead of 'fella' or 'buddy.' Kane."

Her mind spun. "Cain?" Okay, wait a minute. The Bible story about brothers. "Like Abel and Cain? I mean, demons never took Abel." Sympathy wafted through her. "Do you think you're Cain?" Poor guy—and the one shrink in town was usually drunk.

He lifted an eyebrow and shook his head. "Ah, no. Kane with a *K*. And no, the demons didn't have Abel from the Bible." His look whispered he was doubting her intelligence. "I'd rather discuss this privately, if you don't mind."

"I mind." Butch grabbed for Kane's wrist.

The air moved. Somehow Kane reached his feet and trapped Butch against the table, arm pinned between his shoulder blades. "No touching . . . *fella*."

Amber stepped back, her breath quickening, goosebumps springing to life along her arms. Who the heck moved that fast? "Let him go."

Kane immediately released Butch and backed away from the red-faced brute.

"Get out," Butch hissed through gritted teeth.

Kane nodded, his gaze on Amber. "We're not finished." Smooth strides and he was out the door.

Good Lord. Who was that fast, strong, crazy man? And he'd forgotten his change.

Butch rounded on her. "Who the hell was that guy?"

"I don't know. At first I thought he was one of Hanson's guys, but he denied it. Just some lunatic who likes beer." She shrugged off the unease. They were finished—whether tall, dark, and smooth liked it or not. She had enough problems, including the two drunk morons at the bar.

Before she could give Butch a hint, the mammoth

grabbed both guys by the necks and tossed them out the door.

Grinning, Amber finished busing her tables. Handing Butch his share of tips, made much larger than usual by Kane's fifty, she dodged into the back room and grabbed her coat. Tugging her calculator from the pocket, she double-checked her math to make sure she'd been fair with Butch. Yep. It was after two in the morning, and her yawn cracked her jaw. The other two waitresses had already headed home; one with a sleek-looking cowboy, the other to pick up her kid at the sitter's.

"Wait a sec, and I'll walk you out." Butch threw a towel into the sink and squinted past the small windows to the snowy world outside. The phone rang and he grabbed it, his wide face splitting in a smile.

Amber laughed. "Say hi to Sandy for me." No way was she waiting until Butch got off the phone with his sweetheart, who was attending a real estate conference in Wyoming.

Tugging on threadbare gloves, she slid outside into snow and beauty. Soft, the moon glinted across sparkles of now-peaceful snow, more than a match for the myriad of stars now revealed since the storm had passed. But thick clouds were quietly moving in again.

Drawing her coat closer around her shoulders, she glanced around the quiet parking lot, ready to run back inside the safe bar in case the drunks hadn't left.

The door opened and nearly smacked into her back. Butch stomped outside. "I said I'd walk you to the car." He held out his arm like a prince at a ball.

Amber grinned, sliding her hand along his elbow. "I figured you'd be a while."

He shrugged, the cold not seeming to bother him even in the thin T-shirt. "I'll call Sandy later tonight."

Ice and snow slowed their progress toward Amber's ancient Volkswagen Bug, but they finally crossed the parking lot. The metal had faded to a barely-there green, but the car ran. Amber stomped snow off her feet, glancing at the blue tinge marring the powder. "You said you'd switch de-icers to an environmentally safe type. This stuff will poison any animal that tries to eat the snow."

"I will. As soon as I use up the old stuff." Butch scraped ice from the windows with a credit card.

"Fine." The old stuff was going to magically disappear the next night Amber worked.

Butch shook snow off his hands. "How's your granny, anyway?"

Amber slid inside the car and turned the engine over, leaving the door open. The Bug sputtered to life. "She's better. I mean, I think she's better. Her color is good." Grandma Hilde had been kicked in the head by one of their horses the previous week and remained unconscious in the small county hospital. The fact that the horse was one that never riled up was yet another mystery to solve. "I'll give her a kiss for you when I visit tomorrow."

"She'll be okay. That woman is a tough old bird." Butch slammed the door shut.

Amber nodded. Grandma Hilde had to be okay. After waving at Butch, she meandered down the quiet street.

As Colorado towns went, Natureville was pretty sweet. Quiet, peaceful, and with roads easy to maneuver.

She'd driven about three miles outside of town when her engine clunked. Once and then twice. The vehicle lurched and rolled to a stop. What the heck? Pumping the gas, she twisted the key in the ignition. Nothing. Not even a sputter.

A deep breath centered her. Okay. She could handle this. Maybe she should take an automotive class when she signed up for community college. It'd been six years since she'd earned her GED, and it was definitely time to get an education.

Snow covered the pine trees on either side of the road. No nearby homes offered a way to call for a ride.

Quiet slammed all around her.

The bar was about five miles behind her, and home was even farther the other direction. Hadn't she read that staying with the vehicle was the best move? But the temperature was falling rapidly. Her feet were already dead tired. The thought of walking home in the thick snow made them hurt more. Things were just not going her way.

Lights in the rearview mirror blinded her until she looked away. High lights, bright, obviously part of a truck. That truck rumbled to a stop behind her. Her breath speeding up, she tried to squint in the side mirror.

Nobody got out.

Every scary movie she'd ever seen flashed through her head. Slowly, she reached over and locked the door.

Her heart picked up its pace, and her harsh breathing was the only sound in the world besides the ominous growl of the truck. Puffs of clouds came from her mouth. Panic froze her in place as the windows began to fog.

Clouds wandered above and partially covered the moon. Oh God.

Butch drove a Suburban and lived above the bar. She didn't know anyone who had a truck lifted at least two feet like the one behind her. Why the heck wasn't the driver getting out?

Scrambling for her purse, she grabbed a ballpoint pen. Yeah, that'd help. A slightly hysterical giggle rippled from her chest.

Both doors opened on the truck, and two men jumped to the ground, snow billowing up. The drunks from the bar.

Amber licked her lips. Okay. That might be okay. Or a

complete disaster. Either way, she clutched the pen so hard her fingers ached. As a teenager, hadn't she snuck to watch a movie where the heroine jammed a pen in the bad guy's neck? She turned her head to watch the guy on her side of the car stumble along until he finally knocked on her window.

A slightly blurry face bent down. "Hey, baby. Your car lasted longer than we thought it would."

Heat filled her head until her ears rang. Although his voice was muffled, the quiet night allowed the words to penetrate past the filmy glass. She lowered her voice into an authoritative tone. Hopefully. "I have a gun and have no problem shooting you between the eyes, jackass. Get lost."

He threw back his head and laughed, the sound obnoxious in the peaceful woods. "You're one of them eco-nuts from the farm. No fucking way you got a gun."

No, but she had a pen. "What do you want?" The question held risk, or rather the answer did. But sometimes a girl had to know in order to make a plan.

A *smack* to the passenger window had her jumping and biting back a shriek. The second guy leaned down and pressed his mouth against the window. "I'm Chuck." Full, sloppy lips left a round mark.

Didn't the dumbass know not to kiss anything icy? Hopefully he'd stick.

Drawing in a deep breath, she wiped her window clear. "Well?"

The guy outside her window smiled. "We're, ah, here to talk you into selling to Hanson. You crazies don't need that much land, now, do you?"

Relief, raw and hard, ripped through her so quickly her knees weakened. "The land?" Thank goodness. They wanted the land. Something a woman alone could be happy about. "Yeah, sure. I'll talk to the others."

He smiled, menace tipping his lips. "Well, now, we're supposed to convince you. Come out of the car, pretty lady."

Fear rushed back.

A shadow caught her attention. One second the moonlit road was clear . . . the next a man wearing all black stood with long overcoat flapping in the wind.

He came out of nowhere. No vehicle, no hint, just a tall figure in black like something out of a movie.

The clouds parted and the moon slid down to highlight him. Hard, primitive, predatory, fierce eyes lighter than possible stared out of a chiseled face.

Amber slowly sat back as far as possible in her seat. "Kane."

CHAPTER 2

Amber bit her lip, her gaze on the figure dead-center in the quiet road. His name fell easily from her cold lips. Instinct whispered the two guys flanking her car were silly jokes compared to the motionless man taking in the situation. The clouds groped the moon, plunging half his face into darkness.

Her shoulders shuddered from something other than the cold.

"What did you do to the vehicle?" Low, male, Kane's voice carried through the night and past her windows.

The jerk on her side of the car took several lurching steps toward Kane. "None of your fucking business." Fumbling in his jacket pocket, he yanked out a gun.

Amber gasped and reached for her window. Quick motions had the glass partially rolled down. "Wait a second, here. I know Hanson wouldn't want you to kill anybody." Okay, probably not true. Hanson had plenty of blood on his hands. "Let's all pretend this never happened and go on our ways."

Kane settled his stance. "Drop the gun or you're really going to piss me off."

What a terrible idea. That was no way to negotiate with a drunk on a mission. Should she get out of the car and try to defuse the situation? Seemed like a bad move, but staying inside wasn't a great idea, either. The Bug was dead, and at some point, she needed to get out. Or at some point, one of the menaces around her would break a window. While she didn't trust Kane, him getting shot and leaving her with the two brutes held little appeal.

With a quick prayer, she unlocked the door and stepped outside.

"Get back in the vehicle." Kane kept his gaze on the man in front of her.

Yeah, probably a good idea. Keeping the door open and her body protected by metal, she bunched her knees in case she needed to jump back inside. "We all need to stop this, right now. This has gone too far." Though Hanson's men had intended to take it further. Fear and cold set her teeth chattering.

"I'll ask you again—what did you do to the Volkswagen?" Kane's hands remained relaxed at his sides, his voice calm, his tone slightly irritated.

Chuck leaned against the front bumper of the car, the metal protesting his massive bulk with a loud *crunch*. "Shoot him, Alex."

Kane sighed, the sound carrying on the soft wind. He dodged to the side and cut in, grabbing Alex by the neck and slamming his head into the Volkswagen. A sickening thud filled the night, and Alex slid to the ground.

Amber gasped, her gaze on the streak of red now smeared across the faded metal hood.

She swallowed, her entire body going stone-cold. Gravity dropped her to the seat. As her butt hit the torn leather, her brain fired awake. Panicking, she grabbed the door handle and yanked it shut, slamming her fingers on the lock button. What was she going to do?

Wide-eyed, she stared out the front window. The clouds deserted the moon again, allowing streaming light to illuminate the entire area.

Kane scratched his head, his gaze on her, one eyebrow lifted. With a shrug, he turned toward Chuck. "Before I knock you out, would you mind telling me what you did to the car?"

Chuck stepped away from the Volkswagen, his red flannel coat bright in the moonlight. "Why?"

"I need to know if I can fix it, or if I need to borrow your truck." Relaxed, calm, Kane's posture nevertheless hinted at a hard edge.

"You're not takin' my truck." Loud and slurred, Chuck's voice carried on the wind. Visibly gathering his courage, he shot forward, his head down. Three long seconds later, he smashed into Kane's gut in what should've been a powerful tackle.

Kane didn't move.

Chuck dropped back on his butt, and snow sprayed over the hood. The *clunk* of his head against the Bug's grill vibrated the entire car.

Kane frowned, rubbing his chin and eying both downed men. His gaze lifted to her as he stalked toward the grill.

She swallowed and pressed back into the torn leather. What were his abs made of? Steel? He had to be wearing a bulletproof vest to have knocked Chuck out so easily. Reaching out, she twisted the key several times. Please, God, let the ignition start. Nothing happened.

Kane reached the grill. "Pop the hood, *Beag Gaiscioch*."

Little Warrior? Amber lifted her chin—boy, did he have her pegged wrong. Poor, crazy, tough guy. She rolled her window down an inch so he could hear her. "Listen, ah, thanks for the rescue, but I'm no warrior, and you need to leave me alone." Rationalizing with the crazy man probably wasn't going to work.

"So you do admit to your heritage." He gestured toward the hood. "You speak Gaelic."

"My grandmother is Irish, and she insisted I learn."

Amber reached for the lever. No reason not to let him
take a look. "You need help, and I have some ideas."

"Good." The hood popped open, and he leaned down.
"The demons are coming, and we need to get you secured." His voice rolled underneath the hood and straight
to her chest. Sexy and low.

Why in the world were all the sexy guys nuts? "I know
a good shrink in town. He can help you."

"Stop playing games with me, Amber. My patience has
ended." Kane sighed loudly. "They pulled the oil plug and
drained all the oil. Your motor overheated. *Damno is totus
ut abyssus.*"

"Overeducated rich guy," she muttered. How many
languages did Kane know, anyway? "That wasn't Gaelic."

"No. Latin." He slammed the hood closed. "Get out of
the car, darlin'."

How had he heard her? She'd barely whispered. "What
did you just say in Latin?"

"Damn it all to hell." He stalked around the car to place
a hand on her door. "I didn't want to swear in front of
you. Now get out."

Great. The lunatic had a sweet side. Didn't they all?
"No."

"Yes." He leaned down, dark face blurred beyond the
icing glass. "You'll freeze to death in there. Please get out."

"If I don't?" A smart woman always examined all op-
tions.

"I'll break the glass, probably on the other side so you
don't get cut, and then I'll lift you out." Reasonable, he
sounded like he was discussing the weather.

"That's assault and kidnapping."

"Actually, it's battery and kidnapping." He pulled up on
the lever, which didn't give. "Though I promise I won't
hurt you."

"Until you get me to your spaceship and start probing

me." Why hadn't she gone to college and taken an auto-repair class just for basic knowledge? She didn't even know if he was telling the truth about the car, and looking inside the hood wouldn't help her. She reached for her purse with her left hand, keeping her right wrapped around the pen. Her only weapon.

He frowned, his puzzlement clear even through the fog. "Why are you playing games? I don't have time for games."

"Please leave me alone." Cold permeated the silent car, and she began to shiver. "Why are you wearing body armor?" Cops called bulletproof vests "body armor," right? No way was the dark-eyed warrior a police officer.

"I'm not. Get out of the car." He stood, taking that handsome face out of sight.

"Are, too. Chuck hit your stomach and was instantly knocked out."

"This would be so much easier if you trusted me." Kane released the door handle and yanked open his silk shirt.

Abs. Powerful, well-defined, and sexy-as-hell abdominal muscles filled her window. The guy had a decent tan as well. "See? No armor."

She tried to swallow and choked instead. *Wow.* Those things were more of a weapon than a defense. "Ah, yes, I see." Maybe Chuck had been really, really drunk. Yeah, that was it. How in the world was she going to get away from Kane if Chuck couldn't take him down? Reason and kindness. She had a brain and could be quite persuasive when necessary. "I'm not defenseless."

"I'm aware of your power. That's why I'm here." Graceful movements propelled Kane around the vehicle. "Cover your face."

She yelped, scrambling to unlock the door and jump outside to glare over the Volkswagen. "Do *not* break my window."

"Of course." Rebuttoning his shirt, he strode around the hood and grabbed her arm. "We'll take the truck."

He smelled like warm cedar and maleness. They'd made it halfway to the vehicle when realization dawned. She tried to dig her feet into the snow and halt his progress. "Wait a minute. You can't leave those guys lying in the snow."

"Why not?" Kane continued on, tugging her along as if she were a wayward toddler.

"They'll freeze to death."

"So?" He reached the truck and yanked open the door, both hands wrapping around her waist to lift her two feet into the cab. Like she weighed absolutely nothing.

A flutter that had nothing to do with the winter chill wandered through her. "You're strong."

He shrugged. "Strong enough. Scoot over."

Panic swooshed out her breath. "No. We can't leave them to die."

Exasperation rode his strong sigh. "Why the hell not?"

So much for not swearing around her. "It's murder."

He glanced back at the quiet scene. "Not really." Examining Alex still lying on the ground, Kane cocked his head. "I'd say it's more self-defense, and well, death by being a moron." He glanced up at her, and his lips tightened. "I don't think their plans for you were very honorable."

"Maybe not." Dread and relief at her escape from the two henchmen commingled through her. "But we're not leaving them here to die." Swinging toward Kane, she angled her legs to kick him in the chest. "Either help them, or I will."

More Latin spilled from him as he pivoted and stomped toward Alex, effortlessly lifting the unconscious man and carrying him to the truck. Shoving the front seat out of the way, he tossed Alex in the back. Seconds later Chuck landed on top of Alex. Kane pushed the seat back and jumped inside to slam the door, muttering as he put the truck in DRIVE.

Kane's strength was unreal. He wasn't even breathing hard.

Amber scooted to the far door. "You swearing in Latin some more?"

"Yes." He backed the truck down the empty road until reaching a turnaround. "I have a niece I try not to swear around. Latin used to work. Well, until she learned Latin." He frowned.

"How old is your niece?"

"Twenty." He rubbed his chin, the frown deepening. "Suddenly she's all grown up. Well, kind of. Twenty is still young. Too young."

"Too young for what?"

"To save the world."

So many thoughts zinged through Amber's head, she pressed her free palm to her eye. "Does your niece know that fact?"

"Know what?" Kane maneuvered the truck around a downed pine and back onto the main road.

"That she's supposed to save the world." Hopefully he didn't have some hapless woman imprisoned somewhere. How crazy was Kane?

"Sure. Janie gets visions." Kane flipped on the wipers to combat the beginning of another snowstorm. "But we're trying to make sure she doesn't end up in danger or with the world hanging on her shoulders—we're hoping to end the war soon."

"War?" Amber eyed the quiet forest outside the truck. If she jumped out, could she outrun him? "What war?"

Kane sighed. Again. "The war. Vampires, Kurjans, Demons . . . even the shifters. Please don't pretend you are unaware of the war. Your playing dumb insults us both."

Well, shit. She sure didn't want to insult the crazy bastard. "Sorry."

"Apology accepted."

Sympathy for the poor niece, if she really existed, tightened Amber's shoulders. "So, this Janie. She's your real niece?"

"Sure." Kane leaned forward to peer into the darkening storm. "She's been my niece since she was four years old—what an amazing little kid she was. My brother adopted her when he saved his mate from the Kurjans."

Okay. Which word to tackle first? The most intriguing one. "Um, mate? Your brother has a mate."

"Yes. My brother Talen took Janie's mother as a mate. He was a bit overbearing at first, but you have to know Talen. His vision of the world is pretty set in stone. Though, to his credit, he found the right mate for him and everything worked out."

"Overbearing, huh? Hard to imagine." Kane spun quite the story—wasn't most genius close to madness? Poor guy. "Um, at the risk of insulting you again, what's a Kurjan?" Amber might as well get all the facts she could in order to inform the guys who'd want to put poor Kane in a straitjacket.

Slowly, deliberately, Kane turned his head to pin her with a hard look. "Stop it."

"Okay." Agreeing seemed wise. A few more minutes and they'd be back in town. She'd run for it the second he stopped. Her gaze caught on a water bottle peeking out from under the seat. "For goodness' sake. Why in the world would you buy bottled water?"

"Ah, I was thirsty?"

She shook her head. "So drink from a fountain. Do you know what that plastic does to the environment? You should care, darn it."

"I won't buy water in a bottle again."

"Thank you." The earth wasn't going to last if people failed to start taking care of her. A smart man like Kane, regardless of his insanity, should realize that fact.

He frowned, clearly puzzled.

"What?"

"I'm trying to figure out how to handle you," he said.

Her eyebrows rose until she could feel wrinkles. "Excuse me?"

He glanced back at the road. "Three of my brothers have mates, and they all handle their women differently. I was trying to figure out the best way to handle you because I've had enough of the games."

Fear wandered down her spine on the heels of irritation. "Your brothers hurt their, ah, mates?"

"No, of course not." He shrugged. "Though most often, a mate ends up over a shoulder heading elsewhere. I always thought brute strength a silly way to end an argument." His gaze raked over her. "Now I'm seeing the reasonableness of the act."

She cleared her throat. "They don't harm, their, ah, mates. Right?"

"Never." He shook his head. "A vampire would never harm a mate."

Oh, Mother Earth. He said *vampire*.

CHAPTER 3

K ane drove the truck through the archway of the small town, his gaze on the snowy road, and his mind on the quiet woman in the passenger seat. She hadn't used her right hand since getting out of her car. What kind of a weapon did she hold? Probably not a gun, or she would've pointed it at the drunks trying to accost her.

Most likely she held a knife.

An odd choice, really, considering she must know he was a vampire. She'd have little chance of harming him. While she was a demon destroyer, a powerful mind warrior . . . she was still human. Still so very fragile.

The vulnerability she'd tried to hide in those stunning black eyes had stopped him cold. He'd even saved the two drunk morons who had planned to hurt her—an unnecessary and truly time-wasting act. But she'd asked, and he'd hurried to do her bidding.

What in the world was wrong with him?

He'd told Dage he could handle the mission. Talen would've just hog-tied the woman and dragged her home. Same with Conn, their other brother. But Kane had hoped to reason with her.

Why did she have to be so stunning? Beautiful enhanced women were a distraction. One he couldn't afford, even if the world hadn't gone to hell. Two huge goals

loomed before him. First and foremost, he needed to save
Jase. Then he needed to cure a virus created to take out
his loved ones.

But now, he needed to find patience and some sort of
camaraderie with the woman. The sooner she made her
move with the weapon, the sooner he could illustrate
there was no hope of escaping him. She needed to help,
and she would.

He cleared his throat. "Where should I take the snoring
drunks?"

She jumped, swinging her torso toward him, those
pretty eyes wide. "Ah, good question. There's an all-night
restaurant north of the bar—we can drop them off in the
parking lot."

Her voice trembled and her shoulders stiffened.

Wonderful. She'd make her move at a public place. He
shook his head. "Whatever you're planning won't work."
It was only fair to give her warning. Maybe she'd heed the
threat.

"I'm not planning anything."

Nope. The woman wasn't going to heed shit. "Is there
a reason you won't help me?"

She picked at a loose thread on her jacket. "I don't believe you about the demons." Her lips quirked. "I'm sorry."

Oh. Well, that was an odd one. "Why not?"

"Demons don't exist." She scrunched up her face. "I
mean, probably."

"You can trust me." While he understood the need to
hide her gifts, he couldn't allow the subterfuge to continue. The sooner they got that unpleasant reality out of
the way, the sooner she could help him find Jase.

"Sure. Yeah, you're totally trustworthy."

He turned west along darkened streets toward the bar.
"The demons took my youngest brother hostage four
years ago—and you of all people know what they've done

to him." A rare rage heated in Kane's gut, and he shoved all emotion down.

"Me of all people?"

"Yes. As the only demon destroyer we've ever found, you must know what they can do. What they will do."

"Demon destroyer, huh?" She shifted in the seat. "You sure you have the right gal?"

His hands tightened on the wheel. "I'm sure."

"You poor, crazy man." She sighed. "How many brothers do you have?"

So, she was going to humor him. "I have four brothers—Jase is the youngest."

"Where do you fall in the lineup?" Her smile whispered sweetness.

"Smack-dab in the middle." He fit the middle child cliché to a T. The peacemaker, the brilliant one, the one in the middle. "When the first war intruded, and my older brother had to step up as king, we all fell into place. I'm his confidant when he needs logic and order. And a plan."

"Sounds lonely."

How odd. Kane narrowed his eyes, glancing at the woman. "No. We all do our jobs."

"What about when you don't want to be logical? What about when you're angry and want to hit something?" Streetlights from quiet storefronts glinted off her nearly white hair, turning her into an angel.

He shrugged. "That's an indulgence I can't allow. The king needs me logical, so I am."

"Maybe that's why you went a bit . . . off the track."

Good Lord. Was she back to that? "Stop playing with me, sweetheart. Logic can kick your butt as quickly, if not more efficiently, than a good broadsword."

"Was that a threat?" Her posture went ramrod straight.

"Would a threat work?" he asked, an unwilling smile tingling his lips.

"No."

That's what he thought. Bright lights spilled from the all-night diner and cut through the softly falling snow like an invitation. He maneuvered the truck into the parking lot. Regret filled him as he grabbed Amber and hauled her across the seat. "We can't have you jumping out, now, can we?" He turned to shove Chuck in the shoulder. "Wake up."

Chuck groaned.

Good enough. Kane cut the engine. "They'll awaken soon and head inside. We need to get out of here." Jumping out, he kept a firm hand on the woman, even while helping her to the ground. What kind of a moron lifted his truck so high a lady needed assistance getting out?

Her boots scattered snow as she landed and then regained her balance. "Thanks." She kept her gaze on his chest.

"Sure." He shut the door and waited patiently for her to make a move.

She remained still. Snow billowed softly to coat her lovely hair. A small shiver racked her shoulders.

He peered down at her. "Amber?"

"Yes?"

"If you're going to attack with whatever's in your right hand, could you hurry it up? We need to get going."

She started, her gaze slashing up to him. "How did you know?"

He shrugged. "What kind of a knife do you have?"

Her cheeks pinkened, and she drew her hand forward. "I have a pen."

A blue ballpoint pen. He blinked twice, his gaze on the harmless tool.

Maybe it was the ridiculousness of the pen. Maybe it was the woman's courage in planning to use it on him. Or maybe it was the sheepish half-smile she gave.

Either way, his heart rolled over.

Warmth flushed through him, so hot, so fast, his ears rang. His mind blanked. For the first time in centuries, his brain shut off. The woman was crazy. Stepping in, he grasped her chin and tilted her head back.

Her eyes widened, and then her gaze lowered to his lips. A soft sound of surprise emerged with her breath.

He dove in, allowing the animal within to awaken. For the first time in three centuries, there was no thought. All instinct ruled as his mouth took hers . . . no finesse, no calculation, just pure, raw need. He shoved her against the truck, his other hand clutching her hip as he went deeper.

Honeysuckle exploded along his taste buds as his tongue swept inside her mouth. Not gentle, not persuasive, just taking. Claiming.

And it wasn't enough. Not even close to enough.

Pressing into her, body to body, heat to heat, something clicked. Beyond his brain, beyond his body . . . somewhere deeper.

Finally, he found home.

Her nails bit into his skin as she rose to her tiptoes, meeting him more than halfway. A small whimper escaped her as she tightened her hold, her nipples pebbling against him.

A low growl centered in his chest, and he palmed her butt, yanking her into his erection. At the contact, fire rippled up his spine. He needed to be inside her . . . now.

Her flesh filled his hand and he squeezed, feeling her moan inside his mouth. The jeans were a hindrance. With a growl of impatience, he slid his palm beneath her waistband and found silky smooth skin. No underwear—or she wore a thong. He slid his finger over. Yep. She was wearing a thong. Jesus, his head might blow off. As he kneaded her butt, awareness pressed in. She was cold. Or rather, her rear was cold.

He broke the kiss, breathing heavily, his gaze on her upturned face. Snow fell on her lashes as her eyelids fluttered open. Her cheeks were rosy, her mouth bruised. Tempting lips formed a perfect *O* as awareness filtered into her eyes.

Flattening her palms against his chest, she tilted her head to the side, a question pursing her lips.

The restaurant door burst open, and several men wearing faded flannels stomped out. They stopped. The one in the front, bushy beard covering his face, frowned. "Amber? You okay?"

Thoughts scattered across her face.

Realization slammed Kane, but before he could react, she shoved him back. Hard.

"Yes. I need to get inside," she breathed. Pivoting, she hustled through the snow to the front door. "Have a good night, boys." She darted inside the restaurant.

The men glared and then plodded toward their various rigs to take off.

Kane stood alone in the dark, snow cooling his face, his cock throbbing, his temper spiraling. Wait a minute. He didn't have a temper. Damn it. Without question, he needed to get himself under control before yanking Amber back outside. His palms itched with the need to finish what they'd just started.

The phone in his back pocket buzzed. A quick glance confirmed the call came from headquarters. For once in his life, Kane ignored the king's call. Shoving the phone away, he eyed the restaurant door. The phone buzzed again, somehow more insistently. Jesus. He flipped the lid open. "What?"

There was a pause before Dage spoke. "What's wrong?"

"What's wrong?" Irritation had Kane's voice emerging hoarse. "What's wrong is that I'm on a mission and people keep fucking calling me. That's what's wrong."

Silence reigned for a minute. "Well, I'm fucking calling you because we intercepted a communication—two demon scouts are heading for you right now. You have about an hour before they arrive."

"Now that's a good reason to call." Kane rubbed his eyes. "Thanks for the heads-up."

"I'll send Talen for backup."

Kane's eyes flashed open. Talen had no finesse. "Keep Talen home. I've got this." No way would Kane let one of his brothers manhandle Amber. Even as the thought zinged through his head, he acknowledged the irony. One kiss and he wanted to protect the woman. "I need to get a grip."

"What was that?"

Shit. He'd said that out loud. What the hell was wrong with him? "I said, I have a good grip on her. I'll be in touch." He flipped the phone shut.

The stress of failing time after time to rescue Jase would cause anybody to lose control for a moment. Kane straightened his shirt, taking several deep breaths of the chilly air. Calm settled over him. He hadn't slept in too long—an easily remedied situation, and one he'd take care of the second he delivered Amber to headquarters.

Squaring his shoulders, he swiveled around and reached the door in two strides. Tugging the thick oak open, he stepped inside. A cash register sat before him. The main area of the restaurant lay to the right, an alcove to the left. The scents of burnt bacon and scrambled eggs hit him as he viewed the mostly empty booths lining the window. Nobody sat at the stools lining the counter. Small and not even close to quaint, the restaurant didn't do much business at three in the morning. An inebriated trio of women sat in the farthest booth—the women who'd ridden the saddles earlier. One wore a drink-riddled sash with the words FORTY AND FANTASTIC bedazzled across the middle.

She caught his eye, smiling widely as she teetered in the booth.

He gave a short nod and glanced around the room. Amber wasn't in sight. Lifting his head, he inhaled. The scent of wild heather lingered under the bacon smell. Following the scent into the alcove, he stopped short in front of two restrooms, one labeled with the word HEIFERS, the other BULLS. And people thought he was clueless when it came to women. If someone called one of his sisters-in-law a heifer, they'd die. Painfully.

He rubbed his chin and frowned at the paneled walls. *"Damno is totus ut abyssus."* Shaking his head, he shoved open the door for heifers. Empty. Yet her scent clung strongly to the room. Cursing his stupidity, he strode across damaged tiles to the half-opened window at the end of three stalls. He peered out and glared at her perfect boot-prints in the snow.

Yanking his overcoat closer, he stuck one leg over the sill, scooted under, and dropped to the ground. If his brothers could see him now, he'd never live it down. He'd lost one tiny human, and he'd just jumped out of a heifer bathroom. "Fuck." No need to swear in Latin. His desire turned to extreme irritation. When he found Amber, and he would, they were going to get some damn things straight.

He followed the footsteps back to the bar and an empty parking spot. She'd borrowed the Suburban that had been parked next to the building all night. Snow flew as he stomped his boots clean. "I'm the smartest fucking person on the planet," he muttered.

Glancing around the deserted parking lot as snow bombarded his overcoat, a smile rose from deep within him. Then laughter. Throwing back his head, he laughed until his ribs ached. Finally, he sobered and wiped his eyes.

Now wasn't the time for laughing.

She'd impressed the hell out of him. Maybe he'd finally found the one person smarter than him—he'd never been outmaneuvered like this. Another chuckle escaped him as he turned to run after the most exasperating woman he'd ever met.

But man, could she kiss.

CHAPTER 4

Amber tiptoed into the ancient farmhouse and paused as reality set in. Grandma Hilde was in the hospital. No need to be quiet. With a sigh, she stomped her boots free of snow on the threadbare rug and then sat on the polished wooden steps to yank off the boots.

A low meow echoed before Picard wound around her legs. The gray tomcat had lost an eye and was missing fur down the right side of his body from some tragedy that had occurred before he'd adopted her. She picked him up, rubbing her nose against his good side. "I know I left you enough food, so stop asking for more. You wouldn't believe the night I had."

Her lips still tingled.

She shook her head. The best kiss of her life had come from a nut job. A crazy, sexy-as-hell lunatic. Life was *so* not fair.

Picard purred against her for a moment and then struggled to get down. She released the finicky animal so he could dart into the kitchen.

A clock ticked in the quiet gathering room, and darkness cascaded from the kitchen. The only two rooms on the first floor were empty without Grandma around. Amber stood, peering out the window at the snow outside. So pure and fluffy—yet so dang cold. The sun would rise in about an hour, and she should try to get some sleep.

Glancing toward the living room, she gave a short laugh. "Kirk and Worf, get off the sofa."

The two battered but now healthy black labs didn't even stop snoring. She'd rescued the dogs from an abusive situation a year ago, and they'd quickly taken over the house.

"Whatever," she muttered. There was no sense shoving them off as they'd just jump back on the second she went upstairs. "Do you want to go outside?"

They didn't even open an eye.

She shrugged. Someone from their small community had probably let the dogs out earlier. "Fine. See you in the morning."

An ache set up in her back that traveled to her neck as she climbed the stairs toward her bedroom. Two bedrooms shared the second floor with a bathroom between them. Old, clean, and comfortable, the house had been Amber's home for nearly twenty years, since they'd settled in the eco-village.

But the farmhouse didn't seem like a home without Grandma Hilde.

Amber trudged into her bedroom, flipping on the light. Papers spread over the wedding-band quilt Hilde had sewn for Amber from her old baby blankets. With a sigh, Amber sat and shoved the college admission papers to the side.

The community college had open enrollment, so even though she'd only earned the GED, she'd get in. But how would she fare in the classes?

Sure, her grandma and their small community had homeschooled her, teaching her everything from math to germ warfare. But it still wasn't a public education. Had she learned everything the other people had? At least since it was a community college, she'd be among other twenty-five-year-olds and not a bunch of teens.

She blinked, wincing at the dust on the hand-carved dresser across the room. A member of her community had given the stunning piece to her on her sixteenth birthday, and even the dust didn't take away from its beauty. The house definitely needed a good cleaning before Hilde came home.

The old-fashioned green phone on her nightstand rang. She grabbed the receiver, her heart racing to life. "Hello?"

"Hi, baby girl. I got your note," her grandmother said.

Tears sprang to Amber's eyes. "You're awake." She'd known her grandma would wake up and had left a note that she was to call immediately, regardless of the time. "The doctors said your concussion was really bad."

"What do they know?" Hilde coughed. "Though, whatever they gave me, I'm groggy as heck. There's something I know I need to tell you, but my brain won't kick into gear. What happened, anyway?"

"Jonsie went crazy and kicked you." Amber shook her head. The mild old horse had never even snorted loudly before.

"Oh no. Is he okay?"

Amber smiled. Leave it to her grandma to be worried about the horse. "Jonsie is fine. After he kicked you, he smacked his nose into the wall and needed stitches. We think he must've been drugged."

"By Hanson," Hilde breathed.

"Probably. But we don't have proof, and the sheriff is Hanson's brother-in-law, so . . ."

"I'll figure out something when my brain starts working again. Darn drugs." Hilde slurred the last part.

"Okay—I'll come down there right now."

Hilde sighed. "No, you get some rest. I'm really tired."

Amber nodded, relief making her voice husky. "Okay. I'll come visit you in a few hours."

"Visit? Come get me in a few hours. I'm coming home. 'Night."

Amber hung up the phone and blinked away tears. Thank goodness. Hilde was the healthiest person she knew, never even getting a cold. As usual, she'd gone down to the community barn to feed the horses. When Jonsie had knocked her out, she'd looked so fragile and suddenly old, lying on the ground.

Picard jumped on the bed, purring as he settled into Amber's side. She leaned over and flipped off the light, then curled around the rumbling cat. "Everything will be all right, baby." Finally, she closed her eyes and slipped into sleep.

Morning came far too early. A hot shower erased the aches of the previous night before Amber threw on old jeans and a sweatshirt. After she fetched her grandmother from the hospital later in the morning, she would finally register for those college classes. Hopping downstairs, she let the dogs and cat out.

Winding into the kitchen, she glanced at the canning jars lined up on the counter. Maybe she'd take huckleberries from the freezer and make jam after retrieving her grandmother.

A knock sounded on the door, and she paused in place. "Come on in."

The door opened and her friend Mason stomped inside, followed by two elderly ladies, Mildred and June.

"We heard you ran into some trouble on the road." Irritation darkened Mason's faded blue eyes as he hurried into the kitchen. He rubbed the gray whiskers on his chin, a sure sign of his agitation.

Darn Butch. The overprotective bear must've called when she'd had to borrow his Suburban. He, of course, had made her tell him the entire story before handing over the keys.

"I'm fine. Though we really need to talk about Hanson

because he isn't going away," Amber said. In fact, Hanson had upped his campaign with those drunk morons to get their property significantly. The jerk wanted the land to build a high-end golf course community by the northern rocks.

Amber gently removed Mildred Mallosee's coat from her frail body and helped the elderly woman to a chair at the table. "Grandma is awake and thinks she can come home today."

Mason dropped into a seat with a sigh of relief. "That's good news. The doctors weren't hopeful she'd wake up, but I knew she'd make it."

Yeah. The doctors had no clue how strong Hilde could be. Amber soothed her palm along the table. Hand-carved and long enough to seat their entire village of twenty people, the table bore grooves and scars showcasing family gatherings. For two decades, since Grandma Hilde and Amber had relocated to the small community farm, every community meeting had taken place at the table.

The scent of Hilde's natural and homemade lemon cleanser hung comfortably in the air.

Matching oak cabinets held an eclectic mix of home-made tableware for the group. They had more than a couple of skilled potters in the community. Amber eyed the ancient coffeepot near the stove. "Anybody want coffee? I just bought organic beans."

June Parrymore leaned forward from her place at the table, her unruly gray hair tucked somewhat up in a hat. She tapped a huge syringe filled with a golden liquid against her large hand. "I knew Hilde would be all right— I'll go with you to pick her up later. But forget coffee. We need to talk about the guy who kidnapped you. Was he one of Hanson's men?"

Kane. The mysterious, sexy-as-hell, unfortunately crazy Kane. "I don't think so." Amber dropped into a seat, her legs softening in relief after being on them all night. "He helped me get away from the two guys and seemed to be another lost soul. I'm sure he's long gone at this point."

"What if he isn't?" June's lips firmed into a white line. Where Mildred barely took space, June dominated it.

Amber blew out air. "If he isn't, we're in a world of trouble."

"Meaning what?" Mason asked.

"Meaning, Kane didn't seem like a guy who loses often. But I really don't think he was with Hanson."

June pursed her wrinkled lips. "I don't like the sound of him."

Yeah, but the guy could kiss. Amber shook her head. Where was her brain? She pointed to the syringe. "What's in the vial?"

June shrugged. "Tranq. We were heading down to the southern barn to knock Jonsie out so we could take a look at his stitches."

Amber nodded. The group all shared a love for animals. Ages mostly over forty . . . six men and fourteen women, a community who'd gathered to live together and take care of the land as much as possible. They lived off the land, protecting it.

More than ever, Amber needed Grandma Hilde home since Hanson had picked up his campaign of terror in an effort to get the northern rocks.

Mason cleared his throat. About sixty years old and honorably discharged from the military, he'd somehow become the unofficial leader of the group. Even with his gray hair to his shoulders, his bearing confirmed his military background, which was as far as he'd go in talking about his past. Everyone had learned not to ask.

He rested calloused hands on the table. "Did you call the sheriff about last night?"

"No." Amber shook her head. Butch had argued they

should call the police. "But I'll head over there later in the morning and give some type of a report, though considering he's related to Hanson, I don't know what good it'll do." Besides, she couldn't prove that Hanson's men had messed with her car, so the trip didn't seem worth the effort. Also, Kane hadn't really kidnapped her, so why bother filing a complaint about him? But she'd promised Butch, so she'd go.

Mason nodded. "I'll go with you."

A tingle warmed the back of Amber's scalp. A slight pain, more of a tickle, but something strong enough to catch the breath in her throat.

She started to turn just as the front door ripped from the hinges and flew hard into the stairs. Splinters cascaded in all directions. Leaping to her feet, she pivoted to put her body between June and the threat. Mason was faster, reaching the end of the table and settling his stance.

The wind threw snow to cover the wooden floor.

Two men stomped inside. Huge men, they wore black uniforms with an odd silver insignia across the left breast. White-blond hair and deep black eyes made them almost twins, but their faces lacked similarity. Large and trim, their shoulders drew back as if at attention. The one in the lead lifted his head and sniffed the air. Seconds later he zeroed in on her, sharp canines flashing in a smile. "Destroyer."

The tingle exploded in her head. She staggered back. Sparks flashed so hard behind her eyes her eyelashes singed. Pain, internal and complete, compressed her lungs.

She shook her head with a whimper.

Mason leapt for the guy, one hand going to the jugular, the other punching to the gut. The guy growled, slamming a fist on Mason's head. Her friend went down hard.

June screamed, and Mildred clutched her chest.

Sucking in a deep breath, Amber crept toward Mason and dropped to one knee. A sigh of relief escaped her as she checked for the pulse in his neck, even as agony spurted behind her eyes. She glanced up at the guy in front. "Who are you?"

His eyes morphed to yellow and then back to black.

She gasped, leaning over Mason to shield him. Shaking her head, she shoved down bile. Okay. Something was going on with her head and eyes. Some sort of extreme migraine. Grandma Hilde had migraines. Maybe the condition was hereditary, and Amber's escape of them had ended.

The guy grabbed her arm, yanking her up. "We have orders to take you, Destroyer, but killing you is permissible." Rough and gravelly, his voice passed beyond hoarse.

Permissible? Who talked like that? What the hell? She swallowed. "What am I, some sort of prize in a nutso scavenger hunt?" Kane had called her a *demon destroyer.* "What is really going on?"

The long fingers around her arm tightened, and she bit her lip to keep from wincing. No way would she give the jackass the satisfaction. His fingers chilled her flesh even through the shirt.

He leaned down, breath somehow cold against her ear. "Leave with us now, or we kill everyone here. With great pleasure."

Amber stilled and glanced at her family. Mason was unconscious, and not one of the elderly ladies could take on two huge guys. A vibration uncoiled in her gut—fear. She'd never truly felt terror until that moment. She forced her face into calm lines and whispered back, "What do you want with me?"

"We're going to kill you." His soft tone matched hers. "At some point. But first, we will figure out your gifts."

A shiver shook her shoulders. "I don't have gifts." Besides having the greenest green thumb around, she had no true talents, or the last job she'd take to pay Grandma Hilde's hospital bills wouldn't have been in a Western bar.

"Let's kill them anyway." The other guy ground out his words as if gravel lodged in his throat. "They've seen us."

Okay. There didn't seem to be any way to reason with them. She was a pacifist, but she'd protect her family with any means necessary. If she kicked the guy holding her and he went down, did she have enough strength to take down his buddy?

She'd left her ballpoint pen in the car.

Her thoughts crawled through her brain as if mud had been inserted in her skull. What was wrong with her? She shook her head and focused. If nothing else, she needed to get the guys away from her friends. "Let's go now, and I won't fight you." For now. Once she was away from June and the others, she'd figure something out.

The one holding her nodded and jerked her toward the open doorway. "I'll take her out, and you get rid of these people."

The other guy purred and pleasure lit his dark eyes.

Heated air spiraled down Amber's throat. "No." She wrenched away from the brute, yet he held tight, tugging her toward the doorway.

Dawn light glinted off the snowy entryway, peaceful and serene, even with the freezing air riding its beams. Amber folded at the stomach, her butt out, struggling in his grasp. "I'm not leaving them to die."

"Yes, you are," he said in a hoarse monotone, pulling her into the morning.

"No, she isn't." Strong and dark, Kane stood on the porch, long coat flapping in the wind.

Her kidnapper halted and released her arm. "Kayrs."

Chapter 5

Relief rushed through Amber so quickly she stopped struggling, her eyes widening on Kane. Two seconds later, her brain kicked in, and she shot a kick toward the guy's knee. Her foot hit to the side and bounced off like she'd attacked a brick wall.

With a hiss, he took a step forward and swept his hand toward her head.

She ducked.

Then Kane was on him, grabbing the guy around the neck and throwing him into the living room. He settled his stance, his back to Amber. "Leave, now."

The other guy in black smiled again and dropped into a crouch. "Killing a Kayrs will make me a legend. Hand-to-hand?"

"No." Kane yanked out a glowing gun and shot the guy in the chest. Green lasers rippled from the weapon, impacting the man. The jerk stumbled back, blood squirting from the wounds. "You should watch more movies, asshole," Kane muttered. Three steps had Kane at the end of the stairs, gun pointed at the man rising to his feet. "Where's my brother?"

"Dead." The guy lifted his chin, his lips tipping.

Kane shot him in the knee.

The guy fell to his one good knee, a low groan escaping his destroyed voice. "Still dead."

Kane's shoulders vibrated. "We both know that's not true." He spoke softly, a promise of death in the low tones. "You know who I am?"

"Yes. Kane Kayrs . . . the smart one. Useless in a fight." Grabbing a sofa-end, the man shoved to his feet.

Kane chuckled, the sound emerging harsh. "Right. I've spent centuries learning your anatomy. There's a reason you sound like a Halloween ghoul, and I know all about making your vocal cords hurt even more. I can keep you alive for months during torture. Maybe years."

Yellow swirled in the guy's eyes again, and his face paled. "Possibly. But I'm sure it's nothing compared to what your brother goes through on a daily basis. No matter what you do, no matter whom the king sends, you'll never get the youngest Kayrs back in one piece."

Kane's head jerked up. "Thank you."

Surprise had the other guy stilling. "For what?"

"Confirming he's alive." Kane fired three strange green shots into the guy's neck and sent him sprawling into the old brick fireplace. Turning toward her, Kane's face lacked the charm from earlier, leaving a hard predator in its place. "Believe me now?"

"No." She choked, coughing and glancing from the two downed men to Kane. "I don't understand what's going on. What is going on?"

"What's going on"—Kane tucked the gun in his coat—"is that I have to decapitate these two, and then we need to get on the road. More demons will be coming."

Jesus. Maybe she'd taken him too literally. Maybe "demon" meant some sort of weird cult. "So these guys are demons?" Regardless of their affiliations, and death threats, she couldn't let Kane cut off their heads. They were dead.

Someone needed to call the sheriff. Though, what could the two dead guys possibly have wanted with her?

"Yes, these are demons." Kane removed an eight-inch double-edged knife from his boot. "Surely you sensed them—your head has to hurt."

Actually, her head had stopped hurting the instant Kane shot the second guy. What was up with that? She dropped to the stairs and pressed a hand to her heated forehead. "I'm fine. Though now I'm really hot." Biting her lip, she barely kept from swaying.

Kane lifted an eyebrow and glanced at her face. He reached out, placing a cool palm over her forehead. "You're burning up." Stepping back, he rubbed his chin. "Interesting."

No wonder her head had hurt so badly earlier—she was coming down with the flu. "I don't see how my being sick interests you." She needed to get a grip on reality and call the police.

He shook his head. "No. You're not sick. You were fighting their powers just like white blood cells fight any infection in your body, resulting in a fever. Damn. I wish I could test your blood right now."

His eyes sharpened, his focus solely on her as if he'd forgotten all about the men he'd just killed.

Mason stirred and shoved to a seated position. His blue eyes took in her, the downed men, and Kane. "What in the hell?"

Kane eyed him. "You in charge?"

"I used to be in charge in the military. Here at home? Depends on the day." Mason lurched to his feet.

"I'm the good guy"—Kane swept his hand toward the two dead men—"they're the bad, and we need to get going."

"Sure." Mason leaned against the wall, his face pale, his shoulders down. "I'm confused."

He probably had a concussion. Amber pivoted to shield

Mason. "You'll be all right. We'll get some help." Even though Kane had killed two men, something in her whispered he wouldn't hurt her. Just like a psycho fan wouldn't hurt the object of his affection. Well, until he did. Shit.

The odd tickle in the back of her head sprang to life.

Seconds later, the man Kane had shot in the torso leapt up, arms encircling Kane's chest and knocking him into the wall.

Amber shrieked. How did the guy get up after being shot three times?

Kane snarled. Fangs ripped down from his mouth. He blinked twice, and contacts fell from his eyes. Deep violet swirled with black as he gave a cry from hell, arms shooting up to break the guy's hold, his head darting forward with a head butt. He impacted with the crunch of bones breaking.

The other guy went down again.

June cried out, "Devils. Oh my god. Devils."

The pain ebbed in Amber's head, but her gaze remained on Kane's fangs. He had metallic violet eyes. Reality took several long seconds to arrive. Could he be wearing some intricate costume? If so, why in the world would he do that? "You look like a vampire."

Irritation swirled through the odd shine of his eyes. "Of course I'm a vampire." He dropped to one knee and flipped the unconscious man facedown. Quick motions had his knife plunging in the center of the neck before Kane sliced left and right.

Decapitation sounded like fabric tearing. Who knew. Amber swayed, the blood deserting her head.

Kane grunted at the last pull of the knife, and the guy's head rolled toward the living room, thumping along the uneven floor. Blood spurted out on the way and left a trail of glistening red. The body relaxed in death.

Amber gagged and stumbled back against the wall. Bile rose quickly, and she shoved the nausea down, her brain fuzzing.

Without bothering to wipe off the blade, Kane rose and stalked toward the other fallen man. His movement was measured and sure, his flak boots clomping rhythmically with each deadly step. Blood dripped from the blade and dotted the floor with splatters.

"No," Amber whispered. Her knees trembled with the urge to run, but her feet wouldn't cooperate.

Kane leaned over and plunged the knife into the guy's throat, sawing until the head shoved free with a squish of sound.

Air whispered by Amber's arms as Mason rushed by, syringe in hand. Panic fired her brain to life again. She reached out to stop him and missed. Jumping forward, the ex-soldier pushed the needle into Kane's neck.

Roaring, Kane reared up and flipped around. Mason flew into the side of the couch and dropped to the floor, inches away from the dead guy.

Kane's eyes morphed black through the violet. Fangs dropped lower than before, and rage cut into his hard face.

Oh, Mother Earth. Amber gasped, her head jerking to the side. That was no costume.

Growling, blood dripping from where it had sprayed across his jaw, he pried the syringe out of his neck. "What?" He staggered forward, his head rolling to the side.

"Horse tranquilizer," Amber whispered.

The black of Kane's eyes completely covered the violet. He dropped to his knees and dented the floor. The fangs retracted. His dark hair flew as he shook his head like a dog with a face full of water. "We need to . . . go." Swaying, his eyes shut and he plunged face-first onto the wooden floor slabs.

For a moment, nobody moved.

Mason staggered to his feet. "June, go get four stakes and some rope. Run."

The ex-dentist nodded, grabbed her cane, and hobbled from the room.

Amber ran a hand through her hair. The smell of blood and death threatened to suffocate her. "We can't kill him. That's not who we are." Vampire or not, Kane was alive. And her family did not kill. The fact was even listed in the charter for their community.

Mason rubbed a swelling bruise on his jaw, his eyes hard. "We're not going to kill him. The sun is."

Wet and cold snow permeated his body before Kane's mind cleared. They'd removed his coat. He opened his eyes to a cloudy sky. He lay on his back on the frozen ground, arms and legs stretched and secured tight to rusty posts. The wind whispered through evergreens and pines, spraying snow across his face. The sun lit the eastern sky with the golden hue of a western winter, its tendrils of light beginning to wander through the gray. The light crept closer to his booted feet.

He shook his head and winced as barbells ripped behind his eyes. Good God. What had been in that syringe?

Forcing his chilled hand into a fist, he yanked against the restraint. Nothing happened. Whatever they'd given him was still slugging through his veins. If his brothers could see him now, there'd be no living at headquarters. Ever again.

Grimacing, he turned his head toward the main house. Several pairs of eyes stared out the window. "The sun doesn't hurt me," he croaked, not nearly loud enough for them to hear. At least they hadn't plunged a wooden stake into his heart. Oh, it wouldn't have killed him, but man, healing a heart took some time.

A chill swept along his skin. The snow spread far, coating a decrepit wooden fence about a mile away. Sighing, he glanced at the sun visible through a row of bristlecone pines. At some point, the light would hit him. What would the humans do when nothing happened?

A struggle sounded from the farmhouse porch. He turned his head again.

Amber shoved against the ex-soldier, Kane's coat in her hands. Her eyes sparked a deep black, and her cheeks had turned a lovely crimson. The soldier held her upper arms in his beefy hands.

Kane let a low growl loose.

Amber turned her head, eyes widening. "The sun is coming." Kicking the soldier, she jumped off the porch, heading straight for Kane with his coat.

He opened his mouth to stop her when she took a flying leap and landed full force on him, covering him with his overcoat.

Her knee hit him squarely in the balls.

"Holy fucking Christ." He bent at the waist as pain shot down both his legs. Nausea swirled in his belly. A frightening numbness followed the pain. He opened his eyes and only saw dark fabric.

"It's okay." Amber pressed down on his throat, frantically patting the coat around him. "I won't let the sun get you, but you're only covered to your knees. Will you burst into flames?"

He coughed for air. "Get . . . off . . . my . . . windpipe." His breath bounced off the material and warmed his face.

She released him and tucked the wool around his head. "Sorry."

He'd laugh. Really, he'd laugh at the ridiculousness of the situation if his testicles weren't on fire. And not in a good way. "Amber?" The coat muffled his voice.

She stretched across him, keeping him covered. "It'll be okay. Should we try to run for the house?"

Enough. "Hold on, sweetheart." With a growl, he yanked both arms up and in, using physics and his rapidly returning strength to rip his arms free. His shoulders protested, but the ropes gave. His hands gripped her thighs, hauling her into a sitting position as he sat up. The coat fell between them.

Surprise widened her eyes as she straddled him. "Kane?"

"The sun doesn't hurt me." As he spoke, the sun filtered down to warm their heads. He lifted an eyebrow, his groin feeling suddenly better with her perched on it.

"Oh." She frowned, thoughts scattering across her face. "I, ah, don't understand."

She really didn't. How was that possible? "You don't know anything about vampires . . . or demons, do you?"

"Um, no." She gently pushed against his chest and attempted to rise.

He tightened his hold to keep her in place. "Stay." Releasing one thigh, he grabbed the rope tied around his ankle and jerked it free, following suit with the other leg.

The soldier edged toward them, a baseball bat in his hands.

Amber shook her head. "Mason, now isn't the time to hit people."

Kane stood in one swift motion and shoved Amber behind him. "Don't make me hurt you."

"Why didn't you fry?" the soldier asked, his knuckles turning white around the bat handle.

"Legends are bunk." Kane stiffened as the sound of Amber's teeth chattering filled the quiet morning. Half-turning, he slid his coat around her shoulders while keeping his gaze on Mason. "I'm not here to hurt anyone."

"You're a vampire." Mason shook his head, his fear scenting the day with old grass and sulfur.

"Yes." Kane scrubbed both hands down his face. "Vampires are just a different species from humans. We don't take blood unless we need it in battle, we can't turn you into one of us, and we mean you absolutely no harm."

Well, they took blood in sex, too. But Mason didn't need to know that.

"Another species?" Amber stepped even with him, her gaze thoughtful as she peered up. The coat covered her to her toes.

"Yes. Different genetic composition." Unease had Kane clearing his throat. One of their laws included keeping his people a secret from the humans—was he failing on this mission or what? "I'd appreciate it if you would make up a story for the rest of your group, Mason."

The soldier frowned and shook his head. "This is unbelievable." He gestured with the bat toward the farmhouse. "Were the two guys you killed vampires?"

"No. Demons, who are another species." Kane was taking a huge risk in trusting the old soldier. "Bury them later today. The demon nation will leave you alone once I get Amber out of here."

"She's not going anywhere." Mason settled his stance.

"The demons will keep coming until they get her." Kane glanced down at the quiet woman. "They'll kill you all and then her."

"Why?" she whispered. "Why do they want me?"

How in the world could she not know who she was? "You have powers that hurt them, sweetheart." Kane scratched his head. "Though I don't know why you're broadcasting your skills all of a sudden. Has anything changed in the last couple of weeks?"

Amber shrugged, then paled. "Well, Grandma Hilde has a head concussion and is in the hospital."

The air whooshed out of Kane's lungs. "You have a grandmother?" Holy hell.

CHAPTER 6

Amber clutched the armrest of the truck, her heart beating so hard she needed to throw up. "There's no cell service this far out."

Kane flipped his phone shut. "No kidding." He drove the truck at unsafe speeds, somehow keeping all four tires on the ground as he sped over ice and around corners. He had nice hands. Tapered, strong, and capable, they handled the steering wheel of the Suburban with ease. As the SUV whipped around dangerous curves over black ice, Amber reached for her seatbelt. His nice hands wouldn't save her from crashing through the windshield if he hit a Ponderosa pine.

He glanced her way. "How long has your grandmother been in the hospital?"

"Just a few days." Amber settled in the seat and forced her shoulders to relax in case they crashed. "One of the horses got antsy and kicked her in the head."

"Ah. Any other relatives? Do you have a mother or father?"

"No. I never knew my father, and my mother died when I was a baby—some weird cancer."

"I'm sorry." Kane turned his attention back to the road just in time to slam on the brakes, flip around a corner, and punch the accelerator. The rear of the SUV fishtailed before sailing straight. "Is your grandmother gifted, too?"

Amber dug her nails into the armrest, stiffening in her seat. "Gifted?" Psycho Bend was around the corner. "You need to slow down." If he didn't, no way would they make it around the hill.

"I'm fine. Years of defensive driving training." Kane ran a hand through his hair. "Yes, *gifted*. You sensed the demons earlier, didn't you?"

Amber sighed. "If you mean my head wanted to explode in pain, then yeah, I sensed them." She retracted her nails from the leather and clasped her hands in her lap. Once the pain receded, her brain had been working overtime. "This is so confusing."

Kane nodded. "I'm figuring your grandmother knows concealing spells—something probably handed down through your family. That's the only conclusion I can come up with."

That was too unbelievable. Amber took a deep breath. "Grandma Hilde performs both morning and evening prayers . . . more like chants." Amber had promised she'd continue the tradition if anything ever happened to her grandmother, but she'd been so busy lately, she'd shrugged them off.

"Chants?" Kane maneuvered around Psycho Bend without a hitch. "In Gaelic?"

"No. Just a series of sounds . . . almost like humming an old song without words." While there had to be some sort of logical explanation for everything, there was no doubt Kane had fangs. Real vampire fangs. Maybe the two guys sent to kidnap her had been demons. And if demons existed, maybe so did destroyers.

If somehow she had a gift, and it had been hidden since her grandma had taken ill, then the chants had to have been important. "I'm in the dark here, not clueless." She said the words for herself as much as for Kane.

"Chants in song form without words. Very interesting." He took a deep breath. "Do a chant. Now."

"No." The response came naturally, easily. "Do you boss everyone around, Kane?"

"Yes." The calm inflection in his deep voice didn't change. "When it comes to experiments, medicine, and science, I do tend to give orders. I apologize." His smile reached his odd violet eyes. He hadn't bothered to put the colored contacts back in. "Would you please do me the honor of performing one of your grandmother's chants?"

Amber's lips twitched. "Do all vampires have charm, or is it just you?"

Surprise filled those eyes as he glanced at her. "Nobody has accused me of having charm. Ever."

What a load of baloney. "I watched a movie once where the vampires were charming and handsome because they were the ultimate predators. You know, they drew in prey and then . . . bammo."

Kane barked out a laugh. "Bammo?"

"Yeah." Amber shifted in her seat, heat climbing into her face. "Bammo. They sucked the poor humans dry."

"Sunshine, I promise you, I've never sucked a human dry." His voice lowered just enough to cause a fluttering in her lower belly. "Now, how about a quick chant?"

"Why?" Could she trust him? The guy had fangs, for goodness' sake.

"Good question."

The approval in his voice should *not* cause such warmth in her belly. "Thanks."

"Most immortal species can sense other species as well as enhanced humans. You're an enhanced human, and you're broadcasting strong enough to bring wolf shifter

scouts from miles away to check you out. That's how we
found you. I want to see if your chant shields you from
detection."

"Wolf shifters? Like people who turn into wolves?"
Where had reality gone to? Maybe she was in the hospital
with Grandma.

"Sure. Several of my friends can turn into animals."

Amber shook her head, searching for calm. "What
kinds of animals?"

"Most kinds. Shifters have three main classifications: feline, canine, or multis, who can turn into anything except
felines or canines."

She tilted her head to study him, her mind spinning. He
couldn't be serious. "You really are saying that shifters live
among us."

"Yes. You have my word."

Wow. Not only was that incredible, it was awesome.
Her mind ran through various possible scenarios. What
would a person look like who could change into a wolf?
Had she ever met a shifter and not known it? "Good God.
Have you ever seen a jackalope?"

He laughed. "Of course not. Jackrabbit and antelope
mixture? That's a Pacific Northwest joke. No such thing."

"I don't believe you." Her mind spun with the new
knowledge. "Man, I want to see a jackalope."

"There's no such thing in the immortal world, sweetheart."

She wasn't so sure. A second ago she hadn't thought
wolf shifters existed. "So, immortal? You guys can't die?"

"All species can die. Some of us are just harder to kill.
You have to behead a vampire, otherwise, we can repair
ourselves. And we only need your blood in extreme cases
of battle . . . or well, sometimes sex."

Amber swallowed hard. Okay. Taking blood during sex
was gross. Definitely gross. The butterflies in her stomach

were from nausea, not interest. No way. She was not interested in the sexy-as-hell vampire driving like a capable stunt driver. "So you take blood. What happens if you run out of blood?"

"We basically go brain dead. So we try to never run out of blood." He flashed a grin.

That grin was beyond sexy. Concentrate. She needed to concentrate. "You say I'm enhanced. Some sort of demon destroyer. Am I immortal?" Now that would be cool.

"No."

"That sucks."

"You could always mate a vampire, shifter, witch, or demon." Kane sped through the entrance to downtown. "Then your human chromosomal pairs would increase until you were immortal."

"I am so far down the rabbit hole." Much better to concentrate on the possibility of different species on earth than the word *mate*.

"The chant?" While he phrased it as a question, the tinge of a command echoed in the low tone.

She rolled her eyes. "Fine." Taking a deep breath, she closed her eyes and centered her thoughts.

Peace lowered her shoulders.

Calm stilled her movements.

The tune rose easily to her lips, soft and sure, the melody without words.

Humming through all five verses, she opened her eyes as Kane pulled into the parking lot for the hospital. Goosebumps rose on her arms as she finished the last note, pitching her voice just high enough to hit it.

The air in the front seat heated. Pressure popped her inner ears.

Kane's eyes widened. He grabbed her head and shoved her face toward her knees. "Get down."

With a shattering crack, the windows exploded. Cold

wind whipped inside. The world stopped moving for two seconds. Amber lifted her head, her heart pounding. "What the heck?"

"That's some power you have." Kane released her seatbelt, gently wiping snow off her cheek.

"No." She hadn't broken all the windows. "That's never happened before. We don't break glass with the chant."

"Well"—Kane rubbed his chin—"maybe since you haven't shielded yourself in a week, the power came out stronger. Or maybe it's because your grandma isn't here to help temper the power. Either way, that's all you, sunshine."

Amber blinked against the freezing wind, taking in the damaged window. Glass had flown far enough to hit the few snow-covered vehicles in the silent parking lot. "Butch is going to kill me." The bartender loved his refurbished Suburban.

"Windows can be fixed." Kane jumped from the vehicle and quickly crossed to open her door. "You're shielding now. I can't get a sense that you're enhanced." Intrigue and calculation filtered across his amazing face. "We'll have to figure out how that works. For now, let's get your granny before the demons find her."

Amber jumped down, her boots spraying snow as she landed. Panic had her shoving away from Kane and all but running toward the door. She tripped in the snow. Strong arms caught her seconds from falling.

He held on until she regained her balance, his heat reaching through the back of her coat. "Slow down, Amber. I'm sure your grandmother has continued to shield herself."

Maybe. But the woman was in a weakened condition, so maybe not. Amber nodded and stepped gingerly around clumps of snow to reach the door of the small, two-story building. Cedar lined the sides, creating an atmosphere of safety and coziness rather than a sterile hospital feeling.

She slid on the sparkling tiles toward the front desk, which was empty. Grabbing Kane's sleeve, she tugged him to the left and down a long hallway, passing several empty rooms. "She's at the end."

Amber quickened her pace, her heart thrumming. Everything was going to be okay. They'd grab Grandma Hilde and head straight for the sheriff's office. It was time to involve the police. Even if Kane was telling the truth and wasn't crazy, even if Amber wasn't crazy, Grandma Hilde would need police protection from the demons. Or the cult that thought they were demons.

She shoved Hilde's door open.

The bed lay empty.

The world stopped cold. The room tilted. A swirling began in Amber's head. She stumbled toward the wrinkled covers on the bed, reaching out a hand. The blankets were still warm.

Kane rushed across the room to the slightly opened window.

Amber followed, crashing into his back. She stared out the fogged glass. A black truck careened out of the parking lot, a HANSON Farms logo on the side. "That bastard." Pivoting, she bunched to sprint.

A strong hand held her in place. "Wait."

"No." Amber turned and shoved Kane in the gut. "We have to get to the police." Who knew what Hanson would do to Hilde. It wasn't like Hilde would remain quiet. She'd try to escape no matter how weak she felt.

"No police." Kane's grip firmed around Amber's bicep. "Tell me everything about Hanson and these northern rocks."

"Let go of me." Amber tried to break free with little success. "I'll scream."

"You scream, and I'll gag you." Calm and reasonable, Kane's voice remained pleasant as he issued the threat. "No police."

Ass-hat. Amber opened her mouth to shriek.

Kane's palm instantly fit over her lips, stifling the sound. His free arm banded around her waist, lifting her almost two feet so they were eye-to-eye. Then he waited, no expression on his angled face.

Fury shook her shoulders. She kicked out, aiming for his knees. Kane turned them, smashing her between the wall and his body.

His body was harder than the cedar.

Amber struggled, mostly immobilized, the heat from Kane sending her senses reeling. Anger melded with something hotter in her blood. She tried to bite his palm.

He pressed harder so her teeth couldn't find purchase. "I bite back, sweetheart." His fangs dropped low with the warning.

She stopped struggling. Her eyes widened to let in more light, and heat slammed down to her abdomen. His obvious control over himself even while trying to frighten her gave her an odd sense of security along with a bizarre desire to challenge his control. What was the vampire like when he actually let loose?

When had she truly begun to think of him as a vampire? His fangs remained low, leaving her no mental way out. Vampires truly existed.

One of his dark eyebrows rose. "Have we reached an understanding?"

Slowly, she nodded.

"Good." He removed his hand, and his fangs retracted. "Now I'm going to put you down, and we're going to walk nicely through the hospital to the parking lot. Understand?" Waiting for her second nod, he set her down.

She bit her lip as she calculated the odds of getting away

from him. But did she even want to? A vampire, one as strong as Kane, would come in handy with Hanson and his men. "Will you help save my grandma?"

"If you promise to help save my brother."

She breathed in through her nose, mind reeling. "By fighting demons."

Kane jerked his head and grabbed her hand in a firm hold. "No. You're not going to fight demons." He frowned, heading for the door. "You'll shield with your mind but from a safe place. I won't let you get harmed." His jaw set hard at the end. "Trust me."

Famous last words. "What if I can't figure out how to help you?" What if he was wrong, and she wasn't gifted? One tiny headache didn't mean she had a gift. Wouldn't she know if she had some weird mental ability?

"Let's get your granny back, and then we'll figure out how your gift works. One thing at a time." His voice stayed low, but a tenor of urgency ran through the dark tone.

Maybe the vamp wasn't as in control as she'd thought. She followed him into the still-quiet hall and out the front door. The wind whipped into her face as she glared at the Suburban. "We don't have windows."

Kane exhaled a puff of breath in the cold as he eyed the parking lot. "Any idea who owns the brown truck?" He pointed to an older Chevy half-hidden under snow.

"No. That truck has been there since Grandma was brought in. Maybe a patient owns it."

"Good." Long strides helped Kane draw her across the lot. "Let's wipe off the snow." Using his bare hands, he shoved several inches of snow off the windows. "What does Hanson want with the northern rocks?"

Amber shuffled snow off her boots. "My community owns fifty acres, and the northern rocks make up three acres. This is all about water rights. Well-testing around the rocks show plenty of water, and Hanson wants to put in several high-end subdivisions centered around a golf course. We won't let him."

Kane smoothed snow off the hood of the battered truck. "Your community? What kind of community? Like a commune?"

Amber laughed. "Well, kind of. We don't go around naked or anything. But we have banded together in an eco-village to live as much as we can off the land. Even my VW Bug is frowned upon. Most people only use vehicles in emergencies."

"Yet you work in a bar." His expression remained neutral, yet there was a hint of—what was that in his tone?

She bristled. "Don't judge me, rich boy."

One dark eyebrow rose. "Rich boy?"

"Yeah. That coat costs more than most people make in a month. Heck, in three months." Snobby people should have to live off their wits and the land for an entire year. They'd probably only last a week.

He frowned down at his coat. "Oh. My apologies, I didn't mean to sound judgmental."

"Accepted." Amber couldn't help a small smile. Kane had no problem apologizing when he was wrong, now did he? Confidence and fairness in such a sexy package—were all vampires so cool?

Kane dropped to his haunches, inspecting the front tire. "As a race, we're rather protective of females. Sometimes too much so. My sisters-in-law would never be allowed to work alone in a bar—just for safety reasons." He stiffened, catching his breath. Then he stood and whirled to face her. "Don't ever tell them I used the word *allow*. God. Ever. Please."

Amber laughed. "No promises." What were these sisters-in-law like? "Are they vampires, too?"

Kane frowned. "Ah, no. Vampires are male only. We

have to mate a female from a different species, and even then we only produce male vampires. Two of my sisters-in-law were enhanced humans, the other is a witch."

There was that *mate* word again. One simple four-letter word shouldn't send tingles down her spine. "A witch? A real witch?"

"Yes. Moira is incredibly powerful—you have a lot in common."

"What's an enhanced human?"

"A female with gifts—psychic, empathic, and so on." Kane banged the windshield wipers back onto the glass. "So, why are you working in a bar?"

"We make enough money to live off the farm by selling vegetables, fruits, and jams in the summer, and Christmas wreaths in the winter. But hospital bills are expensive, and we don't have health insurance." Amber shrugged.

"So selling the land to Hanson would give you much-needed money." Kane held out a hand.

Amber took it, allowing him to lead her around the truck to the passenger door. "Yes. But we'd be sacrificing the land and our way of life for money. Not a good sacrifice."

He opened the door and lifted her into the truck. "Interesting. Okay, let's go get your granny."

CHAPTER 7

Jase Kayrs settled against the rough stone wall, his gaze on the myriad of earthy colors in the rock across the small cell. Slowly, methodically, he listed every shade of brown he could see. Tan, beige, mud . . . the list went on and on. For every new shade he noted, victory filled him that his brain still worked. Somewhat.

Take that, demons.

A crude window had been cut high above to let in light during the day. Once in a while the wind would blow hard enough he'd get a whiff of the sea, but usually the smell of dirt filled his small space. There was a time he could control the elements and heat the small area, but no longer. Cold permeated through his skin to his bones—no muscles. Idly, he wondered how much he weighed now. Not much.

Water dripped down the grooves in the rock and splashed onto the hard ground. The *tip-tap* of it faded away into the familiar, no longer causing spikes of irritation to dig at his neck.

That had taken about a year.

Sometimes he saw faces in the rock. After particularly bad sessions with the demons, those faces would speak to him. And when he was at his lowest, he'd talk back. These days he seemed to be talking to the rock often.

A massive metal door took up one wall of the four-by-six prison. He'd tried to break the locks for so long without success. Now the sound of the locks engaging sent peace through his body.

Something told him that wasn't a good sign.

But for now, he was late for a golf game with his brother Kane. He and Kane played golf once a week, well, approximately. Time had ceased to be linear during Jase's captivity, but he was fairly sure today was golf day. So he shut his eyes, resting his head against a smooth area and sending healing cells to the kidneys his captors had beaten with metal poles earlier.

The image took longer than usual to fill his brain. Evening out his breathing, he dug deeper.

Sun shone down through pretty pine trees to glint off the grass, which was a lovely turquoise. Or should the fairways be green? His memory failed him. The scent of freshly cut grass infused his senses, and he inhaled deeply.

Kane strode out of the trees, two golf bags over his shoulders. He dropped one in front of Jase. "You're still visualizing. Nice job."

Yeah. Their oldest brother had taught them necessary skills for dealing with captivity and torture. Every time Jase played an imaginary game of golf, he won a small victory over the demons. Those victories kept him from going completely mad. At least, they had for some time. "I'm trying. I kicked Dage's ass in a boxing match yesterday." Or had it been last week?

"Now I know you're imagining things," Kane said with a smile on his angular face. "We're getting closer to finding you."

"No, you're not." It seemed shitty his imagination was fucking with him. "The real Kane wouldn't lie to me. I need the real Kane to show up." Of course, Jase was arguing with his own brain.

A tapping against metal jerked Jase from the daydream. Fury filled him. They'd interrupted his golf game. He shoved to his feet. "Bastards," he muttered to the morphing face in the rock.

Needles instantly ripped into his brain. The pain shot neurons into life and he gasped, dropping to one knee. The sharp stabs of pain cascaded down his spine to his tailbone. "Now that's new," he hissed.

The rock face nodded.

The door slid open.

He lifted his head, and his breath caught in his throat. "Female."

"Yes." The demon wrapped a chilled hand around his chin, turning his face. Her mental attack faded.

Jase shrugged away, stumbling to stand tall, at least a foot taller than the woman. Female demons were notoriously tiny. Blanking his expression, he stared down.

Black eyes, white hair, smoother than possible pale skin marked her as a demon. "I'm Willa."

"I don't need your name."

Her smile revealed even white teeth. "Oh, you might change your mind about that." She retreated, and two demon guards moved to grab his arms and haul him from the cell.

He rolled his eyes. At least, he thought he rolled his eyes. Months ago he'd lost some muscle function in his face. "Field trip?"

Long hair cascaded over her shoulders as she threw back her head and laughed. Throaty, hoarse, the chuckle confirmed her lineage as a purebred. Only pure demons had the odd configuration of vocal cords that created such hoarseness. Unfortunately, on the female, the tenor was almost sexy. She led the way through the underground labyrinth dressed in a tight blue sheath that showed off a toned butt.

"I bet I could bounce a shilling off your ass," Jase muttered.

The guards tightened their hold on his arms. The woman laughed again.

Shit. He'd said that out loud.

They reached a fork in the tunnel, and Jase braced himself for the right turn toward the room he'd dubbed "the torture cell." The demons had used both physical and mental torture in the rock-covered room, usually at the same time. In fact, the red stains on the walls were from his blood.

Sometimes he spent hours counting the different colors of red in the old blood versus the new, just to keep his mind on anything but the pain. Oddly enough, the rock faces never ventured into the torture cell with him.

They probably figured they'd never make it out.

The woman turned the opposite direction.

Eying the two huge guards dragging him along, Jase counted the closed doorways along the way. Then he cataloged each step for when he escaped. That probably wouldn't be soon. While he stood to six-foot-five, the demon guards were several inches taller, and certainly broader. How much weight had he lost, anyway?

Willa opened a door into a spacious room and swept inside, settling herself on a feminine divan. A plush Persian rug covered the rock floor, and priceless oil paintings adorned the walls.

Jase eyed an oil of the Northern Sea. Dark thunderclouds mirrored the tumultuous ocean, the scene both mysterious and somehow threatening. "I doubt Brenna Dunne would appreciate demons having her painting."

Willa shrugged. "Her oils will be worth a fortune someday, and our people need money as much as yours. Besides, Dunne seems to understand the demon mind-set with dark works like that."

Odd, but Jase hadn't noticed that dimension to Brenna before. "If you say so."

Will nodded. "The value of that work will soon increase—considering she won't have time for painting with Virus-27 affecting their kind."

Jase stumbled. The virus did affect witches?

The demon smiled. "Oops. That's news, huh?"

"Yes." His mind reeling, Jase allowed the brutes to shove him into a plush leather chair situated off the rug. Virus-27 had been created by his enemies to harm vampire mates—to take them with their twenty-seven chromosomal pairs from immortal down to human or maybe worse. Nobody had realized the virus would affect witches. But considering witches only had twenty-eight chromosomal pairs, apparently they were susceptible.

Vampires with their thirty chromosomal pairs were safe.

The tallest guy reached for a set of restraints hammered into the floor.

"No. I want his hands unbound." Willa crossed her legs, revealing silky skin.

The closest guard stiffened, turning toward her. An apparent, silent battle of wills ensued. Finally, the guard dropped the restraints and grabbed another set, clasping them around Jase's ankles. With a growl, he and the other guy stomped from the room, slamming the door.

What kind of game was this? Jase tugged a little on the restraints—not very impressive . . . he could probably break free. Even in his state, he had to outweigh the small demon. He lifted an eyebrow. Maybe.

She smiled, sliding to her feet and sauntering over to a bar set in the corner.

The stunning painting of the Northern Sea caught his eye again. There was a time he'd spent hours running along the beach, feeling the salty spray on his face.

Willa turned with a low hiss. "You like the painting."

"Yes." Lying seemed to be a waste of time.

"Or is it the artist who has captured your attention?" Willa asked softly.

Jase settled into the chair, surprise jerking his head. "Brenna? Well, she is a sweetheart." Or at least she was last time he'd seen her.

Willa laughed, the sound grating. "That witch is the reject of all rejects. Imagine an eighth sister being born to a seventh sister." The demon shook her head. "They should've killed her on sight."

Jase lifted a lip in irritation. While it was true that a seventh sister of a seventh sister was known to be the most powerful of witches, like his sister-in-law, Moira, maybe it was just coincidence that no eighth sister had ever been born. Well, until Brenna. The young witch's fathomless gray eyes had always intrigued him. "I like her." The words tumbled from him as if he were talking to the rock faces.

"Lucky Brenna Dunne." Willa turned back to the heavy antique. The bar matched the sofa and end tables. Late eighteenth century. Crystal chinked. Turning toward him, she carried a goblet full of red liquid. The smell hit him when she was two feet away.

Blood.

His stomach clenched in pain. Need had his fangs dropping against his will.

She held out the wineglass, and he hesitated before taking it, the world narrowing to the shimmering liquid. She pressed the stem into his hand. Inhaling deeply, the pure scent of copper and life filled his nostrils. No drugs, no substances that didn't belong in the blood were detectable.

Digging beyond deep, he shoved his fangs back up and lifted his gaze to the demon. "You're giving me blood." Now *his* voice sounded hoarse.

She shrugged a small shoulder and glided to retake her seat on the pink divan. "I figure the sooner we start getting along, the better. Speaking of which, I do apologize for the mind attack when I was outside your door. My re-action was instinctual—even now, you have power. Im-pressive power." Her black eyes sparked with interest. "You can drink the blood, Jase."

Saliva wet his tongue. When was the last time he'd taken blood? Maybe a month ago? "The blood is human."

"Yes. Fresh human—female—and no, we didn't drain her. She donated for a generous sum of money and went on her way."

That should fill him with relief. But his only thought remained on the blood. Still, he didn't drink.

Willa tapped a ruby-tipped nail on her chin. "Okay, I'm impressed. You've been tortured for almost four years, have rarely been given blood, and now have the pride to refuse to drink."

So it had been four years. Maybe his golf game had im-proved since he'd played so often in his brain. A part of him wanted to throw the blood in her face. The other part, the one growling for substance, wanted to drink fast and hard. And if he was ever going to get out of this hell-hole, he needed strength. So he took one small taste.

The molecules exploded on his tongue. A low growl erupted from his gut. Hunger roared to life throughout his entire body. He held her gaze, holding himself off from another sip.

A deep flush covered her sharp face. Interest lit her eyes. "That growl was quite sexy, Jase." Her voice came out more of a purr.

The purr nauseated him. "You have got to be kidding." Sending all his internal sensors into alert, he waited to see if the blood had been tainted. His senses were definitely off. The demons could've sneaked something past him.

"Actually, I'm not joking." She reached for a folder set off to the side and flipped open the top. "Jase Kayrs, the youngest of the brothers. Charming, talented, a good sport." One white eyebrow arched as she focused on him. "Yet you killed right along with the king in the last war three centuries ago when you were only fifteen. Something tells me you weren't as carefree as you appeared."

She was correct to refer to Jase in the past tense. The man in the file was gone. Maybe he had been carefree . . . perhaps not. Either way, that guy no longer existed after several solid years of demon mind games. And this was just another one. "So, I've always wondered. As a female, are you a demon or a demoness?"

She shrugged. "Both or either. We really don't care."

Enough with the small talk. Jase shoved his shoulders back. "What do you want?"

Closing the file, she tilted her head toward the goblet. "I give you my word the blood is pure. Drink it because you're going to need strength."

What the hell. He tipped the goblet and drank down the nourishing liquid. His heart flared to full speed. A tingling wandered along damaged nerves in his neck. The healing had begun. He set the empty glass on the Victorian end-table near his chair, tempted to lick the sides clean. But some pride must remain. "Now tell me why the hell I'm alone with a female demon." Female demons were incredibly rare, and this was the first one he'd met in person. The fact that they were alone seemed off.

She sighed. "You've never heard of me?"

"Nope."

"That figures." Pale pink lips pursed together. "I'm Suri's sister."

Suri was the leader of the demons, and a former friend of Jase's family. He'd also enjoyed torturing Jase for the last few years. "We didn't know he had a sister."

"He has two sisters." Willa rolled her eyes. "But of course, we're kept rather hidden. Especially in war."

"Two sisters, huh?" Maybe Jase's head had finally exploded. No way was he alone with a female demon who had just given him blood. No way. He tried to tune his senses to see if anybody was listening but only reached silence. "You're not hiding now."

"Yes, well, Suri has headed over to the States to incorporate some changes in our strongholds there. We're about to make a move on the king."

"My brother will destroy yours."

She flashed a strong smile. "Handsome, you've been in the dark too long. The Kurjans attacked your headquarters in Oregon a few years ago, and Dage hasn't recovered. Nobody has recovered, and rumor has it, your niece was injured. Badly."

Jase kept his face expressionless. The Kurjans had invented Virus-27 and were at war with the vampires, and they attacked every chance they got. The Kayrs family was always prepared. Demons lived for mind games, and this was another one. "Bullshit."

"Then how did we know his headquarters was in Oregon on the cliffs of the ocean?" Smugness lifted her pale lips.

Good question. There wasn't a good answer, so Jase remained silent. Finally, he stood, the chains rattling against the hard floor. "I'm done now."

She followed suit. "We're just getting started. You have a choice to make."

"Which is?"

"Either mate me, or I'll drive you crazy."

He almost sat back down. The air caught in his throat. "Are you nuts?" No way would a purebred demon, one of the royal family, want to mate a vampire. No way.

She cocked her head to the side. "That's debatable. Maybe." Her gaze swept down to his groin and back up. "I'm tired of being under Suri's thumb . . . tired of being hidden. You mate me, I'll get you free. We both know your king will protect me if I do." She turned and swept toward the door. "If you refuse, I'll drive you crazy, which will greatly please my brother. That'll gain me some freedom, but I'd rather have complete autonomy. Your choice."

Vampires mated by marking their women for all time during sex. The Kayrs family had a marking that appeared on their hands during the opportune moment that transferred to the mate as a sort of brand. His sisters-in-law had been greatly ticked off by the branding. "A mating is forever."

"Yes." Willa twirled around, eyes sparking. "We both know many matings have been arranged through the years. You can force the marking on your palm if you wish."

"No." The idea of tying himself to anyone remotely connected to the bastard who'd taken such pleasure in ripping his mind apart made Jase want to puke. "I'm not your solution—get free on your own."

Oil instantly coated his brain and slid through his gray matter with sticky fingers. Images followed next. Horrible images depicting his greatest fears: His niece dying, Dage being beheaded, brothers being brutalized. Jase tightened his knees to keep from falling. "That all you got?" His voice merged tinny as if from a far distance.

"No."

Spikes of pain ripped into his brain, flashing brutal images of blood and death. He staggered back. The chair caught below his knees, keeping him upright. His vision went black.

"My mind is far more powerful than any you've met, Jase." Willa hissed. "Think about my offer."

Blunt pain centered in his cerebral cortex and pounded out. He dropped into the chair.

Time spun away. He may have sat blinded for a minute—maybe an hour.

Chains rattled and strong hands yanked him up and through the door. The world spun several times around. His feet dragged uselessly on the stone. His stomach lurched, and he swallowed to keep the recent meal in. Suddenly, the pain retreated. His eyesight returned. Coughing, he regained his balance.

The guards tossed him in his cell.

Locks slammed shut, and something inside him shuddered. A glance at the rock wall showed a morphing of several faces, all new. Dropping to sit, he pressed his closed eyes against his knees. If his family was coming to get him, they'd better hurry.

But instinct whispered deep inside his mind that it was too late.

He lifted his head to see a large face in the rock nodding at him.

Definitely too late.

CHAPTER 8

Kane shoved a branch down, his gaze on Hanson's sprawling ranch house. Snowcapped mountains framed the log-style mansion, bright lights beaming out the myriad of windows in the morning hours. He'd finally reached cell service a mile out and had called for backup, but it had probably been a mistake.

Amber shook out her boots. "We had to call them."

"Did we?" Kane eyed the two men standing over by the tree line. Mason was definitely in fighting shape, but the other guy had seen better days. A retired pediatrician, he even had a cane. Being human must suck.

"Yes. Besides, you said your friends might not make it in time."

A wolf bayed in the distance.

Lightning ripped across the sky, and the wind whipped into action. A hell of a storm was coming. Kane glanced at Amber, who was now shivering. "Why don't you wait in the truck?"

"No." Her lips firmed. "I'm coming to get Grandma."

"I promise I'll call you when it's time, sweetheart." Earlier when he'd used the endearment, she'd pinkened nicely and almost listened to him. Keeping an eye on her, he gauged her reaction.

She smiled. Very pretty. "Thanks, but I'll stay right here."

Okay, *nice* wasn't working. Next track. "I'm being unclear, and I apologize. You're not going in the ranch house until I determine you'll be safe." Like it or not, he was responsible for her until turning her over to the king. The thought had his mind stopping for a nanosecond. For some odd reason, he didn't want to turn her over to Dage. Interesting.

The pink turned to a fine red blush. "While I appreciate the apology, you can shove it. Stop telling me what to do."

He frowned. How utterly confusing. "Hanson and his men will resist when we go inside. What could you possibly do to help?" She'd get hurt most likely, and he wouldn't let that happen.

"I'm helpful." She lifted her chin, eyes sparking.

He scratched his head. Bodily carrying her to the truck and tying her to the steering wheel seemed silly. Yet allowing her to get harmed for absolutely no reason seemed stupid. "There must be a way we can reach an agreement here." Why in the world was she being so illogical?

Two massive wolves suddenly appeared at his side.

Amber yelped, hand to chest, jumping behind him.

Well now, good timing. Kane grinned down at the largest beast; a fully grown male with rich brown fur. Then he turned toward the men from Amber's commune. "You fellas take the north side exit from what appears to be the kitchen. All I need you to do is make sure nobody escapes that way."

Mason eyed the massive wolves. "Uh, you have wolves for pets?"

"Sure." There was no doubt Kane would pay for that comment. "They'll guard the perimeter." Kane nodded toward the north. "Please take your position."

Grumbling, the humans hurried past the fence-line and around the house, the ex-doctor moving pretty well even with his limp.

If Kane had known Terrent would make it in time, no way would he have invited Mason and the doctor. But they should be safe covering the northern exit to the house. Kane grinned at the biggest wolf. "Thanks for coming so quickly."

Fur receded and the wolf morphed from animal to man with a popping of bones and a snapping of cartilage. Terrent stretched to his full height, shaking his thick head of hair. His dark eyes twinkled. Then he grinned. "Of course."

Kane tugged Amber to his side. "Terrent Vilks, meet Amber Freebird."

Amber pressed into Kane's side, her face a blazing pink, her eyes squarely on the wolf's face. "It's, ah, nice to meet you."

The naked wolf chuckled and captured her hand in his beefy one. He stood as tall as Kane, well over six feet, with a broad chest and powerful legs. "Sorry about the nudity, but clothes don't make the shift."

She nodded and cleared her throat. "Wolves. Shifters. Real shifters."

Terrent gestured to the other wolf; a sandy-furred male who'd remained in wolf form. "This is Joshua—he came along for some fun."

Kane nodded at the teenaged wolf. "Thanks for coming."

The wolf snorted, paws shoving snow out of the way.

Terrent rubbed a hand through his long dark hair. "We approached from the back and took a look in the window. Four men are in a study at the western rear of the house, reading some sort of map. I scented several weapons, but they're not visible. The rest of the house seems empty—no heartbeats or scents. What's the plan?"

Amber caught her breath. "What do you mean? The rest of the house can't be empty. My grandma is somewhere inside."

Terrent gave her a charming smile. Or at least what the wolf probably thought was a charming smile. Even in human form, wolves looked like predators, and Terrent was the predator of the predators. "Maybe we missed her. Don't worry, we'll search the entire house." His gaze met Kane's over Amber's head.

Kane gave a short nod. Grandma was not in the ranch. Damn it. Where had they put her? "Hanson is mine to, ah, question." No way in hell would he allow Amber to watch him torture someone. It was bad enough she'd watched him decapitate two demons. "I'll go in the front—you go through the back, and make sure not to change into human form again. We want to scare in a shock-and-awe moment—no kills unless absolutely necessary."

Terrent nodded. With another mischievous smile at Amber, he turned and ran through the field. Once he was several yards away, he shot into wolf form while leaping through the air.

Kane rolled his eyes. What a show-off.

Josh followed with a short yip. Both wolves disappeared around the house.

Kane forced his face into a frown and grabbed Amber's arms. Her small biceps were buried beneath layers of his thick coat. "You're waiting in the truck. You can either agree, or I'll tie you to the steering wheel." Yeah, he was bluffing. With a growl, he let his fangs drop low. Those were probably scary to someone not used to seeing fangs.

Her eyes widened again. "Fine. But the second it's clear, I'm coming in." She turned and stomped to the truck, his coat dragging in the snow.

Good enough. The thought of such a brave sweetheart being injured by a jerk like Hanson set Kane's jaw until his teeth ached. By the time he was through, Hanson wouldn't even think about messing with the commune.

Kane jumped past the bushes and ran full bore across the snowy lawn, clearing a fence without missing a step. Leaping across the spacious front porch, he hit the front door exactly in the center. Splinters flew in all four directions as the door shot inside to crumble against a marble table. The table smashed to the floor seconds later.

The crash of glass breaking followed.

Men's shouting filled the space.

He ran to the west, dodging through hallways filled with western art to land in a masculine study full of heavy leather furniture. A stuffed wolf's head hung above the fireplace mantle. Terrent was going to be pissed about that.

One man sat behind an ostentatious leather desk while three others stood against the far wall, their mouths open and eyes glued to the snarling wolves that had apparently jumped in the window.

Good old Chuck and Alex were two of the guys. Apparently the drunks had survived the evening.

Glass scattered across the room, shards sticking out of leather furniture and in the oak floor.

The men from the commune stepped gingerly past the broken sliding glass door and surveyed the scene.

Damn it. They were supposed to cover the north side.

Alex made a dash for the window, and Mason punched him in the throat. Alex hit the ground.

Nice move. Kane gave a short nod to Mason, who nodded back, his blue eyes sparkling. The guy was actually enjoying himself.

"You Hanson?" Kane faced the man behind the desk.

Fat jiggled beneath Hanson's jaw as he nodded, mouth wide, thinning gray hair standing up on his head. "Yes."

"Where's Hilde Freebird?" Kane fought a grin as the

younger wolf nipped at Chuck, who shrank back against a billowing velvet curtain.

Hanson coughed. "I don't know."

Sometimes the direct approach was best. Kane grabbed a silver letter opener off the desk and threw it, lodging the sharp edge in Hanson's left shoulder.

The man yowled in pain.

The wolves echoed the howl.

A soft gasp behind him caught him up short. Heat flared along his neck. Amber needed to learn to stay where he put her. He kept his gaze on the bleeding rancher as he addressed her. "You agreed to stay in the car."

"I changed my mind." Her boots crunched through glass as she scurried to his side.

Kane tuned his senses to survey the rest of the house. Nobody else was in the building. "Fine. Go search for your granny." By the time Amber returned, he'd know everything Hanson knew.

Amber nodded and ran from the room. The ex-doctor limped off to help her. Mason kept watch by the gaping hole in the wall, and the wolves remained still.

The rancher sighed. "Listen. I have no clue where Hilde Freebird is. We went to the hospital to get her, and she was already gone. You have my word." He gingerly reached for the protruding letter opener, grimacing as his fingers touched. With a groan, he yanked the weapon out. "Leave my house now, and I won't call the police." Blood slid down his shirtfront and over his protruding belly.

Chuck made a move.

Terrent stopped him, knocking the guy down and landing on his chest, teeth bared. The wolf's paws were wider than a normal man's hands, his claws dangerous and extended. But he hadn't used them. Yet.

Chuck whimpered. "Get him off."

Hanson's other two thugs remained still and silent.

Kane didn't have time for this shit. Reaching over the desk, he grabbed Hanson by the collar and threw him across the room. The man hit the mantel and fell hard. He cried out as his face impacted the floor. A second later the stuffed wolf head landed on his legs.

Grabbing the bloody letter opener, Kane stalked across the room and dropped to his haunches. He placed the sharp end against Hanson's good shoulder. "Tell me where she is. Now."

"I, I, don't know," Hanson sobbed.

Kane pressed the metal into the man's flesh.

The rancher cried out, his entire body shaking. The smell of urine filled the air. "I really don't know," he gasped.

Sometimes Kane just couldn't get a break. Taking a deep breath, he allowed himself to feel. Just for a second. Hanson's fear and pain slammed into him, and he shoved the sensations aside. Then he delved deeper, using the empathic abilities he hated. Irritation and frustration mingled in his gut.

The guy was telling the truth. Shutting off all emotion, Kane tightened his hold on the weapon. "Okay. Here's the deal. We're leaving here, and you and your men won't tell a soul about us. Got it?" He shoved slightly.

"Yes," Hanson groaned, his entire body shaking.

"And you'll forget your plans for the northern rocks and never bother the village again. Right?"

"Yes." Hanson's shoulders slumped against the floor.

Kane turned so the other men couldn't see and allowed his fangs to drop and black to shoot through the violet of his eyes. "If you bother them again, I'll be back. And I'll eat you for dinner."

The man gasped, and then his eyes rolled back in his head. He relaxed in unconsciousness.

Kane rose, facing the wolves. "We're good here. If you wouldn't mind, would you keep an eye on the village for the time being?"

Terrent growled twice, his saliva dropping onto Chuck's neck.

Kane fought for patience. "I know you'd like to kill him, but I'd consider it a favor if you allowed him to live this time."

Terrent gave a disgusted snort, tossing his head toward the mounted wolf head.

"Fine. If you want to kill him, hurry the hell up." Kane didn't have time for this crap.

The wolf smiled.

Chuck whimpered.

Panting, the wolf seemed to consider the situation. Then he gave almost a bored, canine shrug. With a quick swipe to Chuck's nose, he turned and leaped through the window. Joshua followed suit.

Mason scratched his head, eyes alight with intelligence. "Something tells me that was no ordinary wolf."

"No. And I'd appreciate it if you kept that to yourself," Kane said.

Slowly, Mason nodded. "That would be best."

Kane pivoted to find a pale Amber in the doorway. Shock covered her face as she stared at the still bleeding Hanson. "You stabbed him again."

"He'll live." Kane strode forward and grabbed her arm. "Say good-bye to Mason and let's go."

A rustle sounded in warning. Kane shoved her out of the way and turned in time to hear the firing of a gun. The bullet impacted his chest in a burst of pain. Leaping across the room, he grabbed the gun from Chuck and slammed his forehead into the guy's already scratched nose. Chuck flopped into unconsciousness. Kane crushed the weapon into bits.

Mason's eyes widened as he leaned against the broken door frame. "Are you all right?"

"I'll be fine." Kane took a deep breath, his chest hurting like hell.

The ex-doctor ran into the room, his spectacles lopsided on his face. "I heard a gunshot."

"Everyone is fine," Kane said mildly, wanting to snarl instead.

Mason nodded, his lips twisting as he glanced at Amber. "She's not safe with us, is she?"

"No. But we'll keep her safe." Kane took a deep breath.

Mason nodded, holding out his arms.

Amber rushed into them for a huge hug. "I'll miss you."

"Ditto, Freebird." Mason dropped a fatherly-type kiss on her forehead. "When things calm down, you'd better call."

"I promise." She wiped away a tear as she hurried over and hugged the doctor. Then she turned toward Kane.

He nodded. "We have to go."

Quick steps had them through the house and across the lawn. The storm had opened up to shoot clumps of snow down on their heads. The wind whirled more white around them and made sight difficult.

He opened the passenger side of the Chevy and lifted her inside, pushing her to the driver's position. "Drive while I heal." Blood dripped down his chest, not nearly as warm as the irritation filling his gut. Terrent had warned him about the presence of weapons. Two seconds using his empathic abilities, and he forgot logic. Which was why he never used them. What if he'd allowed Amber to get hurt?

With a growl, he ripped off his shirt as Amber pulled the truck onto the main road. A bullet hole dotted an inch above his heart. "Good thing Chuck is a lousy aim."

★ ★ ★

Amber clutched the steering wheel, struggling to stay on the road. Wind threw snow against the windows in a fierce tantrum. She blinked back tears at the thought of leaving Mason, Dr. Bill, and the rest of the family. As soon as she found Grandma Hilde and figured out a safe path for them, she'd call the others.

Kane's blood filled the cab with a copper scent. She coughed, her mind spinning. "I'll take you to the hospital."

"No. Get on the interstate going north. There's a place we can ride out the storm." Kane wiped blood off his chest. Grabbing his cell phone, he glanced at the face and grunted. Dialing, he lifted it to his ear. "Hi. Amber has a grandmother who was taken from Pinecone Hospital a couple hours ago, probably by demons. Send scouts out and find her."

He paused and waited. "I have a plan. No. We have a hell of a storm going on and you can't land. Find the grandma. I'll bring Amber in when the storm passes. She needs to be trained first, anyway." He sighed and listened, hand tapping on the armrest. "No. No training whatsoever. I need some time, Dage." After listening for another minute, Kane hung up.

Amber's mind fuzzed at the thought of her grandma with the demons. "We have to find her, Kane."

"We don't know where to look." He eyed the angry black sky. "But our scouts will find her. Dage will send them to the hospital, and then he'll contact our sources in the demon nation. Chances are they didn't take her far, and we'll get her back soon. For now, we need to get to safety."

The wind rocked the car, and Amber cried out, struggling to stay on the road.

"Pull over." Kane reached two fingers in his chest and

extracted the bullet. His flesh made a squishy sound as the lead sprang free. "Ouch."

Amber swallowed down bile. "Now that's just gross." She rolled the truck to the side of the road, fighting to keep the vehicle stable.

"Switch places with me." Kane threw the bloodied shirt on the floor.

"No way. You're injured." The guy was crazy.

Apparently he was done talking, too. With a sigh, he grabbed her arms and hauled her over his lap and into the passenger seat while sliding toward the driver's seat. Smooth movements had the truck back on the road.

Blood still coated his chest, but the hole was slowly closing. His defined abs tightened as he settled into the seat.

Amber reached for the seat belt. The storm swirled around them, all white and gray. Her grandmother was probably alone with demons. Actual demons. And Amber sat in the middle of a storm with a vampire who tortured a man as easily as most people picked up bread. No emotion, no regret, just pure coldness in execution. As she eyed the still bleeding immortal, her heart sped up.

Who was Kane Kayrs?

CHAPTER 9

The gorgeous cabin fronted a stunning lake with views from every window. Right now the lake churned dark and angry, reflecting the tumultuous sky as the storm raged all around. Amber finally felt herself relax in the plush surroundings. She'd bet almost anything there was a deep jetted bathtub close—and she was heading to soak.

Kane stalked into the room, having found a dark shirt that fit him perfectly somewhere else in the house. A pink backpack hung over one broad shoulder.

"Nice backpack."

He nodded. "It must've been Janie's."

Amber finished surveying the cozy room with its soft furniture and antique blankets. "Your brother lives here?"

"Talen did live here for a very short time." Kane tapped his cell phone against his hand, his frown deep. "When we went to war with the Kurjans, we consolidated at head-quarters, and he moved in with his family."

"I thought you were at war with the demons."

"We're at war with both." With a disgusted snarl at the cell phone, Kane shoved it in his pocket. "Did you get enough to eat?"

"Yes." They'd hit a drive-through window of a fast-food joint an hour after leaving Hanson's. "I'm still full." She moved to sit on a comfortable cloth sofa, very pleased it wasn't leather. She hadn't met Talen, yet she already liked the guy. He was probably a sweet-hearted pacifist like her people. "So, demons fight with mind control. What about Kurjans? What are they like?"

Kane tugged her up. "We don't have time to sit, darlin'."

She frowned and stumbled behind him through a beautiful hallway lined with Western oil paintings. What about a quick bath? "About the Kurjans?"

Kane shoved open the door to a home office that had a huge bookshelf lining one wall. "Kurjans have fangs and take blood like vampires. But they're white-faced, creepy, and the sun fries them."

The image made her wrinkle her nose. "Like vampires of legends."

"Yes." He grabbed two books off the top shelf and revealed a keypad.

"Why are you at war with the Kurjans and the demons?" One would think immortals could freaking get along.

Kane punched in a code. "The Kurjans declared war on us because they want Janie, my niece. She's been prophesied to change the world, and no, we don't know how. So when Talen got to her first, war ensued. Plus, they can only mate with enhanced females, just like vampires. So we're always competing, I guess."

"And the demons?"

"That's more personal. We made one of their enemies our friend, and well, the demons are basically assholes." Kane stepped back as the entire shelf slid to the side.

Guns.

All different kinds, a myriad of guns, lined the two walls. Vests and shields hung from another wall. Knives and swords lined the fourth. Kane grabbed a black vest he tugged over her head, fitting the Velcro tight. Following suit, he began shoving weapons in vest pockets, his waistband, and finally in his boots.

She tried to step away. "What are you doing? We don't need vests and guns." She needed a bath, darn it.

"Yes, we do." Grabbing a green gun, he pressed the cold metal into her hand.

"No," she protested, trying to shove the weapon away, "I don't shoot people."

"You do now," he said grimly. "Keep ahold of it." Taking her hand, he yanked the cell phone from his pocket to glare at the screen. "Still no service—probably from the weather."

As if on cue, the storm increased in force outside, smashing debris into the windows.

Amber jerked her arm free. "Is somebody here? I mean, do you sense demons—or Kurjans? Or whoever else wants you people dead?"

"No." Kane took her hand and led her around the house, grabbing his coat from the chair to yank over her vest before heading to the back deck. They stepped outside to be bombarded by blowing snow and cold. The sun had disappeared to leave a dark storm in its place. "There's usually a boat hidden down by the trees. We'll have to go for it."

Taking a boat in a storm like that? "You have got to be crazy."

"No. Crazy would be staying here," Kane shouted above the storm. "The demons may know about this place, and I guarantee the Kurjans do. I'd be very surprised if the Kurjans don't have satellite surveillance on Talen's old home."

She tried to balk, but his stride didn't slow. The icy snow ripped across her skin. Freezing air dried out her eyes. His coat dragged on the ground—way too long for her. They slugged through the ice-covered snow on the deck to at least a foot of powder on the small lawn leading down to the churning lake.

Glancing behind her, she took one last, longing look at the luxurious cabin. So much for the jetted tub.

The storm raged around them and smashed frozen pinecones into their legs. Kane kept his stride steady, his mind on the human. She stumbled again, and he turned to shield her from the storm.

Her pale skin was too delicate for the angry wind. Tucking her close, he placed a gentle kiss on her forehead. "We'll be safe soon."

She nodded, her eyes blinking rapidly.

Did he just kiss her head? Where was his brain? Comforting her would lead to her breaking down. Kane pivoted and led her down the path to the lake, trying like hell to block her from the wind.

Branches and clumps of snow beat against them as they wound down the obscure path. Kane dragged his feet to clear the way, hoping Amber's boots would keep her dry. Frostbite would be disastrous at this point.

Finally, they reached the beach. Snow mingled with sand to slam into their faces. When would the wind abate?

The metal rowboat sat securely between a massive pine tree and the rocky hill, snow covering most of the bottom. Kane darted forward and yanked the boat free before flipping it over. The metal scraped along the snowy sand as he dragged it to the violent lake.

Waves crashed in, angry and nearly black. But at least the water wasn't frozen.

He held out a hand for Amber.

Drawing the coat tighter with nearly blue fingers, she shook her head and backed away.

He didn't have time for her to fall apart. "Come here. Now." He pitched his voice low to cut through the storm and her panic.

She mouthed the word "no" and kept backing away.

If the woman went any farther, she'd be heading back up the trail.

The cold cut through his silk shirt and pants. If he was chilled, Amber would be freezing. Maybe he could entice her. "Let's go find some warmth, sweetheart."

Snow coated her hair when she shook her head wildly. So much for enticement. He leapt for her, grabbing both arms and swinging her into the air. Three strides had her butt slapping the metal seat, and he shoved the rowboat away from the beach.

With a cry, she jumped for him, arms stretched for the shore.

He sat her down again—this time harder. "Stay still or you'll fall in."

She gasped, gaze slashing to the churning water all around them. Black and merciless, the water mirrored the storm bashing the boat.

He shook her—waiting until her gaze met his. "Hold on for a couple more minutes, and I promise we'll find safety." The second his brother had purchased the lake house, Kane had memorized the layout and properties on the entire lake. There was a cabin on the far side that was only used for two weeks in the dead of summer by owners who lived in Alaska the rest of the year.

She nodded and settled down, her teeth chattering.

Kane grabbed the oars and started rowing, staying along the shoreline as much as possible. Getting caught in the middle of the angry lake was not in the plan.

Amber took a deep breath, her entire chest moving. "Do you need help?"

What a sweetheart. "No."

She blinked snow off her long eyelashes. Odd that Kane had never noticed eyelashes before. But Amber's were thick and dark . . . giving her an ingénue look that distracted him.

Rubbing her nose, she shivered. "You do everything logically, don't you?"

"Yes."

"Like when you stabbed Hanson. I mean, without being mad. No passion. You just . . . stabbed him."

Sure. "Passion gets in the way when you're fighting." Hell, as far as Kane was concerned, passion got in the way, period. Not that he didn't like a wild night with a woman. But in a fight, cold logic most often won.

"Do you regret hurting him?" Her eyes somehow darkened.

While Kane wanted to ease her mind, he wasn't going to lie. "No." His shoulders moved rhythmically, smoothly eating up the shoreline as he angled to the north. "I'm sorry." Well, he wasn't sorry he'd stabbed the bastard, but he could feel an apology for her distress. She seemed to need the apology, so he gave it a shot.

She nodded. "When you kissed me earlier—was that manipulation? I mean, did you feel anything?"

"Yes." While he hadn't wanted to feel anything, his cock had fired to life. There was something so sweet and sexy about the woman. "I wanted you—still do." They were going to need to warm up soon. Skin on skin was the best way to make that happen.

A logical thought, yet his heart sped up instantly. Man, he needed some rest.

The tiniest of blushes filled her too-pale face for a moment. "I don't like being manipulated."

"Okay." Really, who did? A quick turn into a small alcove, and Kane found the cabin he wanted. "We're here." Ramming the boat onto the shore, he forced a smile and helped her from the boat. "Everything will be all right."

Amber stumbled up the embankment, Kane's hand steadying her several times. Finally, the path smoothed out.

He turned to lift and cradle her against his chest. She protested, giving a slight struggle. He must be exhausted. He shushed her, tucking her head under his chin, his movements not slowing.

Warmth flowed from the vampire, and she instinctively snuggled closer. The guy would kill without breaking a sweat, and yet, she'd never felt safer. Well, physically safe, anyway. There was no question Kane was driven and would take advantage of her brain again to get what he wanted. But she could understand the drive to save family—she'd do anything for Grandma Hilde.

"Don't manipulate me again," she whispered against his neck.

He shoved a branch out of their way. His lips brushed her cheek. "No promises."

Tingles spread along her jaw. What would it take to get a promise from Kane? Something told her he was a guy who kept his word, which made him smart enough not to make promises.

Reaching an icy deck fronting a ramshackle cabin, he set her down, waiting until she regained her balance before letting go. Bending down, he surveyed the lock. "Step back."

She stepped away, sliding on the wood and grabbing the railing to keep from falling. The freezing wood cut into her fingers. Her stomach plummeted at the rough shack. They'd left a warm, plush, comfortable home for a crumbling hut? She shivered violently.

Kane kicked the lock, his boot hitting precisely to the left. The door swung inward. Reaching for her hand, he towed her inside a small room with a barely visible sofa and fireplace. "Stay here for a minute."

He crossed the room and tossed old newspapers and kindling into the fireplace. Long matches sat in a box next to the paper and ignited easily. Kane reached up and opened the flue, blowing on the fire before adding more kindling. "Come here, sweetheart."

She stumbled toward him, her gaze on the wonderful fire.

He stood, turned to survey her head to toe, and handed her the pink backpack. "You're soaked. Drop the wet clothes, and find something in here to wear." Reaching behind her, he grabbed a blanket off the one sofa and shook the heavy wool out. "Then cover up with this. I'll be back shortly."

Then he was out the door.

Shivering, her fingers barely working, she tugged off her vest, shirt, and pants, leaving on her panties. Reaching into the girly backpack, she yanked out a brandy bottle and a plastic bag filled with a woman's sweatshirt and yoga pants. Soft and well-worn, they were probably full length on the owner. Talen's mate must've been fairly petite. They fit like capris on Amber. She pulled them on along with the sweatshirt.

Pulling the blanket around her freezing body, she sat on the couch. Guilt filled her from using the wool blanket, but she couldn't throw it off. Poor sheep. But darn, she was cold. Heat from the small fire slowly penetrated the blanket.

Kane returned with arms full of wood. Precisely placing several pieces on the fire, he sat back, satisfaction on his face. "There we go."

Amber leaned toward the heat, her hands keeping the blanket closed. "Are we safe here?"

Kane nodded and held his broad hands out to the fire. "The storm has picked up, and we're safe for the night. My people will be here tomorrow morning after the storm has abated to get us, so no worrying. Just warm up."

Her teeth chattered and filled the silence for a few moments.

Kane reached farther into the backpack to produce crystal lowball glasses.

Amber barked out a laugh at the high-end crystal in the very low-end shack.

He poured them both a glass and settled himself into a purple chair that didn't come close to matching the faded avocado-themed sofa.

Amber took a deep sip, allowing the warmth to spread down to her belly. "I liked Talen's place better."

"Me, too." Kane grinned.

She couldn't help her answering smile. "Is Talen like you?"

"No. None of my brothers are like me." Kane leaned back in the chair. "Dage is the oldest, the king, and is always in charge. Next comes Talen, and he's, ah, a strategic genius as well as being overbearing. I'm next. Then Conn, who's the ultimate soldier and is mated to a witch. Finally, there's Jase."

"The one the demons took."

"Yes." Kane lost his smile. "I should've found him years ago. I've failed repeatedly." Emotion swirled in his eyes, only to be quickly banked.

She cleared her throat. "You scared me when you hurt Hanson."

"I'm sorry." Kane kept her gaze, expression not changing. "Torture is never pretty."

"It wasn't the fact that you hurt him." A hard as the truth was to admit, Amber would've done the same to save her grandmother. "It was the perfect precision and lack of emotion that was scary."

He lifted an eyebrow. "I'm not an emotional person."

"Why do I find that hard to believe?" she whispered.

That dark gaze searched her face, finally dropping to her lips. They tingled in response. The man went beyond good-looking to sex and danger combined. How was that possible? Besides, why would danger be sexy? But on Kane, the danger only enhanced his masculinity. Or maybe his masculinity enhanced the danger dancing on his skin. The intimacy of the quiet cabin and the safe haven from the storm made both elements too appealing.

The wind slammed snow against the windows, and she jumped.

He studied her like a lion that was more curious than hungry. Right now. But the slightest hint hung in the air that he could change his mind at any time. "Amber, I'm by no means a demon, but all vampires have some psychic ability."

Oh no. Did that mean he was reading her mind? "What's your point?"

"I'm going to attack your mind with mine, and you need to defend yourself."

Panic bit into her. "No."

"Yes. We need to start training as soon as possible." His gaze rose—relentless and sure. "Get ready."

"No, Kane—" Pain slammed into her mind so fast she caught her breath. Invisible fingers dug between her gray matter, tearing. "Stop it."

"Fight me."

"No." Her knees drew up and she wrapped her arms around them, shoving her forehead against her jeans. "Stop."

"Damn it, Amber," Kane muttered, his voice hoarse. "Fight me. This is nothing compared to what the demons will do to you—what they're doing to your grandmother right now. Fight back."

Her grandmother. Anger and fear welled up so hard a ringing set up in her ears. "No!" She shoved against the pain, furious at Kane, sending anger spiraling toward him.

Stars exploded behind her eyes into tiny bits, each shard stabbing into her brain like knives. Pain filled her gasp.

She opened her eyes just in time to see his head jerk back.

A slow smile crossed his face. "Nicely done."

The pain receded.

Amber jumped to her feet. "Fuck you." Turning on her heel, gulping back tears, she headed for the door.

He beat her there and blocked her way. "I'm sorry."

Her knee moved of its own volition straight for his balls.

Pivoting, he grabbed her arms and shoved her against the wall. "Hate me all you want, but you need to learn how to defend yourself." His hold tightened until she faced him. Emotion, raw and pure, swirled through his odd eyes. "I really am sorry," he whispered. One hand released her so he could wipe a tear from her face with his thumb. "There's no other way."

"You just want to save your brother." She gulped back more tears.

Surprise filled his eyes that he quickly banished. "For a moment, I forgot Jase." Kane frowned, shaking his head. "I do want to save him. But I also want to save you—and the demons know about you. The sooner you learn to control your gifts, the safer you'll be."

"Do you really think they're hurting my grandmother?" She wouldn't cry anymore.

"No. I assume they really want you, sweetheart." He cupped her chin. "I said that to motivate you. I was wrong, and I'm sorry."

Her gaze dropped to his mouth. "I'm a pacifist, damn it."

A cell phone buzzed. Kane started, and then stepped back, yanking the phone from his jeans and putting the device to his ear. "Finally. Cell service. What?" He listened, then let out a strong breath. "Excellent. Nice job, Dage. I'll call you tomorrow." The phone clicked off.

Amber clutched his shirt. "What?"

"We have your granny." A relieved smile crossed Kane's face. "The demons took her straight to the airport and had to make an emergency landing in the storm over Utah. Dage had been monitoring all transportation and had allies ready to take her. She's been taken to wolf headquarters and will be moved to our headquarters as soon as possible, where we have excellent doctors. I promise she'll be okay."

Relief flowed through Amber so fast her knees buckled.

"Easy darlin'," Kane murmured, picking her up to set down on the sofa. Frowning, he pressed a hand against her forehead. "You're hot again. Must be something about fighting the infection of battling someone else's mind. I need to get a blood sample as soon as we get to head-quarters." Thunder growled high above and sleet blasted against the windows. He sighed. "Which won't be any-time soon."

Amber settled against the threadbare cushions, her mind fuzzing. The fire warmed the space, its soft light not quite reaching every dark corner. Outside the storm bellowed and tried to get inside.

Kane grabbed the brandy glasses. Handing her one, he retook his seat in the chair. "Drink."

"Stop being bossy."

"Sorry." Slowly, he took a sip, gaze watchful over the rim.

She drank a healthy gulp. How was she supposed to act normal with a sexy vampire studying her? "Stop staring."

"No." He licked a drop from his lip.

She fought a groan. The brandy warmed down her throat to her abdomen. Wind whistled outside, lending an intimacy to the fire-lit area inside. Her eyes half-closed in reaction. Tingles set up in her knees—most likely from the mind war she'd just fought. But the confusion came from her reaction to the vampire. "You shouldn't have kissed me last night."

"I know," he agreed softly.

"Why did you?"

"You're beautiful, sexy, and I want you." His voice was calm and self-assured.

No game playing with that man.

She fought to keep her face calm. He said *want* in present tense. Her body reacted instantly, her nipples pebbling. "That's surprising. I figured you'd go for some robotic scientist type."

"Apparently not."

As people, they couldn't be more different. He was overeducated. She . . . not so much. "I'm a pacifist."

He gestured for her to finish her drink. "Let's talk about that."

She downed the rest of the brandy, a delicious heat sliding through her body. "There's nothing to talk about."

He tipped back his head and drank his brandy, the movement both masculine and sexy. Setting the sifter on the side table, he leaned forward, elbows on his knees. "I've been thinking."

"That's a new one." She snorted.

Vampires had sexy grins. Who knew?

Kane's grin widened. "So, I have a solution for our dilemma. You're a pacifist who shouldn't fight. I am a closet empath who needs to find my brother."

The guy probably didn't confess that fact to many people. She smiled, more warmth coming from his trust than from the alcohol. "What's a closet empath?"

"Somebody who has fought for years to squash down the ability to read emotions from other people." He sighed, stretching his neck. "Though, I can also attack with feelings sometimes. The ability can distract an enemy at the right moment, although I'd rather just use my brain."

"There's nothing wrong with feeling things, Kane."

He shrugged. "Not the point."

"What is the point?" Besides that fact that she was in an intimate setting alone for an entire night with the sexiest man she'd ever met in real life.

"The point is that there is a very simple answer to our dilemma." His eyes darkened and his strong jaw set. "Mate me."

CHAPTER 10

A mber sat back in her chair, a flush engulfing her entire body. "You're crazy."

Kane didn't move, just kept that intense gaze on her. "No, the idea makes sense. When vampires mate, they gain the abilities of their mates. In time, I would be able to shield from demon tactics, and you'd gain the ability to shield even better considering I can negate any empathic abilities I've been cursed with."

Gaining more ability to protect her brain held certain appeal. "I don't even know you," she whispered.

He sighed. "Also, sometimes, I can send out emotions, not really strong, but enough that people notice and might feel the same. That skill would come in handy to someone wanting to mind-attack a demon."

Now that was a very good point. But *mating* him? The idea was beyond far-fetched.

His gaze actually sizzled. "We're attracted to each other—there's no reason not to consider my offer."

Attracted? Frankly, she wouldn't mind getting the vampire naked and exploring that kiss from outside the diner, but mating? Come on. Curiosity buzzed in her mind. "I'm assuming mating involves sex?"

His eyes somehow darkened further. "Yes."

"So we have sex . . . and what?" Heat burst into her face.

He cleared his throat. "Well, I bite you—and, ah, transfer a brand from my palm to you—somewhere. You can choose the place."

Oh, he had to be beyond delusional. "Brand? You brand me like a cow?"

"God, no. The marking is like a tattoo—and you'll gain my abilities and immortality."

How tempting was that? She crossed her legs, curious and oddly aroused. "And when we are finished being mates? Would I still be immortal?"

He stilled. The air seemed to follow suit. "There's no *end* to a mating. You'd be mine forever."

The matter-of-fact tone did nothing to conceal the strong note of possessiveness underlying the words. Then the vampire sat back, patiently awaiting an answer with confidence on his hard face.

Her breath sped up, and she swallowed to keep from panting. "Not in a million years."

Both eyebrows rose. "Why in the world not? You're aroused right now."

She lifted her chin. "Maybe so. You're unbelievably rude to point that fact out, by the way."

"My apologies. But you need to think this through. Our mating solves all our problems."

"Except romance, fun, and happily-ever-after." Three things she'd always strongly believed in. "I won't mate for convenience." Mother Earth. Now she was using the term *mate* like it belonged in everyday conversation. "Why would you?"

One shoulder lifted. His long, tapered fingers spread out over his legs, his hands broad and oddly graceful. "I've always figured I'd mate out of convenience for business, for strategy, or to create an alliance. This fits."

Talk about unromantic. "A business arrangement is no reason to tie yourself to someone for eternity."

"How about survival? Yours and everyone you care about." The set of his jaw promised the conversation wasn't over.

"What about love?"

He sighed. "Love is a chemical reaction induced in our brain to encourage propagating the species. The sensation is merely a scientific phenomenon, like the northern lights."

On all that was holy. "You can't seriously believe such nonsense."

"Of course I do. And so would you if you stopped to think about the idea logically instead of believing in silly movies and sonnets."

Silly movies? How was this the same guy who'd kissed her in the snow and pretty much knocked her socks off? "The answer is no." She was just silly enough she might've believed some baloney story about fate and destiny. But not logic and planning—not when it came to the heart.

He shrugged. "I'm not giving up on this idea, and I can be very persuasive."

So long as he kept his dangerous lips across the room, she was fine. "I am not going to be your mate." Relief filled her as she said the words slowly.

"Your choice. Are you ready to train again?"

"You mean have you rip into my brain?"

He blanched. "Yes. Believe me, my attack was nothing compared to what the demons have in store for you. The sooner you learn to control your gift from a safe distance, the sooner we can go after Jase."

They'd saved her grandmother, and she'd given her word she'd help save Jase. "Okay. Shoot."

"Close your eyes."

Soft, nearly seductive, his dark voice wandered down her spine as if he traced each vertebra with his lips.

Her eyes fluttered shut.

This time, the attack came in the form of a soft glide against her mind. Smooth, even slightly warm, a caress wandered from her frontal lobe to the center of her brain. She shifted on the couch, crossing her legs. A tingling set along her rib cage and wandered south to heat her abdomen. Mentally pushing against the caress, the warmth enveloped her entire brain and provided an electric stimulation that caught the breath in her throat.

Desire ripped through her so quickly her knees trembled. Her sex started to ache. Her breasts pebbled. A slow sigh escaped her.

A whisper of sound floated toward her as he moved, and the scent of male and musk wafted her way. Languishingly opening her eyes, she stared at the vampire. On his knees, he settled between her legs. His heated hands dropped to her thighs.

She should be angry. But her gaze dropped to his lips, and she met him halfway. He swallowed her moan in a kiss that started with anything but logic. Fire engulfed her. Leaning forward, she clamped both hands in his thick hair, opening her mouth to take more of him.

He delved deeper, his tongue possessing, his lips firm and demanding. With a low growl, he tumbled her to the rug, his hard body stretching atop her. Settling an impressive erection between her thighs, his hand slid down and secured her ass, rubbing her against him.

Releasing her lips, he pressed hot, openmouthed kisses along her neck to her collarbone.

The warmth in the brain receded.

She arched up against him, so much need in her breasts they seemed on fire. "Kane."

"No talking." He yanked open her blouse, eyes flaring at the plain cotton bra. A smooth movement had the front clasp springing open. "Very pretty." His tongue flicked out to tease one nipple.

She whimpered, her hands still tangled in his hair and holding tight.

He lifted his head to pierce her with a gaze full of need. "See how good we could be together?"

For two beats her brain failed to connect. Then reality crashed harder than a sledgehammer. "Wait a minute." Her voice emerged husky. "The brain. You stimulated my brain. You planted desire."

"You can't plant desire." He settled himself on his elbows. "I just stimulated the amygdala and nucleus accumbens in your brain—one regulates emotion and the other controls the release of dopamine."

Desire flashed to anger. "You bastard." She'd known him only a day and had already used words she never spoke. "You manipulated me."

"No." His frown matched the slow burn in his eyes. The flash of anger combined with a heat of lust in his rapidly darkening irises. "First, I wanted to show you how else demons could mess with your brain. Then . . . well . . . things got out of control."

Okay. While he was giving his lame explanation, he really shouldn't be pressing the strong line of his erection against her aching clit. Worse yet, she was two seconds away from ripping his pants off. "Get off me. Now."

"No." The grip on her ass tightened. "Not until you at least consider how good we could be."

"From a logical perspective, I can't stand you. In fact, I'd probably kill you in your sleep." She released his hair and shoved both hands against his hard chest. The damn man didn't move.

"Some pacifist."

"See? See what a few hours with you does to me? No way will I mate you."

"Famous last words, gorgeous." He rolled off her,

smoothly pressing his shoulders against the floor and leaping to his feet without using his hands.

What a show-off. But . . . well . . . the move was impressive. Balance, coordination, and strength. If she went
crazy and actually wanted a vampire mate for all eternity,
he'd make a good choice. Lucky for her she wasn't going
crazy. She grabbed the chair and heaved to her feet.
"You're a manipulative jerk."

"That's nothing compared to what the demons will do
if they get a hold of you." Kane shrugged. "Well, without
the kissing part, usually."

His face was flushed, his eyes burning, his body tense.

Oh yeah. She hadn't been the only one affected by the
kiss. Slowly, she dropped her fingers to the buttons of her
shirt to refasten, pleasure filling her when his gaze followed. Take that, buddy.

Then her shoulders started to itch. She glanced down at
the old rug still wearing her butt print. "Tell me that's not
from a real animal."

Kane sighed. "I don't own this place, for goodness' sake.
However, once you get to Realm headquarters, you
should be pleased. We have allies who are shifters. To the
best of my knowledge, most animal-type fabric, rug, and
coverings in every house we own are synthetic."

"Most?"

"I'll make it 'all' as soon as possible."

She smiled. "You're not as much of a jackass as I
thought."

"That's the nicest thing you've said to me." He dropped
back into his chair.

She nodded, fighting to keep from shivering. Whether
from the cold or Kane's kiss, she wasn't sure. Man, she
wished they were still rolling around on the floor. She'd
never felt such need. While she wasn't going to mate him,
they still had this night. A tremor racked her shoulders.

Kane sighed. "You're not warming up."

"Yes . . . I . . . am . . ." She shivered again.

He turned to eye her.

"You mess with my brain, and I'll kick your ass." The time had ended for nicety. "Don't even think of warming me up by manipulating some weird cortex in my brainstem."

"Okay." He tore off his shirt. Defined muscles showed in his broad chest that tapered into an intriguing six-pack. The scientist worked out. He'd healed from the bullet wound completely. His pants followed suit, leaving him in dark briefs. His legs were as sexy as the rest of him. He lifted her and sat on the sofa.

"Hey," she protested as he sat back down with her on his lap. "Why are you getting naked?"

"I have briefs on—and my clothes were wet." He yanked the blanket free before pressing her skin against his and rewrapping the blanket.

His heat slammed right through to muscles and bone. She bit her lip to keep from groaning in pure pleasure. "Stop manhandling me." Her voice came out weak and not nearly as angry as she'd like.

"I like handling you." That deep voice turned thoughtful and a bit rough.

The storm raged outside, the fire crackled inside, and she was sitting on the hottest guy she'd ever seen. "Okay. This is not some big, sexy seduction, we're lost in the storm, let's get it on situation." Her mouth formed the words, but deep down, her body howled in protest.

He chuckled, turning her to straddle him. "Let's warm your back."

Heat from the fire licked down her spine . . . not nearly as hot as the warmth from the hard body heating her front. His thighs warmed the inside of hers. "Kane, stop it." Again, her body ignored the very simple words by her hands pressing against his hard chest, feeling the very, very nice muscles there.

"Stop what? " Dark amusement lifted his lip while those eyes swirled a deep violet.

"Playing with me," she coughed out.

"Darlin', I'm not playing. If I were playing, I'd do this." He leaned in, his tongue flicking along her jugular. His mouth was hotter than possible. "And this." Clever fingers wandered across her rib cage to sweep under her breast.

She pressed toward him, her breath catching.

"And this," he murmured against her neck, tweaking her nipple through the cotton.

With a sigh, she pressed against his sudden erection. "I'm not sure I even like you."

"Most people aren't sure if they like me," he said, lifting away and flashing a grin.

Disarming and charming, the grin heated her insides.

Vulnerability gentled her hands as she framed his face. "What are you really like?" She frowned, her body on fire, her mind curious, her instincts whispering she should run.

He tilted his head. "I don't know what you mean."

"I think you do." She settled against his erection, enjoying the instant flare of lust in his dark eyes. "I'm not easy, and I'm not simple, Kane. I want you. But even though we're fleeting, I don't want a rational, this-is-a-reasonable-way-to-calm-down-and-ride-out-the-storm lay."

His eyebrow lifted. "Did you just say *lay*?"

"You know what I mean."

"Darlin', I'm all brain, no heart. That should make you happy considering the pleasure centers are in the brain."

"No." She shoved against his chest, the movement rubbing her suddenly aching sex against a hardened cock too impressive to easily ignore. "This isn't about thinking. This is about feeling." Staring him right in the eyes, she tried to penetrate to his hard brain. "We both know you can feel, whether you like that fact or not."

Irritation flashed bright in those eyes to be quickly blanketed with humor. "That was a secret."

Her hands dropped along with her gaze. "Whatever."

He sighed. Running both hands through her hair, he gently tugged her head back until her eyes met his. "Amber, I like you. Against all rational thought, I like the way you think, the way you move, even the way you feel everything too strongly. And I want to have one night with you—not to relieve some stress, although it would—not to cement your help, although it might—and not to further any of my rather pressing goals. I just want to get inside you and drive you crazy until you scream my name."

She opened her mouth but no words formed.

His hold tightened. "But you should be very careful what you ask for." The predator he'd been hiding rose to the surface.

All amusement and charm disappeared.

Awareness slammed through her. She'd misjudged him. Sure, she'd seen him kill demons. And she'd known he was a vampire. But he'd seemed like an intellectual, somewhat safe. The male trusting her enough to reveal himself right now was nowhere near safe.

"You want the real me?"

She nodded slowly.

"Then say yes."

Her mind spun. Rational thought whisked away. She should think about this. There was no doubt they'd be parting ways after she fulfilled her promise and helped him with Jase. She had to get Grandma Hilde to safety and off the demon radar. But she never wanted to look back on her life and wonder . . . what if? So they had one night. "Yes."

At her acquiesce, she expected him to react. To delve deep, to pounce.

Instead, his eyes darkened to beyond black. A slow smile, wicked and sure, slid across his handsome face.

She shivered.

He tugged her sweatshirt over her head. His hands went to her bare shoulders, sliding down until reaching her wrists. Then he tugged her to him and kissed her. Warmer than imaginable, his mouth slanted over hers, his lips firm and demanding. His tongue swept inside her mouth, sending her sliding full force into arousal. She tried to lift her hands to his chest, but they remained in place.

Strong hands banded around her wrists and trapped her hands on her thighs. She couldn't move.

Shock, then fire ripped through her. Her panties dampened even more.

His mouth worked hers, taking. Long fingers threaded through hers, sliding her hands behind her back to press against her hips, dragging her clit along his shaft. Sparks flashed behind her eyes. She whimpered.

He lifted away, a dark flush across his high cheekbones, his nostrils flaring. Hunger glinted strong and bright in his eyes. "Now that's a pretty sound. Make it again." Pressing her hands against her butt, he rubbed his cock against her.

She whimpered again.

His smile revealed more of the animal he'd kept hidden.

Doubt broke through the clouds in her brain, and she opened her mouth to protest.

"Too late." His mouth found her nipple, his strength easily keeping her in place.

Where he wanted her.

Sharp teeth nipped and then his tongue soothed. Electricity flared from nerve to nerve, making her nearly desperate to move against him. Yet his hold stayed firm, not allowing her to move an inch.

The helplessness compared to his strength rippled shivers of need down her spine. "Kane."

The world tilted and she found herself lying on the blanket near the fire, the vampire kneeling between her legs. He ripped her pants and panties off. "Oh," she protested, mind whirling, her hands suddenly free and reaching to push against his shoulders.

One dark look froze her in place.

"Hands down." The set of his jaw hardened.

She couldn't move . . . could only stare.

"Put them down or I'll tie them down." No mercy showed in his deep eyes.

Her hands dropped to the blanket as if gravity worked for him. She shook her head. "I don't . . ."

"You do." He plunged one finger inside her easily. Too easily.

She arched up in response, a strangled groan emerging. Internal muscles flared to life and clamped down on him. Her arousal was obvious. "Stop playing."

"I'm not playing." His finger found her G-spot, and she nearly shot off the blanket. With a deep chuckle, his mouth dropped to her clit.

No easing, no teasing . . . he sucked hard.

She exploded with a strangled cry, the entire room sheeting white. His fingers prolonged the orgasm until she wanted to beg. Whether for him to stop or keep going, she wasn't sure. Finally, she came down, her entire body nowhere near sated and truly on fire. Her body protested when he removed his hand.

While it had been awhile, in the past, one orgasm did her just fine. Now one wasn't nearly enough. Somehow Kane had driven her even higher, somehow he'd perched her entire body on the edge, waiting for him. "I hate you."

He chuckled against her clit, sending her senses spiraling. "I'll have to change your mind on that." Slow, delicious licks had her squirming on the blanket, her hands itching to grab and take him. But she had no doubt he'd meant the sensual threat. He really would tie her down.

The idea almost sent her into another orgasm. She shifted to the side to get his mouth where she wanted it, and he clamped both hands on her thighs. "Hold still, darlin'."

"No."

The slap to her thigh made her gasp.

"Yes." His shoulders settled into place, keeping her open to him. Whether she liked it or not. "You have quite the rebellious streak, don't you? Let's see what we can do about that."

Who was this guy? She levered up to tell him off when his mouth got serious. Coughing out a sob, she dropped back to the blanket. Man, he was talented.

A rumble of pleasure echoed against her flesh as he went to work. Alternating between soft caresses and more intense licks, he had her mind spinning and her body gyrating within minutes. A bite to her thigh made her cry out. Then his mouth went back to her core. Minutes later she couldn't tell the difference between pain and pleasure.

Minutes after that she was begging in incoherent sobs.

Finally, he lifted up, a pleased smile curving his lips. "Now that's better."

The words didn't register. Her entire body was alight, in definite pain, in a craving too intense to be real. Yet it was. Somewhere in the recesses of her mind, she knew she was going to kill him the next day. But for now, she almost sobbed in relief when he yanked off his briefs and settled against her. Finally.

He plunged inside her with one strong stroke.

Pain. Her entire body arched in denial. He was too big. She shoved against his shoulders, her breath catching.

"Give it a second," he whispered against her neck, his heated breath sending shivers along her collarbone.

With a catch in her throat, she nodded, settling back down.

Her body relaxed, accepting him. Her eyes fluttered shut at the exquisite pleasure. Who knew?

Slowly, he drew out and then plunged back inside her.

She gasped, both hands clutching into his tight ass. "Again."

Warning hinted in his sudden smile. She should've kept quiet. He shook his head, dark hair moving around his shoulders. "Giving orders, are we?"

"No." Quick, her response burst out before she could think.

"Hmm." Staying inside her, filling her beyond what she thought she could take, his mouth dropped to her right breast and engulfed her nipple in fire. His wet tongue flicked and teased the peak.

Her nails dug into his butt, trying to get him moving again.

His teeth closed and nipped.

The breath swooshed out of her lungs as she paused. Too fast to track, he grabbed both her hands and flattened them against the blanket under his. "Not that I mind wearing your marks, sweetheart, but a man does like to take his time."

"I'm going to kill you." She wrapped her legs around his hips, holding him in place. "Tomorrow." After their one night.

His smile lightened something inside her. "Then I really should enjoy my last night on earth." Deadly fangs dropped low. His eyebrows rose in question.

All instinct and without conscious thought, she turned and exposed her neck.

His low growl of satisfaction echoed throughout her body to where they remained joined.

Seconds later sharp points embedded in her flesh. A flash of pain was brushed away by intense satisfaction.

But the intense pleasure wasn't hers. The feeling, dark and deep, came from Kane. Was this part of her gift? Or was this part of Kane's talents? Either way, she relaxed into the sensation, letting the raw thrill take hold.

She'd accidentally taken some mushrooms once that apparently were as strong as LSD. That was nothing compared to the feeling shooting her neurons into flight as Kane Kayrs took her blood.

Giving a low groan, Kane released her hand to grab her butt, moving out and in. His fangs retracted and he licked her neck. Increasing his speed, he began to pound in a fierce rhythm.

The pounding matched the wildness pouring through Amber's veins. Her thighs tightened as she clasped her ankles together, meeting his thrusts. A spiraling started deep inside her. Breathing became impossible. Then breath became unnecessary.

The only thing that mattered was where that spiraling sensation wanted to take her.

His cock was hard, pulsing, somehow demanding. He thrust harder, angling over her clit.

She broke with a cry, tidal waves of pleasure crashing through her. Her internal muscles spasmed around him as he continued to thrust, sharp fangs embedding in her neck again.

With a low growl, he stiffened against her as he came.

Sighing, her entire body went limp against the blanket.

Kane licked her collarbone, raising up to flash a satisfied smile.

She smiled back. "That was well worth the one night."

His grin turned wicked through the firelight. "Ah, darlin'. We're nowhere near done."

CHAPTER 11

A weak morning sun tried to filter through the swirling snow outside the small cabin. Amber had been awake for about ten minutes, listening to the crazy storm and wondering where Kane had gone. She gathered the blanket closer and stumbled toward the window. Multiple muscles flared to life in protest.

She had been well and truly fucked.

Kane Kayrs, vampire, now knew her body better than she did. He hadn't missed a millimeter in his exploration.

Like the scientist he was, he'd discovered her every secret. And then some.

Jesus. She could barely walk.

Stifling a whimper, she glared out at the still raging storm. Just how long could Mother Nature keep up the violence? No way could Amber survive another night with Kane, and no way would she keep her hands off him if left alone into the darkness again. Her well-used body needed a doggone rest.

Closing her eyes, she repeated her grandmother's chants. Never again would she forget that morning ritual.

The door opened with a bang. Kane stalked inside, raking her with that serious gaze. "Are you all right?"

She straightened and forced a smile. "I'm fine."

"Good. Get dressed." He turned and began gathering

the weapons he'd left on a sofa table. "The storm is still raging, but we need to get out of here. The Kurjans will have been watching Talen's house and are not smart enough to wait for the storm to pass."

"I'm not going back in that boat." She reached for the clothes Kane had laid out on the mantel to dry the night before. Holding them against the blanket, she shifted her feet. "Um, turn around."

Sinful and quick, his smile flashed. "No."

"Yes." The urge to stomp her foot tightened her leg muscles.

"Amber, I know every inch of your body," he drawled. "It's a little late for shyness."

Some scientist. The guy was actually a rake. Vulnerability lifted her chin. "The night is over. Now turn around."

He prowled toward her and covered her hands with his. Dropping his head, his mouth pressed hard against her lips, his tongue sweeping inside. Taking. Warm, sure, and demanding, his mouth took hers like he owned it. Maybe after the previous night, he did.

She was gasping for breath when he lifted his head to survey her neck. A slow glide of his thumb along her jugular sent electricity zapping through her veins.

He smiled. "The puncture wounds haven't quite healed. Interesting." Raising his head, he pierced her with a dark gaze, intrigue filling his eyes.

"Why is that interesting?" she asked, her voice hoarse.

"Usually when we lick a wound, *if* we lick a wound, it disappears. You're still wearing my mark, darlin'."

She lifted her chin farther. "Why does that please you?"

He started. "I have no idea." Both eyebrows slashed down. "Though I have to admit, the fact pleases me greatly." His frown intensified.

She drew back. "Last night was a one-shot deal." If she ever recovered, she was running fast in the other direction. One more night like that, and the vampire would own her. Without question, he'd claimed her in a way she'd never forget, probably never find again. But she couldn't stay with him. "I believe, remember?"

He growled low. "Yes. Happily-ever-after and all of that. Love and emotion." Then he sighed. "Okay, get dressed. There's an old truck in the shed outside. We'll head to town and find a land phone that actually works." Releasing her, he moved to blanket out the fire.

She hurried to dress, scrambling to yank on slightly wet jeans. A warm shower would be heaven.

Kane finished and reached the door. "Do you want a gun?"

"Yes." Well, actually she didn't want a gun. But she took the one he offered and shoved it in her waistband. The metal chilled her flesh.

He held out a hand. "The storm is pretty bad, so hold on and we'll get to the shed."

She hesitated only a second before sliding her hand into his. Warmth enveloped her fingers.

Tugging her outside, he led her over the deck and around a small side yard. There he stopped cold and lifted his head into the wind.

Two tall figures rushed around the faded shed, guns drawn.

Amber gasped. They were the stuff of nightmares. Blood-red hair with black tips, swirling purple eyes, crimson lips, and skin bleached of any possible color. Beyond white.

Dressed in all black, they stopped and pointed weapons.

Kane shoved her behind him. "Damn Kurjans. Don't move, Amber."

She couldn't move if she wanted to. Her feet grew heavy, fear weighing down her limbs. Monsters. True monsters existed.

Kane held his hands up, body relaxed. "You need to get out of here. The entire property is land mined, and only I know where the explosives are located." He yelled to be heard.

The monster in the lead threw back his head and laughed, the grating sound echoing even through the storm. "We've had this entire lake under surveillance for years, and you can bet we conducted satellite imagery of the ground. Nice bluff." He yelled louder than Kane.

Amber wasn't going out like this—not with creepy, white-faced monsters. Sliding forward an inch, she pressed the side of her gun into Kane's back, tucking the barrel in his waistband. Everything she'd ever been taught centered around the fact of not hurting another being. She couldn't shoot them.

But she could hand the gun to Kane. Yeah, it was a moral gray line, one she'd worry about later.

Movement sounded behind her. She whirled around to find a tree spinning by in the storm. Holy Mother Earth. An entire tree.

Kane blocked her completely from the Kurjans. "Maybe so, but there's no way you have reinforcements coming in this storm. You're all alone out here—and will be until morning."

"And everyone says you're the smart one," one of the monsters yelled.

Kane partially turned his head. "In two seconds, you hit the ground. Understand?"

"Yes," she stuttered, her mouth almost too cold to make sound.

"Now!"

She dropped, covering her neck with her arms and making herself as small as possible. Snow slid down her shirt, freezing her skin. Cold pierced her eyes, but she kept her gaze on Kane.

Quicker than she could track, he grabbed the gun and fired. The odd *ping* of those green bullets echoed. They slammed into the closest Kurjan, throwing the wide-eyed monster three feet back.

Fangs flashing in his nightmarish face, the other guy charged.

Kane crouched for the blow, waiting until the Kurjan reached him before throwing his weight to the right and away from Amber. The guy hit like a truck. They landed hard, sending snow spraying. Kane grunted as his ribs protested.

All emotion shut into a box, he jabbed his knuckles under the soldier's throat, impacting the larynx. Leaping up and back, he calculated the Kurjan's weight and arm span—about an inch shorter than Kane's. Interesting. Most Kurjans reached almost seven feet tall. Not this guy.

The guy rolled backward through the snow to his feet, purple eyes swirling with fury and pain.

He charged again.

Kane waited until the last second and kicked out, breaking the guy's jaw. Even through the furious storm, a painful *crack* echoed.

The soldier staggered back.

Tuning in his senses, Kane counted the Kurjan's breaths. Yeah, he was panting. One more blow to the face should do it.

Darting forward, he punched for the nose and karate-chopped the throat of his opponent. The Kurjan dropped to the ground.

Yanking his knife from his boot, Kane dropped to his haunches and jammed the blade in the Kurjan's sternohyoid muscle to the side of the jaw. Shoving in harder, he yanked to the right, slicing through bone.

Blood sprayed along his chest.

With a grunt, he forced the knife the other way, effectively decapitating the soldier.

Pushing the body away, he hustled to the man he'd shot, plunging the blade in the unconscious body. His aim was off this time, and he had to fight the hyoid bone. He was the one panting when the Kurjan's head slid free.

Wiping the Kurjan's blood on the snow-covered body, Kane stood to face Amber.

Her skin was whiter than the snow.

Standing, she swayed in place, the storm battering her. Those black eyes were wide, the pupils huge as she stared at the dead Kurjans.

She was going into shock.

"Amber!" He lowered his voice to command and slid the knife back in his boot.

Her head jerked up, and she stumbled back.

Wind blistered his face, but he leapt forward and grabbed her arms. He shook her. "Snap out of it. Now."

He was such an asshole. But they didn't have time for her to fall apart right now. Pulling her to him, he gave her a quick kiss to the top of the head. "Hold it together."

Amber looked up at the fierce warrior. Had he just kissed her on the head?

Two more Kurjans ran up the embankment from the lake, and Kane pivoted to shield her.

Movement echoed behind her and she spun around. Fear rammed into her gut. More monsters.

Scooting so her back settled against Kane's, she dropped into what seemed like a fighting stance. Maybe.

"How many?" Kane ground out.

"Three." So, five more scary monster freaks against two good guys, one of whom was a pacifist. Life sucked sometimes. Odd that her mind had blanked and was thinking rational thoughts instead of her heart stopping in a huge attack. Maybe it was the adrenaline ripping through her veins yelling at her to flee. But there was nowhere to go.

The Kurjan closest to her sniffed the snow-filled air and then frowned. He sniffed again. "Destroyer?"

Kane stiffened against her.

Instantly the other Kurjans focused on her, all sniffing the air.

Okay, that was just weird. What in the world did she smell like to these guys?

"Amber," Kane hissed in a hoarse whisper, "as soon as you feel me move, hit the ground."

"You can't take out all five of them," she muttered back, panic threatening to send her to the ground anyway.

"Not much of a choice." Hopefully the wind camou-flaged his voice from the Kurjans. "Drop, I'll take these two guys out and then flip over you for those three."

Maybe she should've kept a gun. She could've at least threatened them with a weapon. Evened the odds at least. "This is crazy." How many times had she said those words since meeting Kane? "What if I charge these guys—try to throw them off balance?"

Kane paused before answering. "No."

Too bad the guy hadn't realized she wasn't very good at taking orders. She bunched her muscles to leap—

And a helicopter spiraled out of nowhere to drop next to the shed. Snow scattered in all four directions, com-pletely obscuring the area. Two huge men jumped out, bullets already spraying. The Kurjans dropped to their bel-lies, returning fire from the safety of the snow.

Kane whirled and tossed her over his shoulder, running full bore for the open door of the 'copter. Leaping inside, he shoved her behind him, gun out and already firing.

The massive bird lifted into the air. The two men from the 'copter sprayed bullets and kept their opponents on the ground as they ran and jumped for the seat facing her. The door shut, and the helicopter rose into the storm.

Gasping, she plastered herself to Kane's side.

One of the men leaned a gun out an open weapon and continued firing until they were roaring away. Then he leaned back with a grim smile. "Nice morning."

The wind beat against the machine, sending it rocking. Kane shook snow from his hair. "Good timing. How?"

"Satellite. Saw the Kurjans send a force this way, figured the soldiers were coming for you." The guy's golden eyes swirled with emotion—maybe anger, maybe fear. Perhaps both.

Kane nodded. "Amber, this is my brother Talen." He pointed at an equally large guy with deep green eyes. "And my brother Conn."

"Ma'am," they said in unison.

They were as big as Kane and had metallic eyes. And she had been dead wrong about Talen being a pacifist. He was all massive soldier, intense and deadly. She coughed out air. "More vampires."

Conn nodded. Talen let fangs flash, his eyes glowing. Oh, for goodness' sake. For some reason, Amber had figured it was just Kane having odd eyes. "Thanks for the rescue."

Talen cocked his head to the side, and he studied her like a wolf considering dinner. "I'm getting very faint vibrations from her, but nothing that would lead a pack of shifters to her door. Are you sure she's a destroyer?"

"Yes." Kane settled back in the seat, somehow keeping her close. "There's some sort of shielding spell—very powerful. Once the shielding wears off, she's like a beacon."

The pilot, his hands working the stick, turned around. Silver eyes took her measure. "I'm Dage."

"The king?" she asked before she could stop herself.

"Yes. Thank you for agreeing to help us." His gaze returned to the snow outside.

So the king went on dangerous missions. Interesting. Or maybe he'd come since his brother was in trouble. Well, Amber understood family. "Ah, I heard you found my grandmother?"

"Yes." Conn's gaze raked over her. "The storm is still over Utah and Hilde's being treated by Realm doctors at wolf headquarters. The doctors are watching the head injury closely, but she's strong. And stubborn."

"That's an understatement," Talen muttered. He flushed and then leaned back with an apologetic smile. "I, ah, video-conferenced with her about safety and protocol. She, ah, didn't care to listen."

Dage flashed a quick smile Amber barely caught.

Great. Her grandmother was causing havoc already. "Does she, ah, know . . ."

"Yes." Conn leaned forward. "Your granny is well aware of demons, vampires, and Kurjans."

"Then she has some explaining to do," Amber murmured. How could her grandmother keep such information from her for so many years? If the demons were eventually coming calling, Amber should've been told. Head injury or not, Hilde was going to come clean.

Wind gushed against the helicopter, sending the machine spiraling to the side.

"Sorry," Dage muttered.

Kane exhaled loudly. "All three of you out in this storm isn't wise. You know that."

"We're family," Conn said simply.

Kane shook out his wet hair. "I thought you were heading to Ireland."

Conn nodded. "I leave in the morning to help my mate out with a small problem the witches are having." He shrugged. "Nothing big—someone misusing magic. I'll bring her home after that."

Amber fought a yawn. "How does somebody misuse magic?"

Conn gave her a gentle smile that somehow made him almost seem approachable. "Witches use quantum physics to alter matter and make spells. If somebody misuses quantum physics . . ."

"They might blow up the world." Even at the dangerous thought, Amber's eyelids grew heavy.

"Exactly," Conn said softly. "My mate is an enforcer for her people, so she deals with such threats. With me by her side, of course."

With the large vampire in front of her, most likely. Amber nodded.

Kane smiled at his brothers. "Thanks for coming."

"Sure." Talen kept his gaze on Amber, making her heart beat faster.

A strong arm banded around her shoulder. Kane's scent surrounded her. He leaned to whisper in her ear. "Take a rest, sunshine. We'll continue training once we get safely home."

Amber nodded, her brain all but shutting down, but not before catching an odd look that passed between Talen and Conn. What was that about?

Warmth from Kane's body seeped into her skin, into her bones. After the fear of the day, after having her mind messed with several times, and after a night of amazing sex and no sleep, she went under just enough to relax.

Kane kept his voice soft. "She's had no training and we need to step it up. While she's promised to help, I don't want her anywhere near danger. We'll take turns training her, but nothing too intrusive. I mean it."

"We'll do what we have to do," the king countered from the front of the craft.

"No. We'll train her the right way," Kane said calmly.

Amber giggled, half-asleep. "I thought he was the king."

Kane started. "He is."

"Then why are you the one barking orders?" she mumbled sleepily.

She wasn't sure whether it was Conn or Talen who burst into laughter. Either way, it was a nice laugh to fall asleep to.

CHAPTER 12

Jase hadn't been tortured for some time. In addition, fresh female blood had been provided for him every day. He'd even received new shorts. For whatever reason, the demons had altered their approach. So when his door finally rattled, he gazed up with more curiosity than dread. What were the bastards up to?

Two beefy guards dragged him through the same labyrinth of tunnels as last time but continued past the meeting room. Several hallways later he was shoved into a dimly lit room smelling of spiced oranges.

His eyes had become accustomed to dimly lit rooms. The door shut behind him, and he surveyed the plushest bedroom he'd ever seen. A red velvet duvet covered a bed large enough for several vampires. Pillows in sensual colors—ranging from purple to midnight—scattered across it. A dresser lay to the right, a fully stocked bar to the left.

A painting of a naked woman, strapped down for a man's pleasure, adorned the entire wall above the bed. All four limbs were stretched tight, her body hair free and finely toned. On her face sat an expression of anticipation melded with fear. Definitely not one of Brenna Dunne's works.

Willa stood near the bar in a long red negligee that revealed more than it covered. Black sparkles adorned the hem and rode up the slit for one leg.

Her hair was down and long, and midnight blue makeup enhanced her immortal eyes.

Against his will, his body sprang to life.

The lights were low and a dark melody hummed from the speakers. Nothing lighthearted or full of love . . . the song was haunting and sexy . . . almost as if claiming the inevitable.

He stepped into the room, his bare feet smashing the thick carpet. "Seduction won't work on me, demon."

Her dark gaze dropped to his groin, and she licked her lips. "Your body says otherwise."

"My body has been without a woman almost four years." He stalked into the room, heading for the bar. If she wanted to play games, he'd join in. "And you don't count."

She nearly purred, running her finger around the rim of a crystal goblet. "Have you ever made it with a demon, Jase?"

"No. I've never made it with a snake, either."

She pouted her full lips, anger swirling in her eyes. "You don't have to be so mean to me. It's not like I have much of a choice in this life, either."

Maybe not. Five years ago he'd have felt sorry for her . . . probably would've come up with a way to rescue her. These days he couldn't even rescue himself. Sympathy for a demon was no longer an option. "Fucking me isn't a choice that's open to you, either."

"How about you fuck me?" She gestured toward the painting depicting the BDSM scene. "I have more toys under the bed than you can imagine."

Damn if his cock didn't swell more. "No."

A slight probing filtered along his brain and slid down his spine. He mentally shoved back.

She faltered, her eyes narrowing. "You have some serious power."

Not as much as a demon. Well, not as much mind

power as a demon, but enough to combat a seduction of his brain. Some time ago he'd been able to harness the elements. Gathering his strength, he shot liquid into oxygen.

Nothing happened.

Surprising that sorrow could fill him after so long of a time. He reached for a decanter of scotch, pouring a shot and gulping the harsh liquid down, knowing the entire time it was a bad idea. No way was his system prepared for booze.

Turning, he flashed his fangs at the demon. "Stop the attempts at seduction. You help me get out of this hellhole, and I'll keep you safe for life." Even if he couldn't, Dage would. Chances were, even if Jase found freedom, he wouldn't last long. He wasn't sure if he wanted to last long. Going back to his old life wasn't possible. The Jase Kayrs they'd all known had been as good as dead for years.

He faced the demon, forcing all expression off his face. "Your people can't break me. You know that, they know that, and this is just a new tactic." No, they hadn't broken him. Broken things could be rebuilt—they could eventually be fixed.

He was beyond that.

"I don't want you broken." Her tongue darted out to lick liquid off the glass. "I want you to save me. To save us both."

If he did, he'd finally win. "I've given you my best offer."

"No." Her dark eyes flashed and she gestured toward the bed. "Your best offer happens there, for all time." Pleading and a dark vulnerability turned her eyes the softest of purple. "I've read your file and everything we've ever compiled about you. You don't have a woman waiting for your return, and you're not promised to anyone as a mate."

A mate? Shit. He wasn't complete enough to go solo much less give half of himself to someone else. "There will be no mate."

"So take me." Tipping back her long hair, she swallowed deeply. "We both get saved, and you can go on your own way afterward."

For almost two seconds he considered her offer. Why not? No way would he ever mate. The woman was sexy and in trouble. Somewhere deep down, in a place the demons hadn't touched, maybe a trifle of nobility remained. He could save her before checking out.

Reality smacked him in the head.

With mating came responsibility, and he couldn't handle it. Not even with someone he didn't give a shit about. "No. I won't mate a demon."

"If you don't, I'll destroy you." Her voice lowered, those eyes glowing with a new light. Insanity? Desperation?

He couldn't read people any longer. The bitch was probably nuts. "Good luck with that."

Instant pain flowed through the center of his brain. As if the sides completely divided, neurons flared like heated knives to rip through gray matter. Darkness cut across his vision.

Gravity claimed him, and he hit the floor with an impact that had his jaw snapping shut.

Unconsciousness came as an explosion behind his eyes. Finally.

Amber waited next to the elevator, her mind swirling. Kane had all but deserted her, leaving her with his pretty niece, Janie. With her light brown hair pulled back in a ponytail, the twenty-year-old looked like she should be playing volleyball on a Mexico beach during spring break— and not someone who was supposed to save the world.

Until you looked at her eyes.

Dark blue, serious, full of intelligence, those eyes spoke of a truly old soul.

Amber forced a smile. "I can't believe there are real vampires."

Janie shrugged. "Sure, you can. You just don't want to believe it's so easy to believe there are vampires." Her grin was all imp.

Amber couldn't help but smile back. "That's quite a statement."

"Yeah, I'm known for that." Janie jammed a finger against the DOWN button again.

Amber glanced around the alcove set into an Oregon cliff. Janie had led her around a big lodge and back alcove to a hole cut into the rocks. "So you have an entire head-quarters underground." How weird to be going into the earth. Grandma Hilde wouldn't like living underground. Amber's heart began to beat quicker. Was her grand-mother all right?

"Underground is safe. Sometimes if you listen really closely, the earth will whisper her secrets to you." Janie ran her hand along the rock wall. Then she turned and grinned at a stoic vampire standing guard next to the elevator.

At least, Amber assumed the guy was a vampire. At six and a half feet tall, his light brown eyes were reminiscent of a predator peeking around a tree just before striking.

Janie started. "I've completely forgotten my manners. Amber, this is Max. He's my bodyguard and one of our top hunters."

Max looked like a killer. "Ma'am," he said, a smile soft-ening his broad face.

Amber nodded, fighting the very real urge to step closer to Janie.

Max turned his attention to Janie. "My Sarah tells me you aced the MCAT's last week."

Amber paused, turning toward the young woman. She'd heard of the difficult test students had to pass in order to be considered for certain medical schools. "You're going to medical school?"

Janie snorted. "No. I just took the MCAT's for fun. Sarah's my teacher and Max's mate."

Obvious pride filled the vampire's deadly eyes. "Sarah's a sweet one, she is—smart as anything, too."

The obvious affection the soldier had for the mysterious Sarah made him almost approachable. But the gun at his hip and the hard set of his face would frighten anybody. The elevator door opened, and Amber sighed in relief while jumping inside.

The door shut, and Janie pressed a button somewhere in the middle of a bunch of round, unlabeled buttons.

Amber frowned. "Why aren't there labels?"

Janie grinned. "On the very distant chance that an enemy found our elevator, we wouldn't want them to find their way, now, would we?"

"No," Amber said weakly. Of course, she couldn't find her way now, either. On the very real chance she needed to get free of the vampires, she wouldn't know which buttons to push. "Are you sure my grandmother is all right?"

Janie's face lit up. "Better than all right. She's awesome. Man, you should've seen her ignore my dad when he called and lectured her about safety protocols. I sat in on the call. It was hilarious."

"Now, ah, your dad is Talen, right?"

"Yep."

The scary soldier wasn't somebody who should be ignored. "Oh my."

"Yep, and he's been really cranky lately since my mom and brother went back East to assist the feline nation with some inoculations." The door opened and Janie led the way into a spacious gathering room sporting a pool, several dartboards, and a big-screen television. "But don't worry. Hilde had my dad eating out of her hand within seconds. Charmed the heck out of him."

Now that would be something to see. "Um, will Kane be along at some point?" He was the only person Amber knew.

Janie shrugged. "He's always in the lab—unless he's hunting werewolves."

Amber started. "Kane hunts werewolves."

"Sure. And by himself sometimes, which really makes Uncle Dage mad. But Kane says he needs the solitude once in a while."

The man sought solitude by chasing werewolves. Amber swallowed loudly. "Um, why doesn't the king stop him?"

Janie grinned. "Stop Kane? You're kidding, right?"

Good point.

The door opened and a stunning woman with long black hair swept into the room. She wore a white smock over what appeared to be tattered jeans and a ROLL TIDE, BABY T-shirt. She flashed a smile. "Hi. You must be Amber. Do you mind if I take blood?"

Amber stepped back.

Janie laughed. "Amber, meet my Aunt Emma and the queen of the Realm. She's married to my Uncle Dage."

While beautiful, the woman couldn't look less like a queen. Amber forced a smile. "Um, you want blood?" Okay, she hadn't gotten the full scoop on vampires yet, but hadn't Kane said they only took blood during battle or sex?

"Yes. I have a lab just down the corridor," Emma said.

Janie shook her head. "Okay. We were going to play a game of pool and get acquainted. Manners, Auntie Emma. Manners."

Emma lifted her chin, thoughts scattering across her face. She lifted a pale hand to smooth tendrils of the dark hair out of her deep blue eyes. "Oh. Um, yeah. Sorry. It's nice to meet you, Amber. Do you have any questions about the Realm?"

She had so many questions she wasn't sure where to start. "Ah, well, why do you need blood?"

Emma glanced at a fine gold watch on her thin wrist. "Well, rumor has it you're a demon destroyer, the first we've found, and I'd like to check your blood. Also, since you slept with Kane last night, I'd like to see if there's been any change in your physiology."

Amber tried to swallow and ended up in a coughing fit.

Janie clapped her on the back. "Really, Emma. Manners."

Emma groaned. "I apologize, but I don't have time for manners. We need to find Jase. And, um, Kane didn't tell me, so don't worry about that. Dage smelled him on you, or you on him, either way, Dage let the secret loose."

"He smelled me?" So vampires were advanced in more than strength and speed.

"Sure." Emma tapped a calfskin-smooth boot on the floor.

Amber frowned.

Following her gaze, Emma gestured with both hands. "The boots are fake. No worries. No animals were harmed in the making of these very gorgeous, often used to kick Kane, boots." Tucking her arm through Amber's, she started for the door. "Dage said you lived in some sort of commune . . . eco-village. Very cool."

Amber stumbled toward the door. "Are you sure you're the queen?"

"That's what they tell me." Emma quickened her pace. "About sleeping with Kane, don't worry that he changed you. Chances are since the brand didn't appear on his hand, and he didn't try to mate you, you probably won't be changed in any way."

Amber had thought maybe Kane was exaggerating the whole marking aspect of mating. "Um, about that brand. It's for real?"

Emma paused. "Oh. Yeah, well . . . prepare yourself because it's an odd one. When a Kayrs male finds his mate, a brand appears on his hand that transfers during sex. She ends up immortal afterward, which is awesome. The brand? Not so much. Archaic, if you ask me." Emma tugged her T-shirt to the side and turned toward the wall. "See?"

A beautiful, raised black tattoo spread over the queen's shoulder. An elegant *K* sat in the middle of a stunning Celtic knot. "It's beautiful," Amber breathed.

Emma settled her shirt back in place. "Maybe so, but branding is still archaic." She tugged Amber farther down the hallway. "The marking is only a part of a mating, a huge part. But don't worry, your physiology is probably just fine."

Amber's brain reeled. Why hadn't the brand appeared on Kane's hand? She didn't want to be mated, but hey, shouldn't the brand have appeared since she and Kane had sex? Wasn't she good enough? Geez. "That's a relief to hear. Are you sure?"

"Not really." Emma shoved open a large door to a spacious lab complete with examination table. "The vamps I'm related to are mostly mated, and Jase has been kidnapped, so I don't get to test many women who've, you know, done a vamp."

"What about Kane? I mean, he's not mated." She shouldn't have asked that, darn it. But she held her breath and waited for Emma to respond.

"No, but the guy is seriously discreet. I mean, I wouldn't even know about you and Kane if Dage hadn't spilled the beans." Irritation had Emma's fine lips pursing. "Though my sister and I have talked about Kane—he is always so detail-oriented, he's probably, well, you know. Thorough." She lifted an eyebrow.

Amber slid her arm free of Emma's, heat climbing into her face. "Um, yes. Very thorough."

Emma nodded in satisfaction. "I figured. Well, that's good."

Amber eyed the smooth paper on the examination table. "Well, okay—blood then?"

"Yes." Emma turned toward a dark granite counter holding several quiet machines and grabbed a syringe from a small tray.

"So, you're a doctor?" Amber sat on the paper, rolling up her sleeves and crossing her ankles, swinging them slightly.

"Yeah—in genetics."

Figured. Everybody in the Realm world was seriously educated. Even Janie could go to medical school if she wanted. Amber fought a sigh.

The door opened and Dage stalked inside. Graceful and smooth, the king of the vampires nevertheless hinted at a danger that made Amber's legs stop swinging. Who were these people?

He sighed. "Emma. We wanted to ease Amber into helping us." Wrapping a broad hand around Emma's nape, he drew her close for a quick kiss on the lips. Drawing back, his eyes darkened to deep silver. "I believe I told you to take a quick break and get some rest."

A small smile lingered on the queen's lips as he drew away. She approached Amber and swabbed her elbow with alcohol. "There's no *easing* when it comes to the Kayrs family, you know that. I'll rest when we find Jase, just like you."

"You'll rest today, either on your own or with help, love." The king's voice lowered to a tone of pure danger.

Amber's breath caught in her throat. Her heartbeat picked up.

Emma rolled her eyes. "Don't you have an entire universe to go rule?"

Was the woman daft? That was not a man you messed with. Amber tensed in case she needed to jump from the table. Then the king threw back his head and laughed, causing her to freeze in place.

"Yes." He grinned, the smile turning him almost charming. "But it's so much more fun to rule you."

Amber cut her eyes to Emma. The king was as bad as Kane. "Are they all like that?"

"If you mean obstinate, stubborn, and over-the-top dominant, then yeah. Vampires are all like that." Emma pressed the needle in, humming while blood filled the vial. "Of course, I guess they have their good points, too."

"That's nice to hear," the king grumbled.

The door swept open and Janie hurried inside. "Uncle Dage, there's a problem with the wolves."

Kane entered on her heels. "You are not already taking Amber's blood, damn it."

Emma removed the needle and pressed a cotton swab on the wound. "Yep. Just finished."

Kane growled low.

The room froze. Or rather, the people in the room froze.

Janie huffed out a breath. "Did you just *growl*?"

Amber frowned. "He always growls."

"No, he doesn't," Janie said.

Amber wrinkled her brow as everyone turned to stare at Kane. Well, everyone except Emma, who was studying Amber with delighted interest sparking her blue eyes.

CHAPTER 13

Kane tried to shrug Dage's hand off his shoulder, barely keeping from growling again when he failed. Sure, he could knock his brother on his ass, but what would that accomplish? So he tromped through the sparkling underground corridors to Dage's private study.

The small room sported several chairs around a sofa table. No desk for the king—he preferred an informal setting. No paintings adorned the walls, no feminine touches hinted Dage had let Emma mess with the room. Only family was allowed in the underground study—well, family and Max. But Max was family.

Once inside, Dage released him and pressed a button next to the door. A full screen instantly covered the far wall, and seconds later, Terrent Vilks filled the screen.

Kane nodded. "How's Hilde Freebird?"

"She's a pain in the ass." Terrent tied his thick hair back from his scowling face. "The doctors reduced the extreme swelling in her brain, thus healing the concussion. She had a hairline fracture along her skull, and they applied laser treatments to heal it, though it'll take a couple more days. Yet somehow from a hospital bed, she's managed to organize a boycott on the delivery of my favorite fruit. Something about pesticides." The wolf growled low. "I'm immortal. Pesticides don't hurt me."

"When will she be fit to travel?" Kane asked mildly.

"Three days—I tried for two, but the doctors vetoed me." Terrent rubbed the scruff covering his rugged jaw. "She's doing her chants every day, and I can't get a sense she's enhanced. Quite the talent she has. Any luck with the daughter finding Jase?"

"We'll conduct tests soon," Dage said.

"I'll conduct tests, and she's not doing anything until she's ready," Kane countered, his voice lowering.

Both of Terrent's dark eyebrows rose. "Interesting. I'll let you two deal with that. For now, we have a problem with the inoculation of wolf shifters."

Kane breathed out hard. "I don't have time for a problem." He'd invented an immunization for all shifters against Virus-27, which had turned them from shifters to pure animalistic werewolves . . . with no way to turn back. Personally, he'd had to take down shifters he'd once considered friends after they'd been infected. He'd been ecstatic when discovering the cure for shifters, and hoped to take that and find a cure for vampire mates and witches, thus rendering the virus moot. Hopefully before the damn thing went airborne. "We've been inoculating shifters for two solid years without problems—we should be about done."

Terrent shook his head. "There's evidence the inoculation isn't working."

"Bullshit." There was no doubt the cure worked. Kane stepped closer to the camera.

Terrent's eyes flared black. "Let me rephrase that. I believe, based on tests of the immunization, that someone has tampered with the concoction and made several of our vials useless."

Kane rubbed both hands over his face. "Who would do that?" He shook his head. "Okay. If someone got close enough to the vials to tamper with them, it's someone close to you. The Kurjans have a mole in your organization."

"I contacted the feline nation, and they're experiencing the same problem. Somebody has gotten to the vials, and we don't know how far back the tampering goes. We'll have to immunize everybody again just to make sure. In the meantime, my people aren't protected, and the virus is still out there."

Kane swallowed. "You're right. The only smart thing to do is to inoculate everyone again. Test the vials, find the good ones, and use them. I'll step up production of more vials in our labs to send to you." The ticking clock on his back just increased in speed. At some point, the Kurjans would figure out how to make the virus mutate and go airborne. It was merely a matter of time. He needed a cure before that happened. A cure for all beings. He'd find one, after he got his brother back.

Terrent tugged on his ripped T-shirt. "We need to come up with some sort of plan for who's doing this." He glanced at his watch. "Also, the demons have increased the bounty on Maggie's head. You need to send the little wolf to a new location—everyone knows she's at your headquarters."

Dage exhaled. "Any idea why the demons want her?"

Terrent focused back on the camera. "No. No clue. But I do believe the lass is in danger."

Kane frowned. Something was off there. Was Terrent lying? It was incredibly rare for the wolf to lapse into the brogue since it had been centuries since he'd lived in Scotland. Maggie was a little wolf shifter who had been captured by the Kurjans and infected with the virus, resulting in amnesia. She had no clue who she was and had sought refuge with the vampires. Why would Terrent lie about her?

Terrent tapped an ear communicator that had been hidden and then nodded. "Okay." The smile he flashed held way too much amusement. "Hilde Freebird would like to speak with you."

The screen went black. Two seconds later, a woman sitting in a hospital bed and covered by a hand-sewn quilt squinted black eyes at them. Curly blond hair had been pinned up on her head, and pale, smooth skin covered delicate features. She looked to be about forty years old. Living on the farm had been good to her. "You the king?"

"Yes, ma'am." Dage gentled his voice.

Fire flashed in her dark eyes. "You keep your grubby, vampire hands off my granddaughter—got it?"

Dage bit his lip. "Yes, ma'am. I won't touch her."

"Humph." Pale hands clutched into the quilt. "I know you vampires—not a one of you can keep it in your pants. One of you seduces my sweet Amber, and I'll behead you myself."

Heat started to climb into Kane's face. "Maybe you should've told sweet Amber about her gifts . . . about immortal creatures."

Dark eyelashes fluttered as Hilde turned her attention to him. "Which one are you?"

"I'm Kane."

"Ah." A small smile pursed her fine lips. "The smart one. Good. Make sure you explain this carefully to your brothers; my granddaughter will not be messing with demons. The second I'm healthy to go, we're going. Understand?"

No. But arguing with a lady sitting in a hospital bed seemed like a bad idea. "We'll keep her safe, Ms. Freebird. I promise." Kane donned his most charming smile.

"Don't even think of bewitching me, dumbass. I've known plenty of vampires in my day. You're all full of charm. And don't think for a second I'm unaware of how often you mate to gain the gifts of enhanced females. You even think of having a vampire mate Amber, and you'll regret it. My powers go a lot further than just destroying demons."

Kane coughed twice. Okay, so he'd considered mating Amber. Shit. He was still considering the possibility.

Dage nodded. "It was nice to meet you, Ms. Freebird, and I hope you feel better soon. We have to go now." He hit the button on the wall, and Hilde disappeared.

Thank God.

"Fuck." Kane shook his hands out to stop the adrenaline ripping through his veins. "Why can't anything go as fucking planned?"

Dage headed straight for the bar set in the corner to pour two scotches. "Any more word on the internal struggles of the demons?"

"No. Apparently whatever was going on has been handled. The demon nation is strong enough to deal with us now." Kane rubbed his chin. "I wish we had found out what type of insurgence was happening."

Dage returned and shoved a full glass in Kane's hand. "Sit down."

Kane tipped back his head and downed the liquid before sitting in a thick leather chair, his boots settling on the neutral Persian rug. Warmth coated his throat to land in his belly. "This had better be fake leather."

Dage sat in a matching chair, facing him. "You've never given a shit about leather before."

"I give a shit now." Kane met his brother's stare evenly, irritation clawing down his spine.

"That is a faux-leather chair." The king took a small swallow of the smooth drink. "What's up your ass?"

Who the hell knew? "We're the most powerful race on earth, and you'd think we could sit our butts on something other than pure leather. How hard is that for you to understand?" Kane's fingers curled over in the absurd need to hit something. Was he turning into Talen or what?

Dage's smile lacked any semblance of humor. "Do I need to handle you?"

"Handle me?" Heat burned inside Kane's head so fast, so hard, he was shocked steam didn't flow with his words. "I fucking handle *you*, king. That's my job."

"Is it, now?" Anybody remotely familiar with the king would recognize the soft tone of voice as something to run the hell away from.

Kane was beyond running. "Yes. From day one, I'm your fucking advisor. Your sense of logic in a violent world. You wouldn't know how to handle me." The words spewed out too fast for him to stop, even while he knew he was being unfair. Horribly unfair to a guy who'd never wanted to lead—never wanted to be king.

"She is a beautiful woman." The king took another drink.

Kane stopped cold. His mind blanked. "What?"

"Amber. She's stunning and has the sweetest smile I've ever seen. Very pretty girl."

Taking a deep breath, Kane sat back in the chair. His mind clicked to life. "I was rallying about the unfairness of life and how I have to be logical when Talen gets to just hit things. Could we get back to that?"

Dage shrugged. "That's boring. And your lot in life isn't why you're acting like you have a stick shoved up your ass."

If Kane had the energy, he would hit his brother. Right now, the world on his shoulders was holding him down. "I offered to mate her."

Coughing, Dage wiped liquid off his chin. "You did *what*?"

Kane shrugged. "I mean, before we, well, you know—

I offered to mate her. To get her abilities so she wouldn't have to use them. So she'd get mine. You know how I can shield all emotion, as well as throw emotion *out* in rare occasions."

Dage set his glass on the polished oak table. "That's a very logical reason to mate a woman, Kane."

"Exactly." Thank God somebody understood. "She refused, saying she wants love and all that crap. But our mating really was a good idea."

"So after she refused, why sleep with her?" Dage's silver eyes narrowed.

Why, indeed? Kane brought his glass to his mouth, frowning when he realized the crystal was empty. "Well, we'd just rowed across a freezing lake, and I needed to warm her up." The reason even sounded lame to him. He flashed a smile. "And like you said, she's stunning."

"You like her."

"Sure. She's smart, sexy, and dedicated to what she believes in. She said she'd help us save Jase." What wasn't to like? Her idealistic view of the world was silly, but not unlikeable. "I still think mating her is a good idea."

"Maybe. Though you should be careful, the marking is just one part of a mating. Emma's genetics started to change even before I marked her. Of course, I knew she was destined to be my mate." Dage's eyes darkened as he talked about his woman.

Speaking of which—sometimes his brothers were little old ladies who gossiped. "You didn't have to tell Emma that I'd slept with Amber."

"I know." Dage sighed. "But you of all people know that our scientists need the facts when doing research. Emma wanted to take Amber's blood immediately, and she needed to know you'd been intimate. Just in case."

"I hate when you turn my logic against me." Kane shook his head. He would've done the same thing.

Dage leaned forward. "Amber's gifts are unique, and she's definitely an enhanced female, or potential mate. Maybe we should find someone else to mate her—a vampire who believes in love and all that crap, as you put it."

Kane's shoulders went back. Heat spiraled through his spine. "If she mates anybody, it's going to be me."

One dark eyebrow rose. "Why is that?" Dage asked mildly.

"Because she's the only demon destroyer we've ever found. That kind of power should stay in our family." Now that made sense.

"Interesting." The king sat back in his chair. "So, at what point did the mating brand appear on your hand?"

Kane frowned. "Huh?"

Dage pointed to Kane's right hand. "Your palm."

Almost in slow motion, Kane turned his head to view his palm. Dark and raised, an intricate Celtic knot with an elaborate *K* in the middle stood in strong prominence, filling his entire palm.

The Kayrs marking.

He dropped his glass to the floor. "Holy hell."

CHAPTER 14

The ocean rolled far below them and sent the slightest spray of salt up to the small courtyard. Amber perched on a weathered bench to face the sea. She took a cleansing breath of fresh air and kicked her shoes along the frozen grass. There wasn't snow on the cliffside, but the air was still cold. The sun shone weakly down, creating a lovely late afternoon with no real warmth while thick pine trees shielded her on either side. The rock entry to headquarters gaped open behind her.

She sighed and lifted her face to the sun. "I love this courtyard."

Kane settled his bulk next to her. "You're safe here. Well, now."

"This area hasn't always been safe?"

"No. We were breached a few years ago and had quite the battle right here. But we have sensors all around the forest as well as around our subdivision to the south, and we control several satellites. You're definitely safe here now."

"What about from an air attack?" she asked lazily, keeping her eyes closed. "I mean, what if a suicide bomber decided to hit your headquarters?"

"We have missiles in the ground to take out anybody we don't recognize."

Her eyes flipped open. "Really?"

"Sure." Kane shrugged, his gaze remaining on the quiet ocean.

For some reason, he'd been avoiding her gaze since escorting her outside. She tilted her head to the side. "You mentioned a subdivision."

"Yes. We own a small subdivision on the other side of the forest so we can live aboveground when it's safe. The community is gated with excellent security. This is a nice place to live, Amber."

The emphasis on the last sentence rose her chin. "I'm not mating someone for convenience, Kane." The guy could at least try to get a little romantic considering the previous night was, well, freakin' fantastic. Why couldn't Kane be one of those guys who waxed poetic after a good romp?

"There's nothing convenient about us," he muttered. The sun danced around his chiseled face, angling in the hollows beneath his high cheekbones and along the strong line of his jaw. His forehead was broad, his face symmetrical, his lips full. The dark brows over his odd eyes showed masculinity, while his eyes glowed with pure intelligence.

She really needed to get a grip and stop mooning over the vampire. "You said I could teleconference with my grandmother today."

"I'll set the visit up after we practice your skills outside where we can relax. I don't know about you, but I'm tired of the labs."

A knuckle popped when she clenched her hands together. "You're quite the scientist."

"Yes."

"Speaking of your labs, please tell me you don't use animals in testing."

He stiffened. "I do use animals. Mice, rabbits, and monkeys. But I don't harm them in any way. My favorite monkey is a fellow named Walter."

"Walter?" She grinned. "You let them have fresh air and organic food, right? No meat?"

"Tell you what. I'll let you handle their diet from now on, if you continue to train."

She sighed. That seemed like a fair deal. "So, are you going to attack my brain or try to seduce me again?"

"Attack." His strong voice didn't change. "If you'd just mate me, then you wouldn't have to train."

The guy wasn't letting go of the thought. "I've seen Emma and Dage. They didn't mate for convenience—they're in love." In fact, the air had almost combusted when Dage had kissed the queen.

"They believe in fate. I don't." Kane shoved his hair back from his face.

"You should. Fate exists." She'd always known that fact, even without being aware of her gifts.

The wind whistled around them and shoved Kane's hair into his face again. He sighed. "I need a haircut."

"Yeah. You don't seem like a long-hair type of guy." The thought of running her fingers through his thick mane clenched her thighs together. Not a good idea. "I can cut hair."

He finally looked at her—violet eyes serious. "I'll take you up on that offer."

She was a moron. "Great."

"Thanks. I've been working so hard to find Jase, and then to find you, I've just let it grow."

"So, brain attack?" She might as well get the pain over with.

He frowned. "I'm going to come at you like a demon. Fight me."

She nodded, closing her eyes again. "Go for it."

Nothing happened. The wind wandered over her face while the sun tried to warm her. Her shoes in the grass began to tingle in coldness. Yet, she waited. Finally, she opened her eyes to see Kane staring at her. "What—"

Invisible knives slashed into her brain. Horrible images of war, death, and dying filled her mind. She closed her eyes, screaming silently. Taking a deep breath, she imagined the sun increasing in strength and shoved heat through the images. Thinking of puppies and glowing fish, she replaced the pictures with scenes of kindness and love. As beauty defeated death, she shoved the pain into nothingness.

Her eyes flipped open to see a pale Kane. Oh, sending the images cost him . . . more than he probably knew.

He nodded, pride filling his smile. "Good job. Now attack back."

"No."

His bottom lip turned down. "This doesn't work unless you incapacitate them. You have to fight back."

"I don't want to hurt you."

His eyes softened. "I'm tough—this is important. Please."

Man, if he used that voice on her again, she probably would mate him. "Okay." Digging her nails into her palms, she recaptured the images he'd sent and tried to send them back. His expression didn't change. She tried harder, a large knot of dread filling her stomach.

Nothing.

Her ears began to ring. Darkness dropped over her vision. She swayed.

"Amber, stop." Kane slid an arm around her shoulder. "Really, take a deep breath."

She breathed deep, her body shuddering. "Did you feel anything?"

"No. But we'll try again later." He pressed a hand against her forehead. "You're burning up. Let's get you inside, sweetheart."

She tried to stand, but Kane was faster. Lifting her and striding for the rocks, he tucked her face into his neck. The scent of male and musk settled her, and she sighed right down to her toes. Why couldn't fate exist?

After being poked and prodded by both Kane and Emma for nearly an hour, Amber was rethinking her stance on passivity. They'd taken blood, tissue samples, her blood pressure . . . as well as measured her brain waves. When she'd been ready to explode, Emma had finally led her to a plush sofa in a quiet room with a big-screen television. The door shut quietly behind the queen. Settling back in the cushions, Amber waited.

Grandma Hilde soon took up the entire screen. "Amber, sweetheart. Are you all right?"

Amber studied the woman who'd raised her. Hilde sat in a bed, her color strong, her pretty black eyes sparking. "Yes. How are you?"

"Good as new." Hilde clapped her small hands together. "So, how angry are you?"

"Very. As well as feeling very betrayed." She tried to keep her voice calm, but a low tenor of hurt cut through the words.

Hilde nodded, truly not looking very sorry. "I don't blame you. But when your mother died, I decided to give you a good life, one without the craziness of demons, vampires, or the rest. You deserved a decent childhood, baby girl."

Awareness sprang to life down the skin on Amber's back. "How did my mother die?" she whispered.

Hilde shifted on the bed. "Well, now. Um . . ."

Hurt exploded fast and hard in Amber's chest. "She didn't have cancer."

"No. She was, er, dating a vampire, and apparently he was also involved with a demon, and things got nasty." Hilde's eyes filled with tears. "Your mama and the demoness fought, and my baby's brain was destroyed, and she died. So easily." Hilde plucked a string from a pretty quilt. "I took you and ran, using the chants handed down from my great-grandmother's grandmother to keep us safe. The demons knew we existed at that point. I promised myself someday I'd tell you everything, but our lives have been so full, I didn't want to lose that. After losing your mama, I couldn't lose you, too."

Amber blinked twice. "Was my father a vampire?"

"God, no. Vampires only make male babies. Your mama, well, she had lots of boyfriends. Well, until she met the vampire. But she was already pregnant with you at that time."

Great. Her mama got around. "So I'm all human."

"Of course." Hilde squinted her tiny nose. "Your gifts are passed down on your maternal side. I'm not sure if everyone knows this, but demon destroyers are enhanced *human* females only." Pride lifted her chin.

"If I mated a vampire, he'd inherit my gifts, right?"

Horror widened Hilde's eyes. "You are not mating a vampire, Amber. For goodness' sake. Vampires are . . . well . . . the soldiers of the immortal world. You are not mating someone who'll leave you and head off to war every other century or so."

Kane might be a soldier, but he was also an intellectual. Though she was not mating a guy who didn't believe in love. Why did Kane pop into her head, anyway? Amber gave Hilde her strongest glare. "I'll mate who I want. Or marry. I'll marry and mate whoever I want."

Hilde rolled her eyes. "You always have been head-
strong. Mate who you want. Make the same mistakes I
did—" She gasped. "I mean, make new ones."

Amber sat up. "What did you just say?"

"Nothing." Hilde's beautiful skin flushed a bright red. "I
didn't say anything."

"Good God. You mated a vampire." The room started
spinning. Reality had just been shot to hell.

"Did not."

"Did, too." Amber shot to her feet. "Of course. This is
why you never age. You still look freakin' fifty."

"Forty-five," Hilde countered, throwing off the quilt.
"Fine. Your mama's daddy died in Afghanistan, and I was
alone for so long. I shielded us well, but one night I was
out, and I met, well, someone."

"A vampire." How in the world could this have happened?

Hilde rolled her eyes and blew out a strong breath.
"Okay, yes. The women in our family have always been
suckers for a handsome man—even worse, for handsome
soldiers. We started dating, one thing led to another, and
we mated."

"Where's your brand?" There was no marking on her
grandmother.

Hilde tugged down her shirt to show twin puncture
marks above her heart.

Heat filled Amber's head. "You said that was from a car
accident."

"I lied." Hilde smoothed her shirt back into place.
"Most vampires mate with a good bite during sex. Only
the Kayrs ruling family gets that funky mark that brands
their women."

"The marking isn't funky." Frankly, the mark was an intricate, beautiful design.

Hilde's eyes widened until the pupils were nonexistent.

"Oh God. You slept with a vampire—with a Kayrs brother." Hilde shook her head. "End it, now. Trust me. End that affair now."

Amber slammed her hands on her hips, embarrassment and anger flushing through her. While her grandmother had always been open and rather liberal when it came to sex, they still didn't need to have this discussion. "I am not taking dating advice from a woman who has lied to me for twenty-five years."

Hilde's bottom lip trembled, and she pressed a hand to her chest. "That hurts. Oh, my heart."

Fire almost exploded from Amber's head. "Stop that. You're immortal. You can't have a heart attack."

Hilde frowned. "Well, damn it. I guess that's true." She chortled, her eyes lighting and her mouth curving in a familiar smile. "I'm not sorry I gave you a secure childhood, sweetie. I'd do the same thing in a heartbeat."

"Who did you mate, Grandma?"

Hilde sighed. "His name was Elliot Metrov, and he was a soldier. Not for the Realm, but his people aligned with the Realm."

"Was?" Amber asked softly.

Hilde exhaled, sadness twisting her smile. "Yes. When your mama was killed, Elliot went after the demons by himself . . . he wasn't thinking. He didn't make it."

Anger and hurt roared through Amber. "So the demons killed both my mother and your mate?"

"Yes."

Amber shook her head. She needed to learn to fight, and now. "What about my gifts? What about yours?"

Hilde glanced down. "Well, now, that's, ah, the other thing."

Dread had Amber dropping back to the sofa. "What other thing?"

Twisting her lip and obviously biting her cheek, Hilde

hunched her shoulders. "We're not all that powerful. I mean, my older sister had the gift, not me. And she died years ago . . . long before your mama was born. I just have a little of the power." She sighed, suddenly looking almost her age.

"Maybe I have more."

"You do." Hilde smiled, pride in her eyes. "You're like a beacon, Amber. I have no doubt your power is exceptional, much more so than mine or your mother's. But I'd always hoped you wouldn't have to use the gift."

"I promised," Amber whispered. "I gave my word if they saved you, I'd help them." Even if she hadn't promised Kane, she'd want to help get his brother back safely. And now, after knowing how much the demons had taken from her, she wanted to be able to defend anybody she loved.

Hilde nodded. "I understand. But keep in mind, I don't really know how to use the gift. My mother worked with my sister only, and I went on my own way. In fact, at that time, I never thought I'd pass on the gift, to be honest. My sister didn't pass it on, either."

"So I may be the only one left besides you." The world suddenly became much heavier.

"Who knows?" Hilde shrugged. "But you have to understand, the demons are born to mess with minds, and learn to do so from birth. You aren't trained, and even with your power, you're in over your head." She pursed her lips. "The whole mating a vampire and giving him your gifts is actually starting to make sense. I can't lose you, pumpkin."

"You won't, I promise."

Hilde's gaze narrowed. "Which Kayrs did you sleep with? The king?"

Amber's head jerked back. "Of course not. He has a mate."

"Oh?" Hilde pursed her lips. "I've been out of the loop for a long time and hadn't heard. So which brother?"

"Kane."

"The smart one."

"Yes."

Hilde frowned. "Well, he's a handsome vampire, but never forget, even if he is the smart one, he's every bit the soldier as the rest of them. The Kayrs brothers were taught to fight first and rule second—as well as to sacrifice everything for the Realm. They will and they have."

The words sent chills down Amber's back. Kane did seem focused and absolutely determined. "I'll keep that in mind."

"Good." Hilde sat back down on the bed. "So, er, about your night together. Vampires are amazing in bed, now, aren't they?"

CHAPTER 15

A way from the Kurjan encampment, Kalin stood in the rain, feet braced, water splashing his pale skin. The cloud-cover in Utah offered him a very rare moment of standing outside during the day, and enjoyment relaxed his muscles. As the leader of the Kurjan military, he never smiled in front of his troops unless the moment involved death. For now, at an odd moment, he stood alone and smiled into the storm.

He had complete faith that his researchers would create a cure for daylight. One day, he'd chase bikini-clad women by the ocean under the full rays of the sun. But for now, his people were cursed with parchment-white skin, blood-red hair, and purple eyes. They lived for the night. Well, most of his people. He had black hair tipped with red and odd green eyes like a human. Once in a while he wore makeup and actually walked among his prey.

And prey they were.

A signal beeped on his watch. So much for peace. He jerked around and stalked back to the rough cabin he'd taken as a temporary headquarters.

His smile disappeared.

Shoving open the door and clomping inside, he stood before a small computer. "Where is he?"

"Coming up," said a computer tech who probably had a name.

Kalin forced down a growl and enjoyed as the man cringed away. The guy was what? Only six and a half feet tall? Very short for a Kurjan. "I told you not to bother me until the call went through."

The screen wavered and a strong face filled the screen. "What the hell do you want, Kurjan?"

Kalin stepped forward, gaze on the man he hadn't seen in years. "It's good to see you, too, Suri."

The demon leader stood straighter. "I asked you a question."

What an asshole. The demon ruler had shockingly white hair, fathomless black eyes, and the mangled vocal cords of a purebred. Dressed in all black, a silver insignia above his left breast designated him as the leader.

Odd, but Kalin had never thought about the similarities in their soldier uniforms. Sure, the demons used silver for metals, and the Kurjans used red, but still, black uniforms were black uniforms.

Vampires didn't have uniforms. Arrogant bastards didn't think they needed them, probably.

Kalin forced a bored look on his face. "I have an offer. A demon destroyer for the youngest Kayrs brother." The offer was too good for the demons to refuse.

Suri raised both white eyebrows. "You have the destroyer?"

"I will in about an hour." Sure, he was going after the older one, but a demon destroyer she was. "You interested or not?"

"I am." Suri nodded to someone off camera. "Call me back when you have her." The screen fizzled to black.

"What a prick." Kalin headed for the stairs. "Keep monitoring the situation, and we'll head out when darkness falls." Without waiting for acknowledgment of his orders, he jogged down the stairs to what had been a fruit cellar. Shoving open the door, he headed for the one cot in the small room. Lying on his back, he counted the divots in the ceiling. For the first time in a long time, he allowed himself to drop into sleep without shielding his mind.

The dream came easily, and he found himself walking in the sun, fighting true joy at the warmth. He wandered along a rough path by a raging river. Finally, he allowed a smile to cross his face.

"You look nicer when you smile."

The feminine voice came from his left, and he turned to see a young woman sitting on a large rock. He paused. "Janie Kayrs. You're even prettier than you were two years ago."

She arched a delicate eyebrow. "I've been having some fairly strong visions concerning you, Kalin."

He clasped his hands behind his back, settling his stance. She truly was beautiful. Long hair the color of burnished teak, deep blue eyes, and very delicate bone structure. "Have you, now? I'm assuming this is why you've met me in yet another dream world?"

"Yes." She took him in, no expression on her flawless face.

"Does your father know we're meeting?" No way in hell did either Talen or Dage know the Kayrs princess was meeting the Kurjan butcher in a dream world nobody controlled.

"Don't be silly." She swung a foot back and forth.

For some reason, the small tennis shoe she wore reminded him of their childhood meetings . . . when they were both young and innocent. He'd left innocent behind years ago. "Nobody has ever called me silly."

Her eyes darkened. "Now that's just sad."

He frowned. "Why are you asleep in the middle of the day?"

"I'm getting a cold and needed rest. Plus, I've been trying to reach you for weeks."

That thought should not send warmth through his chest. He didn't care if she wanted to see him or not. Janie Kayrs was an end to a means, and someday he'd use everything she was to get what he wanted. But today he could allow himself some curiosity. "What do you want?"

She took a deep breath that emphasized pert breasts under a white T-shirt. For the first time since meeting her, he realized she was an adult. He flashed his fangs. "What are you now—about twenty?" *More than old enough to take.*

"Yes—I'm all grown up, Kalin." Her small chin lowered. "And I have a grown-up offer to make you."

Now this was getting interesting. "Is that a fact?" His gaze raked her from head to toe, lingering at the good parts. *It was truly a nice surprise that there were so many good parts.* "What kind of an offer?"

She waited until his gaze returned to her eyes, pure boredom on her face. "I know you're in league with the demons, if not yet, then you will be."

He kept his expression neutral. *The oracles had been correct in that her psychic powers were impressive, far more impressive than anyone realized. To be able to take that gift and use it as the Kurjan leader would be worth all the time he'd waited to make his move.* "And?"

"You get Jase home, and I'll trade myself for him."

Kalin's upper lip twitched with the need to smile. He'd already set that plan in motion. Odd that they were on the same wavelength. "What makes you think I want you?"

She rolled her eyes. "Seriously?"

The tiny, defenseless human actually rolled her eyes at him. An unwilling laugh barked from his chest. "I'd kill anybody else who dared to make such a face at me."

She leaned forward, her eyes intense, her voice soft. Her feminine gaze raked him from head to toe, pausing at the medals adorning his chest before heading up toward his eyes. "You don't scare me—you never have."

Odd, but that gave him feelings of both gratitude and irritation. "Then you're not as smart as everyone predicted you'd be."

"Maybe I'm just more powerful than any of you predicted."

Perhaps so. A new burning filtered through his body. Oh, he wanted the little human, without question.

"So, my offer?" she asked.

Kalin sighed. "You'd willingly walk into the den of the enemy for Jase Kayrs, now, would you?" After all the years of them meeting, the little human still didn't understand him. Not at all.

"Yes."

"What about Zane?" There was no question the fate of the world would come down to Kalin, Janie, and Zane, a partial-vampire who'd also visited the dream world several times, first as a child and more recently as an adult soldier.

Janie blinked twice. "What about him?"

Oh, the girl still had a crush, did she? "I'm fairly certain I need to cut off his head in order for destiny to be fulfilled."

Horror filled her eyes that she quickly banked. But not fast enough. She shrugged. "Zane can take care of himself just fine."

"Deserted you, did he?"

She jumped from the rock and landed a foot away. Tilting her head back, she met Kalin's gaze. "The offer will expire. Think about it." With a sweep of her hand, the world disappeared.

Kalin sat up on the cot. Impressive little human. Yet what she didn't understand was that the last thing he wanted was her cooperation. When he took her, and he would, the little female had better fight. Otherwise, what the hell was the point?

CHAPTER 16

Realm headquarters was beginning to smother him. Maybe it was time to go hunt a werewolf or two. Kane stifled a sigh as he slid open his door and stalked into his underground quarters.

Her smell hit him immediately. Wild heather, just blooming.

The tinkling sound of a waterfall echoed from his wall fountain, and the lights had been turned down low. He focused on the woman sitting so quietly on his wide sofa. "What are you doing here?"

Amber shrugged, her gaze going to the two moonlight scenes decorating his walls. "This place is all zen—much different from what I would've expected."

The dark furniture and thick rug blended with the rock surrounding them and gave him a sense of peace when he needed space to breathe. "I work in labs surrounded by chrome, steel, and glass. Sometimes I want something soothing for a little while." He dropped to the couch next to her. "Do you like my place?"

"Very much," she said softly.

He rested his head back and shut his aching eyes. "Why are you here, Amber?"

"I want to train some more."

Just like that, his entire body tensed. "Why?"

She exhaled loudly. "The demons know about me, and they know about my grandmother. She's not strong enough to stop them, and I need to be. So it's time to train again."

His head hurt and the damn marking on his palm had started to pound the second he realized its existence. Of course, the brand had appeared because he was logically thinking of mating someone and for no other reason. Fate didn't exist. He was in control of his body and the marking. "Let's take the night off."

"I can find somebody else to train me."

The pounding in his hand rippled up his arm and down his spine with claws of irritation. "No, you can't. I'm the only genius empath in town, sweetheart. Deal with it." None of his other people could possibly mimic the effects of a demon attack. Thank God.

"I bet the king can attack brains." Her voice rose in challenge.

Kane's eyes flashed open. The idea of Dage invading Amber's mind pierced heat through him until he growled low. "Dage is psychic and can read minds, but he can't attack them. Period."

"Then get to work." She shifted on the couch, sending her scent to tempt him. Female. His.

Forcing all emotion into the universe, he sighed. "No. We'll start again tomorrow."

The slow glide of heat through his head calmed him instantly. The warmth pulsed, destroying his headache before sliding through the tense muscles in his neck and shoulders. His body relaxed into the couch. The warmth continued, through muscles and tissue, warming him from within.

Arousal followed the heat.

His eyes opened slowly to focus on Amber, who faced him, her eyes opened wide.

Nothing in the world could've stopped him from

reaching for her. Grabbing her arms, he settled her on his lap, straddling him.

Her mouth opened in a silent *oh*. "I felt your brain—the headache—the tenseness leave you." Wonder lifted her lips.

"Yes." His mind, warm and strong, completely blanked as his gaze dropped to her mouth.

She shifted her weight on him, rubbing against his cock. He became instantly and inexplicably hard as a rock.

Her throat cleared. "Ah, I didn't, I mean, well . . ."

Tangling a hand in her silky hair, he tugged her head to the side. All focus, all concentration, centered on that pretty pink mouth. She opened it to say something, and he stopped her with a strong grip on her jaw. The sharp intake of her breath only spurred him on.

Slowly, wanting her to know he was fully in control, he tugged her mouth to his. A small sigh escaped her when they touched. She softened, her body leaning toward his, accepting him.

He nibbled at her lips, tasting and coaxing. Her hands slid to his shoulders, the fingers flexing.

His hold tightened on her jaw, and she obeyed the silent demand by opening her mouth. With a low growl, he went deeper, taking and claiming. His eyes shut, and the world narrowed to the woman he'd so effectively trapped. She couldn't move an inch without him releasing his hold. Yet, as her mouth opened wider, as she matched his kiss, he wondered who'd been caught.

As her tongue touched his, the thought disappeared. The woman held passion tight, and he wanted to be the one to let it loose. To unleash the fire inside a gifted female. To bare her and claim every single inch . . . so she'd have no question who she belonged to. The marking on his palm pulsed hard in agreement.

She moaned into his mouth, her nails biting his shoulders. So soft, so willing, so damn hot.

His mind spun. His slacks became beyond confining. Tugging her closer, he fought a groan as her hard nipples scraped against his chest. She pressed against him like a hungry kitten, struggling to get closer. The heat from her core cascaded right through his pants and warmed his groin.

Jesus. She'd kill him.

He wanted to lay her out and feast for days. Take her slow . . . take her fast . . . just take her.

Keep her.

Drawing back, he looked his fill. Her eyes had darkened so the pupils melded with the irises—no distinction. Sexual need flared hot and bright in those dangerous orbs. Her mouth was swollen, looking properly kissed, and a high flush decorated her fine cheekbones. But there was vulnerability along with need on her face.

The combination of the two made the night inevitable. "You're beautiful."

She started, blinking several times.

No . . . no regaining reality. He kissed her hard, pressing deep until she was moaning and kissing him back. Keeping her mouth busy, he cupped her ass and stood. Satisfaction surged through him when she wrapped her legs around his waist in acceptance. Several strides had them around the couch and in his bedroom, where he laid her down. She scooted up on the bed, her gaze on him.

He was so damn tired of planning, so tired of thinking. For just a moment, he wanted to steal some peace. To get out of his head.

The world focused to one small, sexy, dangerous woman.

The hunger in her eyes sparked a primal possessiveness deep within him. "Take off your shirt." Her tongue darted out to wet her lips, and he fought a groan. "Now."

Her hands shook when she reached for the hem of her

T-shirt and slowly, so damn slowly, tugged the cotton over her head. The saucy smile she gave as the shirt landed on the floor guaranteed she'd teased him on purpose.

He had no doubt his answering smile was predatory. "Be careful who you tease, darlin'."

She reached up to cup her breasts through a flimsy bra. "Why is that?"

A whisper of sound and he was on her, both hands encircling her wrists. The swift intake of her breath had his dick surging for relief. "Let me show you." Quick as that, his fangs dropped into her neck.

She cried out, arching against him, an orgasm sweeping through her body.

The taste of wild heather and honey exploded in his mouth. His cock howled in protest. Two swipes of his tongue closed the wound, and he lifted to smile at her bemused face. He nipped her lip and that feminine mouth opened in surprise. Wandering his mouth along the soft skin under her jaw, an overwhelming need to protect almost banished the desire to possess.

Almost.

He licked the soft spot behind her ear, enjoying her sigh of need. Her hands tugged for release, and he tightened his hold. The pulse in her neck increased its pounding in response. He kissed the life-giving vein in approval.

His fangs dropped again, and he cut her bra in two.

"Hey," she protested, "that's my only bra here."

He lifted his head and slashed through the straps. "If you were mine, I'd never allow you to wear a bra."

She frowned. "Allow—" Then she made a strangled whimper as he flicked one nipple with his tongue. She sucked in a breath to try again, and he flicked the other nipple. She went silent.

Man, she had gorgeous breasts. Full and tipped with strawberry-colored nipples, she tasted like summer and smelled like forever. He swirled his tongue around a nipple, his mind spinning when she arched against him. They had too many clothes on.

Releasing her hands, he removed her jeans and panties in two seconds.

Her nimble fingers went to the buttons on his silk shirt, making quick work of them. He shrugged off the shirt.

"Your pants," she murmured, dark gaze watching her palms sliding along his chest. A pleased smile lifted her swollen lips.

"What the lady wants . . ." He unbuckled his belt and removed his pants, kicking them with his socks across the room. He traced a hand from her knee to her inner thigh. Toned muscle trembled under his touch. Ignoring her sound of need, he played with her skin, marveling at the softness. When she arched her mound toward him, he bit back a smile and ran his fingers along the other thigh.

Would she taste as good as she had in the cabin? Had his imagination taken control?

She shifted on the bed. "Kane, I . . ."

"What, sweetheart?" He lifted up just enough for his breath to brush her clit. Her very bare clit. He did appreciate a woman who waxed.

Her gasp of breath filled the silent room. "You're killing me."

"Not my intention." He licked smooth skin, and she almost came off the bed. "Now tell me what you want."

She stilled. "Um, well, what do you want?"

His woman was shy in bed. Interesting . . . and not what he'd accept. "I want you to tell me what you want." Oh, she was wet and primed. He knew exactly what she wanted—but she'd have to ask. Nicely.

"You're kind of an asshole in bed," she moaned.

A sharp slap to her clit had her crying out. Need and intrigue filled the high sound. She liked this. He rose to pin her with a look. "Is that what you wanted?"

"No," she panted out.

"Then you'd better ask nicely." Her thighs had dampened even more after the quick slap. Interesting.

"Please put your mouth on me."

He smiled. "Gladly." Thank God she'd asked. He couldn't have held back much longer. He ran his tongue through her slit, nearly humming in appreciation. She tasted even better than he'd remembered. Sweet and slightly salty . . . and all his.

Her breath came out in pants, and her body gyrated on the bed.

"I love your responses," he murmured against her skin, smiling as her thighs began to tremble harder.

He pressed a finger into her and easily brushed the bundle of nerves that had her whimpering. The sexy sound came from deep in her throat. Gently, way too gently, he pressed a kiss on her mound.

She pushed up against him, and his free hand flattened on her abdomen to keep her in place.

A frustrated hiss came from the woman.

Lowering his head again, he scraped his fangs along her thigh with just enough pressure to still her movements. Then he returned to licking her . . . never in the same place twice.

Her body drew tight in need. "Kane, please . . ."

"Please, what?" He sunk his teeth into her thigh with enough force to leave a small mark.

"I, ah . . ." She sounded almost mindless with want.

Exactly how he wanted her. Needed her. "You want something, sweetheart?"

She stiffened, no doubt biting back a sharp retort. Smart girl. "You know I do."

"Ask for it."

She huffed in obvious exasperation.

Kane gently drew her engorged clit in his mouth. Then he released her.

Her whimper almost made him give in. But instead, he nipped her thigh again. "Ask me, darlin'."

"Damn it. I'd like to come." Her voice came out fast and hoarse.

He figured she'd sworn more in the short time she'd known him than ever before. Poor thing. He lifted up, resting his chest on her thigh. "I'd like to end the war and make it mandatory for all people to take driving tests every year."

Her eyes narrowed. If the woman had a gun, he had no doubt she'd shoot him. So he wiggled the finger inside her, brushing against her G-spot.

Her eyelids fluttered shut.

Stubborn little thing. He added another finger, working the spot until a light sheen of moisture covered her forehead, and a fine blush covered her beautiful breasts. "Ask me nicely, and you get what you want." His cock was ready to explode. "Keep being stubborn, and you won't like the result." He slid his fingers through her folds, barely brushing her clit before plunging back inside her.

"Please let me come," she whispered, her entire body trembling.

"With pleasure." Rising up, he sucked her clit into his mouth, flicking the little nub with his tongue while also working both fingers inside her.

She arched off the bed, crying out as the orgasm whipped through her. He helped her ride out the waves, prolonging the sensation as long as he could. Finally, she collapsed against the bedspread, her eyes opening on his.

Dragging his fingers free, he smiled as her body jerked

in response. Thank god she liked to play the same way he did.

One by one, he licked his fingers clean.

Her eyes darkened. Then she reached out and took him in both hands.

Fire ripped up his spine. He wasn't going to last long. Moving forward, he climbed up her body to press a kiss against her moist neck.

Grabbing both her hands, he held them immobile at the side of her head. "Ready for round three?"

Her knees widened while her legs encircled him, ankles crossing at his butt. "More than ready."

His heart pounded hard.

A determined shove forward, and he embedded in her, balls deep. Heat swallowed him. She was so tight his eyes almost rolled back in his head. "You're perfect."

She blinked in surprise.

Odd. The woman wasn't used to compliments. Even with his body raging for relief, his mind wondered at the fact. The woman was perfect. How could she not know it? "I've lived for more than three centuries, and you're the most beautiful thing I've ever seen."

Her eyes widened, and a shy smile played with her lips. "You confuse me."

"I do my best." He couldn't help the answering smile. "Keep your hands where I've put them."

Releasing her palms, he grabbed the back of her thigh with his unmarked hand and withdrew, plunging back in. The exquisite friction almost put him over the edge. He pressed the palm with the marking against the sheets. The animal within him, the one he never let loose, howled in protest. The hunger to mate clawed with rough nails through his entire being.

Ignoring the animal, Kane plunged out and back in.

Holding her thigh, holding her open, he began to pound with a ferocity he'd never succumbed to. Faster, harder . . . the only thing in existence was that pinnacle he needed to reach. With Amber. Only Amber.

Her thighs tightened and she gasped.

He shifted his angle to slide over her clit, and she exploded around him.

The waves crashing through her gripped his shaft so hard he saw stars. Increasing his speed, he raced for the end and broke, coming with a low growl.

The need to mark her—to mate her—shot fire through his arm. Coming down, taking a deep breath, he glanced at his hand. The mark pounded in angry pain.

The branding was darker than ever.

CHAPTER 17

For once in Kane's life, the lab failed to provide him with a sense of purpose. What was the fucking purpose? He'd spent years trying to cure Virus-27 with limited success. Mates were still vulnerable. Witches were afraid. And now, the one species he'd been able to save was in danger from faulty vials.

The brand on his palm burned with jagged demand and had for several days. The marking burned when he trained Amber, when he touched her, when he sensed her. Hell, it burned even when he was just thinking about her.

"Fuck." He threw a beaker across the lab, closing his eyes as glass smashed near the open window.

Walter the monkey screeched from his high-end cage. Then he frowned, much too serious for a monkey.

"Sorry." Kane had escaped from the earth to his largest lab so he could open the windows and smell the ocean. Aboveground he always seemed to get more accomplished.

Not today.

Today completely sucked.

Not only had he left the earth, he'd left a sleeping beauty in his bed once again. She'd moved right into his quarters because he'd pretty much insisted on it. An innocent, softhearted beauty he had planned to use against demons.

He felt Dage's anger and worry before hearing the king arrive. Shit. Now Kane couldn't even control his empathic abilities? No. Absolutely not. Shoving his face into calm lines, Kane turned to face his brother.

Dage took a deep breath. "The demons have Hilde."

A roaring filled Kane's ears. He swallowed hard. "Are you sure?"

"Yes." Dage frowned, pacing to the window to stare at the ocean. "Satellite pictures are hours old, but there was some fight between the demons and Kurjans at the wolf compound in Utah."

Kane scrubbed both hands down his face. "What the hell?"

"I don't know. Best guess? Whoever is messing with the inoculations tipped the Kurjans off about Hilde. How the demons got involved, I have no clue. But there was a bloody fight and the Kurjans lost." Dage leaned against the wall, facing Kane. "Talen is in the armory suiting up—we need to go."

"We have someplace to go?" Now that was finally some good news.

"Yes. We traced their movements to the Mexico border—it looks like a temporary stronghold. They won't keep Hilde there for long."

"Let's go, then." The idea of storming any demon stronghold had adrenaline ripping through Kane's veins. "I wish Conn were still here." Conn had taken off for Ireland already.

"Yes. He's halfway across the ocean by now."

The question lurking in the king's silver eyes had Kane's chin lifting. "Amber is not going."

"Your call." Dage headed for the door.

Kane ignored the relief shooting through his veins. "Is Talen trying to bring Terrent up via phone?"

"Terrent isn't at the wolf compound." Dage headed into

the hallway. "The Council went after a hoard of were-wolves outside of Seattle yesterday morning." As the head of the Bane's Council, the group responsible for killing all werewolves, Terrent was always on the move. "The Kurjans probably knew he'd taken off before they attacked."

Kane hustled behind his brother through headquarters to a room hidden behind a blank wall. Sliding the door open, he took the cement stairs down to a tunnel that led to the underground labyrinth.

Dage shot into the darkness. "Are you sure you don't want Amber to come with us? We should test her skills."

"No. I'll mate her and get her skills." The words emerged from Kane's mouth before his brain caught their meaning. With a short nod, he acknowledged mating was the only way to both protect Amber and find Jase.

Dage stopped in the dark tunnel. "That's quite a decision." He didn't turn around.

"Yes, it is. And it's my decision." Kane's steps slowed.

The king shook his head and resumed jogging. The *clomp* of his boots echoed through the rocks. "Are you going to lie to yourself that you feel nothing? That branding Amber is all about duty?"

"No. I like her—a lot. She'll make a good mate." And a good mother to their children someday. The thought of Amber swollen with his son made Kane's heart skip a beat. Pleasure filled him. "I'd like your support in this."

"You always have my support." Dage shoved open a door to reveal an armory sporting every type of weapon imaginable. "Even when you're being an obtuse dumbass." He stalked inside and stopped cold.

Kane barely kept from running into his back. "What?" He stepped to the side.

Amber and Emma stood near Talen wearing identical "don't fuck with me" expressions on their faces.

Emma glared at Dage. "You're the king—you don't need to go fight demons. That's why you have soldiers."

Kane ignored the argument. It was an old one, and Dage always put himself in danger if he asked soldiers to fight. As the royal family, they were the first to go if necessary. He eyed Amber. "I'll bring back your grandmother."

Amber paled, her gaze wandering along the myriad of swords lining the west wall. "I'm going with you."

"No." Out of the air, Kane snatched the bulletproof vest Talen threw, quickly securing the Kevlar over his head. "You don't have enough training."

"And yet, I'm the best you've got." She reached for a smaller vest hanging on a hook. "Either tell me how to wear this thing, or I'll go without a vest."

Talen shuffled his feet. "We could use her help." He glanced at Dage for support.

Dage shook his head, gaze moving to Kane. "She's your woman—this is your call."

Emma's instant sputtering at the archaic language failed to drown out Amber's outraged hiss. Amber yanked the vest over her head, her eyes spitting anger. "I'm no one's woman, jackass."

Emma nodded in agreement, a high flush staining her cheeks. "Yeah. What she said."

"I'd like a moment alone with Amber." Kane reached for the nearest gun to tuck in his waist.

Dage grabbed Emma's arm and tugged her from the room. The queen protested, digging in her heels, but the king wasn't going to be deterred this time.

Talen smiled, a shit-eating grin on his face.

Yeah, this was funny. Kane barely kept from slugging him as he went by. For so long, Kane had been the one laughing on the sidelines as his brothers' mates ran them in circles. Not for one second was Amber going to alter his life, and the sooner she figured that out, the easier she'd find her life as his mate.

He nearly swallowed his tongue when she grabbed a gun and pointed the weapon at him. Keeping her eyes pinned, he stalked forward until the barrel rested against his chest.

She gulped in air, her hand shaking. "I, ah, was trying to make a point."

His chest warmed. The woman had the sweetest heart. "Which was?"

"That I'm, ah, not afraid of guns anymore."

The pallor of her skin proclaimed that statement a lie. Kane gently removed the gun from her grasp. "Guns aren't scary. Having to use a gun, well now, that's frightening."

She nodded. "I know. To save my grandma, I'd use a gun."

Her voice wavered just enough to fill him with doubt. "You don't need to use a gun, Amber. Stay here and I'll bring her home to you. I promise." How the hell he'd keep that promise, he didn't know. But damn it, he would.

She sighed, pressing her hands against his vest and meeting his gaze. "I'm here for a reason. For now, I'm the only person you know who can shield against the demon mind games and maybe even mess with them enough that they leave you alone. I have to try, and I know you understand what I'm saying."

He did. She loved her granny as much as he loved his brothers. Nothing on earth would keep him from going after Jase if Kane had an inkling of where he was being kept.

Amber stepped closer. "Sometimes I can get a sense of what's ticking in a brain—I've been practicing secretly since you told me about my gifts. Maybe I can get a sense of where Jase is."

Clever little female. "You're not ready."

She shrugged. "That doesn't matter—I'm all you've got. Deal with it."

Throwing his words back in his face wasn't nice. He frowned. "I don't think I can."

"I can shield." Her eyes implored him to trust her. "Please give me a chance."

His brain bellowed in refusal even while he spoke, "Okay. But the second you're in distress, we're leaving, whether we have Hilde or not." He blinked twice. What the hell? He'd just agreed to take her into a demon foothold.

She shot out of the room, leaving him frozen in place. While her argument made a logical sense, one he'd responded to naturally, doubt clouded his brain. What kind of a mate was he going to be if he allowed her to seek danger?

"I took Cara raiding a Kurjan hospital where we saved several allies," Talen said quietly from the doorway.

Kane whirled around. He'd forgotten Talen had taken his mate on that raid so long ago. "We used her empathic abilities."

"Yes." Talen's eyes swirled a dangerous green through the gold. He shuffled his feet, his frown deep enough to flash his dimples. "We needed to do so at the time—I don't think I'm strong enough to put her in danger again."

Kane stared at his big brother. Talen was the strongest man he'd ever met. "You would. If you had to." Or maybe not. From the second Cara had given birth to their son fourteen years ago, the man had protected her even more so.

"No." Talen gave a rueful smile. He grabbed several knives from the wall to tuck along his boots and vest. Three more guns found safe purchase where he could grab them quickly. "But for now, in this time and place, there's a reason you're falling in love with Amber Free-bird." Quick strides and he was out the door.

Quiet reigned for the smallest of moments. "I'm not falling in love," Kane said to the empty room.

The words echoed off the weapon-filled walls.

Mocking him.

Taking a deep breath, Amber tried to still the trembling in her knees. She sat between Kane and Talen in the back-seat of a Black Hawk helicopter gliding silently through the night. Heat cascaded off the vampires, keeping her snug and warm. They all wore ear communicators. Talen's legs twitched, and he drummed his fingers on his legs to some tune only he heard.

Kane sat perfectly still. No movement, no agitation, just pure calmness. Pure, cold, calm.

Amber tugged the vest tighter around her waist, her mind spinning. Her heart beat rapidly against her ribs. Was Grandma Hilde all right? What if she wasn't? Hilde had said she lacked power. How much? Could she shield a lit-tle from the mind attacks?

Two similar helicopters followed silently behind them, also filled with dangerous soldiers.

She shivered.

Dage turned the beast into the setting sun, nodding his head toward the massive vampire in the copilot seat. "Os-car, tell the rest of the crew about the last time you dealt with demons."

Amber had met Oscar right before takeoff. The ancient soldier had more experience fighting demon mind games than anybody else in the Realm. His metallic aqua eyes were bright with intelligence, and laugh lines cut into the sides of his mouth. She'd liked him immediately.

Oscar pressed his ear to engage the comm line. "Demons don't incapacitate us completely, but you'll be at about fifty percent of your usual fighting skill. It takes that much energy to combat the brain attack of an experienced demon soldier. Of course, with younger soldiers, vampires might retain about seventy percent of concentration and skill."

Dage nodded. "We're getting close. I'll drop quickly and we'll go. Kane, what's our best move?"

"We go in fast and hard." Kane's voice remained so calm he could've been talking about his favorite beer. "We need their minds occupied as much as possible . . . go either for the instant kill or the most painful injury." He kept his gaze straight ahead. "Amber and I will try to sense her grandmother. Amber, you concentrate on shielding and not on injuring. The injuries will come from weapons drawing blood."

She nodded, even knowing he couldn't see her. Or maybe with his vampire sight, his peripheral vision was good enough.

Dage banked a hard right. "Did the satellite shots give us an idea of numbers?"

"No." Talen's drumming increased in speed. "But the area is rather small—probably something thrown together as they prepare to move Hilde."

How small? Amber turned to view Kane. How was he so calm?

Finally, he glanced at her with those odd violet eyes. No emotion showed in their depths. "Do you want a gun?"

Slowly, she nodded. He reached in his back pocket and handed her a small weapon. "If you point a weapon, you use it. No hesitating, no thinking, no feeling. When the gun is in your hand, you're all soldier. Nothing else exists."

Cold metal weighed heavy in her palm. Death had a sensation. Before the night was over, she might turn against everything she believed in to save the one person she'd always counted on. "I understand."

"Good. There are no pacifists or second chances in battle," Kane said, turning his gaze back to the front.

Dage swung left again and shot toward the ground. "Two seconds and we hit."

The helicopter slammed down and the soldiers leaped out. Amber didn't have time to worry about keeping up as Kane grabbed her around the waist and all but carried her toward a sprawling brick building set against a small outcropping of rock.

With twin *booms,* the other two helicopters slammed into place and surrounded the demon stronghold.

Talen dropped to one knee, a large rocket launcher on his shoulder. "Fire." A missile exploded forward and ripped into the front of the building, shooting bricks high into the sky.

Then everybody moved at once.

Gasping, her eyes tearing, Amber allowed Kane to lead her into hell.

CHAPTER 18

Smoke gave the night a surreal quality. The shouts from angry men came from what seemed a great distance. Particles of brick rained down, and it took several seconds for Amber to realize Kane was protecting her head. In fact, the vampire was protecting her, period. Shielding her with his body, he maneuvered gracefully around debris and two downed bodies in what had been a small room.

Downed demons.

They wore the same black uniforms as the two who had tried to kidnap her from the farm.

Dage dropped and jammed a knife into the closest demon's neck.

Bile rose in Amber's stomach and she turned away.

Pain crept along her cheekbones to pierce her lower eyelids, sliding directly for her brain. With a cry, she smoothed shields into place.

Calmness. Peace. Strength.

Kane stumbled and growled low. Blood trickled out his ears.

Amber grabbed his hand, trying to send strength to his mind. "Don't fight the pain—go around it."

He frowned and then his shoulders relaxed. Blood dripped from his nose. "That's better. Seek your granny."

Three demon solders rushed from a doorway to the left.

Talen and Dage pounced on them, even while emitting growls of pain.

Kane tugged her toward the doorway while Oscar flanked her other side. "Keep shielding."

She nodded, her heart flaring to beat against her ribs in a painful cadence. Seeking with her mind, she caught a faint whiff of something pure. Her grandma. "She's here."

Kane nodded. "Yeah, I can sense her. She's not shielding—must know we're here." His gun in one hand, he grabbed Amber's with his other and darted into the doorway.

A long tunnel wound directly into the rock.

"I was afraid of this." Kane shook his head. "Stay behind me. The second you sense them, let me know."

She gripped his hand tighter. An odd connection flowed beneath her skin and escaped where they touched. Her abilities might help him fight the mental pain. "Don't let go."

He frowned, glancing down. "Are you shielding my mind, too?"

"Maybe. But trying doesn't hurt me or diminish my shield over my brain, so there's no reason not to try." Probably. Heck, maybe not. Her head was actually starting to ache a little bit.

He nodded and glanced over his shoulder. "I have lead. Flank her."

Talen and Oscar both stepped up behind her.

Kane maneuvered around burning bricks, leading her carefully. "I sense two ahead." He pushed her against the rock wall and released her. An instant grunt of pain came from him. Talen jumped to his side, and they both leapt forward into the darkness. The echo of flesh hitting flesh filled the tunnel along with grunts and the shattering sound of bones breaking.

Brutal images of war and death slammed into Amber's

brain. She bit her lip to keep from crying out. Settling her hands against the rough rock wall, she breathed deep and tried to shove the images away. Sharp spikes ripped the back of her eyelids. Digging deep, she eased air into her lungs, gently sliding the bad images away and replacing them with good images.

The pain receded.

She opened her eyes in time to see a demon stop short, his eyes going wide as he struggled as if the air held him back. Talen stood before him, one hand out. Talen jumped forward and stabbed the demon, taking him down to the ground. Seconds later, the demon's head flew down the tunnel.

Talen pivoted and shot into the darkness.

Nausea settled in her stomach, and she had to take several deep swallows not to puke.

Kane reappeared, blood across his face and torso.

She gasped. "Talen made that guy stop moving."

"Yes. Talen has a gift." Grabbing her hand, Kane tugged her into the darkness. "Talen and Oscar are scouting ahead—I sense at least three more."

Yeah, she sensed them, too. Threading her fingers through Kane's, she concentrated on sending whatever power she had through their connection. They jogged deeper into the earth, and she kept to Kane's back, following in his steps. While the darkness hid the ground, she didn't falter.

Kane stopped, and she ran into his back. His hold tightened a fraction before he released her. A gentle push to her chest found her shoulders against the wall.

Strong lights snapped on.

Amber cried out, the sudden brightness attacking her eyes. She shut them, her knees trembling. The sound of metal hitting rock snapped them back open.

A demon swung a huge glinting sword at Kane's head. Kane ducked and leapt sideways, climbing the rock wall to jump for the demon's head. He hit hard and slammed the soldier into the rock.

Waves of pain instantly cascaded from the demon and smacked Amber between the eyes. Unbelievable images, truly horrific pictures of death and torture, filled her mind. A sharp spike of pain cut down the center of her brain. She cried out, her mouth remaining open even when it hurt too much to push out sound.

Kane grabbed his head and stumbled back.

No! Amber sucked in the smoky air and pushed against the pain. Her knees weakening, she slid to the ground. As her butt met the hard floor, she settled and gently slid the horror away. The pain followed.

Kane dropped to one knee, blood flowing from his nose.

The demon grinned sharp canines, sword raising high.

Pressing her shoulders against the wall, Amber sent harsh images of pain and death at the demon.

He paused, gaze roving to her. "Destroyer."

She shoved harder.

His grin lacked any semblance of humor. "No." His empty black eyes pierced into hers. Raw, brutal, and pure agony shot through her pupils right to her brain. She screamed, hands rising to ward off something she couldn't touch.

With a furious battle cry, Kane leapt into the air, both hands grabbing the demon's sword. He shoved the weapon sideways toward the demon's throat.

The demon struggled, a hiss coming from his pale lips.

Kane kneed him in the gut. Once, twice, and then a third time as they struggled for the sword. Blood flowed out of Kane's ears, nose, and even his eyes.

His shoulders went back, and he shoved the side of the blade into the demon's mouth. Bellowing a shout of victory, he pressed in and cut the demon.

The demon cried out, falling against the wall.

Kane stepped back, swung the blade, and pivoted his entire body as he swished the sword through the demon's neck. The head hit the ground with a thunderous *clunk* and then rolled into the darkness.

"Are you all right?" Kane wiped blood off his chin. His blood.

Nodding her head, Amber used the wall to reach her feet. "Yes." She swayed. A roaring filled her ears.

Kane grabbed her elbow, and reality rushed back. Turning, he surveyed the tunnel.

Amber gasped at the crude door set into the rock several yards ahead now guarded by Oscar. Gentle vibrations came from the other side of the door. Hurrying after Kane, she tried to reach with her mind into the room. Nothing happened.

Kane set her behind him and kicked the door precisely at the lock. The door whipped open.

Amber shoved past him to find her grandmother calmly sitting on the floor. Next to her lay an unconscious demon soldier bleeding from his eyes and mouth.

Hilde raised an eyebrow. "It's about time."

Hair wet from the shower, Amber padded into the spacious living room of Hilde's new underground quarters dressed in a fresh pair of borrowed jeans and a snug sweater. The jeans were from Sarah Pringle, Max's mate, while the sweater had been the queen's. A huge television took up one wall, while a comfortable-looking sofa and two captain chairs faced it. A thick Western rug covered the rock floor and pretty watercolors adorned the walls. A stocked kitchen and two bedrooms made up the unit.

The door opened, and Grandma Hilde swept inside. She turned and thanked Oscar for escorting her.

The massive vampire nodded, his eyes sparkling.

Shutting the door, Hilde hurried over to sit on the sofa. She'd also borrowed clean clothing. The king had requested her presence for a debriefing that had lasted about an hour. Finally, she'd returned. She smiled, her dark eyes lighting up. "Is that Oscar a handsome one, or what?"

Amber frowned and dropped to the faux-leather couch.

Hilde cleared her throat and stretched her legs across the matching ottoman. "I mean, I'm already mated, so it's not like I can touch the guy. You know if any male touches a mated woman, he ends up in agony from a rare allergy, right?"

"Yeah, I've heard that." Amber didn't return the smile.

"Well, I can at least look at the handsome vampire." Hilde squirmed into a different position. "So, how about those demons?"

Biting back a sharp retort, Amber glared at her grandmother. The glare turned to wide-eyed disbelief. "You look different."

Hilde shrugged. "Yes. I look forty-five, which I am. The last several years I've had to add a bunch of gray to my hair and use makeup to look older. It's nice to be me again." She rubbed her clean skin with both hands. "I'm not sorry I kept this part of your life from you."

Amber sighed. "I know—and I had a wonderful childhood. But right now, at this time, it'd be nice to be able to lay a demon out like you did." God. She was discussing the very real existence of demons with her grandmother. Where had reality gone? "But you said you didn't have any power."

"I didn't. But I did mate a vampire years ago, and when you mate, you get their skills. He was psychic, and maybe I gained enough skill from him that I have some power now. Who knows." Hilde stretched her neck. "I guess all you do with the demons is shove their power back at them." She held out her hand, which was smooth and missing the dark age spots Amber had gotten accustomed to seeing.

"I did. I tried to shove one demon's power back, and he nearly blinded me." Maybe Amber didn't have the power she'd thought. "So, I slid the pain and images away and at least shielded myself. Oh, and I shielded Kane a little bit when we held hands, I think."

Hilde stiffened, gaze cutting to Amber. "You shielded Kane?"

Squirming on the couch for no logical reason, Amber cleared her throat. "Um, yeah. I mean, I think I did."

"Did he mate you?" Hilde's eyes widened.

"Mate? No."

"Hmmm." Hilde frowned. "You shouldn't be able to shield anyone you haven't mated, sweetie. That isn't done, I don't think."

"I haven't mated Kane." Sure, they'd had sex several times. But if there was no marking, there was no mating. "Maybe the ability to shield other people is my gift and not being able to attack the demons is my curse."

"No. I don't think the ability works that way." Hilde shook out her curly hair.

"Why not? I mean, you have curly hair, and I have straight hair, yet it's the same color and I obviously inherited the color from you. Maybe the gift is used different ways, too." Amber had promised Kane she'd help save Jase, and she would. But the sooner she figured out how to use her gift, the better.

"Perhaps." Hilde's dark eyes turned shrewd. "You slept with him more than once?"

Heat climbed into Amber's face. "Grandma—we already talked about that."

Her grandma reached out and patted her hand. "I'm asking because I've heard the marking is just one part of a Kayrs' mating. Along with a good bite . . . and sex. Maybe you've started to mate him and don't even know it."

Now that was ridiculous. "Speaking of mating, I'm so sorry you lost your mate." She couldn't help it. "You know, Grandpa Dracula."

"Oh, for goodness' sake." Hilde chuckled. "He wasn't that old. And that chapter of my life is long closed. The second you were born, your mama wanted to give you a normal childhood absent any mind torture or knowledge of war. When she and Elliot both died, I followed her wishes."

Love for her grandmother welled up so fast Amber's breath caught. Her childhood at the eco-village was wonderful but hardly normal. "Did you really believe? I mean, in the village and what we've stood for, or was it all a ruse?"

"Yes. The eco-village was off the map and a very safe place for us, I'll admit. But our way of life was a good one there, and I truly believe in saving the environment and living off the land."

Relief relaxed Amber's shoulders. "Even so, thank you for giving up your life to make sure I had a good child-hood."

"Sure." Hilde patted her hand. "So, I'd like to teach you how to use your skill, but we need a demon to attack first. I mean, our gifts only come into play when there's demon energy at work. Well, or a very gifted vampire."

Like Kane. His mind had to be truly amazing to be able to attack, even briefly. Or maybe it was his empathic abilities—the ones he hated. Amber frowned. There was an idea somewhere muddled in that thought, but it escaped her. Her jaw almost cracked when she yawned.

Hilde nodded. "Yes, I'm tired as well. Maybe we should

get some sleep and work hard to figure out our lives to-morrow. I mean, where we should go next."

"I'm not leaving." Amber steeled herself.

Hilde sat back. "You're not leaving?" She frowned. "Are you staying with Kane? I mean, is he the one?"

"No. But I promised I'd help save his brother from the demons if he helped me find you. I gave him my word." Hilde had taught her honor from day one, so surely she'd understand how important a promise Amber had made.

"Too freakin' bad. You're not fighting more demons—you said yourself you can't turn their powers back on them." Fear slid the color from Hilde's face. "Not a chance."

"Yes, I am," Amber said gently. "I can learn to use this gift—in time."

A gentle knock echoed through the door. "Come in," Hilde called.

Oscar poked his head inside and rubbed a hand over his crew-cut. "Ah, Hilde? I found somebody to cover the shifter training tonight. Did you, ah, want to see the new movie the king got for the kids?"

Hilde blushed a pretty pink. "Of course. Amber is tired and is going to bed, but I'm wide awake." She bounded off the sofa and headed for the vampire at the door. Once there, she turned and winked at Amber. "Don't wait up, sweetie."

The door shut.

Amber sat on the couch, blinking rapidly. Where in the world had reality disappeared to?

CHAPTER 19

The next morning Amber shifted on the protective paper covering of the lone examination table, throwing off unease at being in the underground lab. Dark rock covered the floor and matching counters held tons of machines she couldn't identify. A couple of pretty watercolors depicting forest scenes had been attached to the rough walls. They failed to calm her down. She eyed the door. "A mating is forever, right?"

"Yes." Kane lifted away from one of several microscopes lining the organized counter and turned to face her. "Though Oscar and Hilde seem to enjoy each other's company." Smoothly stepping her way, Kane checked the myriad of wires running from several monitors to electrodes attached to Amber's scalp and forehead.

A rhythmic beeping sounded from the monitors.

It figured Kane would know what Amber was worried about. Darn genius. She flattened her palms on her jeans. "He seems like a nice guy."

"Oscar is a good soldier." High praise from Kane. Frowning, Kane pulled the top of her shirt open to place an electrode near her heart.

That silly heart began to flutter. Amber shook her idea to concentrate on the conversation and not the warm hand on her skin. "Do we have to do this?"

"Yes." Kane added two more electrodes, his voice distracted. "When you touched me at the demon stronghold, you took away their mind attack. Completely. So we need to figure out how it works. Everyone will take turns training you and seeing how your gifts interact with ours."

"Sounds like fun." Not.

Kane nodded and continued adding the electrodes. "These will measure heart rate and breathing." He fiddled with the machine, tapping the screen until several lines sprang into view. "The lines show your brain waves, heartbeat, and breaths per minute." He twisted a knob, and the lines brightened.

The vampire wore his customary black slacks and silk shirt, the elegant clothing almost masking the fighter beneath. Not even his full mouth softened his masculine features. Even and strong, truly stunning. When she'd first met him, she thought he moved gracefully, like a dancer. Turned out he moved like a predator. The danger in Kane came as much from his sharp intellect as the animal inside.

She sighed. While she'd dated, she'd learned early on not to lean on a man. This one almost demanded it. "You're hard to figure out."

He straightened to face her, eyes clearing. "Why's that?"

Well, she hadn't quite meant to say that out loud. "You're so logical and orderly in here. But in bed . . . I mean . . ." Heat climbed into her face until her cheeks burned.

His gaze heated. "You like me . . . in . . . bed."

"Do not. I mean, I don't like, well, the . . ." God. Could the floor just disappear and swallow her?

"Being dominated?" His voice stayed calm, amusement lifting his lips in almost a smile.

Man, he had to go right there and say it, now, didn't he? She lifted her chin. "No."

The air stilled. "Maybe we should test that theory."

Her breath caught in her throat at his hungry look. "There's no need. I don't like it."

Before she could blink, he had her flat on the table, hand on her neck. Leaning down, his mouth covered hers in a kiss. Warmth shot straight to her toes. Keeping her in place, he kissed her thoroughly, completely at his leisure. Pinned, helpless, her body flared to life.

Instinct propelled her to struggle, and his hand tightened around her windpipe just enough to hint at strength. Damn if her panties didn't dampen.

He went deeper, taking her mouth, a low growl coming from down deep.

She sighed, opening, kissing him back. Need flushed along every nerve.

His other palm spread out over her abdomen, sending heat inside her skin.

Slowly, he straightened. A dark flush covered his cheekbones, raw need glimmered in his eyes. Tension emanated around him—from him. Turning his head, he glanced at the monitors, which beeped wildly. "You might want to reconsider that 'no.' "

There was no need to look at the machines. Her heart smacked hard against her ribs, and her breath came in small pants. "What do my brain waves show?" she whispered. Damn curiosity.

His smile warmed her entire body. "Brain waves match the rest of your readings." Sliding a hand around her neck, he helped her to a seated position. "Deep breaths. Good air in, bad air out. Slow the breathing, and you'll slow your heart rate." His hand swept down her arm in reassurance.

The beeping got louder.

Kane chuckled, stepping away. "Okay. Deep breaths now."

Jackass. Closing her eyes, she drew air in her nose and forced her muscles to relax. Slowly, the beeping ebbed to normal. She opened her eyes, a slight headache making her wince.

"You ready to start?" Kane leaned against the far wall, strong arms crossed.

"Yes." Amber shot him a glare. The damn scientist would probably compare her readings when she was aroused to the ones he was about to create. He just had to figure out everything. Of course, he'd pretty much figured her out, now, hadn't he? She hadn't even known herself very well. Yeah, he was a jackass.

He took a deep breath. "All right. I'm going to create a very light attack. You send the images right back at me."

Invisible fingers slowly glided against her brain. She shivered. Talk about the heebie-jeebies. An image began to form in her mind, and she gasped. The image was of her nude on the moonlit grass. "I am not sending that image back at you."

Charm filled his grin. "That's all right. I already have that image quite strongly in my head." Then he sobered. "Okay—here comes the ugly image."

A picture of a shiny black widow spider filled her mind. A yellow hourglass covered its dark back, and its long legs twitched along with antennae. Two smaller spiders crawled toward the first one. Amber wrinkled her nose. "I admit I hate spiders, but you're taking it easy on me."

"Not really. Now try to send the image back to me."

Nodding, Amber shut her eyes and drew a deep breath. Tightening her eyelids, she tried to hurl the image toward Kane.

Pain cut into her brain.

She cried out, both hands going to her head. "That *so* doesn't work," she gasped. Shaking her head, she centered herself and slid an imaginary warm blanket over the spiders. They disappeared.

Her eyes opened.

Kane still leaned against the wall, but a puzzled frown made his eyebrows almost meet in the middle. "Hmm." He moved forward to study the monitors. "Now that's just odd."

"Maybe I'm a shield and not a sword." Yeah, that sounded a lot like her.

"Maybe," Kane mused, reaching for a stack of papers being spit out by a printer. He studied them before focusing back on her. "So you can't throw images back. Let's try pain."

Dull aches set up around her brain. Her shoulders stiffened, and she blinked several times. Then she softened, allowing the hurt to spread. Clasping her hands together for balance, she mentally shoved the aches toward Kane.

Instant agony stole her breath. Tears filled her eyes. "Ouch." The room swayed, and Kane's face seemed to stretch.

"Whoa," he murmured, reaching her and lying her down. The pain instantly retreated. "Okay. Apparently you're a shield."

That wouldn't help anybody in battle. Well, unless she could help shield him. Pressing a hand against her forehead, she took another deep breath. "I'm okay. Should we see if I can protect your mind?"

"We don't have anybody to attack my mind." He smoothed hair off her cheek, his palm rough. Very rough.

What in the world? She grabbed his hand, lifting her head to view the palm. Raised and dark, a beautiful Celtic knot wound around with a strong *K* in the middle. Her heart kicked into full gallop again. The machines started beeping like crazy. "Um. Is that what I think it is?"

"Yes. The Kayrs marking in all its intricate glory." Kane kept his gaze on her face. "The brand appeared after I met you. I think it happened during the first night we had sex."

Warmth slammed through her. Calm. She'd stay calm. Swallowing, she forced her face into curious lines, an effort dampened by the still ringing machines. "Really? Does the marking's appearance mean anything?"

"Yes. I asked you to mate me, and the brand appeared. The marking appears because we want it to appear, and that's what happened."

Well, wasn't that a logical explanation? Her heart ached. The beeping slowed down around them. Weird. "I see."

"My offer still stands." No emotion showed on his face, and pure confidence lit his eyes. "We'd gain each other's powers if we mated." He sighed, his eyes softening. "I like you, Amber. A lot. We would make a good pair, and I'd give you a good life. For centuries."

The temptation to live forever warred with her need for love. Sure, she wanted immortality—who wouldn't? But maybe she could find another vampire, one who loved her. Though the hurt in her heart whispered that she'd already fallen for a vampire. A logical, cold, purely methodical scientist. A silly little part of her wondered if she could make him love her. Yeah, that wasn't how dumb girls got hurt—not ever. Geez. "Thank you for your very kind, very logical offer. But no."

He sighed. "I think mating would be the best course for us both. Please say you'll think about my offer."

Stubbornness lined his jaw. While his words were phrased as a question, the determined set of his head made her wonder. How far would Kane go for what he thought was the best course? How far would he go to save his brother? Amber licked her lips. "I'm not entering forever like I'm signing a contract to buy a car. Period."

"Okay." He gently began removing electrodes from her body.

Well, he didn't have to accept her refusal so easily. Sure,

growing up without a father, she might have fantasized about love and what it'd be like to finally have a man in her life. "A lot of people have love. I've seen Emma and Dage—they're in love."

"I don't want to argue about love." Kane finished his task and reached for a notebook, scratching odd equations on a page.

Amber frowned. "What's that?"

"A combination of string theory, quantum physics, and neurobiology," Kane said absently.

The paper crinkled more when she fidgeted. Science had never made a lot of sense to her. "Oh. Have you studied all of that stuff?"

"Yes." He rubbed his chin, frowning at the paper before jotting down more equations. "I'm not sure how many doctorates I have—the diplomas may be in a drawer somewhere."

"Oh." She started to swing a leg back and forth. The guy probably wouldn't be very impressed with her GED—the one proudly displayed in her room on the farm. "So, what about Emma? I mean, does she know physics?"

Kane shrugged, his gaze never leaving his paper. "Maybe some. But her doctorate is in genetics, which has come in very handy. Well, it's also how the Kurjans found her, so maybe that fact hasn't worked in her favor. Then again, Dage saved her from the Kurjans, and things have worked out rather well for them. Her sister's degree is in plant physiology—she always likes to have real plants around."

So everyone had serious degrees—the PhD kind. Amber swallowed hard and jumped off the table. "Well, if we're done here, I'm going to check on my grandmother." She didn't wait to see if Kane gave her an absent nod or not. This place wasn't any different from anywhere else she'd ever been—she once again didn't fit in.

Darn geniuses.

Kane looked up and frowned when the door closed. Where the heck did Amber just go? He shook his head. Man, he hoped she hadn't been talking to him before she left. The readings on the printouts were fascinating. When he'd kissed her, the lateral orbitofrontal cortex in her brain shut down, which was to be expected since it signified control. Satisfaction centered him—the woman had not been in control.

In addition, the amygdala in the brain had lit up, which, considering it dealt with emotions, also made sense. Yet when she tried to attack him with pain or bad images, the thalamus lit up. That area was known to deal with sensory information coming in . . . not going out. Now what in the world did that mean?

Janie slid open the door and glided inside. Her pretty face had gone so pale her lips appeared nearly blue. A much lighter blue than her eyes. "I was trying to meditate and had a vision of Jase. It was seriously dark, and I'm scared."

Settling his face into calm lines, Kane tossed the papers on the counter. "This isn't the place." Taking her hand, he opened the door and led her through several tunnels to his quarters. Once inside, he settled her in the one overstuffed chair and took the sofa for himself.

Serenity flowed through his small space from the deep browns of the rug covering rock to the stunning pictures on the wall. He allowed peace to settle his shoulders. As much as he disliked feeling, he opened his senses as wide as he could. Sometimes he could get readings from a talented psychic. "Okay, sweetheart. Tell me what you saw."

Janie rubbed delicate hands down her faded jeans. "I

saw Jase surrounded by brown rock that kept morphing into faces. The faces told him he was going to die."

The girl's fear slammed Kane right between the eyes. His heart kicked into gear, and heat ran along his skin. Taking several deep breaths, he drew enough of a shield into place to block some of the fear. He needed to think, and feelings got in the way of thought. His mind cleared while his heart slowed down. "Tell me more about the faces."

"I didn't recognize the faces—they didn't seem real," Janie whispered. Her gaze dropped to her hands. "I felt him. He's . . . drifting away."

Chills cascaded down Kane's spine. "Jase is strong—he'll survive."

"Maybe." Doubt clouded her eyes when she looked up. "Mentally, he's almost done fighting. I could feel him letting go."

Kane leaned forward. "But you know he's alive. Jase is alive, and that gives us hope. We need hope, Janie." A stone lodged into Kane's gut. The world was classically unfair to make this precious twenty-year-old child see and feel such despair. If he could take the feelings from her, or teach her to shield herself from them, he'd do so in a heartbeat.

Janie reached out to hold his hands and closed her eyes. "Help me get it out of my head."

Kane scrutinized her pale face. "Deep breaths. One, two, three . . ." He counted to twenty and back down, helping center the girl into almost a hypnotic state. "Now, when you open your eyes, you'll feel refreshed and full of peace. Open your eyes, now."

Deep blue eyes flashed open, clear and calm. She smiled and released him. "Thanks, Uncle Kane." She stood and tugged her threadbare Snoopy shirt into place before stretching her back with a soft sigh. A quick peck on his cheek reassured him and he grinned. Graceful steps propelled her across the room to the door. "I'll talk to you later."

He frowned after her, his mind kicking awake. Janie usually wanted to chat after a meditating session and had never hustled off before. "How odd." With his own sigh, he tried to turn back to the papers, but his mind kept going to his niece.

What was that girl up to?

CHAPTER 20

Janie hustled through the underground hallways, her mind calm and her body relaxed. She knew she could count on Uncle Kane to get her in the right state of mind. Oh, she'd been having the visions of Jase for some time now and hadn't thought sharing them would help anyone. But Kane liked to be in the know, so she'd been meaning to tell him anyway. She'd just waited for the right time.

Arriving at her quarters, she shoved open the door to an empty living room. A thick green couch and two matching seats faced a huge television mounted in the wall. A walkway to the left led to the kitchen, a hallway to the right to the bedrooms. Plants of all different kinds took residence on tables and furniture throughout the entire apartment. Her mother did love a nice jungle wherever she found herself living. Of course, so did Janie.

Gliding inside, she settled herself on a chair and crossed her legs, perching her hands on the armrests. Several deep breaths returned her to the hypnotic state Kane had just created for her.

Drawing deep, she threw herself out of reality.

Her feet padded on a rough trail while jungle surrounded the path. Thick leaves bigger than her father's hands swayed in the gentle breeze while birds twittered high above. Rain filtered down, but only in drips. Interesting that her imagination had cre-

ated a jungle; she'd have to watch her thoughts before trying this again.

For years she'd created a dream world to meet friends, and now it was time to up the gift. Time to meet on her timeline.

A stick cracked behind her and she whirled around.

Zane Kyllwood stood on the trail, his stance set, his gaze sweeping the area. He wore dark jeans and a green T-shirt that matched his amazing eyes. In the two years since they'd seen each other, he'd grown even more, probably topping out at six-foot-six. His black hair had been cut short, and the scar leading from his forehead to his left ear had faded slightly.

Janie stilled to show she wasn't a threat. "We're the only people here."

He kept his hand on the knife handle protruding from a sheath strapped to his leg. "This feels different."

"It is." She spoke softly, trying to reassure him. "I'm awake. Well, kind of. I'm meditating."

"But I'm asleep." He cocked his head to the side, prominent dark eyebrows emphasizing his rapidly narrowing eyes. His eyes were set deep, his cheekbones high, his jawline strong. "Explain."

For the first time, he truly looked like a warrior. In all the years they'd met in dreams, she'd known he'd grow up to fight. But she'd never seen him so distant—as if it weren't the two of them against the world anymore. Sure, with the six-year difference in their ages, he'd stopped visiting her while she was younger, but she was an adult now. There was no reason not to meet each other. Or was there?

She eyed him. "I've learned to meditate and thought if I tried hard enough, I'd be able to reach you this way."

"What else?" He released the knife handle.

"You saved my life once." She'd been in a coma four years ago and had sought out Zane, who'd given her blood in a dream and healed her. Nobody else on earth could've done that. He had powers none of them could understand. "I'm not sure, but when you gave me blood, I think it connected us somehow."

He rubbed his head, his upper lip twisting. "I saved your life, and now you're using my blood against me? Really, Belle?"

The nickname didn't warm her like it used to. The first time they'd met, when they were just children, he'd determined that "Janet Isabella" was too grown up for her and decided to call her "Janie Belle." He'd shortened the nickname to "Belle" some time ago, and he used to say it with affection.

She shook her head. "No. I just wanted to see if it worked. There has to be a reason we've been connected for so many years, Zane. You know this war comes down to you, Kalin, and me." The outcome of the war might affect the entire planet.

Zane rubbed his short hair. "There's no way the three of us will work together—you know that. So, we're working separately. All of us."

The man just didn't understand. She studied him, her gaze going to the masculine lines of his neck. There was something about the cords along the sides of a tough guy's neck that had always intrigued her—Zane was no exception. Tingles set up in her stomach. "I always thought you and I would work together. Where are you?" Rather, who was he? But one question at a time.

He looked at her in silence.

Man, he'd changed. Years ago, he could pass as human. Not now. No way would a human mistake the obvious predator lurking beneath his smooth skin. Seconds ago the dark foliage had dominated the area—now he did. He went beyond handsome to dangerous in a frightening sexual way. Worse yet, her body was responding to him in a new way.

Her breath caught, and fingers danced down her spine. She cleared her throat. "I asked you a question."

"I told you we couldn't meet again. I asked you to find another path and to stay out of the war as long as possible." The deep timbre of his voice failed to give her a clue as to where he was living.

"And I told you that was impossible. We need to work together."

He sighed. "I'm not with the Realm—I never have been."

"I know. Even when your daddy was alive, you were part of an isolated faction of vampires." A group of former assassins who caused the Realm no trouble but refused to belong. When his father had died, he'd moved to live with his mother's people. A people the king had never been able to identify. Chances were he was some type of shifter.

Surprise flashed across Zane's face. "You know who I am?"

She bit her lip in indecision. Could she fake him out? All she really knew was that he was half vampire. "Sure."

Two broad steps forward and he gripped her arms in an unbreakable hold. He lowered his head until his eyes pierced hers an inch away. "Oh yeah? Who am I, Belle?"

She swallowed. Even in the created world, heat cascaded off the man. But no smell. For years she'd wondered what he smelled like. Probably something masculine and strong. "You don't even know who you are, do you?"

Irritation flashed in those deep eyes, and his hold tightened. "Don't play games with me, sweetheart. You don't know me anymore."

Oh, she'd hit a nerve. The guy wasn't thinking if he thought to threaten her in the world she'd created. If she tried hard enough, she could probably turn him into a donkey. Temporarily, of course. Gritting her teeth, she forced words out. "Listen. You don't know me anymore, either. You want to work with me for your own good." On all that was holy—did he think she was some helpless human?

His eyes darkened. "Is that a threat?"

A shiver wound down her spine. From day one of meeting vampires, she'd quickly learned how to cajole and charm. Yet for the first time, she wanted to hammer the hell out of a vampire with an ego. "I'm the one with power here, Zane. Don't forget it."

The smile he flashed showed fangs. "Because I gave you blood."

"Partly." She'd always controlled the dream world.

He released her arms. "Then we should even the odds, now, shouldn't we?" Quicker than a thought, he had one arm around her waist, lifting her. The other tangled in her hair and jerked back.

She gasped, both hands shoving against his chest. She might as well have been punching a brick wall.

Sharp fangs pierced her neck.

Crying out, her mouth opened.

Pain melded with a heated pleasure to blank her mind.

With a low growl, he drank deep, drawing her closer. Heat cascaded along her entire front as she met his hard body. He bent her back, drinking.

Then he gentled. The deadly fangs retracted, and he licked her wound.

His rough tongue sent desire spinning through her entire body as if he'd licked her from head to toe. She bit back a soft sigh of need and forced herself to keep from pressing harder against him. Confusion fuzzed her mind—she'd never felt like this.

He set her down and stepped back. A dark flush covered his face while his eyes had morphed to pure gold. "You taste like sunshine and honey."

She exhaled heavily, her heart racing, her breath fighting to pant out. Instead, she calmed herself. "What the heck?"

Massive shoulders moved when he shrugged. The raw desire on his face belied the casual move. "Now we both can find each other, and don't say I didn't warn you. The last thing you want is for me to be able to find you."

"Would you hurt me?" She lowered her voice to a soft note, holding threat.

He blinked twice. "I don't ever want to hurt you, Janie."

That wasn't a "no." Resisting the urge to rub her neck, she met his gaze. "What are you besides a vampire?"

"I'm the man who now has your taste, sweetheart." The en-

dearment contradicted the angry glint in his eye. "Don't look for me, and don't even think about dragging me into a pretend world again. Next time I'll do more than bite you."

Janie Kayrs had never been a coward. Threats did nothing but irritate her. Putting her hands on her hips, she stepped toward him. "Oh yeah? Like what?"

Admiration filled his gaze while dark amusement lifted his full lip. "You know you're the prize, right?"

"I don't like your phrasing."

"Too bad." He lost his smile. "Every single species out there wants you. Every single species out there has oracles, psychics, and seers who have prophesied your coming. Right or wrong— they're all coming for you."

"So?"

"So, here you are meeting in secret with someone who has clearly told you we're not on the same side. Or at least, we don't want the same outcome. And I—have—your—blood."

Ah, but she had him. "I trust you."

"Then stop it." His harsh tone set birds to fluttering high above. "Grow the hell up."

She smiled and stepped even closer, feminine power flushing through her. "Oh Zane . . . I'm all grown up now."

He put out a large-boned hand to stop her movements. "Jesus, Janie. Don't make this easy on me."

"Easy on you?"

He snorted. "Yes. Easy on me. My God. Do you have any idea the power your mate will have—will gain just by mating you? With not only his people but all of the world?"

Mate? She tried to swallow and ended up coughing instead. Finally gasping a breath, she shook her head. "I wasn't offering to mate you."

"Weren't you?" His voice lowered, and a dark flush spread across his high cheekbones.

"No." Okay, sure she always thought she'd end up with Zane. But she wasn't throwing herself at the vampire, for good-

ness' sake. Doubt clouded in. Would Zane use her to end the war—even if that meant the Realm lost? How far would he go for his people, whoever they were? "Why won't you just tell me who you are?"

"Now that's a question you should spend some time with, Belle." He drew in a deep breath. "You're right that you're an adult now—all grown up. I'm done protecting you for your own good. You yank me into your world again, and I'll do what I need for my people. Believe me, Janie."

At the last entreaty, she saw the boy he'd once been. Young, carefree, full of honor. "I do believe you." Sweeping her hand out, the world disappeared.

Her legs cramped. Groaning, Janie unfurled from her position on the chair and flexed her calves. Silence pounded all around her in the underground haven. She ran her fingers across the twin puncture wounds that ached in her neck. Great. Now she'd have to wear turtlenecks for a week.

An odd thrill coursed through her at the thought of wearing Zane's mark.

She hadn't gotten the answers she'd wanted, but Zane had said enough to make her think. If nothing else, he was still not understanding her. Sure, she'd wanted to work together to end the war. But like Zane, she'd make sacrifices for her family and her people.

The vampire was making a serious mistake in underestimating her. Her relationship with him was turning into more war than love.

But all was fair . . . now wasn't it?

CHAPTER 21

Amber relaxed in the queen's quarters, her shoulders settling down as she sank into the plush sofa. The plush, cotton blend of a sofa.

Emma smiled. "Okay. Now I'm going to try to read your mind, so you think of something fun."

"Can you really read minds?"

"I don't know. Dage can read minds, and I'm supposed to get his gifts at some point, so maybe I can read your mind. Maybe not. But Kane wants to test your gifts against everyone else's, so let's give it a try."

Amber nodded and thought of an old *Star Trek* movie.

Emma took a deep breath. "You're thinking about cows."

"No."

"Chickens?"

"No."

"Ice cream sandwiches?"

"No. I don't think you can read minds." Amber bit back a smile at the queen's disappointed look. "What else you got?"

"I'm psychic." Emma sounded downright sad about that fact. "And I can only see the future once in a while. My sister, Cara, is an empath, and we'll have you work with her as soon as she gets home from feline territory. Both

Talen and Dage have cleared time on their schedules to work with you later today."

A knock on the door drew their attention to the exit. Hilde swept inside, her face a pretty pink.

Amber shook her head. How odd to see her grandmother so young.

Emma stood and gestured Hilde to an oversized chair. "Have a seat, Mrs. Freebird."

"Hilde, sweetheart." Hilde sat. "I want to have sex."

Amber jerked her head and started coughing so hard her lungs hurt.

Emma's mouth opened, but no sound came out.

Hilde rolled her eyes. "For goodness' sake, girls. I haven't had sex in twenty-five years. I want sex." She smacked Amber's back several times to stem the coughing.

Emma shook her head. "Um, Mrs. . . . Hilde, you're, ah, mated. There's no, um, sex."

"I know." Hilde waited until Amber stopped sputtering before sitting back. "Janie was telling me about this new Virus-27 that actually takes away the mating aspect. I want that virus."

"Oh." Thoughts scattered across Emma's face. "Well, the virus does take away the mating aspect, and you, ah, could have sex then. But the virus is still dangerous, and while it's slow in progression, it still progresses. We don't know at what point it will lose potency, if at any point."

"So it could eventually kill anyone who is infected?" Hilde pursed her lips together.

"Yes." The queen clasped her hands in her lap. "We've cured shifters from the virus, but vampire mates and witches are still susceptible. It might take a hundred years for the virus to either kill them or run its course, but we don't know what will happen. Of course, we plan to find a cure long before then."

"The risk might be worth it," Hilde said grimly.

Emma leaned forward and patted Hilde's hand. "You're immortal. I know it's difficult to wait, but let us figure the virus out, and then we can apply the benefits to you."

Hilde's jaw set. "Twenty. Five. Years."

Amber sucked in air. What else could possibly go wrong?

Kane spread the stack of papers over the sofa table, his eyes beginning to ache. He'd turned down the lights in his underground haven as well as engaging the soothing wall waterfall, but sitting on the sofa and hunching over to read was probably stupid. He frowned. There had to be a pattern that showed when the shifter inoculation was doctored. Thick boots sounded in the hallway and caught his attention.

The door opened and Dage moved inside. The rug muffled his heavy steps as he crossed the room and dropped into the oversized chair. "Did you find anything?"

"Not yet. Well, that's not true." Kane grabbed two sheets from the far corner of the table. "All infected vials, even those that ended up in feline territory, were held at wolf territory in Montana."

"So the traitor is a wolf."

Kane shrugged. "That's my best guess right now."

The king leaned over to scan the papers. "I'll let Talen know. He was going to make Cara and Garrett come home, but if the problem is in wolf territory, they should be fine with Jordan at his ranch."

Jordan was the leader of the feline nation as well as being a good friend. Kane nodded. "I'd leave them with the felines—somebody needs to keep any eye on those monstrous Pride twins." He didn't care that adoration coated his voice. He'd adored Sam and Sid since the two little cubs had been born. "They're turning four years old soon." Which reminded him, he needed to go shopping.

"I absolutely can't figure out why you're their favorite," the king grumbled. "You're no fun."

"The twins think I'm fun." Kane smiled. He had every intention of getting them involved in science, so maybe a new microscope set would be a good gift. "Who should I alert about the wolf problem? The Bane's Council or individual Alpha wolves?"

"Neither." Dage closed his eyes and settled his head on the chair with a deep sigh. "I studied the data earlier. Does anything stand out?"

Kane had been trying to figure out a way to broach the subject and should've known Dage already caught the problem. Every once in a while Kane forgot the rest of his brothers were as smart as he. Almost, anyway. "The Bane's Council visits coincide with when the vials were probably infected. All seven times—from what I could see."

"Yeah." Dage didn't open his eyes. "And I have what is probably a terrible idea."

Kane studied the king.

Dage had tied his thick hair at the nape and wore sparring clothes absent any blood, so he hadn't sparred yet. Dark circles spread under his eyes, and frown lines cut on either side of his mouth. His eyes flipped open, a deep silver lighting his face. "What?"

Kane frowned. "When was the last time you slept?"

"When was the last time *you* slept?" Dage asked wearily.

"The night before Jase was taken."

"Me, too." Dage ran both hands down his dark sweats. "Don't you want to hear my terrible plan?"

He didn't need to hear the plan. "You're going to send in a spy—a wolf shifter—to sniff out the traitor. Maybe somebody the Bane's Council has requested to appear anyway, and somebody champing at the bit to have a job and help the Realm." Kane pressed his fingers to his temples, mimicking a psychic. "Let's see ... maybe someone named Maggie."

"You're hilarious." Dage stood and paced over to the wall waterfall. "She wants to go. What do you think?"

That every plan they had would backfire as usual. "I think she wants to go, but not because she wants to help the Realm or meet wolves."

"She wants to help the Realm."

"Not as badly as she wants to pull one over on Terrent." Kane shook his head. The little wolf shifter had been waiting for Terrent to retaliate for her kidnapping him years ago, and apparently she was done waiting. Though, Maggie was a sweetheart and probably did want to help the Realm. "I say you let her go." While the job might be dangerous, Maggie was smart, and wolves protected their own. She'd be protected. Well, from everyone but Terrent.

"She's never been on a mission, at least that I know of." Dage stuck a finger in the water of the tinkling fountain.

"Don't touch that." Kane rolled his eyes. He mulled over the situation in his mind. Maggie had been kidnapped and experimented on by the Kurjans, resulting in her having no memory of her life before the vampires rescued her. Nobody had come forward to say they knew her anyway. Dage, as usual, felt responsible for everyone. But the king would do what was necessary to protect the Realm, and sending Maggie was necessary. What he needed from Kane was something else. Support. "The right decision is to send her."

"Thanks." Dage touched the water again. "Ah, we should probably discuss our other issue."

"There's nothing to discuss."

"Right. I'm going to ask you one more time. Are you sure about Hilde? I mean, about using her for bait?"

Kane shook his head. "No, I'm not sure. But she is sure, and she's a tough woman—she volunteered."

"You should tell Amber."

He'd given Hilde his word that he'd keep Amber safe and in the dark about their plan. What the hell had he been thinking? "I can't."

Dage sighed, shaking his head. "Believe me, learn now not to keep important matters from your mate. They get really angry when you do that, and they make your life a living hell. Trust me."

Kane shook his head. "Amber isn't my mate." The stubborn little demon destroyer refused to consider his offer.

"Maybe you didn't use the right words."

The right words didn't really exist as far as Kane was concerned. But he'd started thinking about just seducing her until she wore his mark for eternity. Although, then she'd really make his life a living hell. He sighed.

A speaker crackled in the far corner. Kane concentrated on the device, waiting until Talen's voice came through. "We have a problem. Meet me in Dage's private control room."

Dage sighed. "I'm here—we'll be there in a minute." He eyed Kane. "This can't be good."

Kane stood, a rock of dread slamming into his gut. "No."

He followed Dage through the underground labyrinth to a partially hidden door that opened easily. Stalking inside, he found Talen and Max standing near the control chair. A conference table took space over to the right, but nobody sat. Instead, they all stared at a blank screen.

Talen's face had paled, and his hands shook. He leaned over and punched in a series of codes. "We received this ten minutes ago, and I watched it before calling you."

"What is it?" Max asked. He settled his stance near the

door, always protecting the king's back. Nobody would ever sneak up on Dage when Max was around.

"You're about to watch a video showing two things. The first thing is that Jase is alive, and the second is that he won't be for long." Talen's voice cracked on the last. "We intercepted the video on the Web, and the guys upstairs should have a location soon—after you watch, be prepared to go the second we can."

Kane took a deep breath and opened all his senses, laying himself vulnerable.

Dage turned quickly, his eyes narrowing. "You sure?"

"Yes." Only the king knew how much opening his senses hurt Kane—not merely emotionally, but every time he tried, his brain waves faltered. The intelligence always returned, but at what cost? Most geniuses turned mad at some point, a fact Kane had long understood. "We need to find Jase."

The king nodded and turned back to the screen. "Press PLAY."

Talen hit a button and the image of Jase took shape. Blood cascaded from his nose, eyes, and ears, while shards of bone shone where his skin had flayed open. As someone struck his body with a metal pole, the youngest Kayrs brother smiled. The smile was one Kane had never seen on Jase. Dark and insane.

Kane searched for feelings and thoughts, catching evil from the demons and stubbornness from Jase. While the king no doubt needed reason, as did Talen and Max, Kane had to forgo their needs in an effort to find clues as to Jase's whereabouts. He got images and thoughts, but nothing concrete, and nothing that made any sense.

The tape played for nearly an hour.

Each hit to Jase's body had Kane's body reacting with pain. Each piercing pain to the mind along with every devastating image thrown into Jase's head had Kane gasping for breath. Yet Kane held on, allowing his mind to be bruised, to be beaten.

When the screen finally went dark, nobody moved.

Talen vibrated in place, raw fury on his face. Dage continued staring at the screen, his expression blank. Max wiped blood off his lip where he'd bitten it.

Kane took in the expressions and emotions around him, adding those to the ones from the torture scene.

He tried to go deeper into his memories, into what he'd felt as his brother was nearly killed. There was so much mental as well as physical pain, it was difficult to sort out.

But one thing remained abundantly clear. Jase had released his hold on reality and seemed pleased to let it go. He was ready to die.

At the final thought, Kane's mind finally blanked.

Darkness swam across his vision. A neon star exploded behind his eyes. With a low growl, he dropped to the ground, unconscious.

CHAPTER 22

Enjoying the late-afternoon fresh air, Amber found Kane in a conference room aboveground. The salt of the ocean swept inside the small area from open windows. The walls were cedar, the floor sparkling teak. "This is my favorite room so far."

Kane frowned as he glanced up from the scattered papers strewn across the polished table. His shirt was rolled up to his elbows and showcased strong forearms. Lines of stress cut hard into the sides of his mouth. "What are you doing up in the main lodge?"

She shrugged and pulled a plush chair out from the table to sit. Then she bounced twice, her hands spreading along the supple material. "Tell me this isn't real leather."

"That isn't real leather."

She frowned. The material felt real . . . poor cows. "Tell me you won't buy any more leather chairs."

"We don't." Kane sighed. "I asked you a question. What are you doing aboveground?"

"Looking for you. Talen escorted me up after training me a little bit. Our gifts didn't seem to do much together." Studying Kane's face, she frowned. A dark bruise cascaded out from his temple in hues of purple and red. "What happened to your face?"

"I hit a counter on my way to the floor," Kane said grimly.

"Are you all right?"

"Yes."

He dominated the room in a way that sped up her heart. The guy didn't just take up space, he overwhelmed it. The vampire owned the area around him in a way she'd never noticed other men doing.

She clasped her hands together in her lap. "I can't find my grandmother."

"She's on a walk with Oscar—don't worry, we have eyes on them at all times." Kane smiled, but the humor failed to reach his metallic eyes. "She's safe, I promise."

Talen hurried his large bulk inside, his face hard. "We traced the video of Jase and have a location on a demon stronghold in Arizona." He tossed a stack of papers at Kane. "Dage is on his way up—we go in half an hour." Then he tilted his head toward Amber.

Amber stiffened. "I want to go—you'll need me to find Jase."

Kane ignored her and studied the pictures. "Tell me about this place."

Talen settled his bulk in a chair. "There's a compound in the middle of the desert—looks like it contains one main building and several outposts. The walls surrounding Jase appear to be some sort of limestone—definitely found in Arizona. My guess is they meet underground in a series of tunnels like we use. No mountains or rock nearby, so the tunnels must lead to a town in case the demons need to escape."

Kane scratched his head. "Satellite feeds?"

"Only show the buildings—nothing underground," Talen said. "I compared them to earlier pictures of the area, and the compound is new in the last couple of months, so the area shouldn't be manned completely."

"Was this place sending or receiving the video?" Kane asked.

"Both." Talen shrugged. "This place was sending the video—so there's a good chance the video was filmed in Arizona. Jase is there—I just know it. Right?"

"I don't know." Kane's face stayed calm. "There's a chance the video has been spread around the demon nation—showing their strength, yada yada, and didn't originate there—this could be a trap for one of us or for Amber."

Amber leaned back in her chair. The scientist was intriguing to watch.

Dage hurried inside, upping the tension in the air significantly. "What do you think?"

Kane breathed out. "I say it's a trap, but we go anyway."

"Are you up to a fight?" Dage popped his neck but kept his gaze on Kane.

Amber raised an eyebrow. "What happened to his face?"

"Nothing," all three men replied without looking at her.

Now that was freakin' annoying. "Right. People bruise all the time." What a bunch of Neanderthals.

Talen nodded and stood, apparently missing the sarcasm. "That's true. But if Kane isn't up to going, Max is champing at the bit."

"I go—and Oscar can take Max's place. Max stays here to protect headquarters." Kane swept his hand out, and the papers magically flipped into a nice order. He stood. "What's the plan?"

"Three helicopters—we hit the main lodge with rockets and go from there." Dage waited for Kane's absent nod before continuing. "If they have Jase, he's underground. Leveling the first ground of everything doesn't bother me overmuch."

Amber stood. It was fascinating how they all relied on Kane's judgment without realizing it—she doubted even

Kane realized how they waited for his responses. "I want to go." Ignoring the questioning looks his brothers sent Kane, she put her hands on her hips. "Listen, my going is my decision. You all came after me for a reason—don't forget it just because I slept with one of you."

Dage turned away but not before Amber caught the amusement on his face.

Talen chuckled and headed for the doorway. "I'll meet everyone who is going in the armory."

Dage nodded. "Ah, yes. You two get this settled, and we'll meet you underground." The king disappeared.

Irritation choked Amber's voice into a raspy tone. "He's the damn king. Why in the world is he letting you make decisions regarding me?"

Kane held out his palm and showcased the Kayrs marking. "This is why."

"You haven't marked me," she whispered. Considering her IQ was probably a zillion numbers less than his, he probably wouldn't mark her—not because he didn't believe in love, but because he wanted to mate with some übergenius to have double-übergenius kids. "So you have no say in what I do."

"Actually, I do." He rubbed his jaw, his eyes tired.

"When will the damn marking disappear?" At some point, if he didn't use the mark, the brand had to go away.

"I have no idea. I'm not sure a mark has ever appeared and not been used." Kane frowned. "If you truly want to deal with the demons, you'll want my skills. I can block and attack—which you'll need to do."

She was tempted and not just on an intellectual level. The man was strong, sexy, and a huge-assed challenge. Could she get inside his heart? Instinct whispered she was already there. He needed her. Heck, he needed somebody to be there for him the same way he was there for everyone else. "I want love. Enough people believe in the emo-

tion that you have to acknowledge its possible existence."
Logic was the key with Kane.

He shrugged. "Okay."

"What if you tried to love? An experiment, so to
speak." She kicked an invisible pebble. "Or is there another reason you don't like me?"

"I do like you."

"I don't have a zillion degrees in a drawer, Kane." Finally, she'd said it. Better to get the full truth out there
right now.

He started. "So?"

"So, I mean, I'm not smart like you." Man, did she need
to draw him a map?

His eyes crinkled when he smiled. "Amber—degrees
have nothing to do with intelligence. They have to do
with time to study. You're plenty smart . . . don't worry."

Warmth flushed through her. Kane didn't lie—he
didn't know how. "Thanks."

He pressed the issue. "If you mated me, you'd have plenty
of time and money to get all the degrees you wanted."

The warmth receded. "That sounds like a business
arrangement."

"Most successful marriages, even among humans, are
arranged. Good, solid, business arrangements."

Man, she had her work cut out with him. "I want to go
today. The only way to see if I can help shield other people is if demons are attacking. I'm going—you know you
need me so you can fight at more than fifty percent of
your abilities. Jase is in Arizona. You saw the rocks." Yeah,
she knew using his brother was a low blow. But if she
could shield Jase's mind, just for a moment, wasn't that important?

"I seriously doubt Jase is in Arizona." Kane drew in a
deep breath. "I don't like the idea of putting you in more
danger, but we do need you, and since the place doesn't

seem fully staffed, it'd be a good place for more training. Besides, you're the only real mental defense we have."

Encouragement flooded her. "So the logical, smart thing to do is to take the one demon destroyer you've ever trained with you. Like it or not."

Frustration curled his lip.

Slowly, he seemed to distance himself from the conversation, from her.

Finally, he gave a short nod. "You're right. You can go. Let's go suit up."

What the hell was he thinking? Kane settled himself more comfortably against the helicopter seat, his arm sliding around Amber's shoulders. The woman had actually fallen asleep within an hour of being in the air. She nestled into his side like she belonged there.

Hell. Maybe she did.

Talen flanked her other side as the bird flew through the cloudy night, his face grim, his fingers tapping on his dark pants. Dage piloted the craft while Oscar rode passenger. It seemed odd not having Max next to Dage, but he was needed at headquarters.

For the second part of the plan.

The part of the plan that would have Amber hating Kane's guts.

Dage's gaze met his in the mirror. "We didn't have a choice," he said through the earpiece.

Kane didn't answer. There was always a choice. "We'll see." The idea of disappointing Amber had an odd feeling lodging in his gut. He didn't want to hurt her. Worse yet, he didn't want to lose her. And considering part B of tonight's plan was allowing her grandmother to make herself bait to the demons, the little pacifist was going to be pissed at him. He couldn't blame her.

His frown made his fresh bruise ache. Speaking of

which . . . vampires had fast reflexes. Not one of his brothers could've caught him before his face impacted the counter? Assholes. He glared at the king.

Dage turned back to piloting the quiet craft.

They rode in silence the rest of the way until the Arizona desert stretched far and wide beneath them. Kane studied a heat signature monitor in his hands—one he'd invented himself. "Four demons in building one, three in the second building, eight in the third." Demons burned hotter than most and were easily recognizable. He sat up straighter. "Blow the buildings to hell—anybody important is underground." He shook Amber awake. "Get ready, sweetheart—let's test your skills."

She blinked twice, her pretty black eyes focusing on him, her face flushed.

His heart thumped hard. "Stay behind me at all times." Jesus. He really couldn't lose her. What was going on with him?

She nodded, her eyes widening as she sat up.

Not by one inch did she belong in combat. He was doing a piss-poor job of protecting his mate.

Not that she'd agreed to be his mate.

He shook his head, trying to focus. Now he was thinking of her as his mate. Damn Kayrs marking.

"Amber, take turns touching the arm of any soldier around you once we're down. Everyone pay close attention to the result," Dage ordered. "Engage missiles."

All three helicopters immediately fired missiles into various compounds.

The explosions spiraled heat back at them. Huge clouds of fire rolled up, debris flying every direction. The helicopters set down with a hard *thump*.

Kane shoved the door open and leapt out, turning to assist Amber. Heat blasted them from the fire. He instantly pivoted to shield her. "We stay here until the first floors are cleared." She clutched the back of his shirt, pressing her face into the cotton. Her "okay" came out muffled, but he felt the word against his skin.

Dage and Talen rushed through the rubble of the largest building while other vampire soldiers infiltrated the ruins of the other buildings. Talen kept to Dage's left, protecting the king as usual. The king swept his weapon around, making a large arc, protecting his younger brother . . . as usual.

Some things never changed.

Kane could make out the bodies of the four demons who'd been in the building. His quick nod had two of his soldiers rushing to decapitate them while they were down.

Talen gave Kane the high-sign. Good. They'd found the basement.

Kane turned and tugged down Amber's bulletproof vest. "Shield your face as much as possible so the heat doesn't blister your skin. Stay behind me and slightly to the left— if you start to feel demons, protect your mind instantly. I want to know before you try to attack them back."

She nodded, her face pale, her eyes huge.

Maybe he should leave her in the helicopter with a couple of guards.

Her small hands shoved at his chest. "Get moving."

An involuntary smile lifted his lips. Bossy little mate. With a mental shrug, he turned away and jogged toward the demolished building. Not that she was his mate. Smoke attacked his eyes and nose, burning deep. He kept to the side of the fire as much as possible, acutely aware of the woman keeping pace with him.

Her bravery made him proud. The thought made him pause. Why did her actions reflect on him? Could Talen be correct? Was he falling in love with the little vegan? An explosion outside ripped him out of his internal debate.

They darted around rubble, ducking the still falling debris. Finally they reached Talen, who pointed to a set of cement steps leading down.

He coughed out smoke. "Dage already went down. You two go next, and I'll cover the rear."

Kane nodded, jogging down the narrow stairs. His flashlight illuminated the steps until they ended against a wall with a tunnel veering to the right.

A warning trilled in the back of his head. He paused. Pivoting so he shielded Amber from the darkness below, he turned his head to listen. Silence met his search. "Do you sense anything?"

"Yes," she whispered, her hand settling on his arm.

Instantly warm, a soothing balm cascaded up to his head from where they touched. The woman had more power than he'd realized. "How many?"

"I don't know." Her hold tightened.

He blinked smoke from his eyes. "Keep your breathing shallow." His lungs were safe from permanent damage, but Amber was still human. "If it gets too difficult to breathe, you tell me."

"Okay." She gave a gentle push to his back. "Let's go."

The skin pricked on the base of his neck. A low bellow wound through the haze.

Every cell in Kane's body froze. He knew that voice. "Jase."

Turning his head, he caught Talen's wide eyes. Then he turned and ran.

Their boots clomped against the stairs as they hurried down, and the air become heavier, more oppressive. Kane opened his senses wide, wincing as Talen's emotions slammed him hard in the gut. Hope, despair, anger . . . so many feelings from his older brother.

Fear and hope cascaded off Amber, as well as determination.

Breathing in the stale air, Kane tried to center himself and seek beyond Talen and Amber.

As he reached the bottom and turned the corner, he stopped short. Two demons flanked Dage with weapons jammed into the king's neck. Dage's eyes had morphed to a fierce vampire blue that emphasized the raw rage on his broad face.

Kane shoved Amber completely behind him and drew his weapon. Talen angled so his shoulder touched Kane's, his gun also pointed at the demons.

Dage shrugged. "I heard Jase and started running."

Both demons had a myriad of silver metals on their left breasts—high-up soldiers. White hair and deep black eyes marked them as probable purebreds. If so, they weren't using their psychic powers at the moment.

The tunnel veered off into darkness to the right, while a rusty metal door was cut into the earth behind the demons.

Kane opened his senses more to seek beyond Dage. Dark emotions of pain and rage shimmered from beyond the doorway. Was Jase in the cell? Kane's knees tightened with the need to rush past the demons and open the door.

Another deep cry echoed—sounding like Jase.

Talen growled and stepped forward.

One of the demons shook his head and shoved the gun harder against Dage's jugular until he hissed. "No. We have reinforcements arriving in ten minutes. Let's all remain where we are until then."

"That's a shitty idea," Kane muttered. "King? Now's the time."

Indecision flickered in Dage's eyes.

"Now, Dage." Kane met his brother's gaze. "If Jase is in that cell, we'll get him."

Energy instantly shot out from behind Kane. A hard attack, devastating images, and shards of pain spiraled toward the demons. Amber gave a soft cry as she attacked.

Damn it. Kane settled his stance. "Stop attacking, Amber. We've got this."

"They have Dage," she whispered, the sound full of pain.

The demons both growled. The shorter one gasped, his eyes widening in pain.

Interesting. Amber was actually hurting the guy. Good for her.

The demon who'd spoken jerked his head.

Agony instantly slammed into Kane's brain. Amber cried out, while Talen grunted. Images of Jase being tortured, the skin peeled from his body, caused Kane to blink rapidly.

A small hand pressed against his back. A soothing blanket filtered over the terrible images, snuffing them out. He took a deep breath. Talen exhaled next to him. Kane glanced to the side—Amber had pressed her other hand against Talen's back.

The woman was amazing.

The hand at his back trembled.

"Now, Dage," Kane ordered.

Tension spiraled through the air, and Dage disappeared. Talen instantly fired into one demon's neck, and Kane took care of the other. Both demon soldiers crashed down.

Leaping forward, Talen yanked a knife from his boot and stabbed it into the neck of the closest demon.

Kane pivoted. Amber's shoulders shook, and her face had lost all color. Well, except for her blue lips. Her eyes were wide and bloodshot, while spots of blood dotted under her nose.

He wiped the blood away with his sleeve. Heat from her skin made him frown. Another fever? "Are you all right?"

She gulped, her wide-eyed gaze on Talen as he decapitated a soldier. "Where did Dage go?"

Kane shifted so he blocked her view. "Dage can teleport anywhere in the world—it's one of his gifts. But teleporting weakens him for a little while."

"Teleports." She arched both eyebrows. "Wow." Then she winced as the sound of Talen cutting through cartilage and bone echoed around them. Her hand trembled as she pushed hair from her face.

"You need to stop attacking demons—it isn't working. Shielding is fine, but no more attacks," Kane said.

She nodded. "Yes. As a demon destroyer, I suck."

"No. We just haven't figured out your gifts completely." These things took time.

Talen grunted. "All done. And as a demon destroyer, you rock. You completely shielded my mind. Thank you."

Relief had Kane turning and examining the door. Triple-locked, solid steel. "We need to blow the lock."

Talen nodded and crouched to set the charges.

Emotions ripped right through the steel. Kane took a deep breath of the death-scented air. Had they finally found Jase?

CHAPTER 23

Amber snuffled back a frightened sob, her face cradled in Kane's chest. Man, musk, and smoke filled her senses. He stood several steps below her, and she was still shorter.

Her mind reeled. For an instant, she'd hurt that demon. With her brain. Then the other guy had retaliated and pretty much shut her down. While she wanted to be one of those tough warrior women from a romance novel, she wasn't. She didn't want to fight in a war.

Talen stood on the bottom step after having planted the charges. "Fire in the hole," he muttered.

The explosion rocked the underground area. Shards of rock and a piece of rebar slammed down. Kane tucked Amber closer, shielding her from the debris.

He was always putting himself between her and danger.

The dust settled. She lifted her head and wrinkled her nose at the burning air. Even in the midst of hell, the vampire protected her in a way that made her feel safe. "If I didn't know better, I'd think you actually liked me."

His eyes darkened, and he brushed dirt off her shoulder. "I do like you. Probably too much."

Was there any such thing as "too much"? She doubted it. Her vision wavered. Darn mind attacks. She had to get that under control.

Talen shouted, "I need help with the door."

Kane grabbed her hand. "Stay behind me while we get Jase."

She clutched his hand as they hurried back down the steps. Talen bent at the knees and pressed one shoulder to the steel door, which hung drunkenly from one corner.

The sounds of battle continued aboveground.

Kane studied the situation for a moment and then released her. "Get ready to shove," he said right as he kicked the door square in the center.

Talen shoved.

The door shot open.

Talen threw the metal against a side wall. His loud exhale filled the sudden silence.

Amber peered around Kane. Two men and one woman sat on the dirty floor wearing filthy and ripped clothing. Bruises covered their exposed flesh. They were emaciated, their eyes darker than black.

Neither Talen nor Kane moved.

"Um, is Jase here?" Amber asked.

"No. Jase isn't here." Kane reached for his gun and nodded at Talen. "Make the call."

Talen glanced at Amber and back at Kane. "You sure?"

"Make it." Kane kept his gaze on the prisoners.

Talen grabbed his phone and texted something. "It's done."

Kane stepped toward the trio. "Jase isn't here. Who are you?"

The nearest man shoved to his feet and then swayed. Long, matted blond hair reached his shoulders. Knife wounds dotted his torso. "Ivan Newtrovsky, vampire." He nodded to the other prisoners and leaned against the wall. "Geo Meloni, vampire, and Sally Rhine, wolf shifter. We were having a nice drink together in Prague six months ago when the demons took us."

Kane kept his gun pointed at the floor. "Why were there only two demons guarding the door?"

Geo pushed to his feet. "They brought us here yesterday. More forces are supposed to arrive today."

A buzz sounded from Kane's pocket. He grabbed his phone and answered it. Listening for a few minutes, he finally nodded and hung up. "That was Dage. They've tracked eight helicopters and several trucks heading this way."

Sally allowed Geo to help her up, fear widening her eyes. A cut above her left eye bled profusely. The shifter had that shell-shocked look of most victims. "They're coming. We have to go. Please."

The desperation in her tone had Amber's stomach lurching. Fear weakened her knees until she wanted to run. "Let's go."

"Not yet." Kane eyed the ceiling, nodding toward the far corner. "I hear a slight hum. We're being recorded."

Talen pointed toward the far wall. "Speaker. They must've played recordings of Jase earlier either to mess with us or to trap Dage. It worked, but they must not have known Dage could teleport." Talen's face held no expression, but his voice rumbled with rage.

Kane shook his head. "No. Dage would've been a nice surprise. They wanted to trap a demon destroyer, or at least record one in action."

Sally tried to rush forward, but her legs gave out on her. Geo grabbed her arm to keep her from falling. She shook her head, blood spraying from the deep cut to hit the walls. "Please. We need to go."

Talen tucked his gun away, grabbing a picture from his pocket. "Have you seen my brother?"

The three prisoners all looked and then shook their heads.

Talen sighed. "I didn't think so." He eyed the injured trio. "We can send them to the Realm hospital up north."

Kane shook his head. "No. They go to the hospital in Minnesota."

Geo frowned. "Everyone knows about that place. The Realm hospital, wherever the secret location, is better. We've been tortured for six months. At least send Sally for treatment."

Sorrow rushed through Amber at the plea. "Kane, please . . ."

He glanced down, his face cold. "They go to Minnesota."

A chill swept down Amber's spine. He had no mercy . . . none. "Why?"

"Because that's what I've decided," he said grimly. Grabbing her arm, he pulled her toward the steps. "Talen, get those three secured on a helicopter heading for Minnesota."

His hold was unbreakable, his face unreadable, and his heart untouchable.

His arms strung to the ceiling, his bare feet scraping the floor, Jase faced his attacker, a low buzzing filling his skull. For a couple of hours he'd counted strikes, and then he'd lost count. So he had started over.

Suri wiped blood off his hands, sighing at the red stains coating his dark uniform. He'd even gotten blood in his silver hair this time, and the red goo covered his two guards. Of course, they'd taken plenty of shots at Jase with poles.

Suri shook his head. "Well, your brothers sure as hell fell into my trap in Arizona, now, didn't they?"

The demon leader had showed Jase the video of the Kayrs brothers infiltrating the demon compound. Seeing his brothers had brought a sharp ache to Jase's chest. "Yet they got away."

"Yes, they did. With prisoners of mine who'll do anything I want."

The demon leader thought he was an expert at brainwashing. Jase forced a chuckle. "My brothers are smarter than you."

"Maybe. But it was also interesting to see the destroyer in action. Her skills are, well, subpar." Suri wiped more blood off his chin.

She didn't seem nearly as talented as Jase had expected. Of course, gifts often manifested themselves in odd ways. The woman would learn to use hers. More interesting was the way Kane seemed to shield her, as if he actually had feelings for the woman. Had stoic Kane finally fallen?

Suri stretched his neck. "Those three were relatively easy to break—I did so enjoy myself with them. Of course, you've been much more of a challenge. I have to admit, I figured you'd be broken by now."

Jase smiled and hiccupped back a laugh. "That's a lame goal, asshole."

Suri flashed fangs. "Think so? I know the king rather well—if I send you back broken, he'll never forgive himself. Never forget what going to war with me cost him."

The feeling had completely deserted Jase's limbs. "Bullshit. This is a game to you—one I'm winning." Demons couldn't stand losing, and so far, Suri had failed. Jase blinked blood from his eyes. "Besides, if you know my brother at all, you know he's going to rip your skin from your body the first chance he gets."

The whip flew out and caught Jase around the neck, cutting deep. Pain flared inside his throat. He hadn't seen the whip.

Suri coiled the leather at his side. "Just give in to the

pain, Kayrs." Low, seductive, the soldier's voice wound past Jase's ears to his brain. "Give in, and this ends."

Jase spit out blood. "I trained my entire life to combat you, dumbass." He'd known Suri's plan from the beginning. Break Jase, rebuild him, and send him back home as a demon spy. "You really don't understand family."

"Family?" Suri roared, his eyes flashing yellow and then back to black. "I know family. And I know my sister met with you—offered herself to you." Rage mottled his face an ugly red.

"I refused." The faces in the wall nodded in satisfaction along with Jase. Shit. He was seeing faces in the wall again.

Images of pain and death instantly shot into his mind. He fought back, trying to draw shields into place, when the whip hit him across the face. The images buried deep. Pictures of his family, of sweet Janie, being destroyed by werewolves, being eaten by monsters he'd never imagined.

He groaned low, and then stars exploded behind his eyes. For once, he leapt into oblivion.

Water shot at him, yanking him back to the present. Only one half of his face worked, only one eye could see. He turned his head from the powerful spray so he could breathe. How tempting to stop breathing.

Coughing out water, he felt a rib break. The pain seemed slight compared to the rest.

The water turned off.

Suri rolled his eyes. "Leave him there. I have business and we'll pick up here in an hour."

A broad face in the wall stuck out its tongue at the demon leader.

Jase chortled.

"I think he's half-crazy," one guard whispered to the other as they followed Suri.

"You're half-right," Jase muttered and then laughed. The face in the rock laughed with him. "I guess we'll just hang out here." He laughed harder, tears running down his face as his ribs protested.

His skin chilled and he fought a sneeze. Too much pain in a sneeze.

The door slowly slid open.

His head lolled as he tried to focus on the doorway. "Willa." Man, she was pretty.

The demon gathered her skirts and stepped through water and blood to get to him. A sharp blade glinted in her hand.

Finally. Jase turned to face her fully—exposing his chest. If she hit his heart, he'd bleed out eventually. It'd be better if she took his head off, but she was probably too small. Then he took a deep breath, waiting.

Her black eyes were wide, and her pale hand shook. Stretching up on her tiptoes, she slashed the knife through the ropes holding him upright.

He crashed down.

"Hold on," she groaned, her arms encircling him as she helped him to the ground. She smelled like spiced oranges, and his stomach growled. They hit with a *thump*. She shook her head. "You got blood all over me."

"Sorry," he slurred.

She reached into her pocket for a large coffee mug. "Here's a fresh dose." Gently, she put the cup to his lips.

The scent of fresh, female blood had his fangs shooting down. Opening his mouth, he drank deeply until the mug was emptied. For the past few days, every time he'd been alone, somebody had secretly delivered him fresh blood. Nourishment from a different female each time. Willa was paying a fortune to buy him blood. "Why are you helping me?"

She shrugged. "Maybe I'm a nice person. Maybe I

think you'll help me get away from my psychotic brother."

Yeah, Suri was a freaking nut job. "I'll help you."

Hope filled her porcelain face. "You'll mate me?"

His retina began to repair itself, and his ribs clicked back into alignment. "We don't need to mate. I can save you." The face in the wall snorted. Actually snorted.

Willa sighed. "You can't even save yourself."

The rock face nodded in agreement.

"What do you know?" Jase growled at the rock.

Willa stiffened and then glanced around the room. "Who are you talking to?"

"Nobody. You need to go—if he catches you in here . . ." Jase ripped the rope bindings into small pieces so Suri wouldn't know a knife had been used. Even so, Jase slipped the knife out of Willa's pocket. He'd get free, and then he'd get her free.

She nodded. "Okay. But we're going to have to move soon—he's sending me away in a week."

"We will."

As the demon slipped out of the room, Jase pocketed the knife. It was time—do or die.

Chapter 24

Amber shivered next to Kane as the helicopter slowly lowered toward the ground. Dawn was breaking over the mountains, sending spirals of pinks and golds across the morning sky.

He slid an arm around her shoulder, tucking her closer. Warmth cascaded off him, and her body relaxed against her will.

The man was a killer. A cold, merciless killer. Yet when he held her, she almost felt safe.

Life used to be so black and white. Killing was bad, nurturing was good. But Kane was a good man. The spinning in her mind was making her dizzy. Her eyes felt like someone had shoved chalk in them. Dry and painful. She hacked out a dry cough.

Kane tightened his hold. "We'll get water and electrolytes in you the second we land. You need nourishment." His cool palm pressed against her forehead. "You're still warm. Damn fever."

Yeah, but she'd succeeded this time. Kind of. If one considered using their own mind, a gift from God, to harm people. Yeah, that's who she had become. "What I did, it hurt that demon." Not only did she know she hurt him, she'd felt the pain as if it were her own. She'd shared agony with a demon. Agony she created.

Kane pressed a kiss to her head. "I know."

She shook her head. Now that she could think clearly and wasn't trying to harm evil beings, her heart hurt for the injured people they'd found. "I don't understand why you sent those poor people to the other hospital and not the good one."

He sighed. "All the hospitals are good. Chances are they wanted to know the location of the one hospital we keep secret so they could report back to the demons."

"That's unfair. Those poor people were tortured by demons." How could he not understand?

Sadness and determination curled his lip. "I know, sweetheart. They were tortured and probably turned. We'll get them medical as well as psychological help to deprogram them. Trust me."

The helicopter set down on the landing pad in the forest, and the vampires jumped out. Kane seemed to steel his shoulders before turning to hold out a hand.

She accepted his help, leaping to the ground. He cushioned her fall and held her until she regained her balance. There was something so darn sweet about him, her mind spun. He'd been so cold in sending those prisoners away, but maybe he was right that they needed psychological help. And she'd just seen him kill. Yet, he'd killed to protect her. She wasn't proud of the fluttering butterflies in her abdomen about that.

As they neared the entrance to headquarters, Max stormed out, his gaze on her. "We have a problem—it's your grandmother."

Amber stumbled. "What's wrong?"

Max glanced at Kane and then back at her. "Hilde's gone."

Fear slammed so hard through Amber that her head began to ring. Her grandmother was gone? "How is that possible? How long has she been gone?"

Kane propelled her into headquarters. "How many came for her?"

"You were right. Full contingency of demons. We sent her for a walk in the woods with someone looking like Oscar, in case they've been watching via satellite the last couple of days." Max marched along next to them toward the open elevator.

All sound, all reality stopped.

Kane nudged her into the elevator and pushed a button. "Thanks."

Max nodded, his hard face concerned as the door closed.

Amber took several shallow breaths. *"You were right?"* Her voice rose at the end.

"Yes."

She kept her gaze straight ahead to keep herself from screaming. Betrayal burned hotter than fear down her throat. "Please explain."

"Your grandmother approached Dage with a plan."

The doors opened. Amber moved into the familiar hall-way as if she was half-awake. "A plan."

"Yes. She's a demon destroyer, and if the demons got ahold of her, they'd probably head right to their headquarters."

"Where they're probably holding Jase."

"Yes. We figured they'd lead us to him."

Rage shot nerves to life just under her skin. "What about my grandmother?"

"She wanted to go." Kane shoved open the door to the rec room.

Hurt joined the anger. Why hadn't Hilde confided in her? Amber slid her hand along the clean bar toward a set of pretty wineglasses. Her fingers wrapped around a stem. "So there was a plan in place."

"We figured the demons would strike while we were

falling into their trap. The plan was Hilde's idea." Admiration filled Kane's low tone.

"So you let my grandmother be kidnapped by the demons." The very monsters that had almost broken Amber's brain.

"Yes."

She swung. No thought, no rationality, she just swung as hard as she could for his face. The wineglass impacted his cheekbone, shattering into pieces. Blood welled in a slight cut.

He could've stopped her. A vampire's reflexes had to be much quicker than a human's. But he allowed her to make contact. To smash the glass into his skin.

Slowly, one dark eyebrow rose. "Feel better?"

No. If anything, she felt worse. She dropped the worthless wine-stem to the rug. "You would never sacrifice your family like this."

He blinked. "You're wrong. I have and probably will again sacrifice my family for this war."

"You had no right," she forced out, her lungs heating.

"She offered, and we really didn't have much of a choice."

Wait a minute. The air compressed in Amber's solar plexus. "When you saw Jase wasn't in the cell—when you told Talen to make the call. The call was to let the demons take my grandmother."

"Yes." Kane didn't blink as he met her gaze, his eyes sober. "I let them take your grandmother."

Hitting him again would solve nothing. Yet Amber's hand clenched into a fist anyway. So much for being a pacifist. "I'll never forgive you," she whispered, the words actually hurting.

"I know." His expression didn't change.

Her smile felt raw. "You really are one cold bastard."

"So I've heard."

Tears pricked her eyes. "How can you not feel *anything*?"

His eyes morphed from violet to black and back again in seconds. "I feel *everything*." He took a step toward her.

She took two steps back. "And yet, you did this." Sleeping with him had been a mistake. Falling for him was an even bigger one, and one she'd have to live with. "There's nothing else for us to say."

"I understand." His mask firmly back in place, he turned and headed for the door. "Emma will be along shortly—she's going to want to take blood."

Amber waited until he'd left the room before allowing the tears to fall.

She dropped into a chair and let herself cry it out until her head hurt and her nose ached. But finally, she felt better.

The king found her there an hour later. He moved silently, grabbing a blanket off the sofa to settle over her, his gaze serious, his movements gentle.

"Thank you," she said, sniffing.

"Anytime." He brushed the back of his hand over her forehead as he maneuvered to sit on a matching chair. "Your fever has abated."

"You mean *gone down*."

"Excuse me?" A dark eyebrow rose over a new black eye.

Irritation huffed out with her breath. What a pretentious lot. They all thought they were so smart. "My fever. It went down. The fever did not abate, diminish, or any other zillion-dollar word. It *went down*."

The king smiled. "Okay."

She glared at him through puffy lids. He did not have to be so agreeable. "Stop being nice. I'm really mad at you."

"You should be."

"Stop agreeing with me."

"My apologies."

Okay. She was starting to hate this guy—and she was starting to feel foolish. "What you did was wrong."

"Probably." He sighed, rubbing both hands over his face, wincing as his fingers met the shiner. "If someone had put my granny in danger, even if she volunteered, I'd probably break his neck."

Amber nodded slowly, studying the king. The decision had cost him. Dark circles lived under his eyes, while tension lines marred his smooth face. Even so, he was nearly as handsome as Kane with his silver eyes and rugged features.

He leaned forward. "I'm sorry."

"I don't want your apology." Sympathizing with the king wasn't going to get her anywhere. Amber narrowed her eyes. "What happened to your face?" He hadn't had the black eye after the battle with the demons.

"Oscar hit me."

"For letting the demons take my grandmother."

"Yes."

Amber knew she liked the massive vampire. "Good for him."

Dage shrugged. "The guy hits like a truck. So, what can I do to make this up to you?"

"I want you to get my grandmother back."

"We will. As soon as we know where they've taken her, we'll get her."

"So, there's a plan."

"We always have plans, sweetheart," Dage said wearily. "Sometimes they actually work."

Now that didn't inspire much confidence. "What's the plan?"

He studied her with those odd silver eyes before speaking. "Well, we think they'll offer to exchange her with you. We'll agree and go in and get her. Hopefully the demons will take her to headquarters where Jase is. They'll want to test her skills on the best, and the best would be the demon leader."

Chills swept down Amber's spine. "So you've allowed the demons to take my grandmother so they can rape her mind, and hopefully they'll do so at headquarters so you can save your brother."

Dage stilled. "No. I mean, I don't think they'll hurt her. She's actually a lot more powerful than she thought—I tested her the other day. Through the years she's accumulated her mate's psychic powers."

"What if the demons don't call?" Amber muttered.

"We placed a chip in her foot," Dage said just as quietly.

"Of course you did." Amber took several deep breaths to keep from hitting the king. "Well, surely you've tracked her. Where is she?"

"We only want to activate the chip as a last resort, just in case the demons do a sweep of her body. They won't find the tracker if we haven't activated it, so we won't do so for a little while." Apology twisted the king's lips. "We need to up your training so you're ready to go when we find the demon headquarters. Talen should be here soon to try his gifts against yours again."

"You think I'm going to help you?" Putting her grandmother in danger was unforgivable.

"Yes. I know you'll help get Hilde back."

Hilde had always charted her own path in life, and there was no doubt the woman had volunteered for the duty. If Amber wanted the right to fight demons, shouldn't Hilde also make her own choices? Amber eyed the king. "I'll help. Now you can promise no more water bottles, no more real leather, and everybody in the Realm turns vegan."

He chuckled. "Okay. No more water bottles or plastic

bottles of any kind, and no more real leather. I can't turn anyone into a vegan, sorry."

"Kane lied to me." The words slipped out before she could stop them. Something about Dage inspired trust and confidence, and she didn't have anybody to talk to.

"Yes."

"Thank you for not arguing that an omission is not a lie."

"*Omission* is one of those zillion-dollar words." Dage grinned, suddenly looking years younger.

"I'm no genius, but I know a couple of big words." Amber wanted to grin back, but her face wouldn't follow suit.

"Kane's not that smart."

"Really?" Amber shook her head. What a lie.

"Really." Dage sat back in his chair, his shoulders visibly relaxing. "Ninety percent of the time, he ends up blowing things into a billion pieces. The other ten percent, he's lucky." The king grinned again. "When we were young, he created a potion to make friends."

"Did the potion work?"

Dage snorted. "No. He ended up giving food poisoning to a bunch of the village kids. My mother was beside herself."

Imagining Kane as a young brainiac desperate to make friends warmed Amber's heart. What a cute little boy he must've been with his violet eyes and dark hair. "He still lied to me."

"I know. He blames himself for our failing to rescue Jase—it's blinded him a little bit."

"You blame yourself."

"I'm the king." Dage shrugged. "The failure is my fault."

And Kane was the smartest guy on the planet, so he blamed himself. Empathy for both Kayrs brothers had

Amber's heart softening. She shifted her weight. "The Kayrs marking appeared on his palm."

"I'm aware of that."

"Do you think the marking's appearance means anything?" She held her breath until the king responded.

"I think the appearance means everything." His eyes darkened.

"Kane doesn't."

"Kane doesn't know everything." Dage leaned forward, his broad hands in his lap. "When we went to war the first time, our parents were killed, and we all were forced into roles for which we were unprepared."

Amber tilted her head to the side. "How so?"

A rueful smile curved the king's lips. "I became king, Talen started plotting strategy, Conn started training with the soldiers, and Jase had to grow up."

"And Kane?" Amber asked softly.

"Kane had to balance all of us. He became my confidant, Talen's reason, Conn's conscience, and Jase's protector. As the smartest and probably the most responsible, Kane took us all on." Dage exhaled slowly. "I didn't realize how very much he'd taken on until the demons kidnapped Jase."

"Kane blames himself."

Dage shook his head. "Jase's disappearance isn't Kane's fault."

"It isn't your fault, either."

Dage smiled, flashing twin dimples. "I have no doubt this is premature, but welcome to my family, Amber Freebird. You're a very pleasant addition."

Warmth flushed through her. "I'm not joining your family."

"Ah, sweetheart. Fate has a way of kicking us where we need to go. At some point, Kane's going to fall in line. Although he took on way too much through the years, he deserves something for himself."

That might be a bit presumptuous. Amber tried to clear her head. "How am I supposed to deal with this?"

"Well, I guess, first off . . . you should make a decision."

The hair on the back of her neck stood up. "Meaning?"

"When we go get your grandmother, are you really ready? If so, how will you contribute?" Dage asked blandly.

Adrenaline shot through her veins. She jumped to her feet. "Oh, Mother Earth. You want me to mate Kane." He would be very dangerous to the demons if he mastered her gifts. Her powers would greatly increase as well.

Dage stretched to his feet. "You might want to consider the idea."

"Why? I mean, you can't possibly want your brother to mate for eternity with someone he doesn't love."

"Now that's what I've been trying to explain to you." Dage loped toward the exit, pausing at the doorway to look over his shoulder. "Who says Kane isn't in love?"

CHAPTER 25

Jase crouched next to the cell door, the knife heavy in his hand. He kept his grip loose so his palm wouldn't cramp. The idea of his hand cramping from holding one small knife would've made him laugh four years ago.

When he laughed.

Closing his eyes, he dug deep for a hint of his power. Spiraling out from his core, he tried to freeze the air around him.

The oxygen didn't even sputter.

For centuries he'd taken for granted his ability to mess with the elements, often sending a steamy slap to burn one of his brothers. Now he missed the gift with a sharpness that made his gut ache. The ability was probably lost forever.

The weird faces in the rock nodded solemnly.

"Who are you?" Jase whispered.

As usual, the bastards refused to answer.

Whistling sounded from beyond the door, slowly becoming louder.

He stiffened in preparation. Seconds passed. Then more. Finally, keys jangled against the steel door.

The door swung open.

Shooting forward, he jabbed the knife into a guard. Blood spread over his fingers. Eons ago he'd learned to fight with cold, hard logic. Now a grunting desperation filled him, elation at striking out clamoring through his veins for more. More blood. More pain. More death.

An animalistic need to survive, to destroy, ripped panting noises from his gut.

The demon inhaled in pain, struggling to retreat. He roared in anger, grabbing the knife handle and trying to twist the weapon away from Jase.

Suri stepped to the side.

Barbs of mental pain slashed into Jase's brain. Screeching followed the pain—some sort of high-pitched animal lived in his skull now. He dropped the knife, both hands clapping his ears. The agony pierced his eyeballs from within.

The crack of a metal pole against his rib cage registered in sound but not sensation, so great was the devastation going on in his head. His skull pounded.

Blood cooled his ear canal and slid down his neck.

The crack of the pole sent him flying into the wall. He chuckled, eyes closed, knowing the wall faces hadn't caught him. "Jerks."

Air swished and a fist impacted his temple.

He dropped to the ground, darkness just beyond reach. Time passed.

More attacks came. Some physical, some mental, but he floated beyond them, feeling nothing. He wandered in the haze between reality and dreams, not unconscious, but not really there.

More time went by. Minutes, hours, maybe days.

Coldness coated his skin, but not enough to wake him completely.

His vision remained black. Odd, but a sadness lingered somewhere inside his gut that he couldn't see the wall faces. Did they miss him, too?

Hard hands grabbed his armpits. His feet dragged on the ground. More haze fell.

Something soft cushioned him.

Warm, healing liquid slid down his throat. Blood. Female and strong. A very healthy human.

More time passed where he tried to ignore reality.

Finally, his eyes opened.

Willa leaned over him, her scent of spiced oranges wafting along his skin. The pale mounds of her perfect breasts spilled over the top of her chemise. Against his will, his body flared to life.

She frowned, wiping off his head with a silk scarf. "I thought they'd damaged your brain."

What brain? He took several deep breaths, glancing slowly around. Wearing just a clean pair of black silk boxers, he lay on his back, stretched out on a velvet bedspread softer than any dream. "You finally got me into bed," he croaked.

She laughed, the sound full of mirth. "Yes. All it took was my brother beating you into a coma with a steel pole."

Jase shoved up on his elbows. His body was one continuous purple bruise, but the open gashes had closed from whatever blood he'd taken. An internal inventory revealed mangled organs, ripped blood vessels, and torn muscles.

The blood he'd taken would slowly help him mend.

For now, he needed to get out of hell. Without question, this was his last chance.

The bedroom remained the same as last time he'd visited, except for a new Brenna Dunne oil painting on the far wall. Splashes of red and deep blue colored the view of a rumpled bed—a bed lovers had just vacated. "Interesting piece." He'd had no idea Brenna harbored such sexuality, but he knew her work well. The painting was definitely Brenna's.

"Yes. I bought the work off a gallery owner in Dublin." Willa tossed the bloody silk onto the floor.

"Hmm." Jase forced himself into a seated position, biting back a wince as his head all but blew off his shoulders at the pain. The thought of sweet Brenna's sexy painting in a demon hellhole bothered him a lot more than it should. "You probably stole it."

Willa lifted a shoulder. "Same thing."

"No, it isn't." He swung his legs over the side of the bed. The room spun, and his stomach lurched. Several deep breaths later, and he could finally focus. "How did I get here?"

"I have some loyal followers." The demon sniffed. She eyed his body with interest, her small nostrils flaring.

"And the silk boxers?"

"Consider them a gift."

Jase flattened his feet on the thick carpet. Standing was going to be difficult. So he focused on the painting, trying to imagine pretty, soft Brenna Dunne in his head. The woman was proof that goodness and purity still existed. Cutting his gaze away from the painting, he wavered to his feet and studied the demon. "Suri will kill you if he finds out you just rescued me."

"I know. That's why you need to lie back down and let this happen." Willa tugged off the chemise and revealed high breasts with light pink nipples.

"You're beautiful." He spoke without thinking, his fangs elongating. She truly was stunning. He'd bet almost anything in the world that her pretty nipples tasted like raspberries in the thick of summer. Man, he was hungry.

"Thank you." Her nimble fingers went to the ties of her skirt, and the heavy silk swished to the floor.

Nothing could've prevented the low growl that emerged from his chest. For a small woman, the demon had long legs and toned thighs. And she was completely bare.

He shook his head. "This is a bad idea."

Her hands pressed against his chest. "This is the only chance we have."

"No." His body protested what his gut told him to say.

"Yes," Willa whispered. She leaned up, her lips sliding against his.

Warmth flushed through him. He dove into the kiss. With a gasp, his mouth moved over hers in a kiss filled with question. He took her deeper, for once seeking pleasure instead of finding pain.

But a clamoring in his brain made him lift his head.

His instincts were all he had.

For the oddest of reasons, the painting by Brenna Dunne seemed to ground him. He couldn't have sex with a demon in front of Brenna's painting. He swallowed, trying to shove need out of his body. "We can't. But I promise you, I'll get you out of here. I'll get you safe."

Willa hissed, her nails digging into his bare chest. "We're as good as dead if you don't do this."

"We're definitely dead if I mate you." Jase shook his head. The woman had helped him on several occasions, and he wouldn't sign her death warrant just because she had a tempting body. A very tempting body. Though, the idea of embarrassing Suri, of using his sister to harm him, held merit.

He'd become a true bastard. Shaking his head, he shoved the evil thought away. Getting Willa out of Suri's reach and to safety would hurt the demon just fine. "Trust me, Willa. I'll get you to safety."

"You don't want me." Hurt turned her eyes nearly purple.

"Of course I want you." He grabbed her wrists to tug away from his chest. How in the hell was he going to get them both out of the stronghold? His powers were gone, and his head very well might blow up. "Sex right now between us is not the answer. We need to survive this, not mate."

"Sex is always the answer," she purred. Tugging her

hands free, she leaned in and kissed the purple bruises dotting his chest. Her other hand went to the outside of his boxers to cup him, her fingers stroking through the fabric.

He bit back a groan. His dick arched into her hand even while he gently pushed her away by the shoulders. For years the only touch he'd felt came from hard strikes with poles and bats. The idea of sex nearly made him forget the very real danger they were in the longer they stayed in the bedroom. Plus, the sexy painting seemed to condemn him. "You need to stop," he groaned.

"Your body disagrees with you." She tightened her grip and stroked harder.

"I said *no*." He yanked her hand away and sidled several steps away. The room spun, and his lungs whistled as if holes dotted them. Concentrating, he sent healing cells to deal with the tissue. "Trust me, we need to leave now."

Her eyes flashed from black to yellow. A dark flush slid over her face. Slamming both hands on her hips, she stomped her foot. "You asshole."

So true. He had no doubt even if he survived this, he'd be an asshole. True caring of anybody or anything wasn't going to happen again. They'd killed him as efficiently as if they'd cut off his head. "I'm sorry."

"Not as sorry as you're going to be." Nodding, she slammed horrific images into his head. Images of kids being shot, of his family being beheaded.

He remained on his feet while his heart seized. The woman was nuts. "Knock it off. A temper tantrum isn't going to help."

The images retreated. She exhaled. "You'll pay for this." The bed protested when she kicked the box spring several times. "I *promised*. I promised Suri I'd get your powers. And now you've ruined *everything*."

Jase stilled. Reality slammed him hard. "Suri? He knew about your plan of seduction?"

Her lips twisted. "Of course. Did you really think I wanted to mate you for protection? I wanted your powers, you stupid vampire—as well as a way to get to the king of the Realm. Now we'll just have to break you and make you help us. But you could've had me."

"Well." Jase forced a condescending smile, his mind reeling in slow motion. "You failed, now, didn't you?"

Her chin lifted slowly, a dangerous glint in her eyes. "We both did." Turning toward the door, she yelled for the guards.

Two guards rushed in, both grabbing his arms.

Willa settled her face, no longer looking even remotely attractive. A dark red covered her cheeks, while her eyes blazed a horrifying yellow. "Take him back to his cell. Make sure he enjoys the view on the way."

Laughing, the guards dragged him out of the sensual bedroom. They trod through several tunnels, twisting and turning as they maneuvered deeper into the earth. Deeper into hell.

His mind reeled. He'd almost had sex with a demon, almost mated her. Who knows if he would've ended up trying. But her attempt at seduction was just another demon mind fuck. Was he ever going to get out of hell?

The guards slowed their pace. The scent of blood overtook the oxygen. His fangs elongated naturally. An opened doorway stood to the left, and Jase glanced in as the guards paused.

A blonde, pretty even in death, hung upside-down from the ceiling, blood coating her hair as it dripped into a bucket on the floor. Her blue eyes were wide in horror, her throat slashed end to end.

Seconds passed as he tried to make sense of what he was seeing. Past the blonde, several female bodies hung dead from the ceiling. All had bled out. All had terror on their pretty faces. There had to be five dead women.

The scents of the different blood was familiar.

He gagged. Something snapped in his head. Or maybe it was in his soul. Either way, something he'd managed to hold on to during his captivity ripped apart.

The tallest guard laughed. "Guess your meals weren't free, now, were they?"

Oh God. He had enjoyed the blood of each one of the victims. They'd died to keep him alive. They'd died as part of a sick game invented by Willa and Suri.

The guards hustled Jase to his cell, where they tossed him in.

The *drip-drip* of the water down the wall sounded like a voice whispering "mur-der." They'd killed the young women to give him blood. Willa had lied. *Mur-der. Mur-der. Mur-der.*

Bile rose in his throat.

Shuffling to the corner, he heaved the contents of his stomach. Blood, tons of red mush, coated the wall and floor. The fresh blood from the blonde.

Gasping, he turned.

A face in the wall frowned, condemning him. Pieces of rock dropped out of the wall mouth. Sharp pieces. Sharp enough to pierce his jugular so he bled out.

Mur-der. Mur-der. Mur-der

After all the blood he'd stolen, he didn't want any. The horrendous liquid had to be taken from his body. Bleeding out was the only solution.

This would finally end.

Slowly, Jase crawled toward the pieces of guaranteed death.

CHAPTER 26

Kane kicked the punching bag and sent it flying through the air. Panting in a deep breath, he glared at the empty gym. Now he was acting more like Talen than himself. He didn't need to punch things to calm down. He was Kane Kayrs, for Christ's sake.

In fact, he'd only gone to the gym to find Talen. His older brother didn't have the decency to be where he was supposed to be.

Heavy footsteps sounded outside, and Talen stomped into the room.

"Where the fuck have you been?" Kane growled.

Talen lifted one dark eyebrow. "On the phone with my mate trying to get her to hurry the hell up and come home. Why are you in the gym wearing silk pants?"

"They're a silk-cotton blend, and my normal pants." Kane crossed his arms. "I'm here looking for you."

"Why?"

"I've been thinking strategy and demon strongholds." Hopefully they'd find Jase and it'd be soon.

"Interesting. So far, the best strategy is shock and awe so we can distract them and cut their heads off before they attack us with their brains." Talen rolled his shoulders. "What are you thinking?"

Kane frowned. "Something about using Amber's shielding abilities with modern witchcraft. I mean, the witches manipulate matter with quantum physics, so why not manipulate brain waves? Brain waves are as real as sound or light waves, so I want to figure out how to bend them."

"Great plan." Talen reached for a knife from his boot. "Something tells me learning to bend brain waves may take some time."

Sad but true. But the war with the demons wasn't ending anytime soon. So Kane had better get started.

Talen twirled the knife, his movements fast, his gaze hard. The glint of swirling steel seemed to catch his attention. "We probably don't have time for a new strategy before we get Jase."

"Probably not, but we should still keep building our resources."

Talen threw the knife up and caught it before slamming the blade back into his boot. Then he frowned and sniffed the air. He straightened, gaze serious on Kane. "You smell like Amber."

Kane stilled. "I do not."

"Yes, you do. While you haven't marked her, her scent is all over you. Mating takes more than just marking, you know."

Irritation pricked the back of Kane's neck. "We had sex, that's all. I'm not mating her. Well, I mean, I asked her, but she said no."

Talen settled his stance. "Did you tell her you loved her?"

"Of course not, asshole."

"Calling names seems beneath you. I can tell you have feelings for her." Talen jerked his head in a tough-guy nod toward Kane's hand. "The marking appeared, so fate has spoken. She's your mate, Kane."

Kane blew out a breath. He opened his mouth to debate his brother's ridiculous claim when the speaker in the far corner crackled.

"Kane, Talen, get to control room one. Now," Dage ordered.

Kane's breath caught. There was only one reason they'd be meeting in Dage's private control room—they'd found Jase. He broke into a run behind Talen, hurrying down stairs and through passageways to the concealed room.

Dage and Max were already in place, facing the huge screen. A smaller screen to the right held Conn Kayrs, who was in Ireland with his mate. His face was pale, his jaw set hard.

Kane's stomach dropped. "What's going on?"

Dage flipped a switch and a dingy cell filled the main screen.

Narrowing his eyes, Kane spotted a thin figure in the corner. "Jase," he breathed.

The figure slowly crawled toward the far wall, picking up shards of rock. Pausing, he seemed to say something to the walls. Then he plunged the makeshift weapon into his jugular.

Kane took a step back. Nobody even breathed in the control room underground as Jase Kayrs slowly bled out. Finally, he slumped to the ground, copper eyes open, chest not moving with breath.

The screen went black.

Pain and rage ripped through Kane so quickly his mind spun.

"The video is a fake," Talen growled.

"The techs looked at it—nothing has been altered." Conn stepped closer to the camera, fury lighting his eyes. "We intercepted the transmission an hour ago and have narrowed the sender to somewhere in Scotland. The witches are trying to pinpoint the location but aren't having much luck."

Dage took a deep breath. "Talen, call the pilots and tell them to stand by—and get ready to activate Hilde's tracker. You and Conn figure out an attack plan once we find a location. Max, you're in lockdown here at head-quarters . . . keep everyone safe."

Talen and Max both nodded, hurrying from the room.

Conn eyed Dage and Kane. "I'll see you both soon." His screen went dark.

Dage continued looking at the dark screen, his broad back to Kane. "Do you think Jase is dead?"

Pain settled so hard in Kane's gut that he groaned. "No," he whispered. Giving the king false hope wouldn't help, but he couldn't take away all hope.

Dage whirled around, his eyes a stark blue. "Fucking tell me the truth—don't handle me."

The vampire in Kane wanted to strike right back, but the brother just felt sorrow. "It's possible for a vampire to die by bleeding out completely . . . but it's more likely he'd just go brain dead. Keep in mind how long it'd really take to bleed out. My concern is that he tried to start the process." Kane's voice broke on the end.

Dage lifted his chin. "We proceed as if he's alive and needs to be rescued." His movements jerky, he yanked his hair into a band to secure at the nape of his neck. "When we get to Ireland, we'll engage Hilde's tracking device. Chances are, she's at headquarters."

Kane stayed silent, his gaze on his oldest brother.

Dage ground a fist into his eye. "Will Amber be com-ing?"

"Yes. We need her," Kane said softly.

"Kane, I know this isn't the time, but if we attack the demons, some of us might not make it back."

"I know." Kane would cover Dage's back if it was the last thing he ever did.

"My point is, if you love the woman, at least tell her be-fore we go." Wisdom lurked in the king's eyes. "You'll be surprised how much stronger the admission makes you."

Kane nodded. "Okay."

"Don't appease me." Dage shook his head and stalked toward the door. "Just once you might consider that other people know more than you do about something."

"I do." But he'd been so up front with Amber about his feelings, or rather, lack of feelings. Sure, he wanted her. And, man, he liked her. Could it be something deeper?

His gut told him it was something a lot deeper.

"Is she still mad about her granny?" Dage pressed a button to open the door.

"Wouldn't you be?" Kane turned to follow his brother into the hallway.

"Hell, yes," Dage said. "Whenever Emma gets really irritated at me, I throw her in the pool. Then we make out. Always works."

Something told Kane that throwing Amber in the pool was a bad idea. "I'll keep that in mind." He needed something far more drastic than a good dunking to appease Amber's anger. "Though I think that our saving her grandmother is the only thing that'll make Amber not mad at me anymore."

"That's probably true." Dage paused and put his hand on Kane's shoulder. "I need to go see Emma before we take off for Scotland." The king sighed. "She's not going to like it." He hurried off for the elevator.

"Well, the pool is probably free," Kane called after him. Then he fell against the wall. Raw claws of poisoned pain ripped through his entire body. Tears sprang to his eyes, and he allowed them to fall without a care.

Was Jase really done fighting? All logic and Kane's own eyes said Jase wanted to be finished.

His younger brother was chasing death. Hopefully he hadn't caught it.

CHAPTER 27

The king's words echoed in Amber's head for the rest of the afternoon. Could Kane be in love with her? If so, he'd never admit it to her, much less to himself. More importantly, how did she feel? Feelings were supposed to be clear and absolute, not convoluted and confusing. Unlike Kane, she did believe in fate. That marking had appeared on his palm the first time they'd touched. That had to mean something.

While she was angry with him about her grandmother, she also knew her grandmother. Hilde offered to go, heck, she probably wanted to go.

If Amber had the right to fight, didn't Hilde?

With a sigh, Amber paused outside Kane's underground quarters.

The last time they'd slept together, something in her had shifted. Something deep—she'd given a part of herself away. Regardless, she steeled her spine and twisted the doorknob. If Hilde had a right to fight, so did Amber. And she needed all the power she could get.

This was going to happen.

Shoving open the door, she paused as her eyes adjusted to the dim light. His back to her, Kane stood near the mantel, staring at gas flames in the fireplace. His broad shoulders sent shadows to dance on the sofa. Music wound from hidden speakers, but not the smooth jazz or classical tones she would've expected. Instead, a fierce metal tone beat through the room, dark and angry.

"Amber, this isn't a good time." His voice rumbled low and gravelly across the short distance.

She shivered and moved inside, closing the door. "What happened?"

Kane slowly turned, the harsh angles of his face hard, his eyes a fathomless black. "Please leave."

"No." The pain cascading off him was palpable. She had strong, very strong feelings for the vampire. There was no way she could leave him hurting. "Tell me."

"Jase tried to kill himself."

Her head jerked back. Pain shot down to her stomach. She'd never met Jase, but the words still cut deep. "Did he succeed?"

"I don't know."

I'm so sorry," she whispered.

"Thank you. Now leave." Kane turned back to the rhythmic fire.

She wouldn't leave an animal in so much pain, much less a man she'd been intimate with. Careful steps took her around the sofa so she could place a hand against his back.

He stiffened and growled low.

Muscles shifted restlessly again her palm. "Kane. Let me help."

"How?" His tone lacked inflection and contradicted the tension pouring off him.

Good question. "Talk to me."

"I did. Jase has given up." Kane threw a shoulder and dislodged her hand. "Now you need to go."

"What about my grandmother?"

"She's on her way to Scotland. We're heading after her as soon as she reaches a location."

Amber inhaled and attempted to calm her nerves. The dark music beat through her skin, making her heart speed up. Thoughts zinged furiously around her brain. The man needed comforting, and she needed his powers. For a woman used to feeling her way, the logical conclusion to their problems came too easily. "We need to mate."

He froze. Slowly, he turned his head, dark eyes flashing. "This is not a good time."

"It's the only time." She grabbed on to his arm, digging in. "I'm sorry about Jase, but I can't let my grandmother die—I know we'll find her. I need your powers to save her." More than anything, Amber needed to be able to attack. If they mated, she'd gain the skill. "Plus, if Jase has given up, we need to save him and now. No more waiting."

Kane whirled so suddenly she would've fallen had he not grabbed her biceps in an unbreakable grip. "You don't know what you're saying."

"I do." The words came out more a vow than a simple statement.

"Mating is forever," he growled.

"Maybe." She kept her voice soft, soothing. "Maybe not. Virus-27 will erase the mating mark if I choose." She'd spent some time talking to Emma before making the decision.

Anger twisted his lips. "You're joking. The infection would probably kill you at some point. That's not an option." His eyes went wild, much more animal than man. Was this the vampire side of him? The hold on her arms tightened. "You mate me, sweetheart, there's no turning back. No taking a virus. It's immortality . . . forever."

She swallowed. Fear cascaded shivers down her back. She didn't know him like this. Deep down, she knew her logical argument was a smoke screen. Having fallen in love with Kane Kayrs, the only way to keep him, the only way to teach him to love, was to mate him. She was a gambler at heart, apparently. "Fine."

He dropped his hands. "I agree that mating is the best course of action, just not right now." His voice shook, while a vein pulsed in his corded neck.

"Why not?"

He faltered. "This isn't a good time. We'll approach the matter later when we're both in more control."

So that was it. The vampire, for once, wasn't in perfect control of his emotions. Well, it was about time. Grabbing the hem of her T-shirt, she yanked it over her head. The cotton hit the floor seconds before her bra followed suit. "I know you want me." Standing in the ripped jeans and plush socks, she faked a confidence she truly didn't feel.

His nostrils flared. "Yes. I want you." Even so, he took a step back. "Our mating right now won't make a difference in time to get your grandmother. We have time to plan this right."

Instinct whispered that their mating would make a difference. A smart woman listened to her instincts. "You don't know that our mating wouldn't help in the next battle."

"No, I don't." His gaze dropped to her bare breasts. A dark flush wound over the harsh angles of his face. "Amber, I'm more than willing to lose myself in you tonight. But there's no way I'll be able to keep from marking you this time. If I were you, I'd turn and run. Now."

Her heart hurt. For him, because of him, for her grandmother . . . maybe even for herself. "I'm so tired of being alone." The words slipped out, coming from somewhere deeper than her brain. "Please, Kane." Going on instinct, she moved forward and pressed herself along his length. Stretching up on her tiptoes, she flicked his lips with her tongue. Her hips bumped his erection. Yeah, he wanted her.

He barely seemed to breathe.

Both her hands dove into his thick hair. Giving him a wicked smile, she bit his bottom lip. Hard.

His top lip pulled back in a snarl. Then he slowly licked the blood clean, his gaze locking on hers.

"I want you, Kane." Hell, she was half in love with the man whether she liked it or not. And she was lying to herself about the "half" part. "I'll give you anything you want." Too bad he didn't want her heart, considering he already had it. "Stop being a coward."

His chin lifted. "I can't be manipulated, sweetheart."

Oh yeah? Her chin lifted just as high as his. "How about the direct approach, then?" Releasing his hair, she ran her palms down the hard planes of his chest, the silk tickling her skin until she reached the button of his slacks. A quick tug had them released. Throwing dare into her eyes and defiance into her smile, she slid her hand inside his pants. His already black eyes somehow darkened further.

Feminine power flushed through her. "I've never seduced anyone before," she said softly, stroking him. The man had gone commando. Yet another surprise.

"Be careful what you wish for, little girl." The warning held both threat and promise.

Her sex softened. "You don't scare me."

"Yes, I do," he said softly.

Maybe a little. Considering she literally had him by the balls, he seemed far too confident and self-assured. So she squeezed.

He moved without a hint of warning. Both hands manacled around her wrists, and he hauled her up against him. Surprised, she tried to yank away. His strength made her slight struggle laughable. Yet neither of them broke a smile.

"Last chance," he murmured, his gaze intense on her face. Too intense.

It was by far too late. "You talk too much, Kayrs."

Slowly, pointedly, he tangled one hand at her nape, tethering her. The movement held the deliberateness of a predator playing with its prey. A quick jerk tilted back her head and made her lips ache for his.

Then he waited.

Her heart thundered in her ears. Manic butterflies winged through her stomach. Anticipation tapped imaginary fingers down her back.

The man didn't move.

Apprehension replaced anticipation. She tried to shove him away.

They remained in place.

He easily, effortlessly, kept her immobile. His head lowered until his breath heated her ear. "Am I making myself clear?"

She shivered and stifled a groan. "Like I said, you talk too much." Her voice came out husky.

Dangerous teeth enclosed her earlobe.

Her knees went weak while her panties soaked.

He sucked, releasing her earlobe to run his mouth along her exposed jugular, those deadly fangs a mere hint against her skin. "I've wanted you to wear my mark since the first time I saw you in that bar." The dark timbre of his voice vibrated against her neck and shot spirals of desire straight to her sex.

Was it possible to orgasm just from a voice?

Her blood pumped in rhythm with his breathing, with the heavy metal music winding around them. "Kane."

"You were so sexy, winding through tables, your hair wild and that low-cut blouse showing perfect breasts." He ran his lips up the other side of her neck, taking time to nip her other earlobe into a throbbing bit of need. "I couldn't decide whether to grab you right there, or cover you up so nobody could see you but me."

Her mouth opened, but no sound emerged.

He lifted his head, his features unyielding. "I don't share, Amber."

She took the statement for the warning it was. "Neither do I."

A low growl, much more animal than man, rumbled up from his chest.

She started, reminded once again that the man wasn't human. "Ah, Kane—"

"Too late. I gave you the chance to run. Now you're mine."

His lips took hers. Hard, relentless, determined. He dove deep, taking, whatever beast slumbering inside him suddenly unleashed.

She could taste the difference.

His tongue swept in a claiming. Nipping her bottom lip, he lifted his head to study her.

Her lips tingled. In fact, her entire body throbbed. "I'm not running." Even if her brain insisted she escape, her body wasn't going anywhere. Need had her trembling in his arms, fighting the very real urge to rip off his clothes. Shifting her shoulders enough to get her hands between them, she tugged on his zipper.

He kicked out of his pants, unsnapping her jeans. "These are in the way."

She paused, blinking, shoving them and her socks to the floor.

His gaze swept her from head to toe, and an appreciative smile curved his lips. "Now the panties."

The vampire sure liked to give orders. With a challenge in her smile, she slid both thumbs into the straps and scooted the skimpy material down her legs, shimmying her hips as they went, making sure to take her time.

His low growl made her smile widen. Oh yeah. He may be issuing orders, but they'd see just who kept in control. She had him, and she knew it.

She nodded at his shirt. "Now you."

A wicked smile curved his lips as he yanked off his shirt. Both hands went to her waist, and he lifted her against him. "Wrap your legs around me."

Instinct already had her doing so before he spoke. Maybe she'd taken on too much with the pissed-off vampire. "Are you still angry?"

"No." Tugging her head back, he nipped the underside of her jaw.

He turned so the fire warmed her bare backside. "I am going to mark you tonight, Amber," he rumbled against her collarbone.

"I know," she sighed, gyrating against him.

"Now is your chance to choose where." His hand swept down her back, the raised marking feeling hotter than the fireplace, hinting at a danger she was about to meet. Then that heated flesh cupped her ass.

"Um, the small of my back," she whispered. For years she'd meant to get a tattoo there anyway. The Kayrs marking would be perfect.

"Excellent," he murmured, pressing his palm to the base of her tailbone.

She stilled. "Are you tattooing me now?"

"No." His hand ventured lower to cup her other buttock. "I need to be inside you to mark you."

The low words sent fire right to her core. "Then we should get to it."

"You know me better than that." His mouth dropped to flick a nipple.

Her breath caught. The man did like to take his time. "Do that again."

"Gladly." He flicked again and then engulfed her nipple in so much heat her eyes fluttered closed. Her hips gyrated against him of their own accord.

He chuckled low, sending fire from her breast to her

sex. Even so, she tried to keep a grip on reality as she opened her eyes. "You'll have to twist your hand so the marking isn't crooked." Last thing she wanted was a half-assed tattoo.

"That won't be a problem." He kissed his way up her neck to peer into her eyes. "I plan to be behind you."

Before she could respond, his mouth was on hers. Heat exploded between them like a gas fire. He held her still as he took her mouth, no games, no playfulness, no teasing.

Just pure, raw passion. Honest and true.

Dangerous as hell.

This was the first time she'd initiated sex with him, the fact giving her a sense of power. Feminine power. Even if she lived forever, she'd never forget the taste of him—rich, spicy, and male. He smelled like cedar and felt like steel. Pivoting, he set her on the sofa table, leaning her back just far enough she had to wrap both arms around his neck to stay balanced. His hands cupped her face, thumbs tracing her cheekbones gently, even as his mouth continued to destroy her.

The gentleness of his fingers compared to the fierceness of his kiss shot her entire body into a mode of hunger she'd never felt. She *craved* the vampire. The desire was so intense the feeling went beyond pain to necessity.

His hips rocked against her, his erection pulsing. He wanted in her . . . now. Even more, she wanted him inside her, stretching her, pulsing her into that orgasm that seemed so close.

Releasing her mouth, he ducked down, his shoulders hitting her abdomen.

The world tilted, and she found herself upside down over his broad shoulder. "Hey," she yelped.

The smack to her ass flared need to life in her entire body.

He chuckled low. "If this is going to happen, we're doing it right. In bed."

Air kissed along her bare skin as he deserted the warm fireplace, stalking through a hallway to the dimly lit bedroom. Her mind spun as he flipped her over to place gently on the bed.

The world narrowed to the two of them. She couldn't look away from the amazing specimen of a male standing buck-assed naked at the end of the bed. Vampires were truly a spectacular race.

One of his knees pressed into the mattress, his head dropping to plant kisses along her abdomen, tracing her hip bones, his hands opening her thighs.

She let go of all insecurity and fear, opening for him. This was a moment, one of a kind, and she was taking it.

His tongue ran through her slit. The sensation spiraled through her, and she gave a strangled cry, arching into his mouth.

Inflexible hands clamped down on her hips, holding her in place.

Oh God.

He shoved two fingers inside her while his mouth went to work. A spiraling started deep inside her and she shoved the sensation back, not ready. Not nearly ready to break.

Chuckling against her mound, his fingers started to play. "Stubborn little demon destroyer, aren't you?"

Hell yes. A smart retort sprang to her brain, but her mouth would only emit a tiny gasp of need. Then he found that hidden bundle of nerves inside her, and her mouth snapped shut.

Every muscle in her body tightened in anticipation.

His lips enclosed her clit and he sucked. His fingers stretched her until nearly the point of pain.

And it wasn't enough. Not nearly enough.

The orgasm started to roll through her. She shoved it back again . . . not wanting to stop. She never wanted this to stop.

Her heart roared between her ears, and sweat slicked her body. He was killing her. His teeth scraped along her clit. Her thighs began to tremble in earnest.

"Kane." The man had a wicked hot mouth.

"Now, Amber." His heated lips clamped down on her clit just as he shoved a third finger inside her.

She broke with a sharp cry, her body stiffening, the world stopping. The room sheeted white as waves of intense pleasure pummeled through her body. The orgasm went on for what seemed like minutes, and all she could do was ride it out.

The powerful spasms finally ended, and she sank back to the bed with a soft sigh. The orgasm was spectacular, yet her body still hungered. She needed to be filled.

An arm beneath her thighs and one under her back flipped her over onto her hands and knees. She gasped, her hands clutching the bedspread as she tried to balance herself. Her core was wet and ready for him.

Hot, strong hands gripped her hips.

Coarse leg hair caressed the back of her thighs.

She stiffened, her body going on full alert.

He slammed into her, the force strong enough to send the bed crashing into the wall.

Her eyes opened wide in shock and her nails dug into the sheet. Pleasure ripped into every nerve she owned. Arching her back, she took more of him.

He filled her completely, the hard ridges of his cock stretching muscles already primed from her climax.

"Kane." She whispered his name, needing to hear it out loud. Needing to acknowledge what was happening.

His hold tightened, and he began to pound. Harder,

faster, deeper than ever before, he hammered into her. His fingers bit into her flesh, and even the hard muscles of his thighs bruised her tender skin.

And yet, she wanted more. Needed more. "Harder."

He pressed down between her shoulder blades, shoving her chest against the bed and her face against the pillows. The bed beat rhythmically against the wall. His knees nudged her thighs farther apart.

She couldn't move if she wanted to.

This was beyond sex, beyond claiming . . . it was a true branding. She hadn't realized the difference until now.

He held her completely at his mercy.

At the thought, energy coiled deep inside her. A glimpse of ecstasy.

His palm slapped down on her tailbone, a heated burn making her cry out in startled pain. Oh God. The *marking*.

The world exploded. A white-hot release pulsed through her in devastating waves of climax. She screamed his name, her body shuddering through the release. She rode the fine edge between pleasure and pain for what seemed like an eternity. Finally, she came down, gasping for breath.

Still, he pounded.

His grip tightened, his thrusts increasing in power. His much larger body angled over hers. Sharp fangs pierced her neck.

With a low growl, he came.

Her entire body relaxed, save for the fiery ache of her lower back.

His fangs retracted, and he licked the wound.

The mating was complete.

CHAPTER 28

He'd never make it back to Kurjan headquarters in time. Kalin leaned against the side of the barn, stretching his legs over the hay. The kill had taken longer than he'd expected, and he'd missed his window to run home in darkness. But what a kill it was. The woman had fought well for a human—and she'd tasted like blueberries. He'd rather have found a witch, but sometimes things just didn't go his way.

As usual, his victim had been a petite blue-eyed brunette. He didn't need a shrink to draw a connection to Janie Kayrs.

Stretching his neck, he finished licking blood off his fingers.

Appeased for the moment, the beast within him relaxed into slumber. Finally. He'd been pissed off since losing the older demon destroyer.

The damn demons.

The bastards had somehow traced his call and taken the demon destroyer from the wolf compound. Of course, the idiots had allowed the Kayrs family to retake the old broad from their temporary location. His enemies were truly morons.

He scooted away from the outside wall as the sun slowly

rose in the sky. Someday he'd stand in the sun. But not today.

Once again his nights were free so he could hunt. Years ago he'd led a group of werewolves, true beasts who loved to kill, and somehow had found an odd relief dealing with them.

He actually missed the monsters.

The Kurjans had created Virus-27 without knowing the full potential of the bug. The virus had turned many of the shifters into hairy werewolves before Kane Kayrs had created a cure.

Kane Kayrs. Supposedly the smartest man on the planet. Kalin would bet his left arm the Kurjan scientists were smarter. They had created the virus, after all. Even after all this time, the vampires hadn't figured out the true purpose of the disease.

Why did all important matters take so much damn time?

Shutting his eyes, Kalin searched for calm. He slipped into a dream world, not very surprised to find himself walking in a tree-filled park. He'd known Janie would call at some point.

The grass was short and green, while the sun poured down with a gentle touch. He lifted his face with a hum of appreciation. Birds squawked in the distance, while a gardenia-scented breeze rippled over his skin.

"I tried to make the sun as realistic as I could," Janie said, her voice melodious in the dream world.

He turned to the side, finding her perched on the back of a wooden bench, her feet resting on the seat. White tennis shoes covered what had to be size four feet. "Are your feet that small in real life?"

She glanced down and shrugged. "Sure. You met me in person . . . don't you remember?"

Of course he remembered. He'd saved her life by throwing his knife into the eye of a werewolf who would've killed her. "Yes. You owe me."

"Not really. You attacked my home in the effort to kill my dad." *Fire flashed in her pretty blue eyes.* "I'd say we're even."

There probably wasn't a reason to inform her he still planned to kill Talen Kayrs. "All right." *As he studied her, he realized the woman from the night before didn't come close to Janie's beauty. Curly brown hair fell to Janie's slim shoulders. Pale skin, smooth as alabaster, covered her fine features. Her body was tight, her breasts high, her movements graceful. But it was the deep blue of her intelligent eyes that haunted his dreams. In all his hunts, no woman had ever come close.*

Janie swung one jean-clad leg back and forth. "I need a favor."

Interest sizzled through his veins. "Go on."

"While you greatly disappointed me by not finding the location of my Uncle Jase, I know you have connections in the demon world."

Sure. The same bastards who had set up him so neatly before. He faked a confident smile. "Yes, I do."

Her pretty face paled even more. "I need you to find out if he's dead or not."

The woman's pain was palpable. Kalin had the oddest urge to stroke her shoulder. Shaking his head, he shuffled his boots. He was the leader of the Kurjan military, for God's sake. "What's in it for me?"

"How about you just do the right thing for an old friend?" *she asked soberly.*

He winced. "I don't work that way, Janet. I want something else."

She took a deep breath. "What do you want?"

Now that was a loaded question. "How old are you now?"

"Almost twenty-one." *She tilted her head to the side.* "Why?"

Just how far would she go for her precious uncle? Kalin moved before she could react, grabbing her by the waist to stand on the bench. For once, they stood eye-to-eye.

She stopped breathing, her gaze on his.

For once, he was glad his green eyes were nearly human. "I want a kiss."

Surprise opened her mouth in a small O. "You can't be serious."

He was deadly serious. Sure, they were enemies. Someday she'd hate him. But she was also right that she was the only friend he'd ever had. He wanted one kiss given willingly before all hell broke loose. "Just one."

While he usually saw fear in a woman's eyes, he could swear curiosity filled Janie's. She truly wasn't afraid of him. Yet.

Her gaze dropped to his lips. "Let me get this straight. I kiss you, and you contact the demons to find out if Jase is really dead or not."

"That's the deal." Now he held his breath.

"Okay," she whispered. Sliding her hands up to his shoulders, she leaned in and pressed her soft lips against his.

Electricity shot down his spine.

Her mouth was tentative and much warmer than his. She tilted her head to the side, opening slightly.

He reacted instantly, grabbing her hips and yanking her closer. Plunging his tongue in her mouth, he took. She tasted like honey and heaven, a mixture he'd never even imagined.

She began to struggle, and his fangs dropped low. One nicked her.

The first drop of her blood ignited a hunger beyond belief.

She sank her teeth into his bottom lip, drawing his blood.

Shock made him step back. They both breathed heavily, staring at each other. She wiped blood off her lips.

He licked his.

A low growl rumbled up from his chest. Her blood was the sweetest thing he'd ever tasted—probably tasted like pure sunshine.

She took a deep breath. "Happy now?" Her eyes were wide, her hair mussed, her cheeks pink.

"Not even close," he said honestly. "I've always known some-day I'd have you, but I'd never realized how very much I'd truly want you." The woman had bitten him. Really bitten him. Mating her would make her immortal—his for eternity. "Prepare yourself because I'm coming for you soon."

Sadness and wisdom filtered through her amazing eyes. "I'd give myself to you in a heartbeat if you'd choose the right path."

He shook his head, his long black hair flying. The woman didn't know what she was saying. "Your path isn't the right one, Janet Isabella. Only one species can rule the earth, and it's my time."

"You'll rule with death and fear." She shook her head, her shoulders straightening.

"Of course." Something told him deep down he'd never kill her. Not like those other women.

She jumped from the bench, her tiny shoes not even sending up dust as she landed. "I'll expect the information from you shortly." Turning on her heel, she walked leisurely down the path toward the edge of the park, her perfect ass swaying in the tight jeans.

He smiled. The woman had guts. What an excellent battle it would be.

"My Janet."

Janie sat up in the bed and swallowed several times to keep from throwing up. She had Kalin's blood. While she didn't know how it worked yet, she knew getting his blood would give her a power over him. One she'd need someday.

Of course, she hadn't planned on his taking her blood. Damn it.

Now both Zane and Kalin had her blood. While they could all work together to end the war, neither man seemed interested. They both had their stubborn plans, and her destiny was to thwart those.

Life truly wasn't fair.

Not for a second did she trust Kalin would discover the truth about Jase. She'd just needed the Kurjan's blood.

It had been so much easier to get that blood than she'd thought it would be.

Her stomach ached when she thought about her Uncle Jase. She'd heard about the video from her father, and his face had been shadowed with pain as he'd prepared her for the worst. Uncle Jase might be gone for good.

For now, she needed to clear her head.

Swinging her legs over the bed, she yanked on sweats. Hustling into the bathroom, she brushed her teeth and washed her face.

Energy still sizzled through her veins from trying to trick Kalin. She definitely needed to go for a run.

The smell of pancakes tempted her as she headed for the door. Poking her head in the kitchen, she found a slice of peace at the sight of her father flipping chocolate chip pancakes. He wore black combat clothes and flak boots with a pink apron tied around his waist.

"Sit and eat," he said, turning around.

He was still the biggest man she'd ever seen. Broad across the shoulders, he had fierce features and hands bigger than dinner plates. She adored him for the hero he was. He'd saved her from monsters when she was four years old and had given her a safe home since. The world had instantly become safer the second Talen became her father.

She slid into a chair at the large table and reached for a plate. "Why are you cooking?"

"I miss your mother." He tossed the apron to the sink, sat, and passed the syrup, his golden eyes dark. "She always makes pancakes on Sunday."

"Today is Tuesday."

"I don't care. I want it to be Sunday—and I want them to come home." A dark frown settled over his broad face.

"Mom and Garrett will be home next week." Janie took a big bite and closed her eyes as the chocolate warmed her throat. Her dad always put in twice the amount of chips than her mother did. "These are awesome."

"I'm a good cook—almost as good as my mate." Talen took a bite.

Janie chuckled. "Some of the shifters think you sound possessive and archaic every time you call Mom your 'mate.' "

He swallowed his food, his eyes thoughtful. "I guess I was so happy to find her, and so proud to make her my mate, I say it to make myself happy." He grinned. "And to remind her every chance I get that she's mine."

Okay, that was possessive and sweet. Would Janie ever find somebody who loved her that much? Would Zane ever love her? "You're one of a kind, Dad."

"Thanks, sweetheart." Then Talen frowned, studying Janie's face. "What happened to your lip?"

She coughed and wiped her mouth on a napkin. "I bit myself when I was training yesterday." The lie heated something in her stomach, probably guilt. But her father couldn't know she'd just kissed a Kurjan in her dream. Talk about explosions.

Concern wrinkled his prominent brow. "You should put some ice on it after breakfast."

"Okay." Then Janie sat back and studied her dad. "You didn't sleep last night again."

He sighed, tossing his napkin on his half-eaten pancakes. "I kept seeing that video with Jase."

Janie nodded, pain catching her heart. "I haven't had a vision regarding him, but I'm still hopeful the video was a trick."

Talen rubbed both hands through his hair. "I hope so, too. We usually rely on Kane for logic, but he's definitely off his game, so I'm just not sure."

Janie shrugged. "Kane's confused about everything right now—give him a break."

"What's there to be confused about?" Talen growled. "He met his mate, the mark appeared on his hand, and now he needs to follow his path. Why does he have to think everything to death?"

"Because he's Kane," Janie said gently. "He blames himself for failing to find Jase, and he doesn't trust his feelings about Amber. He's fighting himself and his feelings."

"I don't see why."

"He's not you. Give the guy a break—you're his older brother. Be on his side." Janie shook her head. Uncle Kane and her dad couldn't be more different, but they needed each other now more than ever. "I haven't had a vision dealing with Jase in the future for some time, and Kane could be right. If Jase really wants to die, he'll figure out a way. Kane is going to need you." Heat filled her head as she said the words . . . if Jase truly died, her heart would break. She'd adored her uncle from day one.

Talen smiled, the dark circles under his eyes standing out. "What are you up to, Janet Isabella?"

Sometimes she forgot her father was a genius, too. "Nothing. Geez."

He lifted an eyebrow and gave his stern look. The worry marks under his eyes detracted slightly from the menace. "Are you dating another shifter?"

For goodness' sake. Like she had time to date between manipulating Zane and Kalin as she tried to end the war. "No. I'm not dating anybody right now, Dad. But I promise, you'll be the first one I tell when I find someone to date. Not." She snorted.

Talen huffed out a strong breath. "You're too young to date."

Three hundred years old would be too young for her to date so long as her dad was concerned. She shook her head. "Stop worrying about me and go help Kane. He needs it."

Talen smiled. "When did you get so smart?"

"I've always been smart." She forced a smile, biting back a wince as her damaged lip protested.

"Good. Smart girls get to do the dishes."

CHAPTER 29

Kane finished his run on the treadmill, sweat pouring down his back. He'd tossed his shirt across the room about an hour into the run. Two hours later, and still his mind remained muddled.

He'd left Amber sleeping peacefully in his bed, looking like an angel. A sexy-as-hell angel. He'd mated her. The moment had cemented itself securely in his soul. Hell, the woman was in his heart.

What was he going to do with her?

Heavy boots clomped down the hall, and Talen stepped inside the gym.

He sniffed the air and straightened, gaze serious on Kane. "You mated her."

Kane jumped off the treadmill. "Yes."

"Why?"

Irritation pricked the back of Kane's neck. "Excuse me?"

Talen settled his stance. "Why did you mate her?"

"What the fuck is that supposed to mean?" While Kane didn't need to resort to violence, he had no problem employing it.

A smirk lifted Talen's lips. "I believe I used one-syllable words. Being such a genius, surely you can answer the very simple question of why you mated Amber Freebird."

Kane lunged. Against all rational thought, he tackled his brother, sending them both sprawling across the mats.

They landed with a sonic boom.

Talen tossed him off and jumped to his feet.

Kane anchored himself with his shoulders and leapt to stand. If he knew his brother, Talen would be swinging all-out soon.

Instead, golden eyes narrowed in sympathy. "Listen, we really don't have time for you to have some sort of emotional upheaval. If my kicking the crap out of you will help, I'm happy to oblige. But if not, what the hell's going on?"

"I'd kick the crap out of you." Truth be told, they were evenly matched. While Talen fought with heat, Kane countered with cold. It'd be a good battle.

"Uh-huh." Talen scratched his massive head. "Let's look at this logically so you understand the situation. I'm sure you told yourself you needed to mate Amber to gain her abilities, and so she could gain yours."

Kane frowned. "Exactly."

"And, now that the mating is a done deal, deep down you feel unsettled."

"Exactly." Thank God somebody understood. Kane studied his brother with a new understanding.

Talen shook his head. "She's not yours, Kane."

Fire bubbled up his throat. "I *mated* her. She wears *my* mark. Of course she's mine."

"You dipshit." Talen flashed a rare smile. "The woman isn't yours until she says she's yours. And *that* woman—she isn't going to say the words until you give her everything. Tell her you love her."

"Love doesn't exist." His voice sounded weak even to his ears.

"Why? Because you can't see it? Can't measure love under a microscope?"

"Yes."

Talen drew in a deep breath. "You're my brother and I'd die for you. In a second and without giving a thought. You know that, right?"

"Yes." Man, was Talen going to kill him?

"How do you know that?"

Kane's frown hurt his head. "I just do."

"Loyalty, brotherhood, and love. Three things you're absolutely sure about, and you can't see or examine any of them." Talen cracked his neck, keeping his gaze on Kane. "Yet you believe."

Kane blew out a breath. There was definite logic in the statement. "Okay. I'll think about it."

"Now that's a fucking shock."

Kane gave his brother a look. They had more important things to deal with than his newfound emotional distress. "I'm going to need your help with Dage."

Talen sighed, anger filling his eyes. "Jase is not dead."

"If he wants to be dead, he's dead." Kane wouldn't truly believe the horrific fact until he saw Jase's body. "We both saw him go for the sharp rock. Frankly, it's amazing Jase lasted this long being tortured by demons."

"He's tough." Talen stepped back, as if fleeing the truth.

"Nobody's that tough." Kane hated the words as they left his mouth, but he needed at least one of his brothers prepared. "It makes absolutely no sense for the demons to let that video loose—they want us to know it's almost over."

"They didn't let the video loose—we intercepted the transmission." Rage and denial flashed hard and bright across Talen's face.

"You don't believe that any more than I do."

Talen's huge hands clenched into fists. "I have to believe he's alive and we'll get to him in time."

"Fair enough. But if we find out otherwise, I'll need

your help with Dage." The king would blame himself, and Kane would need more than logic to help him. The Realm couldn't afford for its leader to spiral down into guilt and depression.

"You've got it." Talen's sigh held both sorrow and determination. "We should have a location on Hilde Freebird soon."

"When we go after her, I'm not sure about bringing Amber." Kane braced himself for Talen's displeasure.

"I wouldn't bring her, either." Talen scratched his chin. Kane started. "But we need her."

"She's your mate. You want her to stay here and stay safe, that's your call," Talen said mildly. "You should already know that."

Logically, he did know that fact. "I'm confused."

Talen clapped him on the back. Hard. "Welcome to the fucking club."

Amber stretched her neck to check out the intricate marking on her lower back, her butt to the mirror. She'd dragged the full-length antique out of the bathroom and into the bedroom after taking a quick shower. "I have a tramp stamp," she muttered. Though, the raised K in the middle of a Celtic knot did look kind of cool.

The brand still burned.

She slid her fingers along the fine lines, wincing as the tender skin protested. Yep. He'd marked her but good.

What in the world had she been thinking to allow such a thing? Sure, with the virus, she didn't have to be tied to Kane forever. But maybe the virus was deadly. Being tied to Kane had to be better than being dead, right?

She smiled. He wouldn't like that line of thinking. Not that she cared what he thought.

Except she did.

She cared what he thought a lot. Her heart had been

more involved than even her body in the marking. What if he couldn't love? Could she love him enough for them both?

Probably not. Besides. She deserved love, damn it. She deserved to be the most important person in the world to somebody. To a man. To the man who held her heart.

She shook her damp hair.

The vampire was her exact opposite and the last person she would've chosen to fall in love with. He ate meat, for goodness' sake. And the guy probably sacrificed animals on a daily basis in the name of research. Well, even if he didn't sacrifice animals, he would do so to cure Virus-27.

Of course, the virus was now a threat to her as well as to the other mates.

Mates.

She was a mate. The thought brought both irritation and an odd warming in her abdomen.

How soon would she have Kane's abilities? He attacked with emotion, sending some kind of waves. Could she attack with the waves? She approached life so differently from Kane . . . maybe she wouldn't ever be able to attack.

Where was her grandmother? How dare she put herself in danger on purpose?

The door slid open and all six-plus feet of Kane Kayrs sidled inside.

He was sweaty.

Amber's heart thumped hard.

The vampire was naked to the waist, the strong muscles of his chest glistening. She swallowed. "You look like a romance novel cover."

He barked a surprised laugh, dark gaze wandering over her nude body. "You look like my greatest fantasy coming to life."

Now wasn't that sweet?

Graceful steps forward and he brushed his fingers over the marking. "Beautiful," he murmured, his voice hoarse.

Tendrils of instant need peaked her nipples and softened her sex. She took a step away from him, reaching for a silk robe he'd left for her earlier. Being naked around Kane was dangerous. She angled the mirror toward him, craning her neck to see.

He frowned. "What are you doing?"

"Nothing." Yep. He had a reflection.

Amusement curved his lip. "Stop believing silly legends."

How the heck was she supposed to know? "Okay. So, what have you found out?"

"Nothing yet. We need to talk. Why don't you go scout out breakfast in the kitchen while I take a quick shower?" He disappeared behind the bathroom door.

Why in the world did he make an order sound like a request? She knew a freakin' order when she heard one.

Shaking off irritation, she padded barefoot through the rooms to the small kitchen. The appliances were top-notch, the counters granite, but the lack of a window made her shoulders twitch. She needed to get outside soon.

A round kitchen table sat to the side with bright yellow cushions. She'd bet every cent she owned that somebody else had chosen the cushions.

Opening the refrigerator, warmth flushed through her. He'd stocked up on organic tofu, nuts, and vegetables. Sometimes the hard-assed vampire could be such a sweetheart.

Maybe they could figure out a way to live together.

She frowned. Not without love.

Grabbing all the necessities, she had tofu omelets almost ready when he stalked into the kitchen.

The vampire wore loose sweats, his feet bare, his chest

broad. Wet black hair curled at his nape, and his eyes had morphed to a dark violet bordering on black. His harsh features seemed even stronger than usual.

Her mouth went dry.

He glanced at the pan. "Yum." The deep tenor of his voice lacked enthusiasm.

She grinned. "Sit down. You'll love properly prepared tofu, I promise."

"Uh-huh." He slid gracefully into a chair, hunger on his face. But he wasn't looking at the food.

Her hands shaking just enough to annoy her, she dished up two plates and carried them to the table. Then she grabbed the organic orange juice from the fridge and poured two glasses.

"Thanks for breakfast," Kane said, his gaze on the tofu.

"Anytime. Stop staring and try your breakfast."

He took a deep breath and then ate a small bite. "Hmm." Eyebrows raising, he took another bite and then frowned. "This is good."

"See? Tofu takes on the taste of anything else you cook with it, and I use a lot of spices." She unfolded her napkin. Maybe she should replace all the eggs in headquarters with tofu. "You don't know everything in the world, Kane."

"Okay." He dug in. They ate in silence for a while. Finally, he cleared his plate. "That was good. But I'm still going to eat meat."

They'd see about that. "To each his own." She finished half her plate, her stomach full. "What do we need to talk about?"

"Demons, your grandmother, and eternity." Kane sat back, his gaze thoughtful.

She coughed on her orange juice, quickly swallowing. "That's quite a list."

He smiled, but his eyes remained focused. "I know."

There should be a law about vampires having to wear shirts when talking about important matters. The hard lines of his very impressive chest kept distracting her from reality. Maybe that had been his intention.

She set down her glass. "Demons and my grandmother first."

"Okay. We're going to reactivate the tracker embedded in her foot soon, and then we'll have to go quickly."

"I'll be ready."

"I don't think you should go."

That was incredibly sweet. She shoved back from the table, the chair squeaking on the hard stone floor. "We mated so I could learn to attack."

"Sometimes it takes years for mates to share a gift. Believe me, you're no stronger today than yesterday." He shook his head.

"Neither are you, then."

"True."

"So together we can use our skills and help save my grandmother, and maybe your brother." She wouldn't believe Jase was gone until she saw proof. There were too many uncertainties in war. "Besides, I'm the best shield you have against demons. You need me."

"I do need you." His eyes darkened.

Was he talking about just with the demons? Or was it something deeper?

He crossed corded arms. "The last two times you attacked demons, you nearly passed out."

Logic was the only way to deal with this particular stubborn male. "You're being an ass."

"Maybe." He shrugged, apparently unconcerned.

Logic, damn it. Logic. "I can shield myself, and if I remember correctly, I can help shield you. Maybe if I shield you, you'll be able to attack and protect us and your brothers. If you're attacking, the demons will concentrate on defense and not on making the brains of your brothers bleed."

Kane's nostrils flared. "That's quite an image you created."

"I find visuals help in arguments." Man, now she was starting to talk like the guy.

He shook his head. "I can't be worrying about you while also trying to keep Dage from going crazy."

Dage? The breath swooshed out of Amber's lungs. "You really do think Jase will figure out a way to die."

"I really do," Kane said softly, the words full of pain. "And it's my job to help my brothers deal with that fact and get out of demon headquarters in one piece while saving your granny."

She studied him, reality smacking her hard in the face. He didn't want to believe Jase was going to kill himself— Kane held as much hope as the rest of them. But as usual, he was trying to be the voice of reason and prepare everyone. "Who covers your back, Kane? Who protects you?" Her heart warmed for the man.

He shrugged. "I'm not emotional and don't need protection."

But he was, and he did. "Let me help shield you and find my grandmother. She's my grandmother, and I have to be there. I just know I have to be there."

He gazed at her, no expression on his face.

Logic wasn't really working. She'd go over his head to the king, but Dage would probably follow Kane's advice, especially since Amber and Kane had mated. "I know you don't trust fate or intuition, but I do. And I need to be a part of the rescue for my grandmother. It's my risk and my chance."

He blinked and rubbed both hands down his face. "I don't know."

Three words the scientist probably hadn't muttered very often in his long life.

Amber sighed. "I do know. You're going to have to trust me at some point, Kane—no matter what happens between us."

His hands dropped to his lap. Calculation entered his gaze. "Okay. We strike a deal. You're my mate, Amber. I let you go into danger against every logical reason I have, and you give us a hundred years as mates."

Surprise shot her shoulders back. "You want a formal contract regarding our relationship?"

"Yes."

What an ass. Temper nearly had steam shooting from her ears. Plus, the thought spiraled through her brain that Kane had always planned to take her on the mission. This was just manipulation. "So, does this contract of yours detail how many times a day I seek your advice? How many times a year we have dinner together? How many times in a century we fuck like jackalopes?"

He huffed out a chuckle. "I told you, there are no jackalopes. And no, all I want you to agree to is to spend the next century living with me as mates. The rest of your list is totally up to you."

A hundred years in exchange for him allowing her to do something she had every right to do anyway. Even so, what was a century compared to her grandmother's life? Amber knew, deep down, she had to be on the raid to rescue Hilde. "It's a deal with one caveat."

"Just one?" One dark eyebrow rose.

"Yes. You can release me from the hundred years at any time. The second you do, I have the choice whether to go or stay." The man had no idea of what she'd do for freedom. He'd want her gone within a month.

He sighed. "Amber, I need to concentrate on curing the virus after we get your grandmother back. The last thing

I'll have time for is you playing a bunch of silly games so I let you go."

"Take the deal, Kane."

"Fine. Just so long as you understand that I'll handle immature behavior as I see fit."

She frowned. "Meaning what?"

"You act like a brat, and I'll treat you like a brat."

Oh, the vampire had no idea who he was messing with. She held out her hand. "It's a deal."

His hand enveloped her in a warm, firm grip. "Deal."

A smile flashed to her lips, and she couldn't help the challenging curve.

Someone knocked on the door.

Kane froze. Releasing her, he stood. "Stay here."

Not in a million years. She followed his long strides through the living area to the door.

The king stood on the other side, his face blank, his eyes a burning blue. "We reactivated Hilde's tracker—she's on her way to Scotland. We should have her final location within a few hours, and then we'll go."

Kane's shoulders straightened as if he were bracing himself. "And?"

"We intercepted a second video. The demons cut off Jase's head—he's dead."

CHAPTER 30

Amber cleaned up the breakfast dishes, her heart hurting, her mind spinning. Kane had left with the king to create battle plans without saying another word.

The rage and pain in his eyes would haunt her forever.

Everything that happened to his family, to his people, wasn't his fault just because he was so smart. Why did he have to take all the responsibility on himself?

She wanted to help him. Truth be told, she wanted to soothe him.

Worst truth? She loved him. Had since he'd rescued her on the side of a wintery road.

Why couldn't he love her back?

Maybe he did and just didn't know it.

She snorted. That kind of thinking belonged in junior high. Yet still . . .

After cleaning the kitchen, she went through the already tidy quarters and tidied up some more. Finally, she made the bed—not that they'd slept much. Her heart beat faster as she straightened the heavy down comforter into smooth lines. The dark gray color was somehow sexy. Or maybe what had happened on the bed made the bedspread look sexy.

Her marking began to burn.

"We go in an hour," Kane said from the doorway.

She yelped, her heart racing as she whirled toward him. "I didn't hear you come in."

"I'm quiet that way." His smile didn't come close to being genuine.

"I'm so sorry about Jase." Tears filled her eyes, and she tried to blink them back.

"Me, too." Kane sat on the bed, still wearing his loose sweats and no shirt. "I really wanted to be wrong—but I saw the video. He sure looked dead."

Kane's pain made the air heavier.

Going on instinct, she moved between his knees, cradling his head to her chest. "Maybe the video is wrong."

"That's what Talen said." Kane sighed, relaxing, his breath warming her skin. "I'm not sure. I watched it three times just to make sure . . . until I couldn't watch it again."

"Tell me what happened."

His shoulders stiffened. "Jase was in the cell, on the ground, and Suri plunged a knife into his neck. Then he twisted."

Okay, there wasn't a decent way to ask the next question. "Did you see . . . um . . ."

"No. I didn't see Jase's head roll free."

"So there's hope."

"God, I don't think so. But maybe." Kane's lips wandered along her flesh.

Desire slid through her veins like warm silk. She swallowed, trying to force it away. Now wasn't the time for sex.

Kane lifted his head, dark eyes full of need. "When we go after your grandmother, some of us may not be coming back. If anything happens to me, you listen to Talen. He's promised to get you to safety."

"You think you're not coming back?" she asked softly, tangling both hands in Kane's thick hair.

He shrugged. "I'll do my best."

Holding him, she leaned down and pressed a gentle kiss to his straight nose. "I'll make sure you survive, Kane."

His rueful grin seemed more natural. "It's my job to protect you, mate."

A logical man shouldn't be so old-fashioned. "I think it goes both ways these days, vampire."

"Not to my people, sweetheart." His hands slid over the silk robe to cup her ass. "No matter how much we plan, how prepared we make ourselves, things go wrong in battle. The demons are waiting for us, and they'll be prepared."

His palms burned through the thin material. She shifted her weight, trying to concentrate on his words and not her need. "I know."

His hands moved to the tie of the robe. Drawing the material apart, he studied her, eyes flaring. "You are incredibly beautiful." The reverence in his voice humbled her. Gently, he pressed a kiss to her abdomen.

Her knees trembled. "Um, I'm not sure—" Then she yelped as the room spun and she ended up flat on her back.

"I'm sure." Kane kissed his way up her torso, nipping and licking in between kisses. The bed groaned in protest. "We're heading into hell. Right now, I want a slice of heaven before we go."

His knee forced hers apart, and she arched against him. For a scientist, the man often sounded like a poet. "You have a romantic nature, you know."

"Right." He nipped the underside of her jaw.

She gasped, stretching up into his hard body. "Trust me."

"I do." His large hand flattened against her abdomen, moving frustratingly slow toward where she burned.

She closed her eyes, sliding into desire. The man needed to stop thinking, to stop hurting, to stop worrying about everybody else. For this moment in time, she could comfort him. She could help him escape, if only for a little while.

She tilted into his exploring hands.

He grinned against her skin. "Will I find you wet for me?"

"Only one way to find out." She dug her nails into his shoulders, her breath panting out.

"Good point." One finger ran along her clit, sliding inside her. "Ah, very wet."

Wet and in serious need. Nerves flared in demand. "I don't want slow."

"Too bad." His tongue traced the shell of her ear. His other fingers rolled her nipple, pinching just enough to have her gasping for breath.

The man was intoxicating. Devastating. Addictive. No other man would ever come close.

Could passion have an owner? If so, he owned hers. She ran her hands down his broad back, reaching his tight ass. She sank her fingers into the hard muscles, grinning at his groan. Oh yeah. Two could play at torture.

This moment was hers. The man needed her. He needed to forget pain, war, and reality for a brief time. That she could help him with.

He lifted his head. A dangerous, wicked smile curved his lips and made her thighs tingle. He slid his finger free, his smile broadening at her whimper of protest. Then slowly, keeping her gaze captive, he slid his hand around her hip to tap on the marking.

Fire shot from the brand through her entire body. She cried out, biting her lip to keep from moaning.

His hand flattened out, his heated palm pressing against the brand.

Her eyes fluttered closed as raw need filled her in a

painful demand. His thigh pressed against her core. He plucked a nipple.

A climax bore down on her, so intense her eyelids snapped open to see the world in a haze. Uncaring of any decorum, she rode his thigh, tears pricking her eyes, sweat blooming across her chest. Shuddering violently, she came down, her body relaxing. Almost.

He planted a hard kiss on her lips. "You're sexy as hell. I very well may adore you." His forehead wrinkled as if he pondered a tough physics question.

Well, it was a start. "You're overdressed." Lifting her knees, she curled her toes in the waistband of his sweats and shoved down.

He chuckled and assisted her by shimmying out of the sweats.

An engorged, fully ready, pulsing erection instantly settled against her stomach.

She grinned. "Oh my."

"Indeed." He levered up on one elbow, leaning to the side and tracing gentle fingers up her torso. "Your skin is softer than petals."

"Poet." She reached for him, running her fingers along his shaft. "You're very well endowed."

He smirked. "You talk too much."

"Look who's talking."

Hard hands grabbed her hips and rolled them over until she straddled him. He put his arms behind his head. "You wanted to be in charge."

She might be on top, but by no means was she in charge. They both knew it. Even so, she relished the opportunity to drive him wild. No matter what happened, she'd make sure he never forgot her.

"You're looking awfully determined," he said.

"You have no idea."

"Show me," he whispered.

Taking him in her hand, she poised above him, slowly working him inside her body. Several times she had to stop and take a deep breath to accommodate his girth. Minutes later, she finally rested against him.

Sweat beaded his upper lip while a dark flush had crossed his hard cheekbones. Beneath her, his body vibrated with need.

She smiled. "How's that for determination?"

His lids half closed. "Watch how you play, little one. My control only goes so far."

"Is that a fact?" She flattened her palms against his pecs, leaning forward to take more of him. Control? The man was about to lose his. For a brief slice of time, she was yanking him out of his head.

He groaned, eyes darkening. "That's a fact."

"Hmm." She lifted her butt and slammed back down hard.

He stiffened, drawing air through clenched teeth. "Amber."

Ignoring the warning, she did it again.

Triumph rushed through her when his hands clamped on her hips. He lifted her, the muscles in his arms rippling with the effort. Then he yanked her down while thrusting up with his groin.

She gave a strangled cry. He filled her completely, almost too much so. Hard, pulsing, his cock laid claim to her internal walls, forcing them to clamp hard around him.

Ripples of raw need spiraled inside her.

He ground against her, nostrils flaring at her small moan.

Then he lifted her, surging inside her, forcing her to ride him with the rhythm he chose. One hand cupped her thigh, opening her wider so he could thrust even deeper. He was ruthless and dangerously skilled.

He went faster, his arms seeming tireless, forcing her to take all of him.

Need went beyond dare. She needed to come. Allowing her body to go lax, she let him set the rhythm, let him take what he wanted. With a low growl, he pinched her clit.

She broke with a cry of his name. The room disappeared, her mind shut down, and pleasure too intense to be real shot through her body in waves of excruciating ecstasy. He pumped harder, prolonging her orgasm until she couldn't breathe. Finally, as she came down, he paused.

Panting for air, she shoved her wild hair out of her eyes. Every breath caused little ripples to shoot through her core.

She felt . . . *claimed*.

Realization came back with a slap. He was still inside her, impossibly hard.

And he'd waited for her to realize that fact.

Her eyes widened.

His narrowed.

Quicker than a thought, he rolled them over, remaining inside her. Both arms slid against the back of her thighs, shoving her legs up and opening her to him.

Then he started to pound.

Hard, fast, completely out of control.

She gripped the comforter to keep her head from smacking against the headboard.

He thrust harder.

Faster.

A spiraling started deep inside her, catching her breath. Her eyes widened. It wasn't possible.

He angled higher.

She arched with a silent cry, her body shooting into a climax so powerful she forgot how to think. The waves ripped through her, relentless in their intensity.

His mouth found her neck, his fangs dropping deep.

With a low growl, he ground against her, his body tightening as he came.

Their bodies relaxed as one, slowly sinking back to reality.

He licked the wound and placed a soft kiss against her jugular before raising up.

She gasped for air, smoothing his hair away from his face. "I love you, Kane. No matter what happens later, I need you to know that. I do love you."

He blinked twice, surprise filling his eyes. Then he opened his mouth.

"No." She pressed a finger to his heated lips. The last thing she needed was a half-assed attempt to make her feel better. She was getting to know him, and he didn't believe in love. Yet. "Sometimes no words are better than the wrong ones."

Puzzlement filled his frown. He shook his head and tried to speak again.

A phone buzzed from the nightstand.

Surprise lifted his eyebrows.

Yeah. She'd made him forget the bad stuff for a short while. Triumph heated through her.

Keeping his cock inside her, his gaze on her, Kane reached for the phone. "What?"

He listened and then hung up. "We leave in thirty minutes."

CHAPTER 31

Kane stretched his neck, cataloging the weapons worn by the large raiding party. Oscar had been ordered to the other helicopter just in case he got it into his head to hit Dage again. While Kane hadn't blamed him, they didn't have time for another fight.

Kane had gotten some sleep on the flight across the ocean and made sure Amber was rested.

She loved him.

While that made it easier for him to keep her as a mate, he doubted his liking her was enough. The idea of her leaving him after the century made his gut ache with an intensity that surprised him.

Was that what love felt like?

Love was supposed to be all silly flowers and dancing tulips.

Not a deep, gut-wrenching ball of pain.

He frowned. Without question, he had been caught up in the moment earlier and would've returned Amber's words if the phone hadn't disturbed them. Feelings were foreign to him—by his choice and his design. Yet he was going to have to tap into them to figure out what the hell was going on with him. After they found Jase.

Across the wide helicopter, Moira Dunne Kayrs studied him with her light green eyes. While he'd missed the little witch, her frown made him feel worse. The witch could often read people, and she was seriously reading him right now.

He growled at his brother. "Make your mate stop frowning at me."

Conn's frown beat Moira's—hands-down. "Last time I made her do something, she burned my eyelashes off. You make her stop frowning." He cocked a gun and shoved it in Moira's vest.

She protested. "I don't need another gun."

Conn tugged one of her red curls. "Yes, you do. Take the gun, *Dailtín*."

Kane settled back, used to Conn's Gaelic term of endearment for Moira. *Brat*.

The witch rolled her eyes but left the gun in place. She smiled at Amber. "We have a support group."

Amber started before frowning in puzzlement. "A support group?"

"Aye. For mates of the Kayrs brothers. We get together and lament our lot in life." Moira's smile brightened her pale face. The little witch had always been a beauty.

Amber chuckled. "I'll join as soon as I get home."

"Ah, Amber, you're already in. Believe me, I understand." Moira shoved an elbow into Conn's gut. "I totally understand."

Conn frowned. "We're not that bad."

"Yes, we are," Talen countered with a broad shrug. "But my mate says we're worth it."

"Usually," Moira muttered.

Kane allowed the banter to flow around him, knowing everyone was trying to keep from thinking about the battle to come. But they had ten minutes until touch down, and it was time to focus. Seven other helicopters flew in formation around them, all filled with soldiers ready to kill. The vampires had brought four 'copters with them to Ireland, while the witches had sent four of their own.

Conn smiled at Amber. "Thank you for coming along—rumor has it you can actually counter the demon mind attack."

She nodded.

Moira shook her head. "That's absolutely amazing. I've heard rumors about your people, but I never thought to actually meet a demon destroyer. The playing field is finally level with you here."

Kane cleared his throat. The statement rang true. Amber's gift finally gave them a chance to fight the demons with their strength intact. "Talen? Please go over the plan one more time." His older brother was the strategic leader for the Realm and always created their plans. His current plan was both daring and destructive.

Talen nodded, pressing a button on his ear communicator so the other helicopters could listen in. "We're going with plan A since the demons haven't sent any planes to intercept us. Hilde Freebird's tracking device is active, and she's there. Make no mistake, they'll be waiting with armed forces ready to go. They'll employ mind games right off the bat."

Kane swallowed, tightening his hold on Amber. She'd need to shield immediately. The woman nodded slowly, understanding his silent command. Smart girl.

Talen continued, "Forces three and four will blow all buildings, while forces one and two will instantly infiltrate. We're not looking for prisoners—aim to kill. Decapitate quickly. If there are children or female demons, try to render them unconscious before securing them in a location we'll determine once on the ground." He paused, his fingers ticking off points as he made them. "Female demons are few and far between, but if we find any, they're masters at mind attacks. You'll need to knock them out immediately. Kill if necessary, but try to avoid doing so if possible."

Kane nodded shortly. The idea of killing a woman, even a demon, didn't sit well with any of them.

Talen shrugged his vest into place. He nodded to Kane. "Primary objective for forces one and two is to find and free Hilde Freebird, as well as locating Jase Kayrs. The remaining forces will protect the perimeter."

Kane leaned back against the metal side, forcing calm into his muscles. Chances were incredibly slim that Jase was alive—just because the tape stopped before Suri shoved his head free didn't mean that Suri had also stopped. They'd find Jase and bury him at home. Damn demons. Kane eyed Dage as his hands worked furiously over the controls, flying the aircraft. The king hadn't spoken much, his jaw set, his eyes hard since showing the brothers the video of Jase being decapitated.

Talen had argued that the video could've been doctored, but there hadn't been time to study it before they needed to head to Scotland. Kane had wanted to agree, but giving his brothers false hope wasn't a good idea.

Though, deep down, a small kernel of hope lived in his gut. *Please, God, let Jase still be alive.*

The idea of God never bothered him and just made sense. Sure, Kane was a man of science, but you couldn't create something out of nothing. A Creator was logical.

Maybe love existed, too.

His mate's scent of wild heather wrapped around his head, around his heart. He leaned to whisper in her ear. "You stay behind me at all times and keep your shields up. Now isn't the time to work on attacking demons. I need you strong and your mind clear."

Irritation flashed in her dark eyes, but she wisely nodded.

"If you fail to follow my orders at any time, I'll yank you onto the nearest helicopter whether we've found your grandmother or not." He'd threaten her in a heartbeat to keep her safe. And he meant what he said.

She stuck her tongue out at him.

He jerked his head, more than a little startled.

Moira laughed long and hard across the aisle. "Oh, aye, girl. You're in the club."

Amber wrinkled her nose, tugging her bulletproof vest down.

Kane's gaze met Conn's deep green one. Amusement as well as sorrow mingled in his younger brother's gaze. Conn tilted his head toward Dage, a question on his face.

Kane nodded. Dage was okay to go, but they'd need to watch his back. If he found Jase's body, he'd try to kill every demon he saw, regardless of his own safety. Of course, Kane wasn't sure he'd be able to keep a clear head, either.

Talen glared at them both, his jaw clenched in a stubborn line. He wouldn't believe Jase was dead until he saw an actual body, a fact Kane admired in his brother. He saw life one way, and that had to be the only way. That made him an amazing leader and an excellent soldier. But the fall from that belief was going to make for a hard landing.

Kane wished just for a second to believe in fate and not reality.

The demon compound came into view.

A small hut sat on the shore of Scotland, facing the North Sea. Beaten, weathered, and appearing deserted, the hut masked the headquarters of the demons. How they'd managed to create a sprawling labyrinth of tunnels on the massive island was impressive, yet devastating. His brother's body was somewhere down there.

The helicopters had flown low, so low that radar couldn't pick them up. Their arrival would be a surprise, though no doubt the demons were prepared. With a rush of air, the birds slammed down.

The force hit the beach, soldiers running, the first line setting charges on the hut. "Fire in the hole," was yelled, and the world exploded.

Splinters of wood shot into the air to land on the rocky beach, smacking into the soldiers.

Certainty that he was making a colossal mistake stopped Kane in his tracks. His mate didn't belong in a war zone. Sure, Moira was a mate, but she was a witch and a soldier who'd trained for a hundred years. Amber was a human who wouldn't even eat an animal.

She shoved him. Hard. "Stop waffling. Let's go."

Pride, unwilling and unwanted, filled him at her courage. Her willingness to run into an inferno to find her grandmother was impressive. Deep down, he also knew his mate came on the raid to aid him. He knew her well enough to understand she thought to protect him with her brain. His heart swelled.

Grabbing her hand, he began to jog with his mate toward a blistering hell.

God help them all.

Amber breathed through her nose, trying to keep the wisps of burning flakes from burning her skin as they wafted down. Soldiers ran all around them, shouting orders, guns up.

They'd opened up the ground. A myriad of stairs led down into darkness, concrete lining the walls.

The demons must've taken years to build the fortress, using concrete that went how far beyond the landmass? How far into the ocean? Intriguing and kind of scary.

A haze covered the air, giving the night a surreal appearance. Everything seemed to move very quickly but in slow motion. How was that possible?

Kane's hold tightened, jerking her into the present.

Faster than lightning, a horde of demons shot from the underground tunnels.

Raw, brutal images of pain instantly slammed into Amber's brain.

From the agonized cries around her, the images hit all the soldiers. Yet, they kept marching forward, guns blazing and knives flashing.

She drew deep and covered the images and shards of agony with a gentle, soft, comforting blanket adorned with teddy bears. Then she shot the image through her skin into Kane's.

He sighed, his shoulders going back. "Nice job."

"Thanks." Saying one of her grandmother's chants, she sent imaginary shields through the air to the vampire and witch soldiers. They instantly sprang forward in strength and action.

Keeping the shields firmly in place, she followed Kane past bodies, past fights, to the crumbled steps leading down into darkness. Her grandmother was down in the earth.

A contingent of soldiers headed down, clearing the way.

Kane released her to stand in front of her, and Talen flanked her back.

"Let's go," Kane ordered.

Talen gave her a nudge. She nodded, one hand on Kane's back while reaching for Talen's hand.

He stilled and then gripped her.

Concentrating, she shoved the imaginary blanket through her skin to his.

Talen exhaled slowly. "Wow. Impressive."

She nodded. Both Kayrs brothers were pain free from the mind attack. Now she just needed to concentrate as she stepped on the crumbling stairs and started descending.

Hitting the bottom, they followed the force of soldiers, led by Dage, through a myriad of tunnels. Demons seemed to come out from the rock in challenge. Grunts, cries of pain, and the scent of blood followed their path.

Amber closed her eyes, concentrating. An empty tunnel to the right held odd vibrations. "This way?"

Kane nodded, gesturing for a couple of soldiers to lead the way.

Amber had no doubt he'd be leading the way if he wasn't flanking her.

Talen gave a frustrated growl from behind her.

Him, too.

They followed the soldiers.

A heaviness blanketed the air.

Suddenly, four demon soldiers leapt out of a side alcove.

Dage instantly engaged one. Two other vampire soldiers grabbed their heads, dropping to the ground.

Kane stepped forward and fired rapid shots into the demons' chests. Midnight black eyes wide in shock, they dropped to the ground. Dage killed the one in his grasp. Shouting sounded from far ahead, and after receiving a quick nod from Kane, the king darted down the tunnels.

The injured vampires reared up.

"Decapitate them," Kane ordered grimly and pointed at the three still breathing demons on the ground. He glanced at Amber over his shoulder. "Your shield is working. Nice job."

A side door opened, and a tall demon slid outside, his hand wrapped around Hilde Freebird's neck.

Amber gasped, her mind spinning.

Her grandmother had a myriad of bruises down her pale cheek, and blood slid from her nose. She gasped for air. "I guess I wasn't as strong as I'd hoped."

Tears filled Amber's eyes.

"No," Kane whispered. "Let me handle him."

There wasn't any way for Kane to handle him. If he shot the demon, the bastard would probably tear off Hilde's head before they could stop him. Amber took a deep breath, shooting waves of pain toward the demon.

He smiled sharp fangs, his pale face warming with a light blush. "Nice try."

The pain and images of dying puppies slammed into her brain. She cried out.

Then, the world went quiet. Dying puppies? Of course. Tightening her hold on Kane's hand, she followed her own path, something she should've thought of from the beginning. Blanketing the pain, she sent waves of peace and love toward the demon, all wrapped up in a pink baby blanket.

He stepped back, eyes widening.

Oh yeah, take that happy thought, asshole. Fighting pain with pain had been a mistake. "I'm a pacifist," she muttered, reminding herself. Then she sent more happy thoughts of puppies and daisies to counter the demon's attack.

He visibly blanched, his hand dropping off Hilde's neck.

Strength filled Amber. Her own strength of goodness. Shooting yet another warm wave toward the demon, she gasped when he growled again.

Kane took advantage of the moment and plunged his knife into the demon's neck, twisting until the head rolled free. Then Kane focused on her. "I don't believe it. You softened him into confusion."

"All I did was counter his attack. If he would've stopped, I wouldn't have been able to continue affecting him." She opened her arms for her grandmother to rush inside. "Are you all right?"

Hilde hugged her tight, sniffing. "Yes."

Amber sighed in relief. "Let's get out of here."

Oscar appeared at her side, a wide smile on his face. "I knew you'd be okay. Let's go."

The rocks crumbled around them, shards shooting toward their skin. Kane ducked around Amber to shield her.

She opened her eyes, dread slamming into her gut.

Five demon soldiers surrounded them. All with a myriad of silver metals lining their shoulders, black eyes narrowing.

Kane snarled, shoving her behind him.

Images, so many, so fast, slammed into Amber's brain. Kane's head jerked back. Oscar gave a pained growl.

Sucking in air, Amber grabbed her grandmother's hand. "Remember when Mr. Doodles had puppies and we put pink bows on them all?"

Hilde nodded, blood sliding from her nose.

"Send that thought out to the demons . . . along with peace. Kindness filled with sugar. Trust me."

Hilde gulped and nodded, shutting her eyes.

Amber centered herself, allowing the nameless chants to course through her blood. Then she sent all the peace and pretty images she could spiraling through the air.

The pain in her head receded.

Kane lifted to his full height.

One by one, the demons stilled in place and then returned to fighting without the mind attacks.

Amber kept up her happy thoughts, keeping an eye on her mate. Kane and Oscar battled the demons until all five were dead.

"That is so freakin' weird," Hilde muttered, her eyes wide.

Kane grabbed Amber's hand. "Must be something about brain waves and turning their own attack back on them. You're a blanket shield, sunshine."

"I'm a pacifist, damn it."

Nodding, Kane led the way through the tunnels and out to the breaking dawn. "Wait in the helicopter." Waiting until she and Hilde sat safely inside surrounded by Oscar as well as other armed soldiers, he headed back into the earth.

Less than an hour later, the battle was over.

Kane assisted wounded soldiers into helicopters that headed off to various hospitals in Ireland.

He and Talen limped toward the helicopter, their faces grim. Dage stalked right behind them.

Kane tucked various guns and knives in pockets along his vest and pants. He shook his head as he neared. "Suri wasn't anywhere here—damn coward. Nor were there any demon women or children. And there's no sign of Jase."

Hilde visibly jumped. "I heard something about a Jase while I was being kept underground." Her face paled and her hands trembled in her lap.

All movement stopped, and the Kayrs men stared at Hilde.

Amber put an arm around her grandmother. "It's okay. What did you hear?"

Hilde twisted her lip in an apologetic grimace. "I heard somebody named Jase died, and they buried him near the beach."

Kane pivoted, his gaze taking in the entire area. Then he pointed toward a sweeping tree, bare branches reaching to the rapidly graying sky. "There's fresh earth."

As one, the Kayrs men ran toward the recently dug grave, digging rapidly with hands moving too fast to track. Dirt flew with their desperation.

Hilde gave a low sob, while all Amber could do was watch, her heart shattering.

Moira stood off to the side, her concerned gaze on Conn.

Talen yelled when he uncovered a foot.

Moving slower, the vampires carefully extracted dirt and rocks from the rest of the body.

The soldiers remaining in the area watched silently, keeping an eye on the Kayrs family while searching for threats.

Amber stood inside the massive helicopter for a better look.

Dage dropped to his knees, his eyes widening. "Jase." The low tenor of his voice wound along with the breeze. Then he brushed off more dirt.

The youngest Kayrs brother was finally revealed, rocks and filth covering his bruised body.

Moira buried her face in Conn's side as he stared down at his brother.

Kane dropped next to Dage, leaning forward with a frown on his face. He reached toward Jase, his hands trembling. Then he gasped, eyes lighting up with—hope. Definitely hope. "Jase's head is still attached—barely." Kane jerked up, his gaze on Talen. "Get bandages. Now."

Before Talen could turn, two soldiers ran forward with a medic kit.

Kane quickly grabbed gauze, wrapping what was left of Jase's neck together. "Give him blood."

Sharp fangs dropped from Dage's mouth that he dug into his wrist. He put the blood to Jase's pale lips.

The liquid poured inside.

Seconds passed.

Then minutes, and nobody even seemed to breathe.

Finally, Jase's chest heaved.

He shoved at Dage, his hands clawing. "Let me go."

"Never." Tears filled Dage's eyes. "Keep drinking." He lifted his head, his gaze on Kane. A slow smile crossed the king's face. "We've got him."

CHAPTER 32

Kane took a deep breath, leaving Jase in the hospital bed at headquarters. The youngest Kayrs brother refused to talk to any of them. His recovery was going to take some time. And the fact that he'd still had a tendon attached in his neck had kept Kane awake and pondering several nights. The demons wouldn't have made that mistake. They'd let Jase live.

Why?

For now, Kane didn't have to figure that out. Now, he needed to help his brother recover.

Every time Kane visited, he opened up his senses along with his emotions. The act was getting easier each time, and soon he'd help his brother heal. No doubt the skills he'd gained from mating Amber would come in handy at some point.

They'd been home for two weeks.

He still hadn't mastered his new skills, but Amber seemed to be doing well with hers. The fact that she'd smothered the demon attack with kindness and gentleness still impressed the hell out of him. She'd found her own way and won.

During that two weeks, Amber had been trying his patience beyond belief. When she wasn't training with everyone who had a different gift, she was messing with

Kane's life. The brat was trying to get out of their hundred-year agreement.

He'd kept her more than busy in bed at night, and each time with her was better than the last. But during the day, the woman had run wild. She'd replaced all his food with organic food, had turned several of his soldiers into vegans, and had gotten his sisters-in-law on her side regarding love and forever.

They pestered him daily.

He shook his head. The idea of losing her made his entire body ache. The woman loved him—shouldn't she be trying to stay with him?

He just needed a little more time to figure things out and find a cure for the virus before the damn bug attacked his mate. He was getting closer, he just knew it. So his mate could just relax. They had eternity, for goodness' sake.

He opened his lab on the third floor and stopped short. Rabbits, mice, and his five monkeys bounded around the room, free as could be. Worse yet, string cheese covered every available space, and empty dented cans were scattered everywhere.

She hadn't.

She truly hadn't given the monkeys cans of string cheese. The very same unhealthy string cheese she'd campaigned against the previous week.

Walter opened his mouth and spit cheese. Then the damn monkey grinned.

Son of a bitch.

Talen clomped up behind him. "Is Jase any better today?"

Kane couldn't answer, his mouth open as he stared at his once pristine lab.

Talen glanced around him and barked a short laugh. "You have got to be kidding me."

"I—" Kane shook his head, gaze dropping to his favorite microscope. A rabbit sitting under the scope twitched its cheese-covered nose.

Talen clapped him on the back. "You'd better get your mate under control and now."

"I'm telling Cara you said that," Kane murmured absently. A beaker crashed to the floor as a mouse ran by on the counter.

"Whatever. Conn and Moira are heading home tomorrow, and my mate will be here tonight."

"So?" Kane growled as Walter threw a microscope at the far wall.

"So, we'll all be in one place if you want to have a wedding."

Kane started. "A wedding? You're kidding."

"Nope." Talen pivoted to go.

Kane turned and grabbed his brother's arm. "You're not helping me clean up?"

Talen glanced over his shoulder at the devastation. "Not in a million fucking years. It's your own fault you haven't told her you love her. Dipshit." He shrugged free, whistling a jaunty tune as he sauntered down the hallway.

Kane took a tentative step into the lab, his loafer sliding on cheese. His arms wind-milled, and he crashed to the ground. Finally, the temper he didn't have roared through him.

Then humor.

He grinned as Walter swung to the far wall, licking cheese off his lips. Kane threw back his head and laughed.

The thought occurred to him that he'd laughed more since meeting Amber than he'd done in three centuries.

His heart warmed.

The brand on his palm pounded.

Reality smacked him hard in the face, nearly jerking his head back.

He loved her.

Not in a running-through-daisies way, but in a forever, he'd-be-devastated-without-her way.

As he finally allowed himself to believe in forever, love, and fate . . . his shoulders relaxed. The world finally made sense.

Oh, he loved the little minx.

But man, things were going to change.

Dage Kayrs skirted the large lab, not wanting to see the mess. He'd talk to Kane later. Maneuvering through the underground hallways, he found his mate at the small lab.

Emma's dark hair was pulled back in a clip while faded jeans hugged her sexy hips. No makeup adorned her pretty face, and the logo on her T-shirt was faded beyond recognition. As usual, the queen of the Realm was at work, her amazing mind spinning as she tried to cure the virus. She stood, reading a file, muttering under her breath.

Dage leaned against the door frame and crossed his arms. "I told you to get some rest."

She looked up with a frown. "I'm just reading. How's Jase?"

"The same, though his neck has finally healed." Dage sighed deeply. "He won't even talk to me so I can help him."

Emma grimaced. "Give him time. They really messed with his head. Jase is strong; he'll heal emotionally, too."

"I hope so." Dage studied his mate. Lines of stress cut under her eyes. "You have a headache."

She shrugged. "A little."

He reached out and wiped his thumb across her head, drawing the pain into his skull. A quick push and the ache disappeared.

"That's so cool how you do that," Emma murmured.

Yeah. Too bad the virus was so strong, or maybe vampires with infected mates could yank it free. Talen had tried so many damn times—without success.

Dage forced a frown. "Rumor has it Kane's large lab was destroyed by a multitude of animals and string cheese." Talen had reported in within minutes of escaping the disaster.

Emma bit her lip. "Now that's unfortunate."

Oh, her stunning eyes couldn't hide the truth from him. "I believe Amber Freebird probably had an accomplice or two, love."

Emma tossed the file to land on the granite countertop between two humming machines. Wincing slightly, she straightened her arms and stretched her graceful neck. "Maybe the monkeys did it."

Dage grinned. "Kane is murderous when planning paybacks, and you're on your own."

Her eyes darkened, and she took soft steps toward him. "You wouldn't protect me from big, bad Kane?"

"Nope." Dage allowed her amazing smile to send peace through his body. Finally, he could relax and focus on family. "You deserve whatever he comes up with as revenge."

She reached him, sliding her hands up to his neck. "Hmm. I wonder if I could change your mind."

The woman was dangerous as hell and could actually destroy his mind. "I don't know. Just how persuasive are you talking?"

She licked her lips, pressing along his length. "I can be very persuasive."

He fought a groan, trying to keep his face set in calm lines. It wouldn't do to let the blue-eyed seductress know how easily she affected him. "We haven't been swimming in a while." Then he ducked, tossing her over a shoulder.

She yelped and smacked his back. "Why do you always do this?"

He grabbed her butt in a strong grip. "So I can do this."

She predictably tried to kick him, so he banded an arm around her legs while jogging down to the underground pool.

"I'm the queen, damn it," Emma hissed.

"You only play the queen card when you want to get out of something." They reached the pool, and he swung her around to cradle easily in his arms. Her narrowed gaze almost made him laugh. "What?"

"Don't even think—" she screeched as she flew through the air to land with a splash.

She came up to the surface sputtering.

He laughed and yanked off his clothes. "Time to play, my queen."

Talen met the helicopter at the landing site and ripped open the door to gather his mate in his arms.

Cara laughed, snuggling close and kissing his chin as he lifted her out. "I take it you missed me?"

The damn world finally righted as he held her, the scent of wild honeysuckle wrapping around his heart and squeezing. "Yes. I missed you terribly. You're never leaving me again, mate." He looked up to give a nod to his son.

Garrett jumped to the ground. The fourteen-year-old stood at six feet with odd metallic gray eyes and a charming smile. "Hi, Dad. I kissed a shifter."

Cara groaned. "Your son is a little Casanova. He had the feline fathers ready to cut off his head."

Pride filled Talen as he set Cara down on her feet. "That's my boy."

"Wrong response." Cara punched him in the arm.

Talen gathered his son for a hug. "We'll talk later," he whispered to the boy.

Garrett laughed, stepping back. "It's a deal." He sobered. "How's Uncle Jase?"

"He's getting better," Talen lied. A long time ago, the carefree look in Garrett's eyes had lived in Jase's. Sorrow had Talen forcing a smile.

Cara leaned into his chest, stroking gently. "Jase will be fine." The little empath always could read him.

Talen nodded. "I know."

Garrett glanced around. "Where's Janie?"

Talen turned to lead his family indoors. "She's learning to play bridge from Hilde Freebird." He paused. "I think something's up with Janie, but I can't figure it out. Probably girl stuff."

Cara raised an eyebrow. "Girl stuff?"

"Yeah, girl stuff." Thank God his mate was home to deal with the confusing girl stuff.

Cara slid her arm around his waist. "Speaking of girl stuff, how is Kane doing with Amber?"

"I think there will be a wedding in the very near future, whether the genius likes it or not." Talen smiled, his heart feeling lighter than it had in a month. Well, since Cara had left to help the shifters.

Cara gasped, a wide smile filling her face. "A wedding? Oh, how fun."

Garrett groaned. "Why can't they elope? You know Uncle Kane will want to just get it done."

Talen shook his head. "That's not how marriage works." Unfortunately. "Plus, just think how much fun it'll be watching Kane run in circles." Oh yeah, this was going to be a lot of fun.

Garrett frowned. "I don't understand."

"That's because you're a sweetheart, Garrett," Cara murmured.

The kid rolled his eyes. "Mom."

Talen grinned at his son. "Don't worry, we'll go later and try the new guns Kane created. They take a tree out at a hundred yards."

"Oh yeah!" Excitement sizzled Garrett's eyes into a deep silver.

They reached the entrance to headquarters, and Talen eyed Garrett. "For now, why don't you go learn how to play bridge?"

Garrett opened his mouth to protest, and then glanced from his father to his mother and back. A pink blush wandered from his neck to cover his angled face. "Um, yeah. I'll do that. 'Bye." He turned and all but ran in the other direction.

Cara chuckled. "You're terrible."

Talen swung her up in his arms, where she belonged. "Let me show you how terrible I can be." His mouth took hers even as he hurried for their quarters. Reaching the door, he kicked the heavy steel open. "I missed you."

She smiled, her eyes a deep blue. "I missed you, too."

The world was all right now that she was where he wanted her. "I'm so glad you're home, my mate."

Then his mouth descended on hers again.

Max Petrovsky frowned at the angry brunette currently shouting at him. His Sarah wasn't a shouter. Why in the world was she yelling? Finally, she wound down, pretty brown eyes sparking.

Her eyebrows lifted. "Well?"

Shit. He'd been so surprised at her yelling that he hadn't listened to her words. "Um . . . I'm sorry?"

Her gaze narrowed. "For what?"

He shuffled his humungous feet. "For whatever pissed you off so much."

Wrong answer. He knew it the second the words left

his mouth. The woman grabbed a vase to throw at his head.

At that point, he'd had enough. Plucking the flying vase out of the air by the little handle, he went for his woman.

She backed up, eyes widening.

Putting the vase down gently because he knew it was one of her favorites, he grasped her by the upper arms and lifted her until they were eye-to-eye. "Now tell me again what's wrong."

Her lips pursed. "What's wrong is that your best friend, and almost-brother, Kane Kayrs, is a complete ass who needs to pull his head out of his butt and make Amber happy."

How the hell was that Max's problem? "And?"

"And you need to talk to him and get him to fix this."

"Why in the world do you think I can get him to fix this?"

Her voice softened. Her pretty chocolate eyes darkened. "You see things, Max. You notice things nobody else does, which is why you are such an excellent hunter, and the bodyguard most trusted around here."

Charm. The woman was trying to charm him. Based on the warmth sliding through his veins, she was succeeding. "What else, *Milaya*?"

A light pink covered her freckled face, and not from him calling her "my pretty one" in Russian.

Max frowned. If he was reading her right, and he was, that was guilt in her eyes. And her big defense was a yelling offense that had quickly turned to charm, which was totally working on him. "What did you do?"

Her eyes widened and those long eyelashes fluttered. "Do? What do you mean? I didn't do anything."

"Sarah." He lowered his voice to the growl he used when training the young vampires on the field.

She shivered and swallowed. Her tiny fingers began to play with the buttons on his shirt, while her gaze concentrated on his neck. "Well, I may have helped Amber, ah, sabotage Kane's lab."

"Sabotage?" Everybody knew not to mess with Kane's lab. "Are you crazy?"

She shrugged. "Maybe. But Emma and Janie helped."

"What did you do?"

Then she told him. Sure, he tried to keep a stern face, but when she got to the part about the monkey, he couldn't hold in the laugh. He laughed until his eyes stung.

Winding down, he sat and pulled her to straddle him. "Kane is going to get you all back . . . you know that, right?"

Sarah shifted on him, rubbing her core against Max's already aching erection. "I thought maybe you'd protect me."

He threaded his large hand through her silky hair. His heart was at peace whenever she was near, and he thanked God daily for her. Yet a vampire had to have some fun. "Now, why would I do that?"

She grinned, slowly undoing the buttons on his shirt. "Because you love me."

"That I do, *Milaya*. But it's going to cost you." His fangs dropped low.

Damn if her smile didn't widen.

Dangerous women, all around.

Across the ocean, Connlan Kayrs rubbed a broad hand through his hair, glad the mass was finally reaching his shoulders again. He had yet to pay back Moira for singeing it all off. Sure, he'd been trying to mess with one of her spells, but the little witch hadn't needed to booby-trap the spell.

While he liked Ireland, he was more than ready to go home.

Studying their spacious penthouse with the amazing view of the Liffey, he stretched his neck. Okay, this was home also.

He kicked back on the sofa, his gaze on the water, his boots on the sofa table.

His witch walked leisurely in from the kitchen, her hands full with a tray.

His eyebrows rose. "You made dinner?"

"Aye. Get your boots off my coffee table." Her green eyes flashed with irritation.

"Our coffee table." He dropped his feet to the polished wood floor.

"Our coffee table." She slid the tray before him. "I fig-ure we'd better eat all the steak we can before heading to Realm headquarters." An adorable grin lifted her saucy lips.

Suddenly, he was hungry and not for steak. A quick grab had his woman on his lap.

She laughed, shoving at him. "I cooked, now you eat."

He ran his mouth along her smooth skin. "I'm not giv-ing up steak just because Kane mated a vegan. Period."

"I know," Moira breathed, tilting her head so he could continue his wanderings up to her ear. "But we might want to cut down for a while until she gets used to all of us."

"No." Conn nipped her ear. It was nice to see the smile on Moira's beautiful face. He levered back to study the woman who held his heart. "Thank you for coming to headquarters with me. I know you'd like to stay here."

She nodded. "Jase needs us, so we go. Once he's better, we can come figure out what's wrong with Brenna."

Brenna Dunne was Moira's youngest sister and a mem-ber of the council who ruled the witches. She was also an amazing artist. Lately she'd been pale and greatly over-worked, so Moira had wanted to lighten her burden.

Conn tugged Moira's hair out of the constricting braid
and feathered her wild curls on her shoulders. "We'll
come back and help Brenna as soon as we can."

"I know." Moira reached for the plate, feeding him a
piece of steak. "I do hope things have settled down at
Realm headquarters by the time we arrive."

Conn sighed. "Kane is the smartest person on the
planet. I have no doubt by the time we get home that he'll
have figured out he loves the woman. I mean, he has to."
Thoughtfully, Conn grabbed another piece of steak to feed
to his woman. "But if he doesn't, I guess we'll have to beat
some sense into him." Now that sounded like fun.

Moira punched his arm. "You're such a brute."

He allowed his fangs to drop. "Let me prove it to you."

Amber finished wiping off the table, her mind spinning.
Okay, letting the animals go and giving Walter an entire
case of string cheese might have been a bad idea. Had she
gone too far?

Sure, she wanted Kane to want her around, and hopefully he was figuring out that no matter what havoc she
caused, he wanted her.

At night, he really wanted her. The sex was amazing
and full of emotion.

Why couldn't the stubborn vampire see it was love?

Suddenly, he filled the doorway to the kitchen.

A scratch marred his forehead. He wore dark jeans with
a T-shirt, and his hair curled over his nape. He'd obviously
just showered.

Amber tossed the dishcloth to the sink, forcing a polite
smile on her face. "Hello, mate."

"Where's Hilde?"

Amber shrugged. "She went to teach Janie how to play
bridge. What happened to your face?"

His smile seemed predatory. "Walter scratched me when I took his can of cheese away."

She bit her lip as humor bubbled up. "Well, cheese is bad for monkeys. You did the right thing."

"Yes. And I explained to him that there are repercussions for actions, so he doesn't get a treat for the rest of the week." Kane slowly rolled up his sleeves on both arms, revealing strength and muscle.

"Well, that's just mean." She put her hand on her hips. There was something threatening about the way Kane was staring at her. She took a step back.

He moved before she could blink.

The world tilted and she found herself over a pair of strong thighs. Five hard slaps hit her ass before she could breathe out.

He lifted her to stand between his knees.

Her eyes widened as she realized what had just happened. Her butt smarted. "You ass."

With a shrug, he upended her again, smacking her a good five more times.

The world tilted again as she stared into an amused pair of metallic eyes. "Stop that."

He shrugged. "Are you going to stop messing with my lab?"

Probably not. She tried to step back. "Are you going to admit you love me?"

He studied her for a moment, his expression turning serious. "Yes. I love you with everything I am and everything I'll ever be."

She stilled. Her eyes widened. "You do?"

He grinned. "Of course. You're perfect. Stubborn, impossible, horribly devoted to a way of life I don't understand. I'll love you until the day I die."

Her heart swelled. "You don't mean that."

"Yes, I do. Have I ever lied to you?" His eyes darkened.

"No. But love, I mean . . . love."

"Yes, love." He smiled, the curve of his lip happy.

She struggled not to fall into bliss. "What brought this on?"

"Well"—he tugged her to sit on his lap—"when I was cleaning up string cheese and rabbit poop, the realization dawned on me that I was putting up with such nonsense for only one reason. I can't live without you." He brushed hair off her forehead. "Truth be told, I think I fell in love the first time I saw you in that bar. But it took me a while to realize that it was love."

She played with the wet hair at his nape. "Well, you are kind of slow."

He nodded. "True. It's my cross to bear."

She squirmed to find a more comfortable position considering her smarting butt. "I believe that spanking was inappropriate."

Both eyebrows rose. "You are the definition of inappropriate."

"New deal. No more of that." She tugged hard on his hair.

"No deal. I have no doubt there will be more of the same." He stood, smiling at her surprised squeal. "However, I'm rescinding the deal that you only stay for a hundred years. I want forever from you. Let's go seal the new deal."

She threw back her head and laughed as he carried her into the bedroom. "I love you, Kane."

"I know." He tossed her on the bed to yank off his shirt. "I love you, too, my sweet demon destroyer."

EPILOGUE

Janie Kayrs stared at the pretty blue bridesmaid dress hanging in her closet. Uncle Kane was getting married in less than two weeks, and preparations had been wild. He'd only been engaged for a week to Amber Freebird.

Talk about two opposites who were perfect for each other.

And better yet, Amber came with a grandmother who'd quickly become a grandmother to both Janie and Garrett.

A grandmother definitely young enough to find love again. Oscar had already made his intentions well known. Though Hilde was mated and would need the virus to take that away. Well, once they mastered the virus and figured out how to use the benefits without harm.

Janie sighed. She had a lot of work to do.

But her father had been correct. It had been so much fun to watch Kane try to get into having a big wedding. But he'd finally put his foot down when Amber wanted him to wear a light blue tuxedo.

Of course, Amber had just been messing with him. The woman did have a wicked sense of humor. When she'd suggested Walter the monkey be a groomsman, Kane's head had almost blown off.

But she'd been dead serious about inviting her family

from the commune, and she hadn't backed down. Humans were actually going to attend the wedding. Very cool.

Closing her eyes, Janie allowed herself to drift into almost a dream state. Slowly, she forced tension from her toes, legs, hips, and all the way to her head.

A mental call almost stopped her heart.

Somebody was calling her. For the first time in years.

Zane?

Taking several cleansing breaths, she slid into the dream world, picturing a relaxing bank next to a bubbling river.

Zane emerged from a stand of cottonwoods.

The dark combat clothes matched the expression on his face.

Janie kicked a pebble across the rocky beach. "You called me. I didn't drag you here."

He stopped a foot away from her. "I know."

"So, what?"

He sighed, the green of his eyes darker than usual. The scar along his face stood out in a wicked line, a warning about the life he led.

She tilted her head to the side. "How did you get the scar?"

"A pissed-off demon cut me." He rubbed his jawline absently.

"Those bastards." Someday, she'd pay them all back for what they did to Jase. Of course, he'd be healed by then and would probably want to help. Apparently Zane would want to jump in as well.

"Yes." Zane grabbed a pebble to skip along the water. "I called you because I want to tell you the truth. I'm sorry about how things have gone and hoped I could just—"

Another tall figure exited the cotton stand.

Zane growled. "What the hell is he doing here?"

Janie gulped air.

Kalin picked his way around boulders until reaching the edge of the beach. He wore his Kurjan uniform, red metals shining in the fake sun. The expression on his face was all arrogance. "Looks like I can enter the little world here uninvited."

Damn it. Janie lifted her chin. *"I'm sure that ability is temporary."*

"Maybe, maybe not." Kalin flashed sharp fangs. "But I promised you an answer to your question."

Zane jerked his focus to her. "You've been meeting with Kalin?"

She kept her gaze on the Kurjan. "Once. I needed something." She lifted an eyebrow.

Kalin barked a short laugh. "Jase Kayrs was not killed by demons."

No kidding. "Your news is old."

"My apologies." He bowed at the waist, all sarcasm. "Next time I'll . . . satisfy you quicker."

Unease had a shiver running down her spine. The heat from Zane's temper actually warmed the air around her. "We're not meeting again, Kalin. I'll figure out a way to keep you out of my dream worlds."

He licked his pale lips. "Now that I've had your blood, probably not."

Zane stiffened, his eyes flashing. "He's had your blood?"

Kalin laughed, the sound grating. "That's not all I've had." Then he turned his head toward the woods. "I have to go—duty calls. I'll see you both again soon."

The air relaxed slightly as he exited the private world.

Tension still vibrated from Zane. He stepped closer. "How did the Kurjan get your blood?"

Janie faced him squarely. "That's really not your concern. I have his blood, too. As well as yours."

Irritation had Zane's eyebrows drawing together. "How the hell did you get his blood?"

"I tricked him." Janie shrugged. "Why do you care?"

Anger sparked the oxygen around them. Zane stepped forward, hauling her up against him. "The only way you could've gotten his blood was to bite him. How did you get close enough to bite a Kurjan?"

"I kissed him." Janie lifted her chin.

Zane's hold tightened. Disbelief curled his lip. "You kissed that . . . monster?"

"Yes." Temper flashed through her so quickly her knees went weak. "You're not the only one with plans for the ending of this war, Zane. Don't you ever forget who I am."

His lids half closed. "I don't think I knew until right this second who you were."

Butterflies zinged to life in her stomach. He was so warm and so close. The vampire was also hard—head to toe. Such muscle, so much strength in her childhood friend. "What did you want to tell me?"

His eyelids lowered to half-mast. "Apparently I don't need to tell you anything—you've got it all figured out." He grabbed her chin, his hold warm and firm. Tilting her head to the side, he planted a hard kiss on her lips. "We're nowhere near done here, Belle." Releasing her, he stepped back.

Her lips tingled while her entire body lit on fire. "Then why are you leaving?"

His nostrils flared. "I have plans to make. You might want to do the same." Pivoting, he strode toward the forest.

"What the heck does that mean?" she called after him.

He turned, eyes blazing, jaw set hard. "It means, get ready. I'm coming for you, Janie Belle. Soon."

The dream world disappeared.

Janie Kayrs sat up in bed, her hand going to her still tingling lips. "Well, it's about time."

Did you miss the other books in Rebecca's
DARK PROTECTORS series?

Fated

Marry Me . . .

Cara Paulsen does not give up easily. A scientist and a single mother, she's used to fighting for what she wants, keeping a cool head, and doing whatever it takes to protect her daughter Janie. But "whatever it takes" has never before included a shotgun wedding to a dangerous-looking stranger with an attitude problem. . . .

. . . Or Else

Sure, the mysterious Talen says that he's there to protect Cara and Janie. He also says that he's a three-hundred-year-old vampire. Of course, the way he touches her, Cara might actually believe he's had that long to practice. . . .

Claimed

A Daring Rescue

Emma Paulsen is a geneticist driven by science. But she's also a psychic, so when a dark, good-hearted vampire frees her from the clutches of the evil Kurjans, she realizes he must be the man who's been haunting her dreams. But with a virus threatening vampires' mates, Emma may discover a whole new meaning of "lovesick." . . .

A Deadly Decision

As King of the Realm, Dage Kayrs has learned to practice diplomacy. Still, it's taken three hundred years to find his mate, so he'll stop at nothing to protect her—even if it means turning his back on his own kind. . . .

Hunted

Ready or Not

Moira Dunne is a witch—the quantum physics kind. Time and space are her playthings. Which might explain why her one-night stand from a hundred years ago has turned up to "claim" her—and request her family's assistance with the war he's brewing. But the more she learns about Connlan Kayrs, the more she comes to think this is normal behavior for him. . . .

There's Nowhere to Hide

When Conn and Moira tumbled on the moonlit grass, Conn hadn't meant to mark her as his mate for all time. She was only twenty! But it wasn't easy to wait for her. It was even harder to forget her. So when he finally returns for his wicked-hot witch, he's ready to let the sparks fly— even if he burns up in flames. . . .

Consumed

Sometimes You Mate for Life

Katie Smith is the best of her class, part of an elite hunting force trained to eliminate werewolves from the hills of western Virginia. She's good at it because she has the kind of focus and drive that won't back down no matter how steep the odds. Call it Southern sass. Whatever it is, there's no denying her willingness to risk everything for the only man she's ever cared about—a man on the verge of losing his very humanity. . . .

Sometimes You Mate to Stay Alive

For the past ten years Jordan Pride has dedicated his life to protecting his people from a deadly shifter virus. But in a rare moment of distraction, Jordan's guard drops just long enough for his fate to take an irreversible twist. Unless the woman he loves surrenders everything to him, again and again, under a full moon rising. . . .

Printed in the United States
by Baker & Taylor Publisher Services